Type I

Type I

Max Parnell

Dostoyevsky Wannabe Original
An Imprint of Dostoyevsky Wannabe

First Published in 2021
by Dostoyevsky Wannabe Originals
All rights reserved
© All copyright reverts to individual authors

Dostoyevsky Wannabe Originals is an imprint of Dostoyevsky Wannabe publishing.

www.dostoyevskywannabe.com

Cover design and typesetting by Max Parnell
Editor: Kirsty Dunlop

ISBN: 978-1-8380156-3-3

While innumerous people influenced the writing and content of this book, I would like to give special thanks to those that assisted me during the final editing process: Frank Oldfield, Rojwan Lemoine, Denise Bonetti, James Cullimore and Lucian Moriyama. Most of all, I would like to thank Kirsty Dunlop for working as my editor throughout 2019. Without her insights, support and dedication, this book as it is would never have been possible.

57°59'06.6"N 0°16'52.3"W

It's not about the data or even access to the data. It's about getting information from the truckloads of data ... Developers, please help! We're drowning (not waving) in a sea of data — with data, data everywhere, but not a drop of information.

— NSA

The sound of beeping snapped him back to his surroundings: rush hour at Bethnal Green station. It took him a moment to locate the source of the noise, his brain slowly moving out of auto-pilot. Averting his gaze from the red light, he looked down at his phone, the tremolo effect of the vibrations slowly fading. For months after, he would cling onto what he perceived to be a meaningful parallel between those two signals.

It was possible that at the exact moment his phone hit the contactless point at Mile End's underground turnstiles, it received a notification. Yet, this unsettled feeling stuck with him. Three sharp vibrations, felt through his finger tips. While his obsession over that one memory had caused its distortion, he remained adamant that one signal had caused the other. As if the vibrations from the notification had extended outwards, confounding the smart payment system. Never before had this contactless payment refused him entry, stopping him in his tracks with two words: 'seek assistance'.

At first he assumed that the rejection of his chip had caused his phone to vibrate. It was only when he looked at the screen that he noted it was a long awaited notification. One email, the coolness of its laconic subject line perhaps intended to cause the receiver to stop in their tracks: 'Date released'. He hadn't even opened it. He'd simply stood there in contemplation, overcome by a sort of emotionless inertia, as if indifference was the result of excitement and fear balancing each other out.

For that brief moment, he'd become completely unaware of his surroundings; deafened to the impatient shouts directed at his back. Somewhere, perhaps in multiple places, the exact amount of time he stood staring through his screen will be logged. But in his memory there was no way of gauging how long it had been. After an indeterminate amount of time, he looked up, or rather, continued to look down but through a gaze that suddenly snapped into focus. The gates remained closed. He turned, staring absently at the boisterous group of commuters who barged past either side of him.

After directing himself to one of the tube station staff, he showed them his online banking screen, held it to a different turnstile, and the gates swung open: an act that failed to explain whether the former glitch was related to his chip or not.

The date's announcement momentarily silenced his concerns. Only later that evening, whilst he sat smoking on the roof of his apartment, looking out across the network of moving lights, would he ponder this potential synchronicity.

ooooo

After receiving the news, he bought a packet of Camel Gold from the small newsagent on Roman Road where the owner, on odd occasions, had a 'cheaper' supply for returning customers. Despite his efforts to perceive the correlations between the day of the month and the newsagent's supply of illegal cigarettes, he never managed to pinpoint when would be the best time to buy from him. Certain, for whatever reason, that it was inappropriate to ask, he instead left it down to chance, both reluctant to admit there was no method for deciphering his import dates, while somewhat enjoying the randomness of it.

With the evening temperature still in the thirties, he made his way through the Green towards Braintree Street. Large groups of children sped

12

around the grass on their bikes, while others sprayed them with water. He stood watching them for a moment, their faces dripping wet as if they'd just emerged from the ocean. As he passed by them and reached the pavement, he stopped in a small greengrocers to pick up some fruit. Everyone inside looked exhausted, their chins against their chests, breathing slowly. The air inside the shop was even denser than outside, with small flies hovering above the wilted fruit. He picked a few oranges that looked moderately firm, always careful not to test squeeze too many; a habit he knew the owner hated. As she placed the oranges on the scale, her lethargic movements seemed almost exaggerated, as if she were protesting silently. A small television set buzzed behind the counter. When she bagged up his fruit and counted his change, he caught snippets of the news reporter's dialogue: forest fires raging in Northern Australia, a hosepipe ban in all EU countries, four more casualties in Montpellier, all elderly, all suffered acute heatstroke. She handed him his change and oranges without looking. He thanked her and wandered towards his building where he climbed the flight of fire escape stairs to the roof.

When he reached the terrace he collapsed in his hammock that was still tied up from the previous evening, giving himself five minutes to catch his breath before breaking open the packet and lighting his first Camel. The heat weighed down on him, and he found no reason to go back down to his apartment. His activity there would have been identical, just without the clarity of sound offered from the rooftop. Even with the windows open, it did seem that some sound would always get trapped on the way through. As if an ultra-thin net, invisible to the human eye, were pinned between the frame. He remembered reading in National Geographic about a special window which prevented birds from crashing into the glass. Some type of 'visual noise', the designer had said. Patterns invisible to the human eye that reflect light and repel the birds. He remembered laughing, wondering how serious the problem could actually be? Did it really kill *that* many birds? Apparently it did, over six-hundred million in the USA and Canada every year. More than oil-spills or pesticides. The article's subtitle had said it all really. 'We can prevent birds from flying into windows with current technologies—experts say we just need the will.'

He lay there all night, not quite sleeping, not quite awake, fading in and out of that liminal space between consciousness and unconsciousness that, in some enigmatic way, seemed to offer him the most preferable state for reflection. He'd never spoken with a psychologist. Nor had the personality test he'd taken for fun — the Myers Briggs test — left him feeling like he'd come to understand himself any better. He'd never quite known if he were answering the questions honestly or not; a sort of meta-test that surfaced from the options and which led him, invariably, to overthink every response. His preference for this space seemed to offer an obscure but pertinent insight into how his mind worked. When he needed to be, he was able to think critically. Outwardly, he'd always had the demeanour of someone who cared a lot for orderliness and precision when it came to language. Yet he knew that, while these were traits that had allowed him to excel in the academic world, there was, deeply entrenched within him, a tendency towards what he'd always considered to be ambient contemplation. This didn't consist of questions to which no concrete answers were possible, but instead ideas — or patterns of ideas — that were perpetually beyond his comprehension. He often experienced this when listening to a piece of music — a certain tone or timbre would unlock a stream of memories that were, as far as he could tell, totally unrelated to his experience of the piece. This had become clear at a young age, but kept occurring all the way through his life. He remembered once, during a concert in Prague, when a piece of contemporary Czech music triggered a frenzy of images of the Blue Mosque in Istanbul. He'd been there once when backpacking in Europe. But the Mosque, as far as he could recall, held no obvious significance. He'd decided not to enter, but had taken a few pictures on a disposable camera, which he subsequently lost in Mostar. He'd put the correlation down to the microtonal patterns used in the piece, something he read were fundamental to the Turkish Makam scales.

He'd tried to explain this to a friend before, when she'd come across him standing in the street looking down at the pavement, with a focus she couldn't decipher. He'd gone on to explain that there was something, some correlation or meaning behind the scent of the Baklava and the Stephan Micus piece that started playing in his mind. It wasn't just the piece, it was that one note, *that* G# that was held on the cello strings and *this* smell, as if it were the sound of the Baklava itself. She'd suggested he take a test for synesthesia, which he already had, having been sure that he didn't have the condition. He'd known that there was no way of her understanding what he was getting at; her puzzled look being the same one he'd seen in his students when they didn't understand one of his explanations. 'There's just *something* in it, I can't quite explain what I mean, but there's something there.'

That evening he knew he was too exhausted to think pragmatically about the news he'd received. He needed a full day, perhaps two, to really figure out the logistics of the upcoming months. That would be before he even had time to consider how the programme would affect him psychologically. These questions, he realised, were better considered with a clear head the following morning. Instead, he lay there all night, the salat al-maghrib and the subsequent salat al-isha harmonising with the other elements of Bethnal Green's soundscape, offering him a soft backdrop to the myriad memories, questions and feelings that surfaced instantaneously, like a time-lapse video of bacteria growing.

Perhaps three hours had passed when the sound of the salat al farj, the morning adhan, became audible. Had he been sleeping inside, it would have perhaps been too faint to rouse him from his sleep — the Baitul Aman Mosque being well insulated. The prayer had blended with the suppressed roar of the Bethnal Green underground, seeping from the ventilation shafts. These two sounds created an ambience that, while having become ubiquitous to the area, never ceased to stir something within him. *That* sound, in that very moment, seemed to be at once both utterly pertinent and totally unrelated to what he was feeling. How could it be related, when it was always there, every morning? How could it not be related, considering he'd rented out this apartment the same day he'd met the other members?

Still contemplating this, he swung his feet out of the hammock and stood up, the sight of the passersby below snapping into his field of vision. He thought about descending to his apartment and showering before heading out, but decided against it. Since receiving the email, the exhilaration sparked by knowing that the start date was released had been balanced out by a certain lethargy towards other more mundane elements of life: basic human hygiene, alimentation, responding to emails from the university.

Stretching his arms above his head, more for the symbolism of waking up than for the actual need to loosen his muscles, he patted down his pockets, confirming he had his keys, phone and cigarettes. With a small skip to his step, he made his way down the fire escape stairs and crossed the road into the Green. Walking around it, he passed by the early morning commuters making their way to the underground, disposable cups of coffee in hand. A jogger ran past him, his headphones playing loudly enough that for a brief second, he heard a muffled fragment of a techno track, the four to the floor kick fading out as quickly as it became audible. His mind flitted to a bar in Tallinn, sat across from Anya, shouting into each other's ears while excessively loud music that no one danced to drowned them out. Reaching the A107, he waited for a small opening in the traffic before darting through and hopping up onto the kerb. Ordering a long black to go, he realised he'd forgotten to bring his cup. He'd made a resolution to himself that one thing he could do to cut down on waste would be to stop ordering coffee in disposable cups, a new consumer choice that was small enough to rarely cause him any hassle, but tangible enough to give him at least some sense of self-worth. Not wanting to break this resolution, he changed his order. An espresso to sit in.

Taking a seat outside, he waited for his coffee to cool, the logistical questions he had decided not to think about the previous evening now sliding into his thoughts. How much time would he take off from the university? Could he partake in the phases while still going in to teach? Or was that overly, or perhaps *stupidly* ambitious? It was hard to tell before being briefed. For now, he'd wait to speak to Anya. Raising the small glass of coffee to his lips, and concluding it was cool enough, he knocked it back in one gulp. Reaching into his pockets, he pulled out his phone and a cigarette. Anya had already messaged him: *Ariana, 12:00?* Even for her this was slightly blunter than usual. But he imagined that she shared his eagerness to discuss in depth what the news meant for both of them. No sense in expressing anything other than practicalities over the phone. He confirmed their meeting spot.

With three hours left to kill, he returned to the Green and walked in his usual loop, anti-clockwise, following the outskirts of the grass. Obsessing over the fact that they were soon to begin the phases, a project they had both returned to the UK to partake in, his mind wandered back to the frightfully cold night at his apartment in Kadriorg, when they'd received the news that their applications had been accepted. It was with a certain melancholy that he revisited this memory, as it had signalled both the end of their time in Tallinn as well as the start of what they both envisaged to be one of the most crucial aspects of their trajectories — as academics as well as human beings. He knew there was a part of him that had wanted to be rejected, as being rejected would have meant he had no reason to return to the UK. For Anya, acceptance provided the perfect reason to leave her life in Tallinn. When they'd embraced each other, celebrating the news, he'd struggled to hide the imminent sense of loss he felt for a city in which he'd started to feel at home. Only his logic, telling him that it was his moral duty to proceed with this new group and their agenda, had managed to suppress such anguish. These musings, matched with his loops of the green, kept him occupied until he drifted back to the present, checking his phone to realise he no longer had time to walk to Mile End. Feeling lethargic from the melancholy that had passed over him, he resolved to focus on the implications of the start date and treat his encounter with Anya as professionally as possible.

Entering through the turnstiles at Bethnal Green station, he heard the double beep of the 'seek assistance' pop up, this time halting a man two turnstiles down. Passing through his, he turned to catch a glimpse of the man fumbling with his card, impatient with a smart system that just shouldn't reject a paying customer. Reflecting on his own rejection the previous evening, he laughed at the instant paranoia that had overcome him. It was a habit he'd found himself paying more and more attention to, oscillating between laughing at his irrational outbursts of suspicion and furious at himself for not taking his paranoia seriously enough. Ever since his work in Estonia, he'd been painfully aware of his movements within the cognitive assemblages of smart cities. An advocate of digitalised societies due to their political transparencies, he'd often struggled to reconcile such praise with his concerns of the traceability of every citizen and their actions. This was data that he didn't feel comfortable with any one person being able to access.

Rushing past other commuters even though he was in no rush, a trait that he had redeveloped since returning to London, he skipped down the escalator and stood eagerly at the edge of the platform, being the first one through the doors when the Central line train came to a halt. Stood at the top of the carriage, he looked down the aisle of passengers: a young girl with cornrows reading on a slim Kindle, a middle aged man in an oversized suit browsing restaurants on his phone, another girl discreetly miming along to the words of a song he couldn't hear, but that he guessed the passengers next to her could. He felt the train slow down as it pulled into Mile End.

ooooo

When he arrived at The Ariana, Anya was already sitting at a small table by the window, texting furiously. He sat down, trying to make her aware that he had arrived; she looked up, briefly smiled and asked him to give her two minutes. They sat in silence. He could taste the now old coffee and cigarettes on his breathe and regretted not going home to brush his teeth. Despite the fact that this was a relationship based on friendship, there was still a part of him that wanted her to be attracted to him. He started to rise from his seat, about to excuse himself and rinse his mouth in the bathroom when she raised her hand, indicating that she'd finished whatever needed sorting. Theatrically, she turned her phone face down on the table and let out a deep breath.

'So, you must have heard the news?'

He lowered himself back into his seat, and responded, trying to direct his speech away from her nostrils.

'Yeah, I got the email last night, but they didn't go into much detail, just

19

confirmed the release date.'

'It's crazy, I mean, just think that it was over *two* years ago now when we got the confirmation in Tallinn that we'd been accepted into the group.'

All his efforts to remain focused on the news, and not on his nostalgia, felt immediately threatened. She continued:

'I feel like over this past year, I've been constantly checking my emails, just knowing that at any moment I could receive the confirmation. It's been quite fucked up to be honest, the amount I've obsessed over this. I'd love to know how many logins I've had to Gmail alone this year. As bizarre as it sounds, I can't remember the last time I sat down on the toilet and didn't see that as an opportune moment to check my mail.'

The image of her on the toilet, trousers at her ankles, aroused him ever so slightly, this unwanted eroticism melding with his nostalgia for Tallinn. Annoyed at himself for becoming emotional, he cut her off, asking what her plans were now that the date was confirmed.

'It's hard to tell right now. My work's quite flexible, but not so much that they'd be okay with me going off the radar. They still require me to update them on my research progress.'

'True. I guess as long as you keep checking in, there's ways of accounting for a lack of material to present to them.'

'The weird thing is that, even though I still care so much about my research, it seems like more of an obstacle now. I mean, it's been great for the last few years, giving me a reason to move here and letting me work independently. But the main reason I moved here was always for VFL.'

'I'm in a similar position, really. I've been less and less interested in teaching this past year. I thought it'd be refreshing, after having spent so long researching. But in truth I miss it, both the lifestyle and the work itself.'

'You're still tied in for a while though, right?'

'For the time being. I'll see out my contract until the end of the year. I'm thinking of running both at the same time, the VFL and the lectures.'

The waiter broke their conversation asking if they'd had a chance to look at the menus. They hadn't, but knew what they wanted, as this was their regular go-to ever since Anya had moved to Mile End. They ordered a mezze, manakish and tabbouleh out of habit, neither of them particularly hungry.

'Will you be able to manage both?' Anya asked.

'I'm not sure yet. I'm going to wait until after the conference before contacting my department. The VFL sent me loads of information regarding the programme and the different branches of research groups — I saw you've got your name down for the outreach branch.'

'I'll have to meet the director first, but yeah, I *hope* to be.'

'Well, essentially they didn't offer *that* much information on the actual testing procedure. Who knows, maybe it's so arduous that I'll need to ask for the whole semester off.'

'Might not be such a bad thing?'

They both let the silence float for a little, giving each other space to ponder; a shared skill they had come to master. Vibrations from Anya's phone broke the stillness, but she placed it in her bag without looking at the message. Through the restaurant windows, a young boy gently poured water into the hanging plants. Glancing at the water running down the glass, Anya realised it had been days since she'd watered hers.

'Funny, I just realised I forgot to water my plants today — *and* yesterday, actually.'

'I'm sure two days won't be enough to kill them.'

'Oh I'm not worried about that. If anything I probably *over*-water them. It's just odd because it's part of my morning routine. There's something quite therapeutic about it, watching the soil darken just after I've brewed my coffee. It's something small, but forgetting to do that says a lot about how the news has affected me. But anyway, did they mention much about the actual technology?'

'The technology?'

21

It took him a moment to remember why they were meeting.

'Ah, right. Funny, you saying that made me realise I haven't watered mine in a while. I can imagine them wilting in that dense air. I've been practically living on the terrace these days.'

'So the phases haven't even started and already our routines are collapsing', Anya cut in, laughing.

Sharing her amusement, Carl shook his head a little. There was comfort in knowing that Anya, with all her enthusiasm, shared his apprehension.

'Well, with the technology itself, there's nothing that we don't already know. I imagine they've been checking for bugs since the last update. But they seemed pretty confident the software was as tight as it could be.'

'I bet you can't wait to try it?'

'Oh for sure. But you know what I'm like when it comes to something this innovative. I don't know if it's some kind of defence mechanism, but I try to not let myself get too excited.' Carl replied.

'What's concerning you?'

'Nothing in-'

He paused mid sentence, letting the young, well-dressed waiter sit the mezze between them. They both took a moment to admire the complex presentation — something they agreed gave the food a certain playfulness.

'This is new', Carl said, pointing towards the almost geometric pattern formed from the thin shavings of lime balanced on the clusters of pomegranate.

'Maybe they noticed our appreciation last time we were here?'

They both glanced up at the waiter, who took their look to mean that something was wrong. They assured him it wasn't the case.

'Anyway, you were saying?'

'Ah, yeah so there's nothing *in particular* that worries me. It's more that I've learnt how easily the smallest of errors could set this project back for months, maybe even *years*.'

'True. I guess it's so unique that they don't have any previous evidence to learn from.'

'Exactly. I think this worry has been there in my subconscious for some time now. Like yesterday, something really peculiar happened. I got this email from Maarja, basically wishing me good luck with the VFL and telling me to keep her updated when I can. Seeing as her English is much better than my Estonian, we normally write to each other in English. But she has this really *peculiar* way of using hyphens.'

Anya let out a laugh, grabbing her napkin to cover her mouth.

'When you said you had something on your mind I didn't realise it would be so severe as someone's use of *hyphens?*'

Still laughing, Carl continued:

'The thing is, it wasn't simply her use of them, but what it reminded me of. She tends to unnecessarily hyphenate certain words, like 'good-luck' or 'bike-wheel'. But sometimes the hyphens kind of float at the end of sentences, like 'speak soon -'. Anyway, when I read her last email I remembered this story about the Soviet Phobos One space mission that failed in the late eighties. Obviously the West had been in this game as well, but this was the *heaviest* interplanetary spacecraft ever launched. But do you know what fucked the whole thing up?'

'A hyphen?'

'A *missing* hyphen.'

Anya raised her eyebrows.

'Essentially the 'end-of-mission' control was missing a hyphen, which caused this command to be sent to the spacecraft while it was en route to Mars, destroying everything they'd worked on for decades. That's all it took: one missing hyphen.'

'The only word that comes to mind is *cruelty*. Like, it's almost *nauseatingly* cruel, no? All those years of work, erased by a hyphen, *or lack of one.*'

'So, this missing hyphen was out there in space floating around, then somehow made its way back to the East and into Maarja's email.'

'And you know what her name means in Estonian, right?' Anya asked.

'I don't, no?'

'Sea of bitterness.'

'*Right.* Sea of bitterness. Maybe that's why this story sprung to mind. Not just the hyphen, but because that's a pretty apt metaphor to describe what the designers must have felt.'

'So you're quite concerned that there could be some tiny, almost undetectable bug in the software which could leave us in the same position?'

'It's always gonna be a possibility.'

Four days remained until the group was required to meet for their brief. He didn't have to be in the university until September, still giving him the entirety of August to work on whatever he wished. The problem he'd found recently was that, since starting his position at Imperial, he'd really achieved very little of his own work. It wasn't that he didn't have the time — his hours required for teaching being generously low — but more that he seemed to have lost the ability to focus since returning to London. He'd anticipated that leaving Tallinn could have this effect. In a sense it was so obvious, seeing as his research had been centred on the city. But having completed a three-year PhD programme, he found himself somewhat lost afterwards. It were as if the completion of the biggest piece of work he'd ever undertaken had left him unsure as to whether something of such magnitude would ever again grow out of merely teaching anthropology. Every time he thought about it, it seemed bizarrely akin to a sort of postnatal depression, as if the climax of publishing his thesis and subsequently landing a comfortable job had left him hollowed out.

These hesitations had been at the forefront of his mind since returning to London, but he rarely had a chance to voice them. When he returned from Tallinn, he already knew that he hadn't retained a social circle. Now, he only tended to confide in Anya. Despite not sharing his reservations about moving to London, she knew him well enough to always offer the right support when it was needed. For her, leaving Tallinn — a city she'd grown tired of — couldn't have come at a better time. She'd long completed her research and could write her thesis from anywhere. So when the opportunity arose to join the VFL, there was nothing left to decide. She estimated that it would take her just less than a year to finish writing her book, *The Socio-Ecological Significance of Gambiarra*. With her field work in Brazil already completed, she returned to Tallinn, the city she grew up in. But soon after, she found herself becoming tired of bumping into fellow writers or researchers in every small café or bar she frequented for her long days of writing.

She told herself that it was normal, that having spent so long out of the country, it would take her time to adapt and reintegrate. After all, culturally speaking, the largest country in Latin America and this small Baltic nation couldn't be further apart. But in a sense, she'd known that it went deeper than this. Having dedicated her research to Gambiarra, a practice based on smart improvisation from what little materials are available, the return to a society as digitally advanced as Estonia had been a cultural shock on a level she hadn't anticipated. If she'd been gone for the entirety of the transformation, as many Estonians who fled during the nineties had, the shock would have been more understandable. But she *had* been there for most of it. She *had* been one of the advocates, a member of the younger generation excited by the millennium prospect of a new e-society that had finally broken away from decades of Soviet repression. What had changed was that, having seen the ecological significance of a practice as humble but nonetheless as effective as Gambiarra, she'd come to question the unwavering faith placed by many Estonians in hyper-digitalisation. Yet despite her skepticism, these were questions that required adequate knowledge of such new technologies. This had been a realisation that she knew was undetachable from her research. Gambiarra was, *after all*, still a form of technology.

She first came across Carl at a panel discussion at the university. He'd been sitting alongside her in the audience, taking sparse notes while the guest speakers discussed the use of blockchain in Estonia's economic system. She'd attended more out of a sense of obligation, having been out of the country for the previous two years while the new technology had been test-run as part of the nation's hyper-digitisation programme. In a country progressing as rapidly as Estonia was, two years was long enough to feel out of the loop. After realising quite early on that much of the information covered in the talk would require weeks of further reading, she allowed herself to relax, taking the odd note from a certain writer or paper she'd find online later. Only when the sound of fingers anxiously tapping away on a small tablet caught her attention, did she catch a glimpse of the man sat next to her. This slightly short man with a neatly shaved head and round glasses, somewhat underdressed for the occasion, was staring down at his screen transcribing as much of the talk as his fingers would allow him. When the discussion drew to a close, she'd turned to him;

'See vestlus peab olema sinu jaoks üsna oluline?'

Caught off guard, as if he suddenly realised he'd been observed, he took slightly longer than was expected to reply;

'Jah... ma mõtlen, et seal oli palju teavet, mida ma tõesti pean uurima. Blockchain on minu jaoks ikka veel üsna uus...'

She guessed from his accent that he wasn't from there. Most of the panel discussions tended to be in English to accommodate for the ever-growing international community at the university. But having noticed him writing in both Estonian and English, she hadn't wanted to assume anything: many members of the university had grown slightly frustrated at having to speak English out of habit, rather than to include non-speakers.

'Ma arvan, et teie eestlane arvab, et te ei külasta linna? Kuid ka teie aktsent ei kõla kohalikult?'

This time his grammar failed him slightly, the talk having exhausted much of his mental energy.

'Noh, ma pole siit pärit ... noh, ma mõtlen ... ma elan siin, aga ... do you mind if we speak in English?'

'Not at all.'

'Thanks. Sorry I usually like to make the effort, it's just that it gets to a

27

certain point in the day when I can't express myself so well.'

His cheeks started to heat up.

'No apology required, I know how it is. I grew up speaking English and Estonian, and lately it's mostly English. But the last two years I've been out of the country. So I can relate to that linguistic fatigue.'

'Oh where were you?'

Glancing around, he noticed that the room had started to clear out.

'Brazil. And you're from?'

'London.'

'I'd ask what brings you here, but I think we need to vacate the room.'

ooooo

They found themselves continuing their conversation on foot, wandering towards the building's exit alongside a steady flux of students and lecturers trickling through the corridors. Only when they passed through the main doors, in the threshold between heated lobby and icy street, did the biting wind cut their conversation. Shivering, they raised their shoulders, breathing in as if to verify the drop in temperature. While she'd found Carl hard to place, there was something intriguing about this quite awkward researcher who clearly had a deep interest in the way her country was run. Not wanting to insinuate that it was a date, she told him bluntly that she'd like to know more about his research in Tallinn. She asked if he knew any places close by, but with a minus five degree wind hitting her cheeks, his inability to make a decision immediately made her impatient.

'There's a place I know a few blocks from here.'

'Sure.'

Even within the first hour of their meeting, two distinct styles of discourse that would eventually play out between them had begun to form. The first was the way they spoke to each other when they needed to make a decision: she was always to the point, a directedness inherent to her character which could often come across as blunt or abrasive. He often tried to match her frankness, more out of imitation than because it suited him. In contrast, their second style of discourse played out whenever they spoke of concepts. This other mode, one in which sentences never seemed long enough to express everything they needed to, felt like a social version of Carl's inner ambient contemplation.

They walked briskly, both of them shivering and sharing few words, as if there were no use in wasting time getting to know each other with small talk when there seemed to be something more significant beginning. The bar was relatively empty, and they found a small seat by the window. She asked him what he wanted, but with the large selection of taps on offer, he let her choose. She ordered two Orange Gose Põhjala's, a beer he hadn't tried. Unsure whether this was now a date, he thought to ask a few light questions, but before they'd barely finished their first sips she went straight to the point.

'So what is it about Tallinn, or Estonia that you've come here to write about?'

'Cultural digitisation. Well political and social as well. Essentially how Estonia's become the most advanced digital society in the world in such an impressively short time span.'

'*Impressively*?'

'Yeah, really. I mean, no other nation has come close to the level found here. Especially considering it's one of the former Soviet states. The chances that any of those republics could undergo such a drastic transformation was... well, the odds *were* stacked against them. It really seems to me like the government decided to take a leap of faith and it paid off. Well, paid off politically and economically speaking. Culturally it's too soon to know the full ramifications. But that's what interests me more — the anthropological significance. Economically, I can see the benefits — I think everyone can. But what's yet to be uncovered is how hyper-digitalisation will affect human relations, both on the micro and the macro level.'

He paused to take another sip of his beer, slightly unsure of whether she was interested or mildly offended by what he was saying. Her silence indicated that it was still his turn to speak.

'The reason I came here is really because I see Estonia, and Tallinn in particular, as an interesting case study when looking at smart cities. I think, well, I think it's going to become a really important model going forward. It's mostly due to the transparency — the fact that any one citizen can see if anyone has viewed their information but also has the ability to view institutional information that's *normally* withheld from the public. This definitely increases people's trust, that's for sure. But to be honest, I'm still unsure of whether I'm an advocate of such technologies. It's been something I've been grappling with for a while now. When it comes to anthropology, the implementation of new technologies on a societal scale seems to be one of the biggest issues, well not issues, but *questions* we need to address. I still find it quite hard to pinpoint where I stand on this.'

'How so?'

'Whatever the given benefits or risks, it's more about how we, as humans, engage with these technologies. I guess I worry about how our belief systems become shaped through how we perceive these networks. I think if you get too caught up in the powers of technology to solve our problems, you end up becoming a cornucopian and holding this unwavering, almost *quasi-religious* belief in the power of smart technologies. I just think that can be a dangerous trap to fall into.'

He paused to take another sip, more to indicate that he'd finished speaking than out of thirst. By now she was smiling, whether coyly or out of agreement, he still couldn't tell.

'It's strange, I feel you've just touched on something I've been questioning since I returned to Tallinn. It became so obvious after returning from Brazil, not because the technologies I was studying there *weren't* technologies, but because there was a *rawness* to them that allowed you to understand exactly what they were and how the functioned. Do you know what Gambiarra is?'

'Can't say I do.'

'It's the Brazilian art of makeshift. There's an Indian equivalent called Jugaad, and probably lots of other forms in different corners of the world that go by different names. But it's the art of creative problem solving through improvisation, of making tools out of what you have at your disposal. Obviously for many people in Brazil's poorer communities, there's not many materials kicking about. So they use what they have to build small objects whose functions aren't dictated by their fabrication.'

'Interesting, what types of things do they tend to make?'

'Oh all sorts, from portable electrical generators to makeshift irrigation systems. I've got whole albums of documentation, so I'll have to show you some time.'

'Yeah I'd be interested to see more.'

Her mention of a second meeting calmed him a little; if he'd offended her, surely she wouldn't have offered to show him her albums? He wondered whether he'd smiled too much when she proposed this, and tried to look more reserved.

'But yeah, what I find interesting when comparing this to Estonia is that we've integrated this enormously complex system into our day-to-day lives — as part of the e-citizen scheme — but no one actually knows exactly *what* it is. You know what it does; what the functions of an electronic ID card, e-voting system or e-health check up are. But on a deeper, epistemological level, it's beyond us. I think the fact that it seems to function so well in a way assures us, *convinces* us that we don't really need to understand it, that on some level there'll always be someone, *somehow,* who will deal with any technological hiccups that may surface. So yeah, whatever the societal implications are, for us and future generations, there's not really any means for us to know.'

The tables around them had started to fill up. Evidently a cue to the bar staff, the music chased after the augmentation of noise — a painfully trendy and characterless techno kick now functioning as a metronome for their conversation. Raising her voice and leaning towards Carl, she continued:

'So what's your take, what are these effects that cultural digitalisation is having on us?'

He breathed in, looking up to indicate that he knew he needed to put something carefully.

'It's a really hard question, not just because of its complexity, but because I'm not even sure if Estonia is, in essence, *that* different from a place like London, or Tokyo or Paris or Manhattan — or any other digitally developed city. Before I came here, I imagined the culture would be predicated upon these new forms of technology, particularly among the younger generation. But the thing is… well I think you already said it. Here, no one really knows what the technology is, they just understand what it *does*, pragmatically speaking, even if they don't understand how it was built or what the risks are. But the longer I've been here, I've started to question whether this relationship is essentially that different anywhere else. If you stopped someone in London, and asked them how fundamental a role their smartphone plays in their life, they'd talk about an ease of communication, e-payments, hyperconnectivity, never getting lost again, never being bored on the tube. They wouldn't talk about the e-trail they leave every time they step outside of their home. They wouldn't talk about how each of their conversations are logged, or the myriad moments in the day — any moment in which they are waiting, for anything — when they reach for their pocket and open their email or their calender or any other app. And that's before we even get onto the issues of the smart phone becoming this almost artificial limb we can't separate ourselves from… But anyway, I'm not criticising this or saying that smartphones are bad. What I'm trying to get at is that with all these new technologies, often the more insidious problems that they pose don't become apparent when you consider them based solely on how they serve you.'

'And that's where the tension lies for you?'

Slightly surprised by the question, he paused, deliberately not reaching for his drink. He was becoming aware during this conversation that their body language was quite different. He was a shifter, someone who continuously touched his face or stretched his arms whenever he sat talking to someone, regardless of the depth of conversation. She moved only when it was necessary, in this case, only to take a sip of her drink. Even this she seemed to do with minimal movement. Whereas he looked up or around or down at his hands while gathering his thoughts, she looked straight at him, in a way that managed to be respectfully intimidating without being aggressive. Trying to mirror her behaviour, as if the question required more stoicism, he placed his hands on the table, and looked back at her.

'That's *exactly* where the tension lies. It's that brittle middle ground between luddite and cornucopian. There's this grey space between the two competing beliefs: we know we need new and radical technologies to help us deal with the plethora of obstacles laid out before us, but we also know that we simply can't view these new technologies religiously. I think we often buy into technological innovations as some other-wordly saviours that will get us through the bottleneck, no matter what.'

Frustrated that the music was hindering her ability to hear everything he said, she signalled to the smoking area. They finished the last of their drinks and moved outside, the winter wind stinging their cheeks as they moved into the courtyard. Around them everyone stood smoking Camels, the transition to e-cigarettes still yet to come for many e-citizens, an irony that never failed to amuse Carl.

'Look, I can't stay any later tonight as I've got a seminar tomorrow morning. But I'd like to talk more. There's this programme in London I've been looking into recently, and I'd like to know what you think of it.'

They exchanged numbers matter-of-factly, before she smiled and parted.

'Head ööd, Carl.'

Just before five a.m., when the temperature had reached its coolest point, Carl shifted in his hammock, trying to remember if the British summers had always been so fatiguing. In a restaurant in Bermondsey, he'd once overheard two red-faced men speaking of how, as the global temperature continued to rise — and as a consequence the soil became dryer — the UK would eventually have the climate of the south of France, meaning that some of the best grapes in Europe would now be 'on our doorstep'. He remembered how no hints of concern were discernible in amongst their excitement for this new economic opening. Perhaps worst of all — a factor he hadn't considered until after leaving the restaurant — was that given their age, neither of them would be alive to see such a change. Just the mere idea of their lineage holding monopoly over the best wines seemed to be something to celebrate. He'd thought about how he might have reacted to this in his younger years, perhaps interjecting in their conversation to lecture them on their gross improvidence. Or, if he'd been even younger, he would have banged his fist on their table, causing the whole restaurant to choke on their overpriced scallops as he tore into the men. He would tell them they were both fucking clueless, asking 'couldn't they see what this meant?' when perhaps he himself couldn't quite understand the full significance.

But that younger self was gone. He'd like to say it was dormant, that when he needed to, he could reach into himself and pull out that former activist. *That* Carl — who wouldn't have worried about causing a scene and arguing what he believed to be *his* case despite who he might have offended — had faded like the patterned tread of a bike tyre. And how *had* he reacted? Had he even given the men a disapproving look as he left? He could barely remember, meaning that he'd probably just paid his bill and left.

Rubbing his eyes, the salat al farj became audible, a cue that signalled the sun would soon rise. The dense heat continued to push down on the city's inhabitants. His mind drifted to Alhambra, to armies of Moors crossing the Strait of Gibraltar, landing in the Iberian Peninsula. Feet kicking through the salamander dust. Grape vines coated with Girih patterns and wine cellars transforming into Mocárabes. Swarms of half-naked figures hurling soft tomatoes in Buñol, the city inundated with the debris of coarse, over-ripe flesh. The clink of two wine glasses, two pairs of rouge cheeks reflected back in stainless steel cutlery. Overturned wooden boats clanking against rocks. A bike bell jingling in the hills. The muted roar of the underground, churning rip currents that tore against the coast of Tangier.

He sat up abruptly, swinging his legs out of the hammock and stepping forward to lean on the low railing. The first rays of sunlight caught his eyes like an inappropriate camera flash. He squinted a little. His mouth tasted of cigarettes, his lips of sweat. Staring down, hawk-like at the morning commuters, he patted down his pockets, before descending to his apartment.

ooooo

That afternoon he'd agreed to meet with Anya and Veronica, one of the designers from the VFL. She'd suggested, or rather had *insisted* that they see the new video installations at the Tate Modern. The piece was by a group called *SuperFlux*, who she'd worked with in the past and whose direction was closely aligned with that of the VFL. Both Anya and Veronica had stressed how important such future collaborations could be when looking to reach the widest possible audience. Despite his lethargy and concerns that he really needed to take care of administrative matters at the university, Carl knew this was true, and found their enthusiasm stimulating. Slightly ashamed that he hadn't heard of the collective before, he decided to spend the morning researching their work, more for wanting to have something intelligent to say in their company than because of Veronica's stress on its importance.

As he descended the stairs to his apartment, he ran his tongue over the front of his teeth and pulled back his t-shirt to smell his chest. The crass, almost animalistic behaviour, as if he were re-discovering his own body, made him laugh at himself. Such acts served to remind him that, as of now, he'd need to start taking better care of his appearance. Fighting off the urge to start tidying his apartment, something he knew could take up the whole morning, he took a cold shower, shaved and changed into smarter clothes. Rather than working from home, he decided to take his laptop with him and spend the morning at a small café close to the Southbank Centre.

Emerging onto the street, he slipped into the stream of commuters headed for Bethnal Green Station and felt almost normal, as if he were repeating the same journey he'd made the previous day, and any other week day before that. The façade of normalcy comforted him, and by the time he was opening his Gmail on the escalator, he'd almost forgotten what he'd been doing for the past three weeks. Only when he was met by a turbulence of unopened mail did the façade undo itself. Without opening one message, he locked his phone and returned it to his pocket.

When the train pulled into Embankment the platform was swamped. Pushing past other commuters, enjoying the physicality of the surge, he feigned impatience and concern at the crowd bottlenecking at the turnstiles. There was something about pretending he were being held up that made him feel reintegrated, that helped him to shed the torpor of recent weeks. He purchased a packet of mints from the small newsagent in the station, unnecessarily rushing the cashier, snatching his change from her as he strolled out into the morning sun. He felt his body perspire. Performatively, he stopped in his tracks, looking left and right as if to size up his options. As he did so, he remembered a small Portuguese cafe Anya had taken him to, insisting — although she'd never lived in Portugal — that it had *really* authentic food. Edging around other passersby, he made his way down Victoria Embankment, turning onto Waterloo Bridge. Reaching the intersection with The Strand, he located the café and entered, grabbing a small table by the window, a socket within a cable's reach. He ordered an *abatanado*, having asked in more patient manner which of the options was a long black.

Opening his laptop, he felt a sense of urgency and importance that was long overdue. After all, he was about to enter into the programme, the sole reason for his return to London. The programme that, as he and Anya had both agreed, was potentially the most meaningful cause onto which either of them could dedicate their academic focus. He felt almost ashamed of himself for having been so idle the past few weeks, as if suddenly being well dressed and back at his laptop around other busy workers had galvanized him. Tapping with excessive force on his keyboard, he found the *Superflux* website and leaned into his screen. He navigated to the 'about' page, and proceeded to read into the ethos of the collective.

The more he read, the more he understood why Veronica had been so adamant that they attend the exhibition. Their ethos seemed uncannily aligned with that of the VFL. Opening his small notebook — the physical act of writing always helped him to remember certain ideas — he wrote down the words 'High Fidelity Futures', underlining it to emphasise its significance. Under this title, he scrawled down several fragmented notes, sipping his abatanado before it had cooled, the searing heat acting as a stimulant.

The tables around him started to fill up. A young couple chatting excitedly about a trip to Seoul — him saying how excited he was to try *real Seolleongtang*, her saying how he was going to *love* it there. To his left, a man with a motorbike helmet assumed his position at the table, his strong figure shifting the table legs, spilling some of his coffee. A waitress approached him, said something in Portuguese to which he nodded, indifferently, as she wiped up his mess.

Understanding better the collective's ethos, Carl navigated to the section on the website entitled 'works'. He didn't care about spoiling the surprise of experiencing the work before seeing it in the gallery. On the contrary, he wanted to be one step ahead when it came to speaking about it with Veronica. Reaching into his pocket, he fumbled around looking for his headphones. Failing to locate them, he rummaged aggressively through his bag, wincing in frustration when he realised he'd forgotten them. Glancing around at the closely aligned tables, he decided it'd be uncouth to subject everyone to whatever audio accompanied the videos. Turning the laptop on silent, he hunched further over his screen, gulping down a hot mouthful of coffee. As he scrolled through the archive, the names, capitalised for added stress, shot back at him:

THE FUTURE STARTS HERE, MANTIS SYSTEMS THE FUTURE ENERGY LAB, HOW WE WILL LIVE, DRONE AVIARY...

Unsure as to where to begin, he clicked on 'Drone Aviary', still frustrated at being deprived of the sound. He sat back while the screen buffered, reading the short caption below the screen:

The Drone Aviary reveals fleeting glimpses of the city from the perspective of drones.

It explores a world where the 'network' begins to gain physical autonomy. Drones become protagonists, moving through the city, making decisions about the world and influencing our lives in often

opaque yet profound ways.

This film is part of The Drone Aviary Project, by Superflux, which investigates the social, political and cultural potential of drone technology as it enters civil space.

The video commenced with a tempo acceleration of a drone taking off from a circular green patch — somewhere he assumed was London. As the drone proceeded through the city, scanning its inhabitants, the screen flitted between aerial shots of the metropolis and a colourful, grid like cartoon of the drone's movement through such infrastructures. Details of cars, civilians and buildings popped up around the respective objects, offering information such as residential status, MOT service information and national security numbers of different citizens. At one point, a young Theresa May appeared on the screen, her mouth miming something he wanted to hear, but of course, couldn't. Quotes from Benjamin Wallace Wells took over a white screen.

Lost in the concern that the drone is an authoritarian instrument is the possibility that it might simultaneously be a democratizing tool.

Had the sound not been muted, a piercing, high pitched noise would have rung through the ears of those sitting adjacent to him. Snatching his pen, he carefully noted down the quote, confidant that this would serve as a crucial talking point later on. He resumed the video, pausing again when another block of text, this time from Donna Haraway, flowed across the gyrating birds-eye-view of the industrial areas stretching out around the Thames.

Our machines are disturbingly lively, and we ourselves frighteningly inert.

The drone continued its journey, passing through central London, above the flux of consumers and Hare Krishna's chanting on a street corner. People of all types were picked up by its facial recognition programme, logging their emotions, 'status' and location, the drone's angle switching from hovering above high streets to weaving deftly through narrow lanes. Another block of text begun to consume the screen:

There are eyes everywhere. No Blind spot left. What shall we dream of when everything becomes visible? We'll dream of being blind. — Paulo Virilo

As the closing credits surfaced, he turned to his left, catching the motorcyclist watching his screen. Staring at him with the same aloof expression he'd given the waitress, he looked back down at his phone. Carl closed his laptop, packed up his belongings and paced out of the café.

When he arrived at the Tate Modern, crowds of tourists swarmed the concrete expanse; groups of French school children, restless and bored; families speaking in different lanaguages peering at their phone screens, shielding them from the sun; couples sat drinking iced lattes at the metal tables clustered at one side of the courtyard. Sweat already forming on his forehead, he also covered his phone. Looking back up towards the building, he called Anya, but spotted them both before she picked up. They were stood outside in the shade, leaning against the wall by the entrance.

'Hey-' she answered, but he abruptly cut her off before she could say anymore.

'I can see you don't worry.' and hung up.

Strolling towards them, he gave a to-the-point wave and tucked his phone back in his pocket. They greeted each other with a kiss on each cheek. Out of politeness, he greeted Veronica the same way. Both being English, and not used to such casual intimacy, they both sensed that the other found it slightly amusing.

'Anya was just telling me about her time in Brazil studying Gambeira.'

'*Gambiarra*', Anya interjected.

'Ah yeah, sorry, *Gambiaaara*. Yeah I'd never actually heard of it before I came across that *Gam-bi-olo-gia* collective, but it's interesting how something that started out as a sort of spontaneous problem solving tool ended up evolving into *quite* a renowned art movement.'

'Yeah, certainly interesting how it paved the way for quite complex sound installations.' Carl responded, catching his breath.

He knew this was a subject that could make Anya instantly touchy. For her, people's focus on Gambiarra in its art form often overshadowed their understanding of it as an ecological practice. Whenever she spoke about her thesis, this was a point she always made clear. He guessed she'd gone slightly softer on Veronica, not wanting to create any tension so close to the launch date.

'Shall we?' Anya cut in.

'Let's.'

As they purchased their tickets, the poster for the exhibition caught Carl's eye. SUPERFLEX. ONE TWO THREE SWING! & Other Works. Superflex. Su-per-fle-x. Something didn't add up. When the cashier turned to speak to him, he realised he was staring at the sign looking almost frustrated.

'One admission to Superflex?'

'Superflex.' He repeated back at her.

'Yes, for the Superflex installations. One admission?'

'Yes, no, I mean it's not that. Yes one admission, please.'

'Everything alright?' Anya asked.

'Yeah it's fine, just gonna head to the bathroom before going in.'

Locking himself in a cubicle, he pulled out his phone and Googled the exhibition. SUPERFLEX. ONE TWO THREE SWING! & Other Works. What the fuck was so strange about that name? It were as if he didn't recognise it anymore. Squinting his eyes, angry that his morning revision seemed to be having the opposite effect, he pulled out his notebook. Superflux. Flux. Superflux. Superflex, superflux. Flex, Flux. Oh *fuck off*, he groaned out loud to himself. Someone in the adjacent cubicle let out a laugh, muffling it soon after, a small giggle still audible as his error dawned on him. He'd researched the wrong collective, Superflux, having meant to research Superflex, the exhibition at which he found himself. Why are their names so fucking similar? he thought to himself, careful to keep this outburst inside his head. He contemplated a quick Google search to see

42

what they were all about, but thought twice about it. Suddenly aware that he'd been in the bathroom for longer than usual, he resolved to return to Anya and Veronica. He'd take the exhibition on face value, analysing it as he could. He was an anthropologist, after all, not an art critic. He'd give his angle on the work, theorise it in a way that illustrated his academic competence. Then later, over drinks, he'd find a way of segueing agilely onto the ideas presented by Super*flux*. Nodding to himself, he realised he was still standing in the cubicle. Pulling the door open aggressively, he pushed past a group of school children playing with the dryers and returned to the gallery.

'Carl, we were thinking... The swings are outside on the top level, but seeing as it's still suffocatingly hot, let's see the films first and we'll head up there later?' Anya asked.

'Yep, makes sense.'

'*So* Carl; Anya was telling me about how you both met in Tallinn, about the work you were completing out there.'

He could see the gallery statement for Superflex mounted to the wall next to the entrance, enlarging, the text becoming easier to read as they approached.

'Yeah it was a really interesting city to be based in, seeing as it was so fresh in terms of the new technologies they were implementing.' This was a line he'd repeated so many times when someone asked him about his research and he didn't care to explain in depth. The fluidity with which he said it felt rehearsed, especially to himself.

As they approached the door, neither Anya or Veronica stopped to read the caption. Anya never tended to read about the works before viewing them, arguing that it gave her a more 'honest' viewing experience. Veronica evidently knew more about the collective than any small statement could offer. He entered blindly, following behind the two of them.

The first video they watched had little effect on Carl. He even found it slightly tedious in its simplicity. Given his background, *What is*

Blockchain — a short film about blockchain and its significance — failed to really offer him any meaningful new vision of what this piece of technology was, either ontologically or teleologically. Rather than sparking a sense of listlessness or impatience in him, he felt calm, secure that the material in this show was unlikely to exceed his expertise. He'd have no problem discussing it with Veronica afterwards, would perhaps even impress her with his knowledge on the subject area. Conscious of the somewhat neurotic thought patterns at work in his mind, he checked himself a little, asking himself, inwardly, why he cared so much what she thought? Was he attracted to her in some way? Well, perhaps, but he certainly wasn't excessively charmed or captivated by her. No, he knew it went beyond this. That, in some way, she represented the VFL to him — that his interactions with any one of the group's members somehow felt like addressing the collective as a whole. He'd always hated feeling like he didn't have adequate metaphors or critiquing capabilities when it came to discussing art. It wasn't that he was overly analytical, but that, at times, condensing his ideas down into concise, sharply intelligible insights proved difficult. The film ended and cut short his self-reflexive pontifications.

'*Well,* I bet that wasn't so exciting for you, *no?*' Veronica let out a friendly laugh.

Bothered both by the fact that he must be so easy to read, as well as intrigued that Anya must have already mentioned his thesis to her, it took Carl a few seconds to respond, by which time Veronica couldn't tell if he were offended. Quick to rectify his aloofness, he assured her;

'No no, I mean, that's what I think is important about collectives like these. Something like blockchain is so complex that I don't think many people know how to approach it, even if they want to. That's why having these creative explanations can be so effective.'

Embedded in his response was a verification of his and her philosophies, of why both of them had joined the VFL. *If they didn't see the value in finding creative ways of helping people to understand the systems in which*

44

they existed, they would never have met in the first place. Luckily he'd finished speaking before he said this last part out loud. He felt himself becoming more neurotic. Perhaps it was the heat. The gallery, despite its air conditioning, still felt unnecessarily dense.

'Ah this piece is *really* good — I think it's one of their best, to be honest. I don't want to spoil anything, but yeah really, let's sit for this one.'

Carl and Anya both nodded enthusiastically as they followed her towards the small cinema room.

'Ah, let's wait for the start. It's better if you don't jump in halfway. Trust me it's worth it.'

Neither of them objected and, before they had a chance to spark up a new conversation, the crowd of viewers began to exit, many of them smiling at each other, exchanging under the breath comments of how *eerie* or *surreal* that was. The three of them entered, followed by a large group of garrulous Italian students, their exhausted tutor hushing them in vain, already defeated. Taking their seats at the front, the black screen leered back at them, waiting. Chatting obnoxiously amongst themselves, the students voices echoed around the room, until their tutor made a last ditch attempt to assert her authority;

'Basta!'

Sensing her tolerance was nearing zero, the group fell silent.

The black screen flickered, before a deserted McDonald's restaurant appeared. There was something instantly harrowing about its emptiness: an abandoned space where human activity was still visible, with traces of half eaten meals and fresh trash lining the tables. A large — in this context, otherworldly — statue of Ronald McDonald grinned back at them through the screen, his smile seeming to evoke fear rather than mirth in the restless teenagers. Carl felt his body perspiring, conscious of the wet patches spreading under his arms. The Mcdonald's continued to gleam back at him. Switching from a wide angle shot of the restaurant, the camera turned to capture the bottom of a door, a thin trail of water

45

creeping forward. The rest of the screening held no coherent structure in his mind. The restaurant slowly flooded. Fast food debris floated in the water, the fryer's oil turning the hue a dirty brown. Eerily — this must have been what the two girls were speaking of — when the water was low, Ronald himself, or his statue, started to float around the restaurant, the affability of his waving hand and smile juxtaposing with the submersion of his surroundings.

This was a smile that would resurface during Carl's blackouts over the subsequent months. There was something in it, something akin to the rising of the wine glasses by the two red-faced men in Bermondsey, the toast to rising temperatures and sea levels. Something in that smile, while he sat there sweating and shifting in his seat, turned his stomach. The water continued to trickle in, happy-meal toys washed off their podiums into the fat-saturated swill that churned below them. Zooming in to focus on the counter, the glowing M flickered, dejectedly, before dying. The restaurant fell into darkness, removing the illumination from the cinema room. As the water continued to rise, the camera descended, floating underwater in amongst the paper wrapping and soggy bread buns that hung poised in the watery expanse. When no one in the room could tell how long they had been present, the screen faded to black, the sans serif title emerging on the screen:

FLOODED MCDONALD'S — A SUPERFLEX FILM

The three of them joined the procession of students, who resumed their energetic chatting. They only spoke when they were back in the glaring whiteness of the gallery space.

'What did you think?' Veronica asked, proceeding to offer her analysis before either of them could get a word in. 'I find it such a clever piece in that it really taps into the apocalyptic but in such a mild, and, I guess *cool* manner. I remember watching an interview with the Danish artists who designed it, saying how it was such a piece of chance; they spent *so* long designing the set, making everything by hand, but then you start to flood it, and there's no going back. You can't just start over again if it doesn't work because you've already *trashed* the set. They were saying how, even though they planned so much, there was no way of predicting how everything would play out. The statue for example: they had no idea it would float around the restaurant before collapsing into the deeper water. And that's what's so *forceful* about it. I don't know about you, but I think that was perhaps the most powerful part of the video. The fact that there's this enlarged plastic icon just waving back at you while the area of human activity becomes inundated. It's so historic, thematically speaking, in that it's this cultural space which is globally recognisable and... are you feeling alright, Carl?'

He hadn't been aware of his outward demeanour, having switched off during her racy analysis. Only the mention of his name brought him back to the gallery.

'Oh, yeah I'm okay. I really enjoyed that, well, not enjoyed, perhaps that's the wrong word, I mean, it was a really disturbing piece, something so hyper-real about it, like you said, with it being a globally recognisable cultural space, and, actually yeah I'm feeling a touch fatigued, mind if we head outside to see the other installation?'

'Of course, yeah. The swings are also really interesting' — a comment that made all three of them laugh.

Stepping out into the mid-afternoon sun, Carl sighed as he realised he'd been cooler inside the gallery. Swarms of children and adults clambered over the huge swings. Screaming infants called out to their parents, who in turn called back to them to give others a turn 'on the art'. Loitering next to the bright orange structures, crowds of visitors waited for their turn to experience the piece. Never before had Carl seen such enthusiasm at a gallery, which had, quite literally, become a playpark. Throngs of tourists bustled, cameras clicking, bodies fighting to be included in the snap.

Edging through them, the three took a seat on a wall near one of the sets. Veronica, perhaps uncomfortable with the paucity of their conversation, continued with her analysis:

'It's really interesting with this piece, how it completely reshapes how you look at the simple play-park object. I mean, it's so rare to see so many people this enthusiastic for something they could use any time they wished. I know, it's the same with any object that you place on a plinth. The position it embodies in that space reshapes how you interact with it. But there's something about taking this playful structure, one that we've all engaged with in the past, and reformulating it within this cultural space that almost *allows* adults to re-engage with their playfulness. As if normally, it would be socially unacceptable for them to just go to the park and play on the swings, but here it's expected of them - '

Neither Carl nor Anya responded: Veronica had already stood up, trailing off from herself. On the other side of the courtyard, a father called out to his children to come join him. Reluctant to lose their space, they protested, before giving into his demands. Wanting to snatch the opening, Veronica turned to them:

'Shall we have a go, before the space gets taken?'

Laughing, they all jumped up to take their seats. As their swinging commenced, Carl's thoughts wandered elsewhere. The sun struck down on his forehead like a beater, matching his swing's pendulum motion. Closing his eyes, the surrounding shouts became cacophonous, eventually fading into white noise. Oily water ran across his pupils, melding with visions of Buñol flooded by tomato juice, a lone plastic hand reaching out from the swell. The clinks of a thousand wine glasses chimed abrasively, creating dissonance with the Salat al-'isha, becoming rain. Blockchain warehouses throbbed in remote Scandinavian landscapes, the Estonian winter hitting his cheeks as he fled across the damp autumn fields surrounding Cruden Bay. A blue flash stinging his retina. He didn't realise he'd fallen until he opened his eyes, staring back up into Anya's, watching her mouth mime

The images continued to agitate. Throngs of vigilantes tearing up the concrete, running their fingers through arid soil. Power cables torn down, tied up, used as clothing lines. A population feeling the collective shadow of their ancestors. Eyes that dilated like oil spills.

When he found himself able to speak, he also found himself aware of the crowd circling him. He sat up, laughing at himself in a manner he could tell everyone perceived as forced. The Salat al-'isha still played faintly in the background.

'Can you hear that?' he asked to no one in particular.

'Hear what, Carl?'

'The Salat al-'isha, I don't think there are any mosques around here.'

Those who had come to check on him allowed Anya and Veronica to crouch beside him, politely dismissing themselves from the responsibility.

'Did you knock your head Carl? It's still painfully hot up here, perhaps you got motion sickness.'

Confused that he could no longer hear the afternoon prayer, Carl snapped his head from side to side, glancing at the surrounding buildings.

'Strange. I could have sworn I heard it. You're sure there's no mosques around here. Can you check, please?'

'Carl, are you sure you're alright? There's definitely no Mosques close to here', Veronica said, laughing a little. She went to make a joke to lighten the situation, but as she caught his eye, his serious expression made her stop. Concerned that he may have heatstroke, but conscious that refusing to check could aggravate his confusion, Anya pulled out her phone and loaded Google maps.

'Hmm, well, there's one.'

'Where?'

'It's the Baitul Aziz Islamic Cultural Centre, but it's all the way down near Elephant & Castle, a good twenty minute walk from here. I doubt you'd be able to hear it from where we are.'

'Oh,' he continued to stare into space. 'Well in that case, never mind.' He stood up, dusting himself down symbolically as if to indicate that he was back with them.

'Shall we get a drink? You mentioned you knew somewhere close by, Veronica?'

'Carl, are you sure you're feeling alright, we can take a minute if you need?'

'No no, I'm fine, honestly. I think the motion just went to my head, what with the heat and the coffee. Let's go find somewhere, I wanna hear more about Veronica's ideas for the VFL design.'

While completely unconvinced by this sudden change of energy, they both exchanged awkward glances, and agreed.

∞∞∞

Half an hour later they found themselves sat outside at a large, open top terrace bar, close to Borough Market. Having returned to full cogence during their walk along the Thames, Carl's earlier collapse seemed less worrying. Not wanting to embarrass him, Anya decided against suggesting he take something soft. Insisting that he buy the first round, he ordered three craft beers and followed them back to their table. Anya lit two cigarettes, offering the second to Carl even though he had his own, something she often did as a mark of affection.

'Mind if I?' Veronica asked, pointing to the packet.

'Sure.'

The three sat smoking in silence, looking out towards the dense, summer smog that circled the tips of skyscraper clusters. Myriad jets following automated flight paths crossed past each other, their white, geometric trails forming magenta halos above the buildings. Pulling a deep inhale from his cigarette, Carl studied the patterns forming in the sky. There was something about the way they faded, at quite drastically different speeds that made him realise he'd had this same thought only a few days ago. He looked down at the white rings of foam falling from the top of his glass. He thought about bringing it up with the other two, but thought that they'd put it down to him hitting his head.

'Thanks for suggesting the exhibition, Veronica. There was really something in the Mcdonald's video. As you said, it takes the theme of the apocalyptic but in such a cool, almost hesitant manner.'

'I'm glad you got something from it. I think it produces quite mixed reactions in its viewers... Like some people just find it purely ominous and *harrowing* in the moment. But I think its significance goes beyond that, like since I've seen it, everytime I pass by a McDonald's I can't help but see it flooded and it just reminds me of — well, I'm not sure *what* exactly, perhaps the fragility of the global food system?'

'Yeah, I think that's really what we'll be looking to achieve at VFL,' Anya cut in, 'I mean, that really has to be the role of what we're making. Not something that is just evocative in the moment, but an experience that stays with you, with countless visual triggers that take you back. I'm genuinely so intrigued to see what effect the sessions in these virtual reality worlds will have on me when I return to the city. I won't make you go into the details just yet, don't worry. I know you've been instructed to not let up too much before we experience the settings.'

'That's the thing, *even if* I wanted to, I myself couldn't really explain exactly what settings will govern each phase.' Veronice responded, pointing her unsmoked cigarette at Anya. 'That's what was so interesting about melding the design team with the computer science strand. We as designers had to put in so much work when it came to creating a visual and audio library, but because the settings work on algorithms, each phase will develop organically as it's experienced. So even though we're restricting ourselves to four virtual reality worlds, the *contents* will keep growing organically. Kind of in the same way that the Superflex designers set up the McDonald's but didn't know precisely what would happen when it flooded, we've programmed the aesthetics but we don't know exactly what form they'll take. That's why it's going to be so exciting to hear your reports. I feel like only then will I get a more lucid idea of the worlds that I've helped to co-design.'

She took a large swig from her beer, wiping the foam from her chin. The four of them sat contemplating for a moment. For Carl, the fact that soon he would be exploring these virtual reality worlds — *leaning from the future* as the VFL phrased it — seemed hard to process. Watching the city wilt under the evening heat, he felt almost nauseous at the idea of spending four weeks immersing in virtual reality worlds.

'It's quite surreal isn't it, to think how much we've spoken about the different worlds, trying to imagine what each one will be like? You know like how before you visit a new city, you come up with all these images of what it will be like, then when you arrive it's never as you expected.'

'The whole thing feels really quite abstract just now,' Veronica cut in, 'but wait until you've heard Anton explain the technology. He's got such a good way at mapping out how the VFL will be igniting what he calls a *technological literacy*. He's all about reshaping the metaphors we use, always saying how the problem with our current relationship to technology is that we don't know how to describe it. I remember when I first met him he wouldn't stop talking about the cloud as a metaphor for the Internet. About how it's so ironic, given that what we take to be the cloud couldn't be less amorphous or weightless. When we say the word 'cloud', we think of invisibility, of some faraway place, when in fact it consists of warehouses full of computers, satellites, fibre optic cables running under the seabeds... Honestly, I think his talk on Monday will demonstrate how our work will really change how people perceive these networks.'

Later that evening, Carl and Anya walked towards Borough Market tube station, the air sponge-like in its consistency. Both of them continuously ran the back of their arms along their foreheads, their shirts hanging loosely from their damp skin. Merging with the surge of human bodies piling through the station, their body odour blended with the crowd — a collective stench of bitter perspiration. As they piled onto the already overcrowded tube, each commuter sought desperately to fold their limbs into a tight space. Bare skin on bare skin. The hot air of the underground pumping through the open ventilation shafts. The train stormed through the tunnel, its passengers swaying, hazily. Anya, who always seemed unnaturally adept at dealing with overcrowding, turned to Carl, sighing.

'I feel like I can barely think straight, and I've only had two drinks.'

'It's this heat, the whole day I've found it hard to gather my thoughts.' Carl responded.

As the tube doors opened at London Bridge, two girls wearing face masks squeezed into the carriage. While the sight wasn't uncommon, some heads turned. A few beads of sweat trickled down their cheeks, creating small dark patches on the turquoise fabric. One of the girls, sensing she was being watched, addressed a man stood across the carriage.

'*What?*'

Fumbling with his phone, he pretended to have not heard, and started scrolling. No one else said a word until they disembarked at Bank.

As they ambled along with the other commuters, catching the escalator to the Central line, Anya turned to Carl.

'It's strange, but I've been thinking recently we should all be thinking seriously about using maks.'

'Because of the dust?'

'Because of the pollution. I think those two girls have the right idea. Only recently my father was telling me about the effects CO_2 increase is having on our cognitive capacities. I've always thought of it as bad for our lungs, for our organs, but for some reason I didn't tend to think about how it affects our brains.'

'Just the fact it's coming from your father is enough to take it seriously. He's... what would you call it, well, the *opposite* of a hypochondriac. Remember when he'd fallen of his bike and fractured his toe but wouldn't believe he needed to go to the hospital?'

'Yeah, I think *anosognosia* is the word you're after. But don't get me started on his stubborness... anyway, the reason I say is because he sent me this paper that was recently published in *Nature*. It was stressing how as the levels rise, our ability to think gradually diminishes. The author was noting how in pre-industrial times, up until around 1750 — *I think* — atmospheric carbon dioxide was around two-hundred and seventy parts per million. We only know this from studying ice cores, which are melting away now. It's kind of a strange metaphor, as the CO_2 increases, knowledge stored in these arctic chambers melts along with our cognitive abilities. So yeah anyway, this rate has been rising even since the industrial revolution. We're now at five-hundred parts per million in many industrial cities. But because it's rising exponentially, we should reach a thousand ppm by the end of the century. And at a thousand ppm, human cognitive ability drops by around... I think *20* percent — but I'd need to double-check. But here's the thing: with many buildings being poorly ventilated, it does already reach a thousand ppm in many of them, mostly in schools in poorer neighbourhoods. There were some schools in California where it even reached *two-thousand* ppm. It's so harrowing when you start to see the environmental crisis this way... Like, I don't know, how the more complex it becomes to tackle these questions the less clearly we're going to be able to think.'

Carl turned to face her, his face slightly flushed, small sweat patches visibly seeping through his linen shirt.

'Can we wait until we're out of the undergound? Sorry, but I can barely keep up with you. Let's jump off at Shoreditch and I'll walk with you back to Mile End.'

Emerging from the station, they leant against the wall, regaining their strength while the sun dipped below the horizon. Carl lit a Camel, offering the packet to Anya.

'Can we share one?'

'Yeah, sure.'

Walking through the high street, tables of diners spilled from the restaurants out onto the patios. The neighbourhood felt unusually busy, even for Shoreditch. All around them, crowds of trendy adolescents stood searching, drinks in hand, for any small space they could occupy. Facing straight ahead as he spoke, Carl begun relating his flashbacks to Anya. She could tell by his body language — the continuous shifting of his shoulders, the looking up to the sky and around him — that his explanation was as much for himself as it was for her.

'I had the *strangest* experience on the swing earlier. Like I really couldn't tell where I went. But it wasn't just that I lost my spacial awareness, or that I started hearing the Salat al-'isha, or that Buñol was covered in tomato juice...'

Suddenly conscious of the fact that Anya didn't have faintest idea of what he was speaking of, he paused, before realising that it was probably okay to continue.

'No what was strangest, about that whole series of stimuli that surfaced, was that I saw myself at the oil rig, or more that I saw myself *fleeing* from it. I mean, it's not that I don't still think about that experience, *quite often actually*. But more that the way I saw it, forming part of that sea of images, was that I felt it was... how would I put it? Like that one experience was presented to me again in that moment as if to tell me something.'

'Do you think it's because you're worried about the VFL? It would be completely understandable. I mean, I have my reservations too. And it would make sense that if you're stressed, such a memory might have resurfaced, a sort of PTSD symptom?'

Carl continued to look ahead, nodding at Anya's question without saying anything. He lit another Camel. Around them the evening light slowly faded, emphasising the intrusively white glare emitted from the sushi bar at the top of the street.

'Perhaps so. Yeah I'm really not sure.' he turned to face her, smiling sheepishly in a way that reminded her both of his proclivity for anxiety and of how much she cared for him. Wrapping her arm around his shoulder, she smiled as they walked in silence through Bethnal Green towards Mile End.

When they reached her front door, she invited him in to sleep on her couch, offering to cook for them tomorrow and spend the day regaining their energy before the meeting on Monday. He accepted — both of them relaxed in the knowledge that at this stage of their friendship, an invite to sleep on the couch was just that. No hidden messages. No subtle suggestions. She showered, before warmly embracing him and giving him the key to the balcony in the front room, knowing he'd most likely sit out there until late.

When she removed her clothes and collapsed into fresh sheets, Carl's voice, wavering and uncertain, started to play. She heard the ethereal voices of the Tallinn chamber choir, performing Arvo Pärt's *Te Deum*, a piece Carl had often left playing on repeat while he sat writing in her small living room — the bright celeste sky emitting the type of light only found in those northern regions. She felt her body start to cool as she recalled the cold autumn air gently pulling at her coat as she and Carl sat smoking on her balcony, the moment they realised they both shared something: two experiences that had led them to Tallinn.

A single drop of water dangled from the tap's lips. It hung there for some time, its movement so slow it wasn't visible to her. She only blinked when it dropped unexpectedly, catching the edge of a stained coffee glass in the sink. She knew she was going to reread it as soon as she woke up. Even while she drank a coffee and smoked with Carl, all she could picture was that one folder, hidden on an old hard drive in her cupboard. He knew something wasn't right; he asked her more than once, maybe even three times, if she were okay? She told him she was fine, just a bit spaced out because of the heat. Funny how the heat had become a way to excuse anything. It reminded her of when she tried to quit smoking a few years ago. Of all the things she'd really missed about it, one of the hardest adaptations was never being able to excuse herself without needing any reason beyond stepping outside to smoke. Any uncomfortable, or even just boring situation could be escaped by simply reaching for her packet of Marlboro and taking off.

She stood up, stretched her shoulders back and tucked her hair behind her ears. Should she read it? There didn't seem any reason not to read it but equally she found no way of justifying spending the morning reading something she already knew so well. No, she should probably just check her emails: with the immersions about to begin at the VFL, there were constant updates being fed back to all members. It wasn't that she needed to be aware of everything, but what if someone asked her something at a conference and she couldn't answer because she simply hadn't read the bulletin? All logic told her to not waste her morning by delving back into that one folder. But as she walked into her office and pulled out the small metal filing box from the top shelf, she just knew that nothing else would hold her attention until she had read it.

The F# chime rang out in her office as she powered up her iMac. She remembered laughing when Carl had said it was a shame Apple had decided to remove that opening chord from their new models. Only he could pick up on such a minute detail that most people wouldn't even notice had gone. She plugged in the hard drive and tapped in the long password that she still remembered as clearly as her own birthday. Scrolling through the sea of files — all of which acted as a sort of camouflage — she found the folder and hovered the mouse over it. A small breeze of warm air pushed through the balcony doors and ran across her bare legs. She lit a cigarette and leant back in her chair. For a moment she thought about putting the hard drive away and forgetting all about it. But the thought lasted for as long as the puff of smoke drawn away by the breeze. Tapping the tip of her thumbs and index fingers together, as she always did when pausing from typing to search for the right word, she opened the folder and saw the two documents, each entitled 'Type I'.

I

In São Paulo, the presence of overt political activism in the academic space was something completely new to me. Many of the students respected my research, admiring my interest in the ways in which sustainable practices grew out of the poorer communities for economic reasons. Coming from post-Soviet Estonia, where the aftershocks of authoritarian silencing were — *are* — still manifest, speaking out didn't come naturally to me. But a lack of fervor did me no harm. Instead, many found my cool sensibility captivating. The fact that, even in my third language, I spoke eloquently and succinctly caught people's attention.

One admirer of mine was Marco, an activist with whom I shared similar political outlooks. Integrating into his group of friends, I found something attractive about their militancy, their desire to implement radical change through direct action: something that I'd always found enticing, coming from a nation in which the citizens had suffered years of oppression. I'd been too young to know these perils, but had learnt through my parents about the 'hypernormalisation' of the society, the fact that everyone knew the system was failing and that everyone was lying about its progress, but couldn't act upon this truth.

During my two years in Brazil, the continued destruction of Amazon regions by oil and logging companies continued exponentially. Following a similar trajectory, Marco became increasingly militant, furious that people came out and protested in the street but never really pushed for direct action. In his opinion, the protests often just ended up in a party and a lot of chanting mantras that never resulted in any change. He often spoke about how Brazil killed more environmental activists than any other nation, of how the authorities wanted to scare them into being too afraid to speak out or act against them. What they needed was to be shown that they too were at risk, that people aren't just going to stand by waving banners. If they're going to act brutally, they too should be scared to walk the streets, scared to continue with their work through fear of also being silenced.

In the final months before our journey to the north, his behaviour turned obsessive, losing all of the previous charm and excitement that had attracted me to him in the first place. He had no interest in anything other than our plan. Even when I continued to work on my thesis, he became cynical, saying that Gambiarra was never going to be enough, that it was stupid to focus on small scale sustainability projects whilst huge corporations continued to rape and destroy their land. Only after I'd fled Brazil, when I was away from him, would I look back on our final two months together and see how my perception of him had warped. I'd become almost submissive, even silencing myself when I felt that he wasn't respecting my opinion. He often questioned me aggressively, insisting that if I really cared about the environment, I'd take real action with them, not just sit on my laptop writing about new Gambiarra inventions. This was my chance to do something that would actually change Brazil, that would send a message stronger than any I would ever manage with 'some thesis.'

One night, staring back into his bloodshot red eyes, I nodded in silence and agreed to go with them. For a moment after, he observed me, almost as if he never believed I'd let myself be convinced. A soft smile spread across his face, any signs of previous tension slowly dissipating. It was the face I'd originally been drawn to; the side of him that had been suffocated by his growing fury and anxiety over the previous months. Any power dynamics between us evaporated. As if everything else were on pause, we left the apartment and sat at the viewpoint on Avenida Paulista. I don't remember saying much, just nodding along in auto-pilot to everything Marco said.

Two weeks later we boarded a flight to Porto Velho, Rondônia. The other three that would be joining us were coming from different cities; two men on a direct flight from Brasília and a woman taking a boat from Manaus. A huge backpack weighed down on her shoulders when she boarded the passenger boat, set to move for three days past small port towns. With no security checks to pass through, she placed her bag in the storage room, the rest of the passengers unaware of the explosives sat nestling inside. After three days floating downstream, she arrived in Humaitá District, Amazonas, during the late hours of the evening. We'd agreed to meet her at the port, where we'd drive together to a small motel. Since Marco and I had left São Paulo, he'd ceased to treat me as his friend. We agreed to board the flight separately, travelling to the airport in different taxis. Once in Porto Velho, we made our way to separate hotels, making sure not to even share eye contact in the airport. With my blonde hair and lighter shade of skin, I checked in at a back-packers hostel, making sure to speak in a broken and 'foreign' Portuguese. When the full group had convened at the port, the two of us had kissed, staring back at each other without smiling, before stepping into the car in silence.

The driver, whose name we weren't allowed to know, drove us without asking any questions along highway 230 towards the Floresta Nacional de Balata Tufari. The rest of the details I always struggle to recollect fully — the feeling of nausea that set in having discoloured my memory. I knew more by reasoning than by recollection that we reached Lábrea in the early hours of the morning and found a small hotel where we paid for two nights. The first day the four of us remained inside the hotel, while Marco went alone to scope out the compound.

During our last day together, we waited inside until nightfall, checking the equipment and reiterating our plan again and again, until it felt like the event we were describing had already happened. At nightfall, we would abandon the hotel room, making our way across the small, deserted town, towards the forest. Moving by torch light, we predicted it would take us less than three hours to return back along the highway until we found the opening. From there, we would move inland, passing along the edge of the woodland so as to duck inside if any car headlights illuminated our path. By early hours, when the sky was still dark, we would cross the vast deforested area and reach the wire fence surrounding the compound. Cutting our way through on the south-west corner, closest to the forest that would lead us back towards Lábrea, we would move across the compound to the edge of the building towards the main generator. As long as we proceeded silently, the guards at the main gate, facing the north, would have no reason to move to the back of the building. Close to the main outside generator that controlled pressure levels, the unnamed woman from São Paulo would plant the device. If any of the guards were to encounter us, we'd shoot to kill, plant the device and flee, detonating it once we'd reached a two-hundred metre distance. With no intervention, we would move back to the forest, still under the night sky, disposing of any evidence in the river when we reached Lábrea. The detonation, unless activated, would be timed for 12 hours, giving us enough time to leave Humaitá District. By Marco's predictions, we'd have enough time to follow highway 319 north, where we'd dispose of the car; this was far enough from Rondônia that the authorities wouldn't have stopped any departures. Stopping in Manaus, we'd each move to separate hotels and wait it out for no less than a week, each posing as tourists. We would remain indoors during the day, only leaving to eat. The following week, we would each catch separate flights to Goiânia, before returning to our respective cities. There would be no further communication between us over the following months.

On the first day, when Marco set out to finalise our route, binoculars stashed in his bag, he passed by each of our rooms, making sure we knew not to go outside until he returned. Had we all been in one room, he would have returned to all of us as planned. Yet his paranoia, perhaps justified, had led him to believe that each of us staying in separate rooms would be the least suspicious option. For this reason, no one noticed when, two hours after he'd set off, I left the hotel and boarded a bus towards Porto Velho. By the time he returned at night, I was already in Lima District, having caught the first available flight out of Brazil. I purposefully didn't check the news until I arrived in California two days later. Only once locked in my hotel room did I learn of Marco's death.

A mixture of grief, guilt, but perhaps above all relief came over me. I waited inside my room for the next four days, desperate to catch my flight to Tallinn. Everytime I closed my eyes, I imagined Marco's face contorting as he pushed open my door, seeing that my bags were gone and suddenly realising that I'd fled. My heart palpitated as I imagined his rage, a rage I felt like a hot lamp on my skin as if he were sitting next to me in the hotel room. I imagined him screaming at the other three, demanding an explanation that none of them would have been able to provide; he would have come to realise the flaw in his own plan. I pictured him frantically trying to call me, redialing my number incessantly and being met each time with the answer machine: my phone was floating at the bottom of the Madeira river that crosses Rondônia. Each time I closed my eyes, I imagined the four of them pacing around the room, accusing me of being a traitor and of jeopardising their plan. Lying on my back, my breaths abrupt, I heard him insisting that they go ahead with the plan, growing furious when any of the other members suggested that I could have spoken to the police and that it was potentially too dangerous. Only when I sat down at one of the hotel's computers and read through Brazil's national news articles circling online did I get a clear image of what had happened.

Four terrorists, three men and a woman broke into the logging compound in the early hours of Friday morning. Having been spotted by two guards on duty, gunfire broke out, the guards both shot dead, along with two of the male terrorists. Having planted explosives in the generator, the remaining pair fled through the Floresta Nacional de Balata-Tufari to Lábrea where, posing as a couple, they boarded the 7a.m. boat towards Porto Velho. The explosive device planted at the compound failed to detonate, and was destroyed by the military at 14:13 hours. Hearing that the two of them had managed to catch the boat as planned made the news even harder to read. I imagined his relief at having thought he'd got away, his mind hyper-focused despite the chaos of the violent outbreak. I tried to picture them in Porto Velho: Marco glancing anxiously out of the window, checking for police presence. My eyes flicking across the text on the screen, I learnt of the final hours of a man whose description suddenly seemed alien. Two days later, one terrorist, posing as a tourist journeying to Bahia via Goiânia had attempted to board a bus in Candeias do Jamari. The Federal Police, who had been informed of the subject matching the terrorist's description, had been stationed throughout the town. When the man attempted to board the bus, two plain clothes officers stopped him, requesting to see his identification. He responded by producing his card, answering the officers questions and opening his small backpack. Despite his proclivity towards anger, I felt cold as I imagined his cool-headedness, his uncanny ability to remain outwardly calm in situations of grave intensity. Yet this time it *was* his anxiety that let him down. As the police led him to the side of the street for further questioning, Marco, perhaps realising that his excuse of a vacation wouldn't hold up due to his lack of possessions, made a last ditch effort to flee. Darting away, two policeman chased after him. As he sprinted through narrow, uneven side streets, sidestepping trash bags and young children on their way to school, a swarm of officers entered the neighbourhood from adjacent streets. Unaware of where his pursuers were coming from, he swung a left and met the barrel of two assault rifles, their bullets tearing through his chest as he tumbled into the dry, orange dirt. The identity and whereabouts of the fourth member was still unknown to the police.

The anxiety that tore throughme transmuted into fear. Would they come to realise that I had, in fact, accompanied the group? What about my friends in São Paulo? I'd finished my research, but hadn't said goodbye to anyone. What would they make of my disappearance? These were questions that would continue to plague me over the next year as I settled back into my deeply insular life in Tallinn. When friends from Brazil asked after me, as they often did, I told them that a family member had suddenly passed away and that I'd boarded the first flight home. Having finished my research, I wanted to be back in Tallinn now, close to my family. But, of course, I said, when I was next in Brazil, I'd be sure to come back and visit them.

I

The night sky was edging out from the shadows, the sun jittering, sinking below the horizon. We all squatted on the edge of the tree line, the roar of the North Sea providing an audible cover. It wasn't yet dark enough for us to take our small boat down to the water: we'd wait for the black sky to swallow the landscape before moving out into the open. The beach was deserted, but we didn't dare risk being seen. Instead, the three of us crouched in between the moist shrubbery, smoke pouring out from the thin holes of our balaclavas. None of us spoke: there was nothing of any importance that needed to be said. The cold wind cut at our bodies as we crouched, staring out towards the horizon.

When the only light remaining was the moon, glowing down on the water through a cloudless sky, we stood up, stretched and looked at one another. One man checked his watch: 17:34. Still unwilling to enter into much dialogue, he held out his wrist to show us. The time of evening made little difference: the rig was active twenty-four hours a day and we'd run the risk of being spotted at any hour. If this happened, the authorities would be alerted and we'd need to get away as soon as possible. The only cover we could rely on was the initial darkness of the sky.

Nodding to each other and extinguishing our cigarettes, we strapped our equipment to our backs and darted across the damp moss, descending towards the beach. Three black silhouettes, the moon bore down on us as we crept, reflecting back from pieces of broken glass jutting out from between the pebbles. With the military-style boat hoisted upon our shoulders, we crossed the beach and waded out into the sea. Salty foam spat up at us, the uneven rocks croaking underneath our boots. With the water at our waists, we lowered our vessel into the churning waves. One by one, we folded our bodies across the rubber, sliding onto the wooden bench. One of the men took out his GPS finder, inputting the rig's position. The screen flashed into life, beeping as it uncovered the distance and trajectory we needed to follow. Tapping the side of the boat, he motioned to us to kick-start the engine. Frothing and spluttering, it burst into action, its iron cough muffled as we lowered it into the waves. The cold air tore at our balaclavas, pouring salty gusts across our eyes. The headlight on the front of the boat drew a perfect beam in front of us, illuminating the warps of the swell.

The lights of the rig became visible before the GPS started to bleep, letting us know we were approaching its field of vision. The man controlling the steering cut the engine and I cut the headlight in quick succession. For a moment everything went quiet; even the wind. The three of us crouched on the deck, almost admiring the godlike figure of the structure, towering above the water. The man at the head of the boat flicked open the GPS screen.

We could still get a bit closer before using the oars. Gently restarting the engine, the headlight now switched off, we crept forward, the wind drowning out the engines faint hum. When we could see the beam of light circling the water below the rig, we cut the power and reached for our ores. Tentatively, we glided forward, edging closer to the nearest of its four iron legs. Peering through my binoculars, I noted a few workers stood at the edge of the metal railings on the top deck. I signalled to the others to move to the left. We'd approach it from another angle.

Small waves slapped against the rig's legs, tossing our boat back and forth as we snuck up and tried to grab a hold of the iron. When we had temporarily secured the boat, we didn't wait to hear if we'd been spotted. The man on the boat's left knew that this was his moment. Opening up his large gym bag, he pulled out the device and placed it into its carefully cut out metal cramps. We held his waist as he leant over and gripped the metal. The boat continued to sway and jolt, making it difficult for him to keep his footing. Securing the clamps to the structure, he breathed a sigh of relief, having always been doubtful that their engineer would have got the dimensions perfect. But there it was: our signal cutter stood majestically, its red light blinking out towards the depths of the Atlantic. Folding himself gently into the boat, he placed his index finger and thumb together, signaling that it was secured. We wrenched at the ores, pulling the boat away through the illuminated waters and crossing the beam's border, immersing ourselves within the safety of the night sky.

When we were at a far enough distance not to be picked up by the lights, we paused our rowing and turned to face the rig. I took out my binoculars, scanning it for movement. Rolling the focus reel gently with one thumb, I stood for a few minutes, breathing deeply. When I lowered them, I turned to the others.

'Nothing.'

'I think we did it, by the time they know what it is, or even locate it, that will already be too late. Their whole system will be down. Even with their back-up generator, they'll encounter the same problem. All signals cut, all lights out.'

'Shall we do it then?'

'Do it.'

The man who had secured the device pulled out a small remote, aiming it like a wand towards the rig. With the dry wind richocheting through our ears, the lights went out. We stood in silence, struck by the black expanse that leered back at us. Within seconds the engine was running and the headlight was glaring out towards the mainland. The man with the GPS stood at the helm, watching over the trajectory. Another howl from the wind. The ocean lit back up. Cutting the engine, the driver swivelled the boat around. In those few seconds, the flash had already dimmed, but out in the distance, orange flames flickered high into the sky. The smell of burning oil drifting towards us, polluting the air.

'What the fuck was that?' The driver screamed. We just stood staring.

'It was meant to render the rig impotent, not fucking send it up in flames? What the fuck did you do to it?'

Ignoring his questions, both because I didn't have the answer and because it wasn't the time for explanations, I turned to the third man.

'Get the engine back on, now.'

Scrambling for the controls, we resumed our positions, careering towards the mainland, the wind screaming for us. When the grey pebbles of the beach became visible, the man at the helm turned to the driver, instructing him to go right up to the shore. When we felt the rudder cracking as it bent into the seabed, we jumped overboard and thrashed through the shallows, heaving the boat out of the sea. Running as quickly as we could, my lungs constricting as I strained my body, we reached the van parked in a small lay-by on the edge of the woodlands. Opening the back doors, we loaded the boat and piled into the front seats. While the off-shore rig creaked and groaned under the weight of the flames, its workers calamitously piled into the small lifeboats; the cold spray of the waves cooling their inflamed cheeks. Across the small stretch of the North Sea, we wound along the coastline road, heading to the borders. When we reached our designated forest, the driver swung left, pulling into the small, deserted car park. The engine cut and we sat in silence, staring into the black expanse of the windscreen. Eventually the driver pulled of his balaclava and turned to us.

'What the fuck just happened there?'

The man who had planted the device turned to face him, breathing deeply as he removed his balaclava.

'I don't know, Anthony said all it would do is blow the power because of the signals being cut. It should have just sent the system into overload and shut it down. Then even when the back-up generator kicked in, the problem would have been the same, scrambled signals, so everything just cuts. He didn't say anything about explosions...'

'He didn't *say anything*? You mean he didn't even *mention* that this could happen?'

'You were fucking *there*. You heard his explanation; he only showed me how the clamps worked. I know as much as you do. There must have been something he didn't predict, some kind of imbalance sparked by the system overload that caused a spark. *I* don't fucking know.'

'That's great. A whole fucking rig of dead people because Anthony didn't quite get how the thing worked. All of us on a charge of multiple murders because he got his predictions wrong.'

'They had lifeboats, they might have got on them before the whole thing went up.' I pulled my balaclava off, my pale face dripping with sweat.

'Oh sure, I bet they're *fine* actually, what the fuck am I worrying about? They had lifeboats. Let's just hope they got to them before they *melted.*'

Batting his head several times against the headrest, he lit a cigarette and closed his eyes.

'Okay look,' he said more to himself than to us, 'we can't lose our cool now. We fucked up, Anthony fucked up — doesn't fucking matter anymore. What happened, happened. We need to stick to the plan. We'll drive down to the scrap yard near the borders. We've made good time so we'll be there way before day break. Get rid of the boat, change the licence plates and head down to London. The quicker we're back, the better.'

The night sky was growing fainter by the time we approached the borders; light just starting to steal over the horizon. Following the GPS, we passed through small towns, our warm breath steaming the windscreen. Winding down empty roads just outside of Dumfries, we followed a bumpy track towards the wire fence of the scrap yard. Pulling up, the driver jumped out and took a cautious glance around. No one. No sound. Opening the gate, stacks of rusty cars and skips piled high with metallic waste were dotted across the mud. Pacing back to the van, he opened the passenger door.

'Let's go. You wait by the gate, keep an eye out. Any noise, we're out of here.'

The other two men wrenched the boat from the back, loading it onto their shoulders. Moving swiftly, they paced into the scrapyard, following the driver's orders to head to the far corner where he'd spotted other abandoned boats. I stood by the entrance gate, fumbling with my lighter, my hands shaking.

The events that followed happened too quickly for me to recall how I acted. The flash of a blue light hit my eyes before I heard the sirens: the deep fluorescent beam darting in between the trees acting as a phantasmic omen of the chaos that was about to ensue. The moment of that blue flash, that lasted less than a second, would play back in my mind over and over again. It would come to me in my dreams, or when I was walking down the street: the blue glare of a kebab shop or the entry to a nightclub. That moment — in which I suddenly registered what was about to happen but knew it was too late to act. Before I could call out, screams of 'armed-police' and the roar of car tyres skidded in the mud as they circled the van. A swarm of officers piled out of the cars, guns raised. Still out of their vision, I sprinted to the edges of the yard, crouching behind a pile of disused cars. I turned to face the other two, but there was no need to warn them; they'd already heard the news.

When I heard the shout of 'clear', and the stampede of boots thundering into the scrap yard, I tucked myself into the passenger foothold of the car I was crouched behind, pulling the rusty door ajar. I heard screams of 'stay where you are' and 'place your hands on your head' directed towards the other two. Feet pounded the floor as they scoured the area. Opening my eyes to glance through the door, my eyes met a tear in the wire fence, two meters from my hiding spot. That was what I remember most clearly about the experience: that dilemma. Should I stay hidden, or should I run? Was I safer tucked in the car, or trying to move through the forest? The sound of car doors being wrenched open, still at a slight distance from mine, answered the question. Crawling out from my car, I pried myself through the wire. A loose end scratched my cheek, drawing blood. Still on my hands and knees, I continued into the forest, panting, whimpering to myself until I was past the first tree line. With no idea where the police were coming from, there was no way of judging what was stealthy. I raised myself up and ran, damp wood chips and leaves spraying up under my feet as I tore into the distance with no direction, my survival instinct overriding my aching body.

Unsure of whether I'd been seen at any moment during the entire mission, I didn't dare enter any public spaces. I needed a train station; needed to get back to London, but if they knew there was a third member, I'd be completely trapped on the train. As I ran across the wet meadows, passing through forests chopped up and segmented by wire fences, I noted a sign informing me that Dumfries was only a 2 mile walk. Terrified of entering it, but aware that with no shelter I wouldn't be able to hide out in the forest, I decided to chance it and look for a B&B. Luckily, my wallet was still tucked in my back pocket. I decided to get the first available room and descended the footpath, the midday sun now warming my skin. Passing by dog walkers, I avoided all eye contact, eventually reaching the town and circling the streets as I searched for a place to hide out. The normality of the setting turned my stomach; families walking with their shopping bags, pubs filled with locals reading their papers, groups of teenagers loitering at bus stops. My heart palpitations shot pains through my chest; my fear that people would *just know* overwhelmed me with paranoia. The idea of waiting there, perhaps indefinitely, sickened me. Going against all logic, I followed the signs towards the station, boarded a train to Carlisle and caught the connection to Euston.

With no official responsibilities tying me to London, I left the UK the following week, heading to Prague with the excuse of needing space to work on my book. Not having a job to quit, or a university position to take time away from, made this transition quite simple. The publication of my masters thesis three months ago had landed me a modest but respectable payment. That, alongside some small savings I'd amounted over the previous years meant that I'd be able to hold myself up for the next few months. Having rented out a small studio apartment in the city's suburbs, I followed the news updates coming in from the UK. To my relief, there had been no casualties at the rig. Flicking through the news channels, a BBC presenter read the facts back to me:

'The explosion, caused by a rapid change in pressure when the system cut out, caused an abnormal surge in one of the pressure tanks. The engine sparked and went up in flames, but fortunately didn't spread quickly enough to engulf the rig before the workers could get into their lifeboats.

With no means of communication, they'd been saved by a local fishing boat that had spotted the flames and called for help. The rig, which had been the terrorists' initial aim, was damaged beyond repair. BP will be looking to dismantle it over the coming year. Two men have been arrested and charged with counts of terrorism and attempted murder.

Authorities were alerted by telephone by a local man who had seen the glow coming from across the water. Asked if he'd noticed any suspicious activity, he noted a van driving at high speed along the coastal path, but didn't get the licence plate or see the driver. All police departments across the west of Scotland were called into action, instructed to stop and search any vehicle matching the description. Only in the early hours of the morning, when notice was given of a van spotted in New Galloway, did authorities rush to investigate. It was at the Cargenbridge scrap yard that the van was uncovered, along with two men attempting to dispose of a boat they used to reach the oil rig. The two men, whose names have not been released, confessed to all charges placed against them. They will stand in the Crown Court in the following week.

While the two men claim there were no other participants, recent investigations have given police reason to believe otherwise. Traces of blood along the opening of a wire fence at the compound have indicated the presence of a third suspect. Their identity is still unknown to police.'

No profile of the third member. No casualties. I lay back on my mattress on the floor, lit a cigarette and stared up at the tobacco stained ceiling. We'd fucked up, hard. Or perhaps not fucked up, got unlucky, you could say. I tried to feel guilty for the other two, but the more I thought about it, the fairer it felt that it had been me that got away. My mind reverted back to the question I'd been asking myself since I got on my flight to Prague. How had I, the classroom anthropologist, been convinced into undertaking such an act? The more I thought about it, the more bitterness I felt towards the crowd of activists I'd fallen in with. My one consolation

73

was that I knew no one in the group would spill anything. All their actions were too interconnected. If I got uncovered, so too would others, and vice versa. For now, I'd take some time away from London. Other members wouldn't try to contact me. I was sure of it.

After returning to his flat in the late afternoon, Carl spent the Sunday evening rearranging his belongings, trying to establish some sort of space he could refer to as his 'area of work'. This consisted of a small desk stationed in front of the window. Most of the papers or other paraphernalia that the flat surface had accrued was packed into drawers inside his cupboard. Two of the healthiest looking plants were lifted from his kitchen windowsill and placed on either far corner of the table, acting as two pillars of clarity that would enable him to work. The only other object placed onto the wood was a clean ashtray. Stepping back to admire the new workspace he'd carved out, he gave an affirmative nod to himself. He contemplated placing some pens and paper alongside the plants, just to highlight that this was now a zone in which reports would be written. Even if the reports needed to be typed, he reached the conclusion that the presence of these objects would help enable his workflow. He rearranged the remaining rooms of his flat, hurriedly piling any clothes into the washer and pushing any excess books or papers into spaces out of sight. When the flat appeared minimal, even clinical, he retired to the balcony and collapsed into his hammock, pleased with the air of orderliness he'd created in his living space.

When the salat al fajr — which now acted as his alarm clock — roused him from his sleep, he got to his feet and stood gazing out towards the mosque, leaning on the rail and stretching. Feeling energised, he took a cold shower with his bathroom window wide open, his eyes closed as the sound of water striking his face slowed his breathing. After dressing, he gave a final patrol of the flat, checking for any leftover mess that could disrupt the tranquility of his writing sessions. Satisfied with the layout, he grabbed his laptop bag, patting down his pockets for his phone, Camels and keys, before making his way to the tube station to meet Anya.

When he arrived at Euston Square, she was outside waiting for him. With over forty-minutes to spare before the meeting commenced, they sat down at a small café with outside tables. Carl ordered them two espressos with a cube of ice in each one, the morning heat already at twenty-four degrees celsius.

'How are you doing after yesterday, do you feel well rested?'

'Yeah, I'm feeling much better after the weekend. I spent the evening organising my flat and managed to arrange a small work space. I think in a way the project starting now is really good timing. I've been in need of some kind of writing work to help structure my weeks. Something stimulating that I can really get stuck into.'

'I guess even though it's not detached from your other work, it will still be something *new*?'

'*Mmm*, exactly. That's the problem with the work at the university. It's never in short supply, but so much of it tends to be so draining. Plus the more I've thought about this over the past few weeks, the more excited I feel to be a part of it. I mean, it could be something really powerful, could be that spark that we've spoken about before. Who knows just now, but yeah, I feel good about it.'

He inhaled deeply on his Camel, before finishing his coffee, careful not to choke on the icecube that was melting on his tongue. He looked back at Anya, suddenly conscious of the fact that recently most of their conversations had revolved around him, around how *he* was feeling, or what *his* expectations were. Slightly self-conscious, he pushed a few questions at her.

'And you? How do you feel? Do you still feel excited for the project?'

Raising her eyebrows slightly, as she often did when asked a question that required much consideration, she looked down at her cup, exhaling a thin beam of smoke.

'Yeah, I think I am. I *think* I am. It feels quite overwhelming, to be honest. To know that the reason I moved over to London, what *two* years ago now? Yeah, two years. To think that this was the driving factor... I mean, it's not that I have doubts, but it's more that I've had so much time to process the ideas behind the project that the same excitement it gave me initially has transformed into a more... what would you say? Professional, outlook — I guess. As if I just *know* this is something I want to be a part of, whether or not the concept of Virtual Future Lessons, *whatever that entails*, has the galvanizing effects I initially imagined.'

'Virtual Future Lessons. It's strange we always refer to it using the acronym. But when you actually say the name, it takes on this other significance. Almost like I'd forgotten what the letters actually stood for.'

They both laughed at this, as the temperature crept up to twenty-eight celsius, informing them that it was time to make their way to the building.

The VFL centre itself, a series of offices and studio spaces, was located within a tall yet unassuming building within the grounds of the University College London. When they arrived, Anya checked the directions on her phone to find out which door led them to the correct lecture theatre. Climbing flights of stairs that smelled like dried floor cleaner, they could hear voices not far above them. As they reached the top floor, the stairwell opened out onto a spacious hallway. A small cohort of casually dressed people stood chatting, turning to face them as they approached through the rotating doors. Large windows ran alongside either side of the building, lines of plants stood wilting in the harsh sunlight that flowed through the glass. Recognising each other, Veronica smiled back, greeting them warmly with a hug.

'Great to see you both,' she said, before skipping any polite small talk. 'I don't know about either of you, but I haven't been able to stop thinking about that McDonald's video. I actually had a dream last night

I was in a mall by myself, with everything as it normally would be during closing hours, *then*, then I just came across this McDonalds, the inside of it completely flooded, so I went to the glass and as I reached out a finger to touch it, the whole thing just *smashed*, shattered right in front of me.'

She let out a laugh that seemed strangely jovial given the intensity of her dream, sparking laughter in both Anya and Carl. A short silence hung between them.

'I wonder what that's trying to tell you?' Anya offered.

'Who knows?' she said with a theatrical shoulder shrug, before resuming a more formal tone.

'Anyway, enough about my dreamworld, how are you feeling, Carl? You're looking well.'

'Much better now, thanks. I managed to get some time to recharge over the weekend.' Aware that the other members had stopped talking and were facing them, Carl directed the conversation away from his health. 'Pleased to meet you all,' he said warmly, addressing the small group.

'Yes sorry, let me introduce you! These three have been working with me recently. Keiran, Sadie, Cara — Carl and Anya are also with us on the project.'

All of them nodded at each other politely. The short space of silence granted Carl enough time to access their appearances. *Pretty casual*, he thought to himself, glancing at their trainers. He wasn't sure what made him more uncomfortable, the silence or the sudden feeling that he was overdressed. Pretty casual, *for a conference*. His anxiousness made way for an inward laugh, his nerves fast tracking to humor as a coping mechanism. Veronica piped up, breaking his neurotic musings.

'These three are working with the publicity for the project. They've already amassed quite the network, contacting publishing companies, journals, universities and other research institutions, making sure they're ready to publish our findings at the end of the phase trials.'

'It's gonna be the first step before we look at how to gain a wider audience.' one of the women, either Cara or Sadie, interjected. 'As I'm sure you know, we're trying to make sure it doesn't just remain in the bubble, so to speak, but that it has quite the far reach. But by starting with these institutions, before moving into gallery and cinema spaces, we'll have the official backing to spread the installations.'

Before anyone could comment, the doors leading from the stairs swung open; another group of members were making their way through the hallway. Veronica turned to them, beckoning with her hand.

'We better jump in and grab a seat before it starts.'

ooooo

All six of them moved inside to the windowless lecture room, the AC's whirring above them. As they took their seats, Carl breathed a sigh of relief, his body cooling down for the first time since his cold shower. From the large illuminated screen behind the lecturer's podium, the words Virtual Future Lessons stared back at him, the sub-caption reading 'learning from the lessons of the future'. Small groups started to file in until the doors were closed just before the clock struck ten a.m. The hall was less than half full. This opening event, of course, was kept private for the official members. The surrounding chatter hushed until silence prevailed, at which point a tall, slim man dressed in a white polo-shirt, dark suit trousers and black running shoes made his way onto the stage. A small burst of clapping accompanied his walk to the podium. A subtle energy pulsed through the room, each member sitting upright, staring intensely toward the stage. There seemed to be a shared understanding that what they had all been waiting for was soon to commence. Smiling back at the group, the speaker greeted them:

'Welcome and thank you all so much for being here. As all of us know, this event has been a long time coming, and first and foremost I'd like to congratulate all of you for your patience and dedication. We're extremely excited to be here to discuss the details of the next step we'll be taking towards releasing the VFL. For some of you, this will be the most important part of your journey so far. But for all of us, the fact that the phases are about to be tested — *and for the first time documented* — is a hugely significant moment.

Now, I know that everyone present here will be familiar with the ethos and ideas that have guided this project into being. But seeing as this is the first time we've all been present in the same space, I'd like to start my talk by running through a little bit about the VFL; how the idea was conceived of, the research that has been put into it, a little bit about the team, how we arrived at the point we now find ourselves, and what our expectations are for the future. When this has been covered, we'll be discussing the role of our phase testers and of what happens at the end of the test period. So...'

He cleared his throat a little, taking a sip from his water and turning to the screen behind him. Noticing that almost everyone around him had a pen and paper in front of them, Carl dug into his rucksack to find his notebook. As he sat up straight, he became aware of the noise he was making. No one turned to look, but he sensed a certain disapproval. He made sure to zip up the bag gently, feeling each of the teeth click together.

'As I'm sure most of you already know, the VFL's inception came in the winter of 2017, during a three month residency hosted by the MIT Media Lab. Those invited for the residency programme were specifically selected for their cross-disciplinarity, a key characteristic not only of every founding member, but of each of you sitting there in the audience. Were you not of this type, you wouldn't have been accepted onto our programme. So, yes, the residency at the Media Lab.

Well, I guess the easiest way to explain it is that MIT thought it'd be a fun experiment to lock up a group of interdisciplinary thinkers; artists, writers, computer scientists, coders, AI researchers, programme designers and the like for three months and just see what happened. We were sort of their guinea-pigs for this experiment'.

He let out a little laugh, looking to the members sat at the edge of the stage on a panel, whom everyone in the audience now realised had also been part of the residency. Carl noted how his intonation rose and fell, almost chiming. For the most part, his speech seemed to modulate quite naturally, and when he wanted to emphasise something, it was clear. Yet, every now and again, a certain inflection would create a white space around the words. His hands moved perpetually in front of him, drawing shapes in the air, as if he were inadvertently placing his words into different spaces on the stage.

'Basically, no one at MIT knew what we'd create, nor what we even wanted to create. Perhaps

if we'd been put together years
earlier,

well who knows what we'd have come up with. But,

as everyone surely remembers, 2017 proved to be a particularly unstable year, where so much of our attention was taken up by

flooding

or droughts occuring in different corners of the globe. Following month after month of news updates covering Hurricane Irma in the Dominican Republic, the thousands of people killed by flooding in south Asia, the aggressive droughts that wiped out swathes of humans and animals alike in East Africa, similar heatwaves in India and Pakistan, or Hurricane Harvey coming from the Atlantic to force thousands from their homes in Texas and Louisiana....

Well, it felt that no matter what background you were coming from,

81

the growing concern for climate related disasters was immediate. Yet what many of us shared,

unknowingly until we met,

was a
latent sense

that the greater the coverage and the more frequent the hypothesis laid out within the scientific community, the larger question of how to act itself became more obscure, more obfuscate.

What I certainly felt during this time was a sense of apathy, of futility... inertia. When I looked around, I couldn't help but think that no matter how intensely these effects were being felt, most people... well, hmm, I guess you could say they still struggled to imagine a world in which these drastic changes would stop being changes and be simply the constant.

During those summer months, I found myself inadvertently falling into the fatalist mindset, imagining our societies gradually imploding as the harsh changes in our climate rendered obsolete the smart systems in which we live.

I'm sure this scenario,

given the current state of affairs in London,

doesn't seem so far-fetched to most of you?'

He looked back at the audience, each member glancing at each other and moving their heads, neither indicating a clear affirmation or negation.

'One of the most complex and overwhelming qualms I had to face up to was figuring out exactly where *I* stood in relation to new technology. What should a computer scientist *really* be doing with their time?

Whatever your domain,

   I'm sure

this is a dilemma many of you have faced:

 the difficulty in trying to recognise how technology can help us to overcome the current ecological collapse, without falling into the trap of *naively relying* on technology to provide answers to the exponentially complex questions that face us.

 This question, I believe, starts with recognising what sort of world we want to live in. If we want to understand and realise different ways in which technology can be used to aid us in our struggle for ecological and political stability, we need to think about the possible worlds we want to live in. Only by imagining new and creative ways to sustainably integrate technology can we start to paint a picture of what our societies of the future might look like. '

 He paused again, taking a sip from his water and looking down towards his feet. He continued to look down, breathing deeply, gathering his thoughts. Carl noted how the more he stressed certain words, the more troubled he looked, as if the very act of enunciating was forcing him to reconsider the very questions he was currently posing.

'Well, these were the ideas I went to the residency with.

  Questions of how to envisage better worlds of the future, worlds that we would actually want to live in, *as well as ones that we want to avoid.*

What I didn't really expect was that everyone else in the group would share similar, if not the *same* concerns as mine.

And,

being at MIT,

more understandable that these concerns would be inextricably linked to technology and the role it could play, both as an aid to the problem and a cause of it.

While we haven't the time to really explore even a *fraction* of the ideas that were shared during our hours of conversation, what all of us unwaveringly agreed on was the necessity to think past the chaos and uncertainty of the present moment, and envisage ways to look into the future to gain an understanding of how to act in the present.

What we mean by this,

essentially,

is the necessity to look not to the past for lessons, but to find a way of

learning from the future.'

This enunciation felt measured, the speaker evidently having pinpointed its delivery.

'So how does one *learn from the future*? It starts here,
in the present moment,
with the *current* data we have at our disposal.

Study the present data to envision future worlds from which we can learn.

This type of analysis,

                              we agreed,

would allow us to create these future worlds from which we can gain insights.

But yeah, *look to the future for lessons,*

                                        I mean

    initially none of us really understood what that meant'.

He let out another laugh, looking back at the intent eyes of the audience with a sincerity that made everyone smile. He seemed to recognise the difficulty of what they were trying to achieve and yet this wasn't any messiah speech: he seemed to have real passion and concern for the future of the planet. His uncertainty, actually, helped to assure them that the project wasn't the implausible vision of some techno-utopian.

The truth was that no one in the room knew the answers to the complex questions of technology's role in ecological stability: they were too multifaceted. The fact that their group's leader recognised this was, for many of them, crucial. He continued:

'Yeah, so, it took us some time to really figure out how such an abstract concept could actually be transformed into something concrete, something viable. How do you learn from the lessons of the future, lessons that can't be lessons because they haven't yet happened? You can imagine worlds of the future, imagine how you'd like or not like the world to be. But you can't gain experience or understanding from your musing on worlds that don't yet exist. In line with this dilemma was the question of whether creating imagined worlds of the future, even if we were able to, would really offer us insights into how to act in the *present* moment. Would creating worlds of the future actually help us at all, if we couldn't understand how we got to them?

The answer we arrived at was,

well, yes,

somewhat,

but not fully.

We all agreed that there had to be some value in imagining better or worse futures, principally because it gives us something to aim towards. However, if we could also come to comprehend *how* to get there, that would truly be something of worth. So where did this lead us to?'

Turning his body towards the panel, his eyes flitted between them and the audience. There was something about his pauses, his glances directed towards the panel that suggested he almost *needed* their verification. Carl started to perceive how, now and again, members of the panel would nod to themselves as they caught his eye contact. Leaning on his hands, he admitted to himself that his interest was falling more on the speaker's behaviour than on the content of his lecture.

'When trying to figure out how to create these worlds, we were fortunate to have both Dr Alice Melynk and Dr Thomas Meyer with us, two computer scientists who have spent the past decade studying the coding process behind the creation of virtual realities.

Coupled with our designers, we knew that there was the potential for us to design worlds of the future that people could step into However, we all agreed that designing these worlds wouldn't offer any solution of *how* to work towards building them.

We easily foresaw the risk of falling into the feedback loop; of being confused by excess possibilities and continually looking for more information to solve the current complexities:

of course

this would lead to even more confusion.

This is a condition that affects us hugely at present. More information does not lead to more informed decisions. Nor would possible future worlds,

which we had no how idea how to reach,

help us take meaningful collective action in the present. What we needed, both as a way of creating the worlds and explaining the paths leading to each one, were the use of

complex prediction algorithms.

These algorithms would not only take vast amounts of information from our present world in order to map out potential worlds of the future. These algorithms would have the ability to *decipher* this information.

What we,

and when I say we,

I mean Dr Joseph Janssen,

was able to bring to the table,

was an AI into which we were able to input data ranging from

                                      diverse areas such as

    political stability,

        world population growth,

        air-temperature changes,

            growth within smart technologies,

to name only a few, which could then be algorithmically mapped on to a timeline of the coming decades, predicting certain consequences of these changes and growths. What was important to note is that these were *predictions,* not objective answers. But what these predictions allowed us to do was alter certain features,

                            let's say,

concrete consumption & population growth.

What would happen if it were to decrease in this continent? Running these changes through the software would, of course, yield different predictions across a multitude of different domains — from CO2 levels, housing developments, the rise of certain political ideologies or the prominence of blockchain technologies. And *these* changes grow exponentially with every alteration you implement. So, by working our ideas into this prediction software, we could start to map out *not only* what different futures could look like, but what actions will lead us in which direction.

But perhaps the most fascinating aspect of Dr Janssen's AI is not merely that it uses a set of algorithms to map out these future possibilities, but that the product, that is the *make-up* of the virtual worlds, are

constantly

in flux.'

Another measured delivery, Carl thought to himself as he watched the audience grow flustered — the description almost arousing the other members.

'What this gives us, in essence, are future worlds that are constantly developing, in real time. With every change that occurs in the prediction software, certain elements of the VR world alter accordingly; the result of this being that no one experience is the same and no one world ever runs the risk of becoming outdated. So, for each user that steps into one of the future worlds, as an accompaniment to each experience will be an explanation of how the software envisioned and predicted such a future, outlining the changes that were inputted into each version to create this specific world.'

He took a deep breath, visibly fatigued by the task of needing to condense the details of such a complex software into a short lecture.

'This may sound grossly oversimplified,

in fact,

I'm sure it does.

But with the complexity of the system's design, we cannot spend our time today going into the finer details — although I do of course encourage all of you to familiarise yourselves with this by reading Dr Janssens work.

So, having come to understand how the system of predictive algorithms could function, this left us with the question of how to translate this into a visual experience. We wanted this experience to be as immersive as possible, an experience that allows each user to temporarily exist as a spectator in one of these future worlds. That's where the expertise of our VR designers, Dr Meyer and Dr Melynk proved invaluable. Not only has their research allowed us to design these hyper-realistic worlds, but their ability to synchronise the graphic make-up of these environments with the prediction algorithms has really allowed us to create something hitherto unheard of.'

He stared back at them for a few seconds, an energy pulsing through his eyes that radiated out towards the audience. Smacking his lips, he continued:

'Studies have shown that VR can affect people's decision making like no other technology.

As I'm sure many of you will have learnt through experience,

when VR works well,

it sticks with you.

What I mean by this is that an experience in VR can really lodge in your memory, can be as beautiful or as traumatic as anything experienced in real life. If VR wasn't so effective at creating these immensely powerful experiences that can really change how people think and act, we wouldn't want to use it.

So what we've got,

well...

let me reiterate it once more.

What we have at our disposal, are real-time virtual realities of the future, each based on predictions that are both reliable *and* decipherable.

What we've done is achieve what we initially set out to do. We've created something that will, for the first time, allow us to look into the future and learn lessons *from* it. Lessons that will help us shape the present world by enabling people to comprehend *through experience*, how our decisions today will affect tomorrow.'

At this, the audience broke out into a steady applause, many members turning to each other to exchange grins and raised eye-brows. An energy of optimism and expectation flowed between them, each member becoming aware that they were part of something huge, something that in years to come future generations could look back on as a turning point in their history. The magnitude of such a possibility was almost incomprehensible. Yet while he clapped and turned to smile back at Anya, deep inside Carl's stomach there churned a feeling of skepticism, one that he couldn't help but think grew out of distrust for the speaker. While understanding that it was due to time restrictions, he felt a certain frustration that he'd brushed over some of the more complex information regarding how the algorithms functioned, and how these could be *translated* into reliable graphics.

Watching the audience around him clapping, smiles beaming from their faces, he felt a certain uneasiness and even a mild repulsion at the faith this audience was putting in such a complex piece of technology. As much as he tried to convince himself otherwise, he felt that the audience's conviction mirrored a certain religious adherence he'd witnessed during his years as an activist. He wanted to raise his hand and request that the speaker elaborated on the data being fed to the algorithms, for evidence that it was reliable and *decipherable*, as he'd promised. But he felt almost ashamed to be that person; the cold skeptic in a room throbbing with confidence. His thoughts were broken when the speaker called for calm, reminding them that they still needed to discuss the next step.

'Thank you, really, thank you, I know how exciting this is for all of us, but we need to go over the testing period before we finish our session today. So, yes, as we outlined in the programme, before we can start hosting public events, we'll need to provide written reports of each of the four worlds. This is as much for our own understanding as it is for anyone else, as before we can allow anyone else to experience the settings, we need to know both that the graphics are reliable, and also that the changes in the worlds do *in fact* synchronise with the algorithms. This is where a select few of our members here today will be starting their contributions towards the project.'

He paused, glancing up from his notes and catching Carl's eye. Carl felt a pinch of heat pass across his chest, almost as if the speaker could feel his doubt. The eye contact lasted less than a second, but was enough to unnerve him. He sat forward in his seat and looked down, reaching for a pen.

'Over the next few months, four of our members, each coming from different academic backgrounds, will be test running the VR and providing written reports on their findings. These reports will serve as documentation of four *distinctly* different future worlds, and will allow us to begin painting a picture of what each of these worlds consists of. By pairing these findings with the data the algorithms are running on, the reports will be the first in our collection of evidence that seeks to document how specific global changes will affect elements of the future. These reports will be presented, along with our project outline, to multiple funding bodies and academic institutions, in what we believe will kick start a growing support for the project.

Of course, at this point we cannot say how readily available the VR will be. This depends entirely on the backing we may receive from certain institutions. However, let me make it clear, we intend to spread this project as far as possible. This is not a technology we wish to restrict merely to tech-focused and academic institutions. The project's success will ultimately be determined by how far it can reach and by how many people it can influence.

Well, I think I've spoken for long enough now and I know our testers are probably itching to know what's next for them. For those of you in the audience who will be partaking in the test programme, the full briefing will be carried out separately in room 203, just down the hallway, at two o'clock. For all other members, further talks will be held in separate rooms until five p.m today. You should have all received the timetable via email and I encourage you to stay and speak with the other members from the MIT collective. We'll all be hosting different talks where you'll get a better understanding of the project.

I'd like to finish by thanking all of you for being here, and for making this project happen. All of you, through your contributions and the expertise you are offering, will be part of something that could change how we engage with both the present *and* the future in a way none of us are presently able to fully imagine. Thank you, *really*.'

The same excited applause accompanied the speaker as he made his way over to the initial MIT crowd to exchange energetic hand shakes and nods of approval. The crowd began to hush, with members turning to each other to speak in smaller groups. Carl felt a hand on his shoulder, pulling him back into the present moment. He turned to see Anya facing him, smiling.

'Quite some talk, no? I mean, most of the information he went over we already knew. But being here today, seeing how many people are already a part of this... there's such an *energy* in the room.'

'Oh completely', Carl responded, trying to match her enthusiasm. 'I mean, hearing everything outlined, especially how the VR is going to be in flux, changing in real time... yeah it's quite hard to really imagine it. Sorry, I'm gonna excuse myself and get some air before the briefing.'

'Sure, do you want company or do you mind if I stay? I want to have a word with one of the designers.'

'No no, go for it. I'll catch you after the briefing.'

ooooo

Outside in the small courtyard at the back of the building, Carl circled a dried up fountain; cracked concrete sporting a few faded graffiti tags. He lit a Camel and paused, looking up towards the large windows of the fifth floor. He could just make out the tops of a few heads, bobbing and jerking in a manner that suggested the people they belonged to were engrossed in animated conversation. Small streaks of water began to slide down the dry glass, drawing pathways in the orange dust that clung to it. At first his eyes followed them, unaware of their source. He glanced up at the cloudless sky, a deep azure glaring back at him. When his vision flicked back to the windows, he coughed violently, smoke trapped at the back of his throat. Rainwater hammered against the window pains. Streaks of water pouring down the building, dripping onto the courtyard. Carl stared back up at the cloudless sky, his head becoming dizzy. He felt the thin cotton of his shirt growing moist as the droplets sank into it, running from his shoulders down his arms. Looking down at his feet, thin paper bags wilted in the puddles that had started to form. Flicking his moist Camel into the fountain, he hurried back into the building, covering his face from the storm as he ran.

On the top floor, he entered the bathroom, grabbing a fistful of paper towels to wipe his forehead. In the mirror, he tried his best to straighten out his shirt, push his damp hair into place. After walking quickly down the hallway to room 203, exchanging a few polite nods with other members, he noticed that the other testers were already inside the room. The speaker, a slim woman with a two-piece blue suit, turned to him as he entered.

'Carl?' she asked, smiling.

'Hey, yes, apologies I'm a touch late, I needed to dry off a bit.'

'Ah, erm *okay*, no problem... I'm Sarah, I'll be giving the four of you your briefing for the upcoming months.'

They exchanged a handshake before Carl took his seat next to the other three testers.

'So, while I've had a chance to read each of your small bio's and to familiarise myself with your work, I thought we'd start by each of you very briefly mentioning your name, your professional background and how you came to be here today, what led you to join the VFL. We'll keep this quick as we need to get through the briefing by five. So, would you like to start?'

She directed her gaze towards Carl, gesturing with an open hand.

'Erm, yeah sure, *so*... Well, I'm Carl, my background is in anthropology and specifically in how changes in technological landscapes affect human behaviour. My PhD research was focused specifically on Estonia and how the rapid digitisation and implementation of advanced blockchain technologies affected human behaviour. It was actually while I was in Estonia that I heard about the VFL. A close friend of mine, who's here today, was really excited about the programme's potential. She's also from a techno-anthropological background, and for a while we'd both been feeling that the research we were undertaking, while useful... how would you say? I guess *fell short* in comparison with the possibilities offered by this programme.'

He realised he'd been looking down at his table, rather than facing the room, a throwback to his early university days when he was too introverted to be able to face his auditors. He shifted uncomfortably in his seat, trying to smile back at the other members.

'Thank you Carl, I've no doubt we'll get to hear more about your research, but for now does anyone else wish to introduce themselves?'

'Yep sure' said the woman sat directly to Carl's left. Turning as she spoke, making sure to include everyone in her roaming eye contact, she commenced:

'So my name's Irma and I'm coming from an economics background.

It's interesting that you mention Estonia.... Carl?' He nodded. 'Yes, it's interesting that your work was based there. I'm from the Czech Republic originally, and my work has focused primarily on the socio-environmental effects of shifting economic landscapes, in particular the Central and Eastern European landscape. Basically my research has been examining how, *if possible*, an economic system can move from linear to circular without destabilising the system. The idea is to essentially move towards ecological stability without *plunging* a country into recession.'

A flicker of anxiety gave rise to a jump in her inflection, as if just saying the word 'plunging' brought with it a fear of shortages.

'And... sorry what was the last question? Ah *yes*, right, how I came to join the VFL. So, that's a bit easier. I came across an article on the MIT review that mentioned the residency the VFL had grown from. While I'm coming from a more traditionally academic background, I've been working with a group in Prague that focuses on using AI, similar to the one mentioned earlier, to predict how certain economic policies will affect the air quality in any given geographic area. It's quite intricate, but as Sarah mentioned, we'll all get a chance to speak more about our research after. So yeah, essentially I saw this programme and thought it could be a really interesting way of allowing people to engage *not only* with climate change, but with the technologies that can, *well*, that can help us in our search for solutions to economic reorganisation.'

The group instinctively turned to face the woman on her left. Her demeanour was more akin to Carl's; shifting in her seat, she slowly cleared her throat and looked forward at Sarah.

'Nice to meet you all, I'm Kristen. So, *yeah*, my background is mostly in geography, but more specifically in city planning and how to use seismic technologies for damage reduction in areas likely to suffer from natural disasters. I've been working in Tokyo for the last seven years, looking for the most viable solutions to dealing with earthquakes. They've got quite a unique approach to disasters there. I mean, beyond all the smart technologies; park benches that turn into cooking stoves, swaying skyscrapers, secret manholes that can be turned into toilets, they have this book that all citizens own, called *The Tokyo Disaster Preparedness Manual*. Not only does it teach citizens how to act leading up to, during *and* immediately after an earthquake, there's also this section on accepting death and returning to life after such a shock. You see, for them it's not a question of *if*, but a question of *when*. And when it does come, they know that the chances of either dying or losing a loved one are quite high. They know that another one is expected soon, as they predict it will be more or less a century after the one that struck in 1923. Through working there and seeing how people are prepping, I guess I came to believe that this type of preparation shouldn't just be limited to Tokyo. I think the type of transformation their society has undergone will soon become a reality for places all over the globe. But yeah, so how I came to the VFL...

Well, in the last year or so I've been following this group in Tokyo who are designing VR specifically to simulate the experience of being on a train during an earthquake. The idea is to make the experience more familiar to people so that when it happens for real, they're already partly accustomed to it. They've been testing it on this group, measuring their heart-rates during these immersions, and by their analysis, they think that these participants already find the event less paralysing than during the first experience. And yeah, over the past year I've become quite fascinated with the potential of VR specifically for panic and harm reduction techniques. It's really quite wild how powerful it can be, actually. Like this hospital in New York that uses VR simulations of Antarctica to cool down the bodies of patients who have suffered second and third degree burns. Their body temperature actually cools *drastically* and so many have said that they didn't even notice their bandages being removed. But *anyway*, apologies, I'm getting over-excited. So yeah, it was the fascination, all the late nights reading through articles from different researchers working in the field, that I came across the VFL. I kinda just knew I wanted to be a part of it.'

She sat forward smiling at the group, rigid in her seat, caught up in the type of excitement that could have allowed her to keep speaking for the next hour. Respectfully, she turned her body towards their final member.

'Pleased to meet you all, I'm really excited to be here.' she smiled back at them. 'I'm Sofia, and I'm a trained psychologist, but currently I don't actually practice it. I stopped seeing patients a few years back and took up a research position at Goldsmith's. It's been a bit of a back-and-forth really, as I come from a literary background, but converted to psychology and now I'm trying to incorporate my literary and cultural theory studies into the research I've been undertaking. I'm essentially looking at the neurological effects advanced urban landscapes can have on us. But, well, how to put this... I guess I've always been eager to lead some of the field research myself, rather than just researching based on other writers' findings. I was always quite obsessed with Guy Debord and the Situationists, so as part of my official research, I've been looking into a sort of 21st century psycho-geographical mapping of London.

I've got a small collective of writers, sound artists and app designers, and we've been trying to find ways of creating this app with these headphones that don't really cancel out urban noise, but convert it into the sound of natural phenomena, mostly wind, in real time. The team working on it have designed it so that the wind has all twelve tones; if there's a certain street where the same distinct noises occur consistently, it should play the same, or *at least* a similar melodic line each time. The wind essentially ends up sounding quite like a flute...' She let out a small laugh, the rest of them joining in, 'But the initial idea was more of a way to reduce stress levels of walkers, without them needing to listen to music and become unaware of their surroundings. With these you can still hear everything that's approaching you, just in a way that doesn't feel abrasive or unwanton. I get that as a technology it's not *that* advanced, but its use comes more in being able to monitor the long term affects of urban noise reduction.

So, the VFL... there's been quite a few people at Goldsmith's talking about it. One of the sound artists working on this app showed me the call for participants and I spent the next two days reading about their residency at MIT. It just seemed very suited to my work.'

'Thank you Sofia, and to all of you for being here today. So, I'm Sarah, and I'm one of the designers working on the VR's graphics. My background is primarily in computer science and VR graphics, which is what led me to look into working at MIT in the first place. And, as you all know, I was one of the members at MIT during the residency programme in 2017.

I've been working with the group since, as the artistic director of the VFL. My job has essentially consisted of studying the huge amounts of data that is input into the graphics algorithms by our other computer scientists. This data is taken from all areas of the net: Google maps, 3D imaging sequences and millions of photographs — all used to build up the AI's photographic world features, *PWF* as we like to call it. That's one of the easiest ways you can visualise the formation of the worlds you'll be entering: a world built on millions of photos, constantly in flux.

So, the idea has really been that we shouldn't be the ones actually *designing* these worlds. Rather, we feed a set of algorithms all of the necessary information for the *software* to be able to form these simulations. Then we have to get checking for bugs. That's not so straight forward with this, not like in video games where you just pay a few testers to walk through all the levels. In actuality, this consists of our AI scanning the code and checking for any 'noise' — that is any formation that jumps abruptly. I don't want to go too deeply into the fine details, as it's not actually *that* relevant for your positions as testers, but all of this is included in the packages you were emailed.

So, let's look at what your testing actually consist of. As I mentioned, we don't need you to be checking for bugs or for abnormalities within the settings. The idea is that you may well be entering some pretty abnormal worlds, ones we can't quite imagine now. The reason we have selected you four is not just for the variation of your backgrounds, but actually for the overlap we see between your work. I'll come back to this point in a second.'

A few rays of evening sun darted through the dusty blinds, falling gently across their white desks. Despite the drop in temperature from its afternoon peak, the seminar room retained a dense air. Carl felt his eyes flick towards the windows. White contrails chopped across the flamingo pink sky. Water becoming ice crystals becoming drawings.

'The idea', Sarah continued, 'the idea is that, initially, there will be four phases, or *futures* if you prefer. We want to start with a small number, as we think this will facilitate a more stimulating and coherent analysis of the changes in each given phase. You'll each participate at different times in different locations, this way when each of you present your final reports of each phase, we will see how certain elements may have changed over the course of a few weeks.

Remember, these changes, the ones that occur in a specific phase, *shouldn't* be that drastic. We've set up each phase to be designed on a set of data that is purposely different from the others. That way, after your reports, we will be able to map out how the present alterations cause specific future effects. This information we are purposefully going to withhold from you until after the final reports are delivered, just to eliminate any possibility of influence in your writing.'

Watching her hands fold, her knuckles letting out small cracks, Carl noted how her style of speaking mirrored that of the previous speaker. As if it were a coping mechanism for passing through such dense amounts of information, she continually shifted her body language to match her intonation. The more he focused on her delivery, the more he saw her as a curator, carefully placing fragments of her speech around the room.

So,

        the phases themselves.

As I mentioned, there are four, and you will experience each one, but on different weeks. Your actual time in the experience will be

        8 hours a day,

for the first 5 days of the week.

                During this week we will be working
    from the

Cheval Three Keys Hotel

and will be renting rooms for each of you to stay in over the course of that week. Please don't

                    underestimate

how

           tiring

being inside one of these settings will be. You'll be given

                high grade

    food supplements before the immersion, and after leaving the setting you'll be taken through

                  a series of exercises

to ensure that your coordination and balance are

in order.

After your evening meal, we recommend that you try to sleep as soon as possible

so as to rest your eyes before the next immersion.

The following three weeks will be your time to return home and write up

a detailed report

of the phase, with no further immersions until the first week of the following month. Our reasoning for keeping each immersion

condensed

and in one week

is to allow you to

psychologically immerse

into each phase — and to do so without any outside distractions.

However,

if at any point during this week

you are *not* feeling physically or psychologically

capable

of completing the remaining immersions,

you *will* be allowed to stop immediately but will remain at the hotel

during that week for us to

monitor your well-being.

I'm going to send a PDF around with all the details, along with the timetable outlining the phase allocations.'

She finished by taking questions from the four of them, elucidating the finer details and offering them guidance for how best to deal with the physical exhaustion that can come with using a headset for hours on end. When they had finished going over the pragmatics, the excitement continued to rise, their conversation quickly racing into each other's research, darting from Prague to Tokyo, across to Massachusetts and back to London, from blockchain currencies and e-citizens to VR harm reduction and AGI. Outside, flecks of orange dust floated in the evening air, the cloudless sky continuing to shift in hues of pink as they lost track of time.

As they descended down into the courtyard, their conversation turned to the question that had been boiling inside all of them more than anything else: what the algorithms would have predicted for each of the phases?

Two days remained before the first phase. The testers had all been instructed to take the weekend to rest, drinking no alcohol and as little caffeine as possible. On the Friday evening Carl left the university, having, to his surprise, secured exactly what he wanted: a generous reduction of his hours of teaching until January, when he'd be required to return to a more comprehensive schedule. But for the next four months he was granted leave to work on his research, with the slight compromise that once a month he'd return to give one lecture on Anthropocene linguistics to the first year undergraduates. Emerging from the university into the evening's humid air, he felt a sense of relief that finally allowed him to be excited for the coming week. Purposefully taking his time, he ambled towards South Kensington, his mind flitting through the possible scenes he might encounter in the first phase.

Jumping on the district line, he stood squashed between the other commuters, his eyes closed, listening to the wind whirring through the small window between the carriages. He had to consciously remind himself that no matter what he imagined, his predictions would undoubtedly miss the mark. He thought about how often he'd tried to imagine the energy, architecture and even smell of a city before visiting it. Each time, of course, his imagined streets and buildings looked nothing like the place. Perhaps it was better not to try to preempt the settings. Hot air churned through the tunnel, tugging at his loose linen collar; the dry breaks scratching the tracks as the train rolled into Mile End.

'So you managed to clear it with them?'

He'd barely sat down before Anya started asking him about the VFL. She was darting about her kitchen, grabbing him a drink while she finished off the last touches of cooking.

'Yeah — oh I better not actually', he pointed to the glass of wine she'd just poured, 'we're meant to keep off all drink this weekend.'

'Ah of course, sure. Mint tea?'

'Sure.'

Moving around her modest but carefully designed kitchen, she started to place small plates of dolmades, baba ganoush, tabbouleh, and flatbreads on the table. The kitchen's layout felt so effortless; the somewhat motley collection of ceramic pots, small paintings and plants could have looked kitsch. But there was something about the way she laid everything out that harmonised the different aesthetics. Taking his tea, Carl stepped out on to her balcony. He lit a Camel and inhaled deeply. The buzz of motorcycle engines moved in squares through the small alleyways lining her street.

'Yeah it's all cleared. I don't quite know how I walked away with such a good deal. I mean, I didn't have that much responsibility before, but yeah, one lecture per month until January. That shouldn't be an issue.'

The lack of movement in the kitchen caused him to turn; their dinner was ready.

'Yeah, I guess it's really hard to know how a full week of immersions is going to affect you. I know they'll be taking you through exercises every evening, but still, that's sure to leave you feeling quite fatigued, no?'

'I think now that it's here, I'm just ready to jump in. Even today on the tube I had to keep reminding myself not to try and imagine what it'll be like. It's strange though, recently I've found myself continuously reflecting on Tallinn, on what took me there, on meeting you and hearing about the VFL together. I know we've always made a conscious effort not to dwell too much on what happened to both of us, but recently it just keeps cropping up, no matter where I look. I'll get flashes of blue light flickering past me, but then when I try to locate the source it seems there's none. There's been a few times where I've been in the street, and turned to look over my shoulder, then suddenly realised there weren't any sirens behind me. I know, it's textbook neurosis, but recently I've started to become... well, not even paranoid, just sort of conscious that I have this moment in my past that has really shaped where I am today. I know when I think about it rationally that the case is closed — has been for a long time. But small elements just crop up now and again. Like this guy watching me at that Portuguese café you recommended. I was there before we went to the Tate with Veronika. It was like I recognised him from somewhere long ago, but not as a friend or colleague. Then later that afternoon, when I blacked out on the swing, I had this vision of myself running through the forest near the scrap yard site. It sounds so unrelated, which I know it is, but it kind of unsettled me, having this guy I thought I recognised looking at me, then that fragment all of a sudden reappearing. It was like he'd triggered it.'

He paused, suddenly aware that he hadn't touched his food. Nodding his head as he swallowed mouthfuls of flatbread and baba ganoush, showing that he approved of the taste, he looked up from his plate. Anya was sat motionless, staring out towards the night sky.

Lighting a cigarette, she poured herself a mint tea and looked back at Carl.

'It's funny, I've also been thinking a lot about what happened. Not specifically about Brazil, but more of the moment when I told you, of that horrible feeling of not knowing how you'd react before you admitted what had happened in Scotland. In some ways, I don't think I'd have really been able to continue with my work, with everything, had I not been able to understand my past *through* yours, if that makes sense? It was really as if by hearing what happened to you, about the persuasion — the kind of toxic pressure to take direct action, that I was able to really understand what had happened to me in Brazil. I really felt when I heard you talk, that

I was looking into a mirror.'

'I think what I found hardest, even harder than hearing what you'd gone through, was seeing how scared you were about telling me: that you had no way of knowing how I'd react. That's why I smiled. Because I knew that even with how traumatic it had been, and how hard it was for you to admit it to me, I'd now be able to open up for the first time, something I thought I'd never get the chance to do.'

She smiled back him as they both sat there in silence. He remembered how she stared at him, his arm on her shoulder, assuring her that she needed to listen, that before he commented on her story, he needed to tell her his. She sat there, completely still as she was so good at doing, listening intently to his every word. Admitting his past had produced so many emotions that he had to stop on regular occasions during his explanation, catching his breath, still not quite believing how he could have met someone whose story was so closely aligned to his. Feelings of relief had mixed with a wave of guilt, a sense that for the first time Anya was learning why he was in Estonia, as if everything else he'd told her had been a set of carefully fabricated lies. Would she still trust him, or even want to know him?

During that hour, he almost forgot that exactly the same questions must have been running through her head. This uncertainty, while anxiety-inducing, brought with it an invitation to work through these memories, ones that still remained present like sharp stones in their shoes.

Just like Anya, Carl went on to explain the trajectory that followed the attack. His cautiousness not to flee from London, but to leave inconspicuously, for reasons that he could easily justify. He went through the details methodically: his stay in Prague, the apartment he rented, following the trial that came six months later, his careful distancing from anyone else in the movement.

Rubbing his eyes and continuing to inhale on his cigarette, he explained how he'd been searching for institutions in eastern Europe that could be interested in his work. He had no desire to return to London, wanting to keep his distance for as many years as possible. He had no luck, and it was only when chatting to a writer he met in a riverside bar in Podskalí that he learnt of Estonia's advanced digital society.

He spent the following months researching the university in Tallinn, drawing together his proposal for a PhD programme. When he was invited to meet the anthropology department, he was unaware that his time in Prague would soon be coming to an end. Due to his respectable academic background, alongside his well drawn out proposal, he was invited to commence his research programme the following autumn. With no further reason to remain in Prague, he packed up his belongings and found a small studio apartment in Sikupilli, knowing that the next nine months would be spent starting his research in this small, Baltic city, soon to become his new home.

After revealing their past, a new intimacy grew between them. Suddenly there was no one in the world with whom they felt closer, and without being able to reveal *those* parts of themselves, there never would be. But this new emotional intimacy brought with it a certain confusion. Up until then, their relationship had been one of close friends who shared academic interests. What had kept their relationship locked in its previous formality was a deep paranoia of having anybody too close to them; anyone that could dig a little too deep into their past.

Since Carl had left the UK, he'd kept his relations strictly casual. Only when he met Anya did this change. Perhaps the only reason it could have changed was due to Anya's near identical behaviour. She too, since returning to Tallinn, had become more reclusive. This happened almost overnight, her excuse always being that she was simply too busy with her research. Eventually her friends stopped asking.

It was only with Carl that she established a rapport that seemed to extend beyond a shared interest in anthropology. After picking up on his eloquence and intelligence, she felt that there was more to his awkwardness and reserved nature than him merely being shy. She wanted to pry a little, to ask him more about his past, about how he came to find himself in Estonia. When she asked him, or heard other people ask him, she noted how he recited the same story, each time, almost word for word. But the fear of having to explain more of her past silenced her curiosity. It was only a year after their first encounter that they eventually opened up.

After that evening, when they sat looking out on Anya's balcony under the small heat of the gas lamp, they felt as if they'd almost declared their love for each other, so strong was the connection.

Some time after that night, they found themselves returning from a bar they'd been to with two other researchers, the winter air stinging their slightly flushed cheeks. Walking alongside each other, they shared a cigarette, both of them unsure of what their next step should be. For Carl, a sense of desire to be with Anya was greater than his lust — as if sleeping together were perhaps a stepping stone to bring them even closer together. For Anya, it was more a curiosity, as she acknowledged that while she had thought of sleeping with Carl, only now had the possibility really presented itself.

They returned to her apartment, both conscious of each others intentions. Yet when they reached her bedroom, almost without speaking, the fluidity of their connection didn't translate into physical actions. Both felt slightly awkward; Carl self-conscious of his drunken manouveurs, Anya soon realising that her love for Carl didn't extend to physical romance. They took each other without ever really finding a rhythm, then lay in silence, embracing in a way both seemed to comprehend as a form of telling the other that, despite the anticlimax, there was no doubting their love for each other.

The following morning she gently woke him, taking him to the balcony for coffee, while the early light of Tallinn's sky yawned above them. Watching the faint cyan stretch out over the buildings' silhouettes, they both sensed that there was no need to explain anything.

At 8 a.m. the following Sunday, Carl boarded the tube to Monument. Even during the early hours of the morning, the weight of the air was oppressive, mingling with the smell of sour rubbish that had started to decompose during the previous night. Carved in the faces of each commuter was an exhaustion gradually turning into frustration, which couldn't be directed at anyone. People were sick of the heat, sick of the sweat and dense air that was now ubiquitous to any tube carriage. Worse still was that more people were now using the tubes. The newly tarmacked roads had become soft during the summer, and many were now closed.

Throughout the capital, overground train lines were also beginning to give in, the heat having buckled the iron tracks in multiple points. Police and the city council were increasing their vigilance on any waste left in the street, as black bin liners wilted, emitting foul odours and liquids that turned the pavements sticky. Many people were now borrowing a lesson from China's citizens, moving everywhere with a small face mask on to avoid inhaling the dust that circulated the streets like an amber ghost, regularly catching peoples' open orifices, leaving them choking or rubbing their eyes.

As the high temperatures persisted, many people complained of their smartphones overheating, sending them into hibernation mode which barred them from transacting. Set up within the tube station were small cold boxes where people could queue up to hold their phones inside for a few minutes, just to cool down their handsets.

Despite the armies of different charities who walked the streets in the searing afternoon sun, lugging huge boxes of water bottles for the homeless, the story of sunburnt, dehydrated bodies being discovered under railway arches and shop doorways was now commonplace. Perhaps more harrowing were the cases reported of homeless people sucked under and drowned in the Thames whilst trying to bathe, a few bodies having been reported reaching as far as Gravesend before being fished out.

With September having arrived, many journalists started to question what kind of transition into the autumn months would follow. Many were worried that the near 40 degree heat would persist, before dropping unexpectedly, potentially bringing with it huge storms. Yet perhaps most worrying of all was the fact that even most scientists were admitting they didn't know what was coming. The climate had simply become too difficult to predict.

When they reached Monument, the surge of agitated commuters bottlenecked at the escalators, the crowd crushed together, forming one entity as each individual perspired, staring at the back of the person in front of them. When he reached the exit, Carl lent against the station wall, pulling out his phone to check the directions to the centre. The message 'your iPhone is overheating' glared back at him. Already feeling slightly nauseous, he moved back inside the station.

A queue of frustrated faces stood staring at the coolbox, currently occupied by three men, their hands held inside. Turning to the guard who worked at the station, he asked him how to get to the Cheval Three Keys, exhaling with relief when the man led him outside to point him in the right direction.

Pacing down the street, his shirt already stuck to his back, he passed by a crowd of people swarming around a fatigued looking worker from Costa standing with a tray of tasters. Forcing his way through the crowd, he snatched up one of the shots of iced tea, returning the cup to her tray as two teenagers beckoned for her to go back in to get them refills.

When he located the large five star hotel that looked out over the

Thames, he rushed through its revolving glass doors, gasping for the cool air of the lobby's air conditioning. He spotted Sarah standing by a window looking out towards the Thames. Stopping to wipe his brow, he cleared his throat before approaching her.

'Hey Sarah.'

'Carl!' she answered enthusiastically, smiling back at him, 'good to see you. Here, let me just get you some water. Have you eaten already?'

'Yes I'm okay for food, thanks. Just some water would be great.'

Nodding, she quickly moved through two glass doors and returned with two glasses and a bottle of iced water.

'Please, have a seat. The other three have just been shown to their rooms, and so will you shortly. How have you been since our last meeting?'

Gulping down his water, Carl breathed in deeply, regaining his composure.

'I've been well thank you. I managed to organise a really favourable schedule with my department at Imperial and since then I've had some time off to rest up for this first phase.'

'I'm glad to hear', she responded. A door swung open behind her and Anton stepped out into the lobby.

'Carl! Great to see you here.' He leant over and shook his hand enthusiastically. 'Thank you for getting here so early this morning. We're going to show you around and then the day will be yours to rest up as best you please.'

'Of course.' Carl smiled back at him.

Leading him through the white-tiled hallway towards the lifts, he felt his body start to cool down. Vibrant green plants lined the corridors, each resting in a crisp white pot. Minimal paintings of small stick like figures positioned at equal distance hung to the walls. When they reached his room, he almost laughed at how grandiose the whole experience was becoming. The single room with its low double bed and small en suite also sported two glass doors leading out onto a balcony from which he could see London Bridge. Placing his bag carefully against the wardrobe, he switched on the air conditioning and turned to face the other two.

'It's perfect, thank you. In fact, significantly better than anywhere I've stayed in the last few years.' He let out a small laugh.

'We didn't want to underestimate how exhausting the experiences may be. So we figured the least we could do was make sure you each had a comfortable living space.'

'There's a phone with both our numbers written down next to it,' Sarah cut in, 'So if there's anything you need beyond room service you can call either of us.'

Having already received his briefing via e-mail the previous week, there wasn't much more for them to discuss. Instead, they gave him a small tour of the facilities; the small swimming pool, the lounge areas and restaurant where they could dine each evening if they didn't wish to eat in their rooms. Finally they led him to the conference space they had booked out on the top floor. The glass windows along the southern facing wall illuminated the room, the sunlight bouncing off the white tables and blue water cooler. Three reclining leather chairs had been positioned at equal distance, a small table placed next to each one.

'This will be where the immersions will take place,' Sarah pointed out to him. 'You'll each have your headset and headphones, and that's all you'll need to worry about. We'll be keeping the room at a cool temperature throughout the session, and if for any reason you do have to leave the phase early, we'll have an assistant here for support. When the immersion is finished, she'll check up on you and lead you through some exercises. Other than your eight hours in the phase, the evening will be yours to rest as you wish. As we mentioned, you'll all be given high-energy meals and hydration tablets beforehand which will keep you energised throughout the immersion.'

When the tour was over, Carl returned to his room, grabbed a large glass bottle of water from his fridge and opened the balcony doors. The blanket of heat that fell over him was almost comical in its intrusiveness. He pulled up a chair and lit a cigarette, staring out towards the blurry landscape: central London warped by hot air. Few cars passed on the roads. For a moment it almost fell still. Flicking the ash from his Camel into the blue porcelain tray marked with the hotel's name, he leaned forward in his chair, staring down at the dry sand lining the edges of the shrunken Thames. A handful of homeless people mingled with the tourists, the former washing their clothes in the warm water, the latter boldly photographing them doing so. Carl sat there gazing at them, unaware of time passing as the light remained stagnated. For a moment, he started to question what was the use in what they were doing? The city was suffocating, people were dying of heat strokes and a national water shortage had been in place for the last three months. Something drastic needed to happen, but no one knew what.

The VFL as good as admitted that it didn't have all the answers, but at least the phases would be a profound new research to present to other institutions. The explanation circled in his head like a mantra. Looking down at his iPhone, the screen had turned black. The same white text as before instructed him to cool down the device. The irony of his situation felt sinister.

Moving inside through the dust-covered doors, he poured another glass of water and collapsed onto the bed. What at this stage could really be of any use? The question continued to loop, his forehead sweating. Visions of dry roads cracking in two, melding with streets of restaurants suddenly submerged in thick green water. The corpses of London's homeless floated downstream, enmeshed in happy meal wrappings and dormant plastic nets rising out from the arid river banks. Blue lights of lost ambulances flashed, GPS screens turned to chalk.

ooooo

At seven a.m. the following morning, his alarm sounded in synchronicity with the small bedside phone ringing. Confused, Carl grabbed at both, muting the alarm before answering the phone.

'Carl? Good morning. This is just to politely remind you that breakfast will be served for all of you downstairs in the main restaurant in half an hour. We'll see you down here.'

'Ah okay, yes, thanks.'

Putting down the phone, he rolled out of the double bed, ambling to the bathroom to wash his face before slipping into the black tracksuit each of the testers had been given. Zipping up the top of the jacket, he caught a glimpse of himself in the mirror and laughed a little. Despite the academic nature of this project, he felt like a teenager all over again, his unshaven chin resting just on top of the black nylon collar.

Jumping in the lift, he hit the first floor button and stretched his arms above his head, pulling at his shoulders and rotating his neck; just wearing a tracksuit seemed to require him to warm up. On the first floor, he followed the signs into the restaurant, his eyes scanning for the group as he entered. Noticing a hand raised in the air, he spotted Sarah sat alongside the other three members, each in their black tracksuits. Standing to greet him, dressed in a white linen shirt and neatly cut black trousers, she smiled and pushed out a chair for him. Nodding to the other members, he took his seat.

'So,' Sarah commenced, 'We suggest that you all have some fresh fruit and water to start out with, just to settle your stomach. Then before leaving here we'll issue each of you with your high-energy protein powder and hydration tablets. Today, we'll take them together so I can talk through the dosages, but as of tomorrow, you're welcome to take breakfast alone before starting the immersion, should you wish.'

They nodded, each member appearing either tired or slightly apprehensive for what they were about to put their body through. Some small talk flitted between them, but overall Carl perceived that the initial

115

excitement they'd shared had made way for nervousness. Crunching on his watermelon, his eyes darted around the table, observing their faces. Perhaps, like him, exhausted after the relentless surge of heat and drought that had wrung the city dry, they too were skeptical of the use of their current project. He pondered this thought a little, but resolved that there was little use in him questioning what they were doing. Too much time, on everyone's behalf, had gone into the project. He felt his body growing warm and lifted the tracksuit over his head. As he tugged, he felt the zip catch his cheek and let out a little groan. As his face emerged, Sofia pointed at his cheek.

'Oh Carl, you've caught your cheek. There's a little blood on it.'

He felt his face turn pale and his palms become moist.

'You okay? It's only a tiny one but you look like you've seen a ghost.'

He rubbed at his cheek and turned his hand to examine the blood.

'Didn't have you down for the *squeamish* type', Sarah laughed, trying to lighten the mood.

'Oh it's fine, just a tiny scratch,' he answered while looking down. 'I'm just gonna head to the bathroom to clean it up.'

Stood facing himself in the mirror, he saw movement inside the tiny incision. Dark waves crashed in reverse. The nose of a van poked out from the mouth of the wave's barrel, gyrating. The blinking of a small light reflected in the dense currents. He quickly splashed some water on his cheeks, dried his hands and returned to the table.

'All cleaned up?' Sarah asked with a smile as he took his seat.

'All good thanks.'

Drinking his iced water in silence, he finished his papaya and excused himself, slipping through the sliding doors onto the sand-coloured terrace. Placing a Camel in his mouth, his thumb had just grazed the metal ring of his lighter when he heard a voice behind him.

'Mind if I grab one of them?'

He turned round to see Sofia approaching him.

'Hey, yeah of course', he said, extending the packet to her, 'how are you doing this morning?'

'Quite badly,' she responded, fishing into the packet and leaning forward for him to light her cigarette, 'yeah quite *fucked*, to be honest with you. I can't take this heat anymore. Like, I know we're all in the same boat, but it's really started to mess with my head. Not only can't I think straight, I'm actually starting to see things. It happened yesterday, when I was looking down Oxford Street, trying to remember this place where I'd purchased an eye-cooling mask, and when I was looking through the hot air, I could just see the texture of *foam*. You know how you get it on the small waves when they break, the whiteish, bubbly stuff. I could just see tiny traces of that passing over my field of vision. I just froze, there on the pavement, started rubbing my eyes then eventually had to use a bathroom in this restaurant to wash my face. It went away, but, I mean, kinda unnerving when you're hallucinating and can't tell what's happening.'

'Anya, my friend who is also on this programme, told me recently about how rising CO2 levels affect our ability to think clearly. Before then I'd always understood it as something that simply damages our lungs, but it really got me when I heard this. It's quite a grim thought, really.'

'Yeah, you're right that is grim. Just this invisible gas whose effects we understand but only see on a grand scale — actually, no. I don't wanna get into this right now.'

'When I look around me at the moment, I, I start to question... yeah I'm not sure...' he trailed off.

'No, *go on*, you were gonna say that it makes you question what we're doing here, like what's the actual *use* in *envisioning worlds of the future to make people more conscious of climate change,* when our present reality is already such a blatant indicator.'

Carl turned to face her, the tip of his cigarette burning away, forming a wilted curve of ash.

'Do you think I'm being cynical?'

'On the contrary, it just caught me off guard to hear that someone else on this project shares my concerns. I'm just not sure whether it makes me feel relieved or more apprehensive. I mean, don't get me wrong, I don't see any point in backing out now,' she stepped forward and aggressively stubbed out her cigarette in the ashtray. 'We're here now and *not* doing the immersions would be far more useless than doing them. It's just that I'm not sure the results are going to really offer us any pragmatic solutions. The problem just seems too multifaceted.'

They both turned at the sound of the glass doors sliding open. Seeing Sarah looking out towards them, they felt almost intimidated, as if their doubts were somehow a blasphemy against the integrity of the project.

'We're gonna head upstairs now and start the main alimentation, whenever you're ready.' And with the same softness with which she had spoken, she smiled at them and turned back into the restaurant.

The four of them stood waiting in the upstairs conference room, the taste of powdered protein and chemical hydration still lingering in their throats. High-grade stuff from Amsterdam, they'd been assured. Some company that fabricates powdered food which supposedly provides its user with the perfect energy balance. Its plasticy banana flavour had been washed away by the hydration tablets, used mostly for cases of severe hydration during bouts of Malaria. All of them felt slightly nauseous, both from the 'food' and the sight of the matt black headsets sat on their tables.

The built in air-conditioning unit whirred overhead, cooling their faces. Zipping up their track tops, they laughed, noting that it was the first time they'd felt chilly in months. When Sarah entered the room, eight minutes before the clock struck ten a.m., they turned to face her. A thin ray of light penetrating through the window clipped her forehead. Without speaking, she moved round to her laptop and flicked on the large screen. A small schedule blinked back at them:

118

Immersion One

Carl Campbell : Phase One

Sofia Horváth : Phase Two

Kristen Jansen : Phase Three

Irma Auer: Phase Four

Assuming a more formal demeanour, she commenced her brief.

'This is the phase schedule for the first immersion. As explained earlier, there will be a rotation each month so that every member experiences each phase. No further information regarding any of the phases should be shared amongst yourselves until all of the final reports are finalised. Only by proceeding in this manner can we ensure that sixteen objective reports are written. Whenever you're ready, please take your seats and our assistants will aid you in fitting your headsets.'

The two men who had been standing at the side of the room walked forward as the four of them sat down. Carl noted the almost static feel of the rubber against his moist skin; a slightly abrasive prickling as he flexed his facial muscles. A few beads of sweat dripped on his cheek. Running his fingers over the smooth rubber of the controller, he took a deep breath, the weight of the headset tilting his chin downwards.

When all of the headsets had been fitted, they guided them through a series of small exercises to ensure their eyes had adjusted. They were asked to pinpoint certain aspects of different landscapes, using their hand controllers to navigate through the glowing spaces that started to render.

The controls, they each confirmed, were remarkably easy to use, their thumbs caressing the small joysticks as they proceeded through the practice urban settings.

'What's important is to not forget about the small button located beneath your middle finger,' one of the assistants reminded them. 'This is the relocate switch, which will immediately transfer your position to another random location in the setting. It's crucial that you don't spend the whole immersion just exploring one area. The idea is that there is a whole world to be discovered, and while we want you to pay close attention to specific elements, it's crucial that you don't narrow your research by forgetting to vary your position within the space. We'll start soon, so I'm going to ask all of you to put your headphones on. When they're fitted, I'm going to talk into them through this microphone. I'll play a series of sounds and I'll ask you to identify them by their number. I want you to each raise your hand when you hear me describing the element you're visualising.'

He commenced his audio testing. Speaking back to the man stood inside his virtual world, Carl noted how freakishly real the interaction felt.

Outside the sun was already in full force. A police helicopter circled overhead, its GPS flickering as it located the registration of a stolen motorcycle. All along the side of their hotel, dust smeared the windows. To the police officers looking in, the vision that met their eyes was four figures dressed in black tracksuits, their identities veiled by their headsets. Two other men edged slowly around them, one speaking into a microphone, the other noting down something on an iPad each time they raised their right hands. All around the hotel, in the barren streets of sticky tarmac, commuters leant against walls, trying to catch their breath or tipping bottled water over their foreheads. A blue light began to flash on the helicopter's GPS screen. Subject located, Birdcage Walk, St James' Park. Tearing off into the distance, the black shadow of the propellers grazed the hotel windows, sliced up into a series of geometric sparks, wanderings across the blinds.

ooooo

Throughout the day, Sarah and her two assistants sat attentively in the conference room. From time to time, one assistant stood up and gave a quick glance at the body language of the researchers, checking for twitching, overly red skin around the mask or severe sweating. Nothing out of the ordinary, they confirmed each time.

Only when the outside light started to dim did they begin preparing the yoga matts, eye drops and hydration tablets. Many of the researchers shifted in their seats. This is a good sign, one assistant assured Sarah. It means they're still active and focusing. Watching the clock attentively, the second hand started to approach the eight hour mark. When it struck six p.m., Sarah triggered the shutdown mode, a small note appearing on each of their headsets informing them that everything would gradually fade to black.

When a further two minutes had passed, their headsets were gently removed, one by one, along with their headphones. Instructed not to move alone, the assistants helped each tester out of their chairs and led them to sit on the yoga matts. Chilled water was served to each of them in large glass bottles, together with a further hydration tablet.

All four of them sat in silence, sloppily drinking their water and staring forward, expressionless. When the assistants came round with the eye drops, he didn't have to ask any of them to open wide and stare up. As if in auto-pilot, their eyes still fixed wide open, they each obeyed with an expression of total submission, their eyes barely blinking as the cooling drops struck their retinas. With the same total compliance, they each moved steadily through the stretching exercises, their faces still suggesting their minds were elsewhere.

When Carl returned to his room an hour later, he fell face down on his double bed, breathing heavily into the fragrance of the pillow. Only when he realised he was about to sleep until the morning without showering, eating, or even undressing did he exert himself, rolling his body one hundred and eighty degrees to stare up at the ceiling. This instant collapse was a reaction they'd been strongly advised to avoid, one that would undoubtedly leave them disorientated by the end of the week.

Urban fragments of unrecognisable technology danced across the beige ceiling. Rubbing his eyes, he sat up and looked around the room, trying to focus his vision. He took careful note of the furniture, the colour of the walls, the small 'no smoking' sign on the desk next to the phone. Moving his aching body into the bathroom, he frivolously splashed cold water over his cheeks, running his wet hands through his hair and over his neck. Looking back at himself, he felt slightly haggard. The bathroom light seemed to give his skin a shade of pale, violet-blue, creating a soft dissonance between his tone and that of the polished tiles above the sink.

Still not hungry, he moved out onto the balcony, carrying his field recorder, his Camels and two litres of water with him. Lighting up a cigarette and messily gulping down water from the bottle, he activated the microphone.

Somewhere in the street below, sirens screeched past, their howl ricocheting off the tightly packed buildings. The latency of blue lights flickered, bouncing off the glass windows of the neighbouring skyscrapers. He waited for the noise to die down, before opening his mouth. A state of aphasia took a hold of him, his words falling out in loose chunks, caught up in the urban vernacular of passing cars, distant rumbling and the Salat al-fajr. Grasping for small details of the immersion, he started to speak.

Later that week when he returned to his apartment, he listened back to the oral notes he'd made to himself during those evenings spent on the hotel balcony. His ability to distinguish between each session was greatly diminished by the identical daily routine: they'd woken up at eight a.m., taken breakfast together as a four, engaging in minimal small talk. They'd been taken through their stretches by the assistants, taken their hydration tablets and high-protein meal substitutes. They'd immersed, each of them for exactly eight hours every day in their given setting. They'd finished at 6pm sharp each evening, been taken through the exact same stretches and given the exact same eye drops. Only afterwards, when Carl had returned to his room, was he unaware if the others had shared such a similar routine. He'd showered, ordered a small superfood salad, and sat on his balcony smoking, speaking into his microphone.

The thought of listening back to the recordings almost unnerved him a little. It was less the content, which was still quite fresh in his mind, that made him uncomfortable. What really concerned him was his ability to piece all the information together into a coherent analysis. And yet despite the self-doubt, the idea of really coming to understand what he'd seen excited him. There were many elements that suggested this was a world they should be aiming to learn from. The bigger — and much harder — question was whether it was a viable future: could the path to such a world ever be constructed?

Lying down in his hammock, he put on his headphones and kicked his leg against the wall. Rocking gently from side to side, his own voice starting to speak back to him:

Relationships infused with technology — Corporate harmonny

Planning algorithms — modulating balance. Demand and Supply.

Evolutionary Recovery Centre — insertion of leaves under the skin

inserting loose fauna or coastal debris in the images — No UBI

experimentation at the edges of the human and the self

fortnightly bird dance — automated robots clear waste

dolphin-like creatures with long tusks — mature blockchain distribution

Corporations collaborating in harmony — Circular economy — State shareholders

Digital fabrication — Infrastructure as public utility Deeply Circular

Small voice box enhancers — 'Creative gain' biosphere stability

dissolve the border between work and play — Deeply circular

filtration systems which ensure the trees are carefully watered

Commodity capitalism — creative gain — autonomous distribution

deus ex machina form of resolution — Deeply circular

The recording lasted for hours. When it had finished he listened to it again, kicking his leg against the wall to keep the hammock swaying. His phone lay downstairs on the coffee table in the front room. Unopened messages from Anya glowed on the home screen. As had been advised, he'd decided not to start his writing that weekend. His eyes were still suffering from a dull ache that dug into his forehead. Even looking at his phone caused him some discomfort.

When Sunday evening came, he woke in his hammock, the dusty fabric clinging to his dry skin. Pulling himself out of the net, he stretched his arms behind his back, before wiping the sweat from his forehead. The small head-rush he received after standing brought with it visions of plant lined tower blocks, the hanging pots being fed by carefully shaped hosepipes. Rain from their smart sprinkler systems fell onto his skin. Feeling the thin cold sprays against him, he let out a small gasp. The sudden urge to commence his writing took a hold of him.

He paced down the staircase of the iron fire escape, forcing his keys into the lock and bursting into his hallway. The air inside was even thicker than on the roof, the density choking him a little. He turned on the kitchen tap and placed his face underneath it, mouth open wide, the water spraying over his cheeks. Grabbing his laptop, he moved back to the roof and into the hammock. Kicking at the wall, he opened his laptop as the hammock traversed its ninety degree curve, its distance dropping as its motion trailed out.

Trying to organise the fragments of information he'd recorded, he transcribed his own voice, creating threads, each word triggering a profusion of memories, flashes of imagery and snippets of conversation. All around him the sky darkened, his silhouette a merging of hammock and body, darting back and forth across the rooftop as his fingers hammered away at his keyboard.

Sat at his desk the following morning, he shifted in his seat looking over his notes. Huge segments on biosphere restoration loomed back at him. Despite having passed most the night in his hammock, he felt strangely refreshed. Almost *too* energised. He flexed his fingers, trying to recommence his writing. Yet something had changed. Everytime he felt words forming, they slipped out of focus before his fingertips made contact with the keys, like a sneeze disappearing after breathing in. He leaned back in his chair, perplexed. With this movement, he felt the words taking shape, but as soon as the chair legs hit the floor they burst. Scrunching his eyebrows, his confusion grew into anger. He violently pushed his chair back from the desk; its legs scratched the wooden floorboards. Deciding that the desk was the issue, he stuffed his computer, field recorder and notebook into his bag and headed for the front door.

The temperature outside had reached forty-five degrees, a now standard temperature for midday in central London. The oppressiveness of the street stopped Carl in his tracks. The idea of being out for too long in the heat was unbearable. He tried to compose himself, figuring out where would be a good place to write. A schoolboy walked past him, his shirt sleeves rolled up, his tanned hands clutching a brown paper bag from McDonalds. Visions of the flood returned to him, the cold water pouring into the restaurant, cooling his body temperature. Clapping his hands together, he let out a sharp 'right'. The boy turned to face him. Ignoring his eye contact, Carl shot off, eager to board the tube at Bethnal Green, his destination already decided.

When he arrived at the intersection between the Strand and Waterloo Bridge, he darted across the road, edging past a cyclist who had to break to avoid him. Ignoring the man's insults, he entered the café and checked for a free table. A few small spaces by the window were unoccupied, the other customers evidently avoiding the harsh sunlight spilling onto the marble surfaces. Dumping his bag on one of the chairs, he approached the counter, recognising the same woman that had served him before.

'An ameri- *abatanado*, please', he said, grinning at her, pleased he'd remembered the right phrase.

'Of course. I'll bring it over to you.'

Taking his seat, he let his eyes scan over his surroundings, catching the attention of the man sitting in front of him. It took him a second to recognise the motorcyclist. Must be a regular. Staring straight at him, Carl gave an overly formal nod. The man, unimpressed, looked back down at his phone. Pulling out his laptop, he plugged in his headphones and started listening back to his notes, skim-reading his writing simultaneously. Some time passed before he realised the waitress had placed his coffee down next to him. Pushing his fingers down on the keys he attempted to commence. Again, something pulled back inside him.

Some hours passed. Quite how many he didn't know.

Rubbing his eyes, his frustration grew in tandem with the inexplicable block preventing him from writing. Leaning back in his chair, he felt a lightness run through his arms, a small slither of clarity pass in his head as his ideas seemed to momentarily lift off the ground with him. Then his chair legs hit the floor, and his mind muddled, nauseously. Perceiving a parallel between this motion and his thoughts, he leant back again, feeling his head clear. He continued to rock back and forth on his chair, the cheap wooden legs aching and creaking under his strain. Pushing himself up and down with his feet, the chair's front legs jumped on and off the ground, scraping and scratching the tiled floor. Alongside this noise came the sound of fingers furiously hammering away on the keys. Large blocks of text under the heading 'Climax Community' started to form, his analysis of the previous week tumbling out of his memory, charging down his arms and materialising as it reached his finger tips.

Breathing in and out, his cheeks red from the leg pumps, he only snapped back into his surroundings when the motorbike man pushed his shoulder violently, pulling off his headphones. Unnerved, he swung around in his chair, slightly embarrassed to see the whole café looking at him.

'Stop fucking swinging on the chair. You disturb all of us.'

'But I have to', Carl responded without thinking. 'I can't write when I'm sitting still'.

Taken aback by the absurdity of this statement, the motorbike man raised his voice, glaring back at Carl.

'Not my problem, go somewhere else.'

'I'll be quieter', Carl promised him. Irritated by the interruption but realising that he could no longer cause such a racket, he placed two wads of napkins under each chair leg and gently rocked his feet up and down. With his headphones removed, he monitored his noise levels, ensuring he wasn't louder than the espresso machine or the till. As his writing continued, he didn't notice his rocking slowly growing. Wearing through the thin paper napkins, the legs started creaking again. Memories of bodily experimentation erupted within him, flooding his thoughts faster than he could type. The intensity caused him to kick violently, his chair almost bouncing off the ground. He swung liberally, in near disbelief as he recalled the surreality of what he had witnessed. A loud snap followed by the tumbling of a table and the shattering of porcelain cups pierced the ears of the other customers. Everyone fell silent.

'Fucking idiot, look what you did,' the motorbike man roared at him grabbing him by his shoulder and leading him to the till. 'Pay now, then you fuck off.'

His back bruised from the fall, Carl pulled out his wallet, apologising, saying he really had no choice, which seemed to confuse more than anger the man.

'Three hundred. For chair, table and cups', the man barked at him. Wasn't that a bit excessive for such small damage? But Carl wanted to be out of there as quickly as possible. Keying in his pin number, he continued to apologise to no one in particular, before grabbing his belongings and scurrying out of the door. Outside the hot air instantly clouded his thoughts. 'Back and forth', he said out loud to himself, over and over, as he paced across Waterloo Bridge, eager to find another place to write. Up and down, backwards, forwards, left, right, swinging,

S

                                        w

     in

                g

       i

                                                n

                             g.

When he stepped through the doors into the Tate Modern, the wall of cold air pumping out from the AC sparked a twitch in his upper body. Groaning with relief, he paused for a moment, feeling the vein in his temple pulsing. Approaching the desk, he smiled back at the same woman who had served him during his previous visit.

'Hey, one standard for Super*flex*, please.'

'Standard for Superflex, that will be eleven pounds, please. Cash or card?'

Hitting his contactless against the reader, he collected his ticket from her and turned towards the exhibition.

'Oh just one thing, sir. We're asking all our visitors to take extra care on the swing installation above the main gallery. Due to the heat we've had a few people becoming light headed and taking a tumble. So just take it easy if you do go on them.'

'Of course, thanks for the heads up.'

Despite her giving the same warning to every guest who entered, the swings were packed. Red-faced children and adults alike tore through the air, sweat pouring from their foreheads. Anxious to find a space, Carl began roaming around the installation, his eyes darting from one swing to another. No one looked like giving up their space anytime soon. Stalking around a set of four swings, he stared back at the children lazily kicking their legs, urging them to grow tired. Eventually one young girl in a blue dress got bored and hopped off her seat. For a moment she stopped in her tracks and turned to face Carl. The pale blue of her eyes clashed with the dark blue of her summer dress. Pointing her finger to the swing, she told him he could have a turn.

'Thank you', he smiled back at her.

About to take his seat, another parent started to protest. Her child, apparantly, had been waiting in the queue first. Impatient, Carl turned to face her.

'I'm gonna be on it a while, so if she wants a quick go she can jump on first.'

Bemused by this response, it took her a few seconds to speak.

'Ermm, okay, thanks?'

'No problem', Carl said, stepping aside and motioning with his hand.

His presence evidently making her uncomfortable, the woman allowed her daughter a very quick spell on the swing, taking a few photos before beckoning her to move away.

'All yours', she smiled back at Carl, awkwardly.

'That's great, cheers.'

Already pulling his laptop from his bag as he took his seat, he opened the screen and gently kicked off with his feet. Careful not to go too quickly, needing both his hands to secure the laptop, he sat hunched over the keyboard, gently rocking back and forth. Exactly as it had happened in the restaurant, the words started to flow forth from his finger-tips. Unaware of his vocalisation, he spoke aloud to himself, his lips mouthing in synchronicity with his fingers, the report starting to take shape.

'Perhaps one of the most striking elements witnessed in this phase was the experimentation at the edges of the human and the self.

It would seem to anyone visiting this world that the traditional societal and familial structures have been totally reshaped.

The members of this society seem... seem to view relationships as consisting of what people can gain from sharing a space or entering into agreements together.

When I say 'gain', this does not signify the traditional economic sense of gain. Far from being a society of advanced capitalism in

which citizens view their own relations as commodity values, this sense of the word 'gain' is tied more closely to the word 'create'.

'Creative gain', as I will now refer to it, is a central tenet of this culture.

One group I encountered, a group of roughly a dozen citizens, cohabited a small space in which they viewed themselves as a 'creative unit', their bonds being formed based on the creative utility of each member.

While their activity could be compared to an art collective in our society, their cohabitation and sense of each member's creative utility seemed to pervade every element of their daily lives.

Their focus was specifically on exploring different uses of bodily augmentation and how this blend between human and technology could allow a certain individual to explore the different uses of their body for creative endeavours.

Yet, as it would seem with almost all elements of this phase, the link between human endeavour and coexistence with the nonhuman is taken as a measure of how valuable a certain artistic expression really is. In the case of this group, their focus was on the augmentation of the human voice

to communicate with animals that were located in their city.

Small voice box enhancers, or 'VBHs' as they referred to them, had been surgically input into larynxes, allowing the

members to perform bird songs, communicate with cats and even imitate the sounds of insects, such as grasshoppers and crickets.

When I first came across this group, they... they had started their training of communicating with each other in bird song. While they had arrived at a

point of being able to comprehend simple questions or directions, their focus was on trying to find ways of expressing parts of their personality through this new language...'

'Hey, sorry if you're just sitting there on your laptop, do you mind if my son has a go on the swing?'

Engrossed in his report, Carl had almost forgotten where he was. Annoyed at having his flow interrupted, he looked back up at her, his face sweating.

'Sorry no, I'm quite busy. Just wait for someone else to leave.' He replied, looking back down at his screen and gently kicking off with his feet.

'You're barely even swinging. If you just want a place to sit, there's somewhere inside.'

He thought about replying, then realised she had no authority to remove him. Completely ignoring her, he continued typing.

'*Prick*,' she snapped, before leading her son away by the hand.

'This new augmentation, while still very much in its early experimental formation, is viewed by other members of the society as having the potential to benefit the population at large.

The population as a whole seem to be incredibly open to radical new forms of technological expression which can be used to bridge the communication gap between humans and nonhuman inhabitants.

Rather than seeing the nonhuman as a cohabitor of the urban space who should merely be respected and protected from extinction, the general consensus of this society is that the nonhuman should have an active voice in the decisions taken in city planning....'

With the afternoon sun continuing to scorch the back of his computer, his screen glitched a little, before going into hibernation mode. Frantic, his face a little sunburnt, he jumped up from his swing and headed towards the shady spot under the pavilion. Here, he could make out the message on the screen:

Engine too hot. Cool laptop down.

Somewhere to his left he heard a child crying, a parent rushing over to help them up after their fall.

'Fuck', he said to himself aloud. He'd only been writing for twenty minutes and already his computer couldn't handle it. Collecting his bag and moving inside the Tate he took out his phone. A near identical message, neatly written under the Apple logo met his gaze. iPhone overheating, please cool down. Breathing deeply, he made his way through the crowds of tourists, heading to the ticket desk.

'Hey, could you to check for any other swings close to here.'

'You mean a park?'

'No, it can't be outdoors. Too hot for the computer. Could you have a look if there's any place with indoor swings. In fact it doesn't even need to be close to here, just in London.'

'Ermm, I can have a quick look on Google, yeah'. She searched a little, slowly shaking her head from side to side, before biting her lip. 'Yeah, no sorry there's nothing coming up. There's only places where you can buy swing sets for gardens.'

Hours later he stood admiring the new arrangement in his living room. A single garden swing, hanging from a green metallic frame. Positioned around it were six fans; a few on the floor, the rest either attached to the walls or placed on shelves cleared of all books and ornaments. Outside, the clouds had turned a shade of dark brown, an ominous overhang that everyone in the street was speaking about. On the news, presenters relayed fragmented information from weather experts. Panel discussions continued to ponder the potential risks each city faced as the climate grew harder and harder to predict. All throughout western Europe the production of sandbags ramped up, with all coastal cities entering red alert. Hot winds screamed above the Atlantic as fibre optic cables fizzed beneath the surface. The air grew thick, and Dutch canals raised their heads.

Not wanting to hear any more information about the latest catastrophe or warning, he closed the news app on his phone and leaned his head back. After spending four hours in the gardening warehouse, testing out different chairs, he'd selected a sleek, wicker-basket seat and found a small wooden panel that could be attached as a table. Lighting up a Camel, he rocked back and forth in his chair, fans whirring all around him, swirling up the smoke into thin streaks that waltzed above his head.

A week later Carl found himself standing in front of a small cohort of undergraduate students in one of Imperial's sleek lecture theatres. The group couldn't have been more than thirty, but being the centre of attention had unnerved him as soon as he stepped up behind the speaker's podium. Knowing that it was his only responsibility — to turn up once a month and deliver a lecture — added to the pressure. Clearing his throat, he briefly introduced the lecture title: Linguistic readings of the term 'Anthropocene'. When he reflected on his lecture later that evening, he couldn't clearly remember, but imagined that he'd opened it with something along the lines of:

'So, when it comes to the ethico-political implications of this concept, there's been a lot of interest — particularly in the social sciences. One thinker who has written extensively on the question of linguistic possession is Dalby, *in his book Anthropocene Geopolitics...*'

Or something similar? Something referential, probably. Closing his eyes, he saw himself again, slightly flustered, fumbling with his notes.

'So, one of his key questions about the term Anthropocene centres around *who* gets to use the term. In this sense, 'who' can refer to groups of people, nations, continents, or even hemispheres that play a role in the construction of this term. The question you should start to ask yourself as you look further into the word's origin is what groups get to invoke the framing of the new human age? This consideration, Dalby notes, is crucial for the planet *and* for different parts of humanity.'

He'd paused, he seemed to remember, sipping his water, which by then

136

was warm. Feeling his words creating a flow, he noted how his heart got a little steadier, his breathing more controlled. Rubbing his eyes, the lecture unfolded.

'Similar reservations', he continued, 'can be found in Latour's work. The Anthropocene, he writes, is not merely an extension of anthropocentrism, rather it is the *human as a unified agency*', he placed both his hands on the speaker's podium, letting those words resonate. This gesture seemed to trigger more of a response than the words themselves, each student quickly jotting down the term; regardless of their comprehension or non-comprehension of its significance.

Now more confident in his orating abilities, he began to slowly walk from side to side across the stage, pausing in between words, letting his chin rest on his fist as if trying to work through his own ideas.

'This *unified agency*, or, if you will, *virtual political entity* -'

More scratching of pens, tense scribbles reverberating through the room.

'This notion is of the human as virtual political entity... as a universal concept that has to be broken down. Divided among many different peoples, each with contradictory interests or, *opposing cosmoses*, as Latour would have it.'

Just relaying this information seemed to open up the possibility for his own personal rediscovery of the concepts. He could perceive a certain tension building amongst the alumni, an expectation that he was building up to something — something that would surprise even himself. Gulping his water, holding it in his cheeks for a moment, he turned back to his notes and continued.

'But here, *here* is where we really get to the contention surrounding the term. Not just a revision of it, a *rejection*. Outright. Off the table. The refusal to accept the term 'Anthropocene' at all. This refusal, I believe, is borne out of what many people see as a parallel between the Anthropocene being described as a geological epoch and its growth *into* an ideological stance. That is, they see the term 'Anthropocene' as simply being an ideological equivalent to globalisation. Within this school of thought, we encounter the notion that the whole earth is becoming conflated with humans, and more precisely with *Western man.*'

Sunlight hit the blinds, a thin shard chipping away at the students' desks and catching Carl's eye: he winced.

'So where does the tension in this argument lie? Is it a fair to name our present geological age 'the age of the human'? Does this somehow expound human attempts to master Earth? Seen in such industries as bio or geo-engineering? Or does this term, *in fact,* offer us the potential of a wake-up call, a slap across the face, iced water over the head?'

The students started to laugh, their smirks urging him to become more theatrical in both his mannerisms and descriptions.

'Is this term, then, really the message we all need, the angry finger pointing towards the dishes piling up in the sink? Or does it unfairly place all humans under the same interrogation — everyone guilty by association? Rural farmer and oligarch alike?'

He stood looking back at them expectantly; no one in the room was quite sure if he actually required a response from them. No one spoke up.

'Let us turn our attention to Weber, and his suggestion of the *Zoocene.*'

As their hands rushed to keep up with his discourse, many looked up in anticipation. His figure loomed static, staring back at them, his mouth half-open, his eyes glazed over. From the students' perspective, all they could decipher was a lecturer paused in a complex thought, one that needed time to work through. When roughly a minute had passed and he hadn't spoken, a few eyes glanced at each other. For that entire pause, a stream of images passed through his mind, erupting somewhere behind his retinas. Images of trapped animals, their cages slowly filling up with deep blue water; a lion's paws treading in the swell, its golden fur turning a dark, muddy brown. White lights bounced off the shallow puddles, reflecting a blue mist towards his gaze. Snapping his head, abruptly, he found himself back in the room.

'Zoocene', he said aloud, anxiously trying to gather himself. 'Yes, the *Zoocene*. Weber argues that our current era should be referred to not as the *Anthropocene*, but the *Zoocene*.'

Despite his attempts to reinforce the term's significance, the effect was minimal, the students still confused. Trying to keep his composure, he continued:

'Yes, as Weber argues, we need to move away from the modern Humanist way of thinking, focusing not on the notion of Enlightenment, but of

Enlivenment.

The word *Zoocene*...'

Seafoam licked gently at his peripheral vision, his body starting to feel off balance. He resumed his pacing of the stage, steadying himself.

'The word Zoocene underscores the Greek word *Zoë*, meaning life in its felt sense, one that extends to the whole animate earth. Whereas the Anthropocene always centres around a discourse on humankind, the Zoocene instead suggests that our consideration of ecological issues in this era should always be considered through a term that takes non-human agents into consideration. This term is our lens, through which all issues should be viewed...'

He had more to say, but the words began to churn violently as images of inundation filled his head. He found himself stuttering, rushing over concepts, failing to lead the lecture across the trajectory he'd mapped out. From inside some distant cages, the howl of a thousand mammals thundered, echoing through his skull. Placing his fingers in his ears he turned his head a little, which only deepened the eruptions. Flashes of paddy fields sprouting alongside the Thames, mangroves uncoiling throughout the underground, their tips pushing through the barriers at every tube station. He found himself pausing again, trying to shake the images from his head. Yet with every word that fell form his mouth, a visual accompaniment sprouted.

'*Capitalocene*', he finally blurted, letting the word ring out a little. The images became watery, loosening their grip on him.

'Let us consider how global capitalism makes the depletion of resources so rapid, unwavering and so accessible, that Earth's systems are becoming frighteningly unstable.'

He continued to talk, but later that evening, when he looked back on that segment of his lecture, there was a significant blind spot. He assumed he went on to speak of climate-change modelling as a positive feedback loop, triggering changes of states in human political and ecological systems. While lying in his hammock, he skimmed through the quotations he took down from Haraway's *Tentacular Thinking*. Tentacular thinking. That was the trigger. He remembered moving through Haraway's paper, laying out her critique of the term 'Anthropocene'. Again, he saw the flood of images that had burst above him as he relayed her words:

One must surely tell of the networks of sugar, precious metals, plantations, indigenous genocides, and slavery, with their labor innovations and relocations and recompositions of critters and things sweeping up both human and nonhuman workers of all kinds. The infectious industrial revolution of England mattered hugely, but it is only one player in planet-transforming, historically situated, new-enough, worlding relations.

He recalled the details: the cargo ships passing across choppy oceans. Stolen fruits mashing together under the strain of the wooden crates. Carefully drawn out maps, dissecting continents. Orange dust hitting khaki shirts. Western diseases landing on the east coast of the Americas. Slave quarters, fingers placed on iron bars. A blue flash shooting from a damp prison, suddenly closer to home. His two friends, stood in their cells. Caged beasts.

He saw them staring back at him, their eyes cold, empty. Nauseous, he moved the lecture towards his final point, one that he hadn't planned to include, but which seemed to assume its own place on his tongue.

'As Brad Lerner notes, with this total instability in our environment, the only scientific thing to do, is *revolt*.'

Revolt. He stood staring back at the interactive screen, passive, taking in his own notes. Revolt. Hearing this word over and over in his head, blue flashes passed across his eyes. His fellow activists' faces reappeared, overexposed behind rusting prison bars. Long grey hair, oily, tentacular. He suddenly felt like Judas himself. The tentacular vines of the garden of Gethsemane, the other disciples looking away from him. Had he betrayed them? Abandoned the cause? Where was the revolt in his life? With every slide he moved through, he felt as ignorant as the students attending the lecture for the first time. Lost in thought again, he stood there for a few seconds, contemplating his own trajectory.

'Tentacular Judas' he said out loud to himself. A burst of mirth broke out in the audience, those unable to control their initial laughter quickly grappling with their bodies, straightening out their faces and looking down at their papers, as if trying to make sense of their lecture notes.

He couldn't recall how the lecture had ended. Lying there in his hammock, rocking himself from side to side, the tube hummed through the ventilation somewhere in Bethnal Green. Images of the underground as one tentacular entity — a rhizomatic tangle extended throughout the capital — whirred in his head.

He lit another Camel and allowed his neck to sag a little. The tube as mushroom, its underground network a mycorrhizal root, formed behind his eyes. Breathing in deeply, mushroom heads sprouted out of the turnstiles, whole stations throbbing with fungi. At the end of his fingertips, he felt three sharp vibrations. A blue light flashing. He looked down at his phone.

Despite his reservations at having to give his only lecture the week following the immersion, Carl felt grateful that it was out of the way. Any additional responsibilities while trying to compose his report would be a hindrance, or at least a minor annoyance. For this reason, he'd contacted his department and requested that each of the classes be arranged earlier during the second week of each month. He was surprised to receive such a prompt response, the department's convener not only assuring him that this would be taken care of, but also mentioning, as a brief endnote, that many students had expressed their enthusiasm for his recent lecture. This relieved him more than anything else. That evening after the lecture his head had been painfully foggy, a swarm of images and thoughts colliding and piling up like gridlocked traffic. He could recall very little of how the lecture had actually played out, save for the strange tentacular outbursts. News indicating that students were eager to hear his next talk put his doubts to rest.

During the two weeks that remained for him to finish his report, his routine seemed to form itself. This was more out of his activity being contained within the parameters of his flat, rather than any prefabricated plan: when he was awake, he would be writing. When he was too exhausted to write but not tired enough to sleep, he would be in the hammock, listening to the sounds circulating around his roof. He ate only when he felt like it, not bothering to stick to a meal schedule. He saw very little use in this, as there was almost no differentiation between his meals.

With the heat breathing down aggressively on the city, he found a sudden taste for tropical fruits, the innumerous middle-eastern grocery shops on his street providing him an ease of access. Often he went days on end where the only alimentation that would pass through his body were watermelon and coffee. Enjoying the physical act of having to grip the huge slices with his hands, sinking his teeth deep into the pink flesh, he relished in the mess it made of his arms and face.

A lunch break didn't really exist in his day, so blended were the movements between eating, writing, thinking and resting. When the hunger grew inside him, he would push his laptop to one side, cradle a plate of melon in his arms and kick at the floor, the swing projecting him backwards and forwards, his body passing through the AC's multi-angular wind tunnel. When he felt quite overwhelmed, his tanned skin drenched with pulp and seeds, he'd spring from his chair and stand naked under the cold shower, presenting his open mouth to the powerful spay that washed any debris from his skin or teeth. Once refreshed, he'd return to his chair and recommence his writing, as if his bursts of hunger were some dirty habit he needed to relieve himself of and forget about soon after.

Often during the early hours of the morning, he went out for a brief stroll around Bethnal Green. These passings couldn't constitute a routine: it made no difference to him if these walks were to wake himself up or tire himself sufficiently to fall asleep. During these circular movements around the park, he fell into a habit of humming fragments from different Arvo Pärt compositions to himself. Often he hummed the same melody over and over, the quaintness of its progression forcing him to wander at a tranquil pace, one foot pressing down on the warm concrete before the other begun its accent.

As he embodied these faint melodies, he didn't only recall memories from Estonia, but was fully transported back there. Remembering what Sofia had said about VR simulations of Antarctica being used to cool the bodies of burn victims, he now found in this exercise a means of dropping his own body temperature — this melodic transportation somehow triggering a cool breeze. As he walked his loop around the dry, dusty grass, he would see snow covered parts of Tallinn, the thin frosted branches of the leafless trees and small air pockets trapped underneath frozen puddles. Sometimes Anya would be standing alongside him, wrapping her scarf over her mouth as she always did, the thickness of the cotton never making her speech any harder to understand. If someone were to look out onto the Green, they would see a man standing in his loose linen trousers and unbuttoned cotton shirt, sweat rolling down his forehead, a mechanical arm feeding his mouth drag after drag from a glowing Camel.

And it would be just this.

Another victim of the heatwave, reduced to walking laps of a dusty park because he couldn't sleep. But behind his eyes, he was somewhere quite distant, sat in the pale blue light of Kadriorg Park, inwardly remembering how fortunate he was to have secured a life for himself there. Often during these walks, a noise within Bethnal Green would snap him back to his surroundings. His body temperature having dropped significantly, he would often rub his shoulders, pacing back to his apartment as if he were underdressed in the depths of winter.

When four days remained before the following immersion, he found himself cleaning out his apartment, tossing out bin liners of coffee tins, cigarette packets and watermelon rinds. Despite the fogginess he'd felt during the last few weeks — a certain heaviness that came over his thoughts at infrequent moments during the day — he'd managed to write his first report, one that he felt proud of. The process of putting into writing the world he'd visited had also given him more confidence for the project itself. By having to not just experience, but anthropologically interpret the worlds, he'd come to appreciate how much effort had gone into the design and formulation of the algorithms, something he hadn't fully valued before. After finishing his analysis, he realised that there was, undoubtedly, vast amounts of information still to be discovered within this single phase. While he wouldn't be able to return to it during this year, he looked forward to revisiting it, and seeing how the world would evolve.

After showering and dressing himself, he stepped onto the rooftop into the late morning sun, the ice cube in his espresso jutting out of the golden foam, melting. Resting his arms on the wall, he smiled to himself. When his phone rang and Anya asked if they were still on for seeing the exhibition, he confirmed the time and wandered calmly down the iron stairwell.

∞∞∞

Hot air danced around the turnstiles in Bond Street. The population of London had grown even more accustomed to the painfully slow queues that formed every time a commuter's smart phone went into hibernation mode. Carl noticed how people no longer seemed angry about the delays. Before the heatwave, he'd perceived London to be one of the most impatient cities on earth. Whenever he'd struggled to get his phone or debit card out in time, he'd felt hatred darting out of other commuters' eyes, striking his back. Now it was different. When there was congestion, people simply looked placidly exhausted, seeming to recognise, as if for the first time, that there was no blame to be laid. Perhaps the temperature had made the city so unbearable that any tiny changes people could make to alleviate the tension of simply moving from one place to another were suddenly seen as sacred. He waited in line with the other commuters, adapting to this new code of conduct.

When he finally made his way out of the station he saw Anya waiting, her back turned towards him. As he approached her, the breeze from a passing bus tugged at her dark-blonde hair, the straight strands gently tumbling back down onto her shoulders. He stopped in his tracks, admiring her. There was something about Anya's unwavering composure, the fact that no matter the temperature, she never showed any discomfort or fatigue. Despite being from the Baltic region, she seemed to have an

145

almost super-human tolerance for the searing heat. All around him people stopped to tug at their moist t-shirts or mop their perspiring foreheads. But there she stood, hands placed on the black metal railing, looking out across the street. Her neatly cut linen trousers, a shade of olive-green that complimented her beige shirt, swayed gentlys. As he stood there, it dawned on Carl that he was unequivocally in love with Anya, and probably always would be. Perhaps it was because he'd known this for some time that such a realisation took little effect over him. He looked down for a moment. Well, of course you already knew this.

Resuming his steps, he approached her and gently tapped on her shoulder. When she turned to face him, she smiled in a way that reminded him they hadn't seen each other for almost three weeks.

'It's great to see you,' she said over his shoulder as he hugged her, 'I'm glad you managed to find the time to come along today.' They started their short walk along Davies Street towards the gallery. 'Ah, just before you start telling me how it's been going, shall we stop for a drink? The gallery is so close and we won't be able to chat inside.'

Carl agreed, and they browsed the street for a café, eventually ducking down one of the side streets when they saw a cluster of small tables tucked in a shady patch. Taking their seats, they each ordered an over-priced espresso and a glass of ice, most of which had melted by the time it reached their table. Taking out a cigarette and offering Carl the packet, Anya turned to face him.

'So, how has it all been going? I can imagine it's been a heavy few weeks what with the report and also needing to be in the university?'

'Well', he let out a little laugh. As he started to relay to her his previous few weeks, he was overcome by a sense of calm. As he spoke, he looked back at her, realising that no matter how much he'd tried to convince himself otherwise, it made no sense to deny his feelings. Rather than making their situation harder, the apparentness of it all showed him he had nothing left to prove. Their relationship was as it was, and he'd grown to accept the dynamic of romance without physical intimacy. The only obstacle up until this point had been his refusal to admit to himself that he was okay with this. He'd tried to convince himself that even if the possibility of an intimate relationship arose, perhaps he wouldn't even want that. This apprehension, despite the level of friendship they had reached, often caused him to feel slightly on edge around Anya. It wasn't really nervousness, but more the recognition that he wanted to present his best side to her. Perhaps subconsciously he hoped that if he maintained a level of unpredictability, this would somehow spark an interest in her, a desire to know him even better than she already did. In his mind this had always equated to physical intimacy, to taking their relationship to a 'higher' level in which there would still be so many mysteries left to discover. Only now, while sat there in the midday heat, did he lose all inhibitions. He no longer felt self-conscious about his own body: his slightly reddened cheeks, his wiry physique, his nervous movements. All worry evaporated.

'It's been great, actually. Looking at the VR through an anthropological lens, I mean, having to really put into writing what the designers have managed to achieve... yeah it's given me a new sense of appreciation for the project as a whole.'

'I've been dying to ask you what you saw, but I know you're supposed to keep the details to yourself for now, right?'

'I'm afraid so. We've been asked not to describe the settings to other members of the group until the testing period has finished. So I'm going to have to respect their rules. But really, it was overwhelmingly powerful. I'd never imagined that it would be so complex, so intricate. It really felt like they'd considered every possible element imaginable, down to the smallest, seemingly most insignificant details. I think before I entered the immersion, I'd become a little cynical, almost imagining it as some gimmicky video game where I'd be flying around some dystopian smart city of the future. But in truth, what I found so overwhelming were the conversations I had with people who, well, I guess you could say *lived* there. The great thing about it is that it will keep evolving, so by the time you get to experience it, everything I witnessed might be in a much more advanced stage. Or you'll just encounter totally different elements, who knows?'

He paused, taking a sip from his lukewarm coffee and tapping the long curve of ash that had built up on his cigarette.

'In all honesty I'd had similar reservations, ones that only really came to me during the last few weeks. Up until then I'd been so confident, but something changed. Suddenly the whole notion of an algorithm being able to dictate how a world evolved seemed almost, well, *far-fetched* — I guess you could say?' Anya asked.

'Totally. I think it's normal to have such doubts. We're certainly not the only ones. When I was outside smoking before the immersion, I spoke to one of the other testers and she also seemed hesitant. I think it's also because none of us last year predicted the chaos of this summer. Of course we were all aware of the crisis, but it still felt at a distance...'

'Then all of a sudden this heat wave breaks on London and people realise it's here, on their own doorstep.'

'Yeah exactly. When it's facing you head-on, you panic and want instant answers and solutions. So some group of researchers saying they've created worlds of the future from which we can learn, seems too abstract.'

'But did you feel that' she paused, trying to find a way to word the question that wouldn't push Carl to reveal any specific details, 'did you feel that there were elements you encountered that we could feasibly aim for, from our current position?'

'Possibly. As expected, some of the innovations seemed otherworldly and, without being able to decipher the changes, almost impossible to reach. *But*, there were some societal structures that would appear as radical as the familiar structures of, hmm, say the Melanesia peoples during the nineteenth century.'

At this Anya raised her eyebrows, aware of the reference.

'But, you know, *as anthropologists we've of course always been taught to break away from ethnocentrism in this world.*' Carl said, gesturing with his hands, making Anya laugh. 'So I think we can implement the same reduction of our societal preconceptions when we visit one of these future worlds. That way, if there is a societal structure that seems to work, one that keeps the human population living in tune with other species, then *at least* we have an idea of what we *could* aim towards.'

'I think that's the point I've arrived at. I mean, even if the VFL does find a neat method of deciphering what changes we can implement, the world will always be in flux and each society would always still need to adapt accordingly?'

'Yeah I think we're on the same page.' Carl nodded, stubbing out his cigarette. 'This is how I'm approaching it — seeing it not as a means of saving ourselves from ourselves, but as a means of offering us a target to aim at, even if the solutions will change along the way.'

When the waiter asked if they'd like anything, they each looked at each other.

'The exhibition is open until six, right?' Carl asked.

'Yeah, it's barely past midday.'

They ordered the same again and leaned back in their chairs. Rays of sunlight fell across the table next to theirs, reflecting off the polished cutlery and piercing the water tumbler. The smell of seared fish seeped out of the kitchen window, as inside the only other customer, an elderly man sat by himself, handed his menu back to the waiter. Staring down at the small beam of light passing through the tumbler, Carl thought back to the hotel, to the light that had fallen through the large windows. The shape, a sort of triangular tube, seemed to mirror the same shape of those blinds. The thought hovered for a moment, bursting when Anya reached for the ashtray, her shadow breaking the thread.

'And how have you been?' Carl broke their silence, again conscious that they'd only spoke about his work. 'Have you managed to work from your flat during this heat?'

'So so. I can only manage for around four hours a day. Then my head just starts aching. It's like a form of humidity that builds up, this sort of damp heat. I often feel totally out of it once I've finished reading.'

'I've had to construct a three dimensional circle of fans in my flat.'

At this, she let out a laugh, coughing a little afterwards.

'I have my one chair, well more of a swing, actually.'

'*Swing?*'

'Yeah, well, something strange happened. I went to that Portuguese café you'd recommended to me. And while I was there, I couldn't write unless I was rocking back and forth on my chair.'

Her laughter resumed.

'Seriously, when I was sat still, I just couldn't get my fingers to transcribe what I was thinking. Then I just started rocking back and forth, just as I do in the hammock. Ah that was it — it was in the hammock that I realised the movement seemed to help.'

Two smartly dressed waiters turned to watch Anya laughing, each of them smiling.

'But then in this café, I ended up snapping the legs of the chair, fell completely backwards and got kicked out.'

'And then?'

'Then in the street, I was just looking for somewhere to sit where I could also move freely, then I remembered-'

'The Tate.' she finished his sentence.

'You got it. But it was too hot. Not just for me, but for the computer. So I ended up buying a small garden swing and about six fans. I've got a small space set up in the flat now.'

'This I need to see. After the exhibition, I'm passing by yours. Speaking of which, shall we make a move?'

They paid, leaving a tip for the two waiters to split. As they walked down Davies Street, it dawned on Carl that he rarely saw Anya laugh. He

150

found it strange that it had taken him up until now to notice this. Anya never fake-laughed to make a situation more comfortable. She would politely smile when someone made a joke she didn't appreciate. The kind of smile which indicated that while she wasn't offended, she certainly wasn't amused. Yet even between them, although he would never have described her as a cold person — for she demonstrated care and consideration for many, often for those she didn't even know — she *did* seem almost always occupied with something that required serious consideration. An article she might have read, an insight that might have come to her and of which she needed to work through. There was always, it seemed to Carl, *something*. This new Anya, one that cried with laughter, seemed almost foreign to him. He felt a certain privilege to have been the one to spark such laughter, before wondering if it was really a new experience for her, or just for him. As the green man illuminated, she turned to speak.

'Do you remember those prints I showed you before, the ones also by Richter?'

He didn't.

'Maybe, which ones do you mean?'

'The silicate ones. The ones we both thought looked like carpet textures.'

'Ah yeah, I'm with you. They're the ones with the grey and black blob-like structures?'

'I only found out this week how he actually made them.'

A bike bell rang, and to their left, a figure shook a cup of coins, asking them for change. Turning to face the man, Carl tried his hardest not to look visually shocked. A man with red raw skin, either sunburnt or plagued by some other type of rash, looked up at them.

'Spare some change?' the man rasped, sweat pouring down his forehead. Carl reached into his pocket, fishing for coins. Finding only a few silvers, he dropped them in his cup, Anya following in suit and sparing the man a two-pound coin. Seemingly too weak to even thank them, he nodded, his eyes quivering as he leant back against the wall, breathing deeply. The two of them continued to walk in silence for a little; any return to conversation feeling inappropriate. When they could see the gallery, Carl reminded her about the silicates.

'So how did he make them?'

'Ah, so he was actually depicting a photo of a computer-generated simulacrum of reflections. These reflections are from the silicon dioxide found in insect shells.'

They paused outside the doors of the gallery, leaning against the wall to shade themselves.

'It's so interesting how when you first look at it, it just looks like an abstract work, this sort of illusion that you can get lost in. But there's so much more happening behind, especially when you think about how the chemical compound is so commonly used.'

'Yeah straight away my mind went to fibre-optic cables.'

'Yeah exactly. Quite beautiful how the piece documents this scientific discovery — all through oil painting, with him having to find the hue that would depict these structural colors.'

'Ah, so the colors weren't contained in the textures themselves?'

'That's what's so cool about it. The structural colors come about through the *refraction* of the textures. They don't actually contain pigment.'

'You'll have to show me the prints again.'

'I will, of course. Shall we take a look inside?'

When they found themselves in the air-conditioned space of the gallery, what seemed most powerful, before they'd even looked at the art, was the transition from overcrowded, overheated street, to the empty, cool whiteness of the four walls. They each stood, breathing for a moment, feeling their body temperature start to drop. A single guard stood by himself in the far corner, rubbing the sides of his arms.

Along each of the four walls, separated into small frames, were the surprisingly small images, each one measuring ten by fifteen centimeters. Pausing to read the statement, printed in sans-serif in neat black letters along the wall, Carl mused over Richter's description of the different mediums.

Over-Painted Photographs

Now there's painting on one side and photography — that is, the picture as such — on the other. Photography has almost no reality; it is almost 100% picture. And painting has reality: you can touch the paint; it has presence; but it always yields a picture... I once took some small photographs and then smeared them with paint. That partly resolved the problem, and it's really good — better than anything I could ever say on the subject. — Gerhard Richter

As he moved slowly along the rows of small images, Carl made no attempt to pause at one. He'd learnt, or perhaps just decided that he didn't want to give each piece equal consideration. He'd leave the pieces to either draw him in or fail to interest him. The artworks themselves would dictate how he'd interact with the space. Anya always adopted the opposite approach, taking her time to carefully consider each piece, almost as if she were studying each one for the information it contained, rather than the experience it might offer her. Passing from piece to piece, the words 'photography has no reality' continued to play over in his mind. He stepped up close to one of the photos. Pink and blue paint erupted from the image. As he stood focusing on the thin streaks of oil paint obscuring the building, he felt he suddenly understood what Richter was getting at.

The photo, in itself, while depicting the place, felt distant, the warmth of the analogue quality rendering it almost dreamlike. The paint on the image grounded it, somehow bringing the building, or his experience of it, into the present moment. Images of the recent immersion started to filter into his memory. This time he didn't feel himself becoming overwhelmed by them, as he had during his lecture. Now the memories seemed to exist as photographs, snapshots from a world that itself had no reality. A world of images built on predictions. The more he looked at the paint, the more tactile the images became, even without him being able to actually touch them.

'Photography has almost no reality', he said inwardly to himself, and then laughed when he realised the irony. Where did that leave the virtual world he had recently entered into, a world of moving photographs one could only look at, but not touch? There was, he realised, *nothing* tactile about the world. Nothing that he could actually grasp. Perhaps until that moment he hadn't quite managed to comprehend how surreal this made the whole experience — the visual and audio stimuli being so overwhelming. Did this reality they had designed, so visual, so one-hundred percent photographic, *elude* reality, rather than construct it?

A virtual reality with no reality. He laughed again, the guard too docile to even send him a disapproving look. Still mulling over this thought, he continued to examine the images, the thick smudges of paint appearing like living tumours that grew out of the photos. The dreamlike past being ruptured by the tactile present. The more he focused, the more Richter's brushstrokes seemed to appear like natural growths. Tree roots or funghi systems that had perhaps always lived underneath the photographs, bursting out when the reality of the moment ended with it being captured by the camera's lens.

He approached Anya, who was stood pensively before an image depicting a man crossing a bridge, a large squeegee stroke of blue, red and white riding across the photograph. They stood together for a little while, observing in silence. Only afterwards, when they had left the gallery, did both of them admit the image had reminded them of Tallinn, even though neither of them could recall a place it resembled.

Behind his swollen eyelids, a photographic reel softened, oil paint metastasizing across the celluloid.

'It's just as I imagined.' Anya said, laughing as she threw herself into the swing. 'How do you manage to keep the laptop steady while you're swinging?'

'I bought this little table you can attach,' Carl responded, waving the small piece of wood in one hand. 'I'm not sure why, but I *do* know that this whole set-up helped me write that report.' He turned to face the desk in the corner of the room. 'I mean, that was the intended space,' he said, pointing to the untouched surface.

'I think this is better, well, certainly more *fun*, she laughed.

'Ah, just a second', he knelt down, turning on the fans. With all of them connected — somewhat dangerously — to an overloaded extension cable, a dynamic wind tunnel formed around Anya. Laughing, she kicked off again, her hair dancing in the wind as she rocked back and forth.

'Would you like a drink?' Carl asked, already walking into the kitchen.

'Sure'. She called after him.

When he reappeared with two small beers, a slice of overripe lime swimming in each one, Anya sprang up from her chair and switched off the fans.

'I feel like I've been walking along the coast,' she said, accepting the drink and clinking glasses with his.

'Shall we head up to the roof and catch the last of the evening light? I've always been envious of the space you have up there.'

His mouth full of beer, Carl nodded.

'Ah, do you have a small speaker? I wanna show you this album I came across. There's a really amazing story behind it. I'll tell you when we're upstairs.'

As Carl hunted for his small portable speaker, he realised that he couldn't remember the last time he actually put music on. Pausing once he found the speaker, he held it in his hand, observing it.

'Is it charged?'

He hit the on button. The green light illuminated.

'Yeah seems so. Really strange, I just realised I haven't put music on in weeks, maybe months.'

'Strange, you used to constantly have your headphones in. Even when you were reading, you'd always have an album on at the same time. I remember because I always found this impressive; I can neither read nor write to music. I don't need silence, but it has to be background noises. Otherwise I just focus on the music and can't gather my thoughts.'

'This whole time, I think I've been listening to music, I just haven't selected any or even chosen to listen in the first place.'

'How do you mean?'

'I feel like a lot of the time, I have this Arvo Pärt piece playing in my head. Normally I'm not even aware of it. It's like a background noise, just circulating. I think I noticed it the other day when I went for a walk during the night around Bethnal Green. I was fucking boiling in here, like *really* couldn't stand to be lying down. Then while I was walking around the Green, I just heard *Credo*. The start where the whole orchestra erupts with the choir and they're chanting 'I believe in Jesus Christ'.'

Both of them burst out laughing.

'Strange, that being the last piece he wrote before his decade of silence. Was this a quasi-religious awakening you had, brought on by heat stroke? Maybe next time you'll awake from the chair with the *Tintinnabuli* chimes sounding. Then you'll *really* know you're ready to produce the report.'

'Maybe', he continued, still laughing. 'The strangest thing of all was that I totally lost track of time. I must have looked mad, just walking in circles around the park, miming those words to myself. But I wasn't even there. I spent the entire walk looking at Kadriorg Park in Tallinn. No, not looking, actually walking *in* the park, experiencing it physically, not just as a spectator. You were there for part of it. We were at that café, just looking out towards the snow-covered fields. You were saying something but the scene was completely mute. As if someone had taken that fragment of my memory and put *Credo* as the score.'

'I remember those afternoons there. I can actually picture the two of us sat there, just as you described it. But did you feel alright after? It does sound like a strange symptom of heatstroke.'

'I felt amazing. My whole body temperature dropped completely. When I snapped back to Bethnal Green, I was almost cold. It's like Kristen, one of the other testers, had described with the VR experiments they did in New York. They hooked up these children with severe burns to a VR simulation of Antarctica while they removed their bandages, and their body temperatures completely dropped. Most of them said they forgot they were even in hospital.'

'That's quite amazing. But has it happened again, the melody circling in your head?'

'I think it's been there for a while, it's just that only *then* I really noticed it. That must be why I haven't been playing other music. My brain's just going into some form of survival mode and triggering that music to cool down my body. Like a form of sweating.'

Still laughing a little, Anya sipped her drink and beckoned him towards the door.

'Well this album is from Cabo Verde, so perhaps not the best if a body-temperature regulator is what music has become for you.'

When they stepped out onto the roof, Anya lay down in the hammock, Carl perching in a chair and propping his feet up on the railing. Scrolling on her phone, she found the album. Jangly guitar blended with a space-sounding synthesizer. Carl lit a cigarette and offered one to Anya. A deep red sky grew darker above them, a thin layer of clouds glowing on the horizon.

'So what's the story behind it?'

'Well, it was in the late sixties and this cargo ship was leaving Baltimore headed for Rio de Janeiro. There was meant to be an exhibition in São

158

Paulo, showcasing the most advanced, cutting-edge synthesizers of that era. But the ship never arrived. There were no reports from the crew, and for *months* people just assumed it had sunk. So, then this very boat gets washed up on the coast of Cabo Verde. There's no crew on board, and to this day people still don't know what happened to them. But the cargo, the synthesizers, these were all still perfectly intact, sealed in their boxes.'

Carl started to smile, seeing where the story was going.

'But once the police had seized the cargo, this anti-colonial leader, I *think* his name was Amí... Amílcar Cabral, something like that, but I need to check. So yeah, he basically declared that the instruments now belonged to the island and that they should be distributed equally to the schools. So all of a sudden, these children who'd never had access to electronic instruments, had at their disposal the world's best synthesizers. There's this one man, Paulino Vieira, who used the synths to modernise their indigenous folk dances. What I love about it is that they still kept using some of the more makeshift instruments they'd always used, blending raw percussive sounds with dreamy synth solos and disco guitars.'

Carl smiled. 'Just brilliant', he said. 'To think that there's a whole genre that comes into being through a navigational failure. That's perhaps the best anecdote of serendipity I've heard before.'

The carmine sky riffed of the ethereal synth chords, the clouds forming to bolero rhythms. As the light faded, the heat emanating from surrounding buildings foggied their panoramic, the distant rooftops bleeding smudged paint. All around them the edifices respired, fatigued concrete aching.

When the album finished, Anya noted that she should probably be getting on her way. Her and a few other members at the VFL were organizing a workshop the following morning. Helping her out of the hammock, Carl accompanied her to the front door.

'Good luck with the next immersion,' she smiled, as they embraced in his doorway.

'Thanks. If you've got time the following week I can swing by and see you again.'

'That'd be great, we'll find the time. Head ööd, Carl.'

'Head ööd,' he called after her as she descended the stairwell.

Closing the door behind him, he picked up his laptop and dropped into his swing, the fall rocking the frame. Lighting up a Camel, he opened his report, deciding to read it once over before finally submitting it.

'But *that's* the most impressive thing about it! Not *what* they managed to coordinate, but *how*.

                    You've seen a picture of one of those old telex machines, right?

                  Piece of shit.

Like,   *really*.

            When I first read about

                                      Cybersyn,

                           it sounded like some
Latin American socialist *sci-fi story*.

But when I read what technology they were using,

                            I mean
          that's no easy gig.'

He recognised his voice as soon as he entered the breakfast lounge. As he recalled his name, *Anton*, he realised he'd been just 'the speaker' in his head. This nameless gesticulator whose words seemed to follow invisible coordinates. *That* was what he'd recognised. Not the timbre of his voice, but its movements.

'Just think about that for a second.

   Five-hundred telex machines. Each one feeding back to the control room in Santiago.

So essentially, every group of workers is inputting their data, then retaining semi-autonomous control over their factories. But there's the *means* in Santiago to intervene when necessary.

       It's all based on a

Viable System Model,

 essentially applying a theory of the human nervous system to cybernetic models.'

As Carl approached the table, his eyes were drawn to two empty espresso glasses in front of the speaker. The faded brown stains looked almost arid against the glass. They must have been chatting for a while.

'Carl!

      Glad to finally catch you in a more

informal environment.

Can I offer you a

coffee?'

'Please,' he responded, taking a seat. He said good morning to the other testers, before reaching for some fruit.

'I was just telling the group about project Cybersyn, the rather

ambitious project

Allende's government took on during the seventies.

It's fascinating, *especially* when you think of the contemporary equivalents, like the

City Brain Scheme

in Hangzhou.

I mean, *sure,* theirs is far more advanced because they're using

AI

and

Deep Learning

to manage the city across many deeply complex levels.

And it works amazingly!

But that's because they've *got* AI. Same for ourselves.

What we're doing with

our system

is unique.

But if someone tried to do it almost half a century ago,

and actually managed to make something that worked!

Yeah I mean, the designer would be worthy of some praise,

no?'

No one else seemed to be speaking, and as Carl was the last to be addressed, he felt obliged to respond for the group. Covering his mouth, rolling his index finger in circles while he finished chewing, everyone waited.

'The most impressive thing about Cybersyn is the decision making tool, its economic simulator, to be precise. Something called *Cyberstride,* this statistical modelling software the team developed. So they didn't only have the means to intervene and control, but to actually predict the outcomes of different decisions, similar to what we're trying to do here.'

He looked back down at his coffee, instinctively patting himself down looking for his cigarettes. He wasn't in the mood for talking about technology. None of the testers were. His answer had been so clinically delivered that Anton seemed taken aback, as if he'd perhaps thought that none of them would have been as clued up as he was.

'Excuse me, I'm going to smoke before we head up.'

Hot air smeared itself on his cheeks. The visceral blare of a thousand car horns sounded, xanthic dust settling on his skin.

Rubbing his eyes he pulled out a Camel and perched on the stair railing. The urban din stopped him hearing Anton approaching.

'What you smoking?

Camels.

Good choice, I must say.

Mind if I take one?

In times of high stress this vape just doesn't cut it.'

Taking a long toke, he exhaled with closed eyes.

'What's stressing you out, if I may ask?'

'Well, certainly not the project itself. *That* seems to be going just fine —

and while I've got you here, *fantastic* write up on phase one. Was just what I was after.

To the point

proper case-studies,

and some *very* pertinent overall analysis.

But anyway, you asked what *is* causing me stress, not what *isn't*.

One word Carl:

reception.

I've been in the public eye a lot recently; giving lectures, partaking in panel discussions, all of it. And one of the most infuriating things I have to come up against is an overall skepticism and aversion to what we're trying to achieve.'

Carl squinted, the high pitched car horns continuing to shriek in the nearby street.

'I guess you must be quite accustomed to having to deal with this though, no? I mean, putting forward an idea as radical as yo- *ours*. I'd imagine that dealing with criticism comes as second nature to you.'

'You're not wrong, Carl. I'm only too accustomed to this now.

But it's not receiving criticism that makes me tick. It's *stupidity*. You're a lecturer so you must know where I'm coming from.

Naivety I can tolerate,

but stupidity,

that's my pressure point, *really*.

Like yesterday, I was answering questions at one of our outreach conferences at Kings, and this guy raises his hand, clears his throat, then proceeds to ask the most obtuse question I could imagine. Something along the lines of *how can you ever expect to have complete confidence in the prediction of an algorithm compared to the prediction of a human scientist?*

Thing is, that's literally the easiest fucking question to turn around. I almost had to try not to laugh, just holding up a mirror and reflecting the question back to him, like,

how the fuck do you know anything about the future?

It's so simple,

I just asked him, genuinely, do you also have concerns about the two

degree rise in global temperature that's predicted and how that would be genuinely catastrophic?

Of course, he answered yes, even deciding to add on *but what does that have to do with my question?*

Stupid prick. I'd have loved to say that to him, *really.*

Like, just stop him there and tell him his question is so obtuse he doesn't even deserve an answer. But obviously, *it's a conference,* so I have to humor him with an actual answer. So yeah, I said to him, why do you believe in the two degree rise theory? 'Well *that's what the scientists are telling us'.* No. It's not the scientists that are *telling* you anything. It's the predictive algorithms they're *using.* They're the spokespersons for these predictions.

They're not sat there reading reports and then banding together to wage their bets on how much the temperature will rise. The only way this two degree prediction could have come about was through atmospheric modelling. Just ask any scientist and they'll tell you that they just take a host of variables and run them through computers and use this to generate thousands of different simulations for the coming decades. When they've looked at the data offered by these *algorithms,* that's when they can predict a two degree rise.

So if you're so easily won over by the use of algorithms in this case, why the scepticism towards our use of them? Like seriously, how stupid do you have to be not to see that?'

Carl finished his cigarette, looking down towards the ground. The outburst of anger had him on edge. He made sure to nod his head a little, demonstrating that he was taking in Anton's words without signalling whether he agreed or not.

'I guess the difficulty with these discussions often comes from a lack of shared definitions', Carl responded. 'Usually when I'm in the middle of one of these conversations, I tend to check in with the other person, making sure what we're both referring to, say, 'artificial general intelligence', or 'life', actually *means* the same thing. This is really what I instruct my students to do during our seminars. You'd be surprised how often two people can struggle to realise that they actually agree on an issue because they haven't comprehended the subtle variations between their own understanding of a term. Like in the case you just mentioned, if this man had actually *known* what an algorithm is and *how* scientists define it — in its most basic form — he'd probably have never asked that question.'

Anton continued to stare towards the glass buildings, his eyes tracing something — quite what, Carl couldn't tell. A long, curved ember hung at the end of his half-smoked cigarette. The fact that he decided not to turn to face him, while contemplating what he had said, seemed measured. Carl felt his shirt growing moist.

'You're right Carl. Strange how the longer you're working on something, you just assume that people are as well-informed and well-read as yourself. Then you get hit with a question that feels so eye-wateringly stupid, and you just flare up, you know? But you're right, really. I'm glad we're on the same page.'

He didn't know what to make of those last few words. What was it that they'd actually agreed on?

In the control room the air conditioning murmured. Views of the metropolis dripped behind the windows. Outside the roads continued to throb. Word of crop failures and potential food shortages had spread like a virus. Cities all over the continent were entering panic mode. All around London, congestion plagued the roads, as those with a vehicle made their way to the nearest superstore, ready to bulk buy as much as they could transport. In a small locker outside the testing room, the testers' phones vibrated with news updates. Governments issuing warnings, pleading with the population to remain calm:

'Panic-buying has to be avoided or limits will be put in place.'

'We need frugality and community values, not a descent into atomisation.'

'Please refrain from driving in the centre when possible.'

Words that carried little weight. A frenzy of gross tribalism simmering.

The testers lay stretched out on yoga matts, the static of their nylon tracksuits flickering against the rubber. Sarah entered quietly and stood behind her desk, waiting for their exercise to finish.

'So, seeing as we've all had a chance to catch up already, let's dive straight in with the new programme.'

Turning to face the screen, she read back the allocated phases.

Immersion Two

Irma Auer: Phase One

Carl Campbell: Phase Two

Sofia Horváth: Phase Three

Kristen Jansen: Phase Four

'Nothing has changed in respect to the amount of time — eight hours — that you'll be in the immersion. Just as before, if you feel uncomfortable or ill during the session, raise your right hand and one of our assistants will help you remove your headset. Please do not do this yourself. Based on your reports from the last immersion — which are *fascinating*, I must say — you all did very well at using the location switcher. Please keep up the good work today, as it is vital you experience multiple different areas of the phases. Are there any questions before we start?'

Their silence answered.

'Great. Well, *you know the drill.*'

ooooo

Sweat beads trickled down his forehead. Taut skin wrapped around strained shoulders. Carl sat on his balcony rubbing his eyes, a deep headache having already set in. He'd read somewhere that rubbing your eyes when tired causes more agitation and damage than relief. Similar to an itch that the relief of scratching only exacerbates. He felt much worse than after the previous immersion, this phase having been brutal in every sense. Thinking back to the previous month, he recalled how rough Sofia had looked each morning at breakfast. Nightmares formed from the day's grotesque simulations, perhaps? Had she been on phase two? He realised he couldn't be bothered to figure it out. His field recorder sat sweating in his hand, the red light blinking. He knew he should speak, try to get some information down. He'd be grateful next week. He opened his mouth, but managed nothing but a sigh. In a way he knew there was no possibility of him forgetting what he'd experienced. In this moment, blanking it out of his mind felt like the healthiest option. Stubbing out his Camel and turning off the recorder, he collapsed onto the bed. The current news updates of potential crop failures felt alarmingly pertinent, the early stages of this potential future world being played out in real-time below his balcony.

Friday morning snapped into focus. The repetitious nature of the week was fuelled by the obligation not to share information about the phases. Carl found himself sat opposite Sofia, the only other tester with whom he'd established any rapport. She looked much better this week. Fresher, less haunted. The breakfast lounge remained deserted, the other members having chosen to order room service. Above the bar, a muted television showed scenes of food riots in Greece. Large swathes of sweating bodies chanting mantras at a static police line. De-escalation tactics faltering.

'Makes you think doesn't it? Like one minute *here we are,* all these pricey fresh fruit, perfectly ripe, sat on our plates. Then the next minute everyone's charging around buying water containers and stockpiling canned goods. *Sinister,* if you ask me.'

His eyes remained glued to the screen. Silent figures with masked faces lifting bricks from the pavement. The images continued to agitate. Throngs of vigilantes tearing up the concrete, running their fingers through arid soil. Power cables torn down, tied up, used as clothing lines. A population feeling the collective shadow of their ancestors. Eyes that dilated like oil spills.

'Do you have a pen, Sofia?'

'I don't, no. Why, did you remember something important?'

'Actually I don't need to write it down, I doubt I'll forget it, seeing as it's just one word.'

'May I ask which word? You've got me curious now?'

'Gambiarra.'

'*Gambiarra?*'

'It's this Brazilian practice of reusing materials to create innovative new devices.'

'Oh, isn't that what your friend Anya is researching?'

'You know each other?'

'Met a few weeks ago at one of the outreach events at Imperial. So anyway, why Gambiarra? Or would that mean we had to start sharing details of the immersion?' she said, reaching for another mandarin.

'Yeah I won't go into details, but there was a lot that I saw which fell under that term.'

'Seems like not much has evolved from when I covered that phase. I didn't know the word Gambiarra then, but after speaking to Anya it felt like the term could be the title of that phase. Pretty grim stuff, no?'

'I feel like shit after this week,' Carl said, rubbing his cheeks.

'Not gonna lie, you look like it too.'

Carl looked up, half-shrugged in agreement and kept eating.

'Get some rest this weekend. I didn't think I needed it last time and ended up being apathetic for a week.'

'And this time? You still feel motivated?'

'Nothing's changed, really. It's like I said to you before, it's hard to see the value in this when outside people are already preparing for the looting. Like, how do you... no; you know what, I don't need to repeat myself. But yeah, as I said, it would be equally pointless *not* to finish the testing phase now. I guess I'll just stockpile supplies on my weeks off.'

She took another bite of mango, wiping her mouth matter-of-factly.

'Thing is, it's not *even* about what's going on outside. It's more to do with Anton and the rest of the *cognoscenti*. I bet — and this isn't a new suspicion — I bet that when it comes down to it, deciphering the algorithms and looking for concrete solutions is gonna prove too complex.'

'I think we both share that suspicion.' Carl agreed.

'*I* think, what we might have on our hands is another AlphaGo situation. In fact, I think they're gonna be pretty fucking analagous.'

Carl looked up from his plate, raising his eyebrows.

'So you know the story?' Sofia asked.

'It's victory over Lee Sedol?'

'Exactly.'

'Yeah, like, four games to one, right?' Carl asked.

'But here's the thing. It's not just that it beat him. It's *how* it beat him. There was this famous move it pulled off. Something that no one has seen in Go before. I don't know all the rules, but essentially the wisdom dictates that early on you should play on the third or fourth line from the edge. Anything else is as good as suicide. Then here comes Google's AI and sits its piece on the *fifth* line. Okay, so everyone's like *'what the hell just happened?'* Most people thought that AlphaGo had fucked up, but some knew it was a calculated move. Sedol had to get up and leave the room and I even read a report of one other Go expert saying it was making him feel sick as the machine wasn't playing *human* moves.

So, sure enough, fifty, *fifty* moves later, AlphaGo manages to manoeuvre from the bottom left corner and collect with that piece on the fifth line. You know already it went on to win by four games to one. But it was *that* move that made everyone, myself included, really consider what we were working with. I think this one Go analyst put it perfectly when he pointed out that even though this game is thousands of years old, we humans have only ever scratched the surface of its possibilities. We simply can't plan fifty, or even *twenty* moves ahead.'

'I see where you're going with this.'

'You see? So it's not even about who is the better player, human or machine. The most important thing to take away from this is that we will *never* be able to understand what that computer did. We can't get the algorithm to explain itself. So even when it pulls off something extremely powerful, for better or for worse, we only see the *effects* but not the *process*. I think that's what we're most in danger of here. Before even beginning to worry about how the wider public will receive it, we need to know that we're not building another AlphaGo.'

An acute pain in his neck told him to stop scrolling through the news feed. Footage of queues stretching out of supermarket doors, interviews with farmers talking of nutrient deficiency in the soil, anxiety dripping into the water supply. Keeping updated with the impending chaos only had so much use before it became numbing.

Kicking gently in his swing, he sat his phone down on the table and leant back, the fans humming noisily around his head. The idea of writing the report made him feel a little sick. He thought that not having any notes, either written or spoken, would make the task seem more daunting. But it was all in there, ticking over. Perhaps after writing the report he could just do his best to forget about it? That must be why he felt so heavy. He couldn't stop thinking about it until he had it materialised.

He stood up, making his way to the kitchen to splash cold water over his face and neck. The pipes chattered as the tepid water spilled out. He let his head hang under the tap, as much for the sound as for the moisture. His chest felt tight, his face red and slightly sore. This hissing sound turned into a shudder, the hard spray beating against the metal sink. He suddenly felt wasteful and turned off the tap.

An hour later he found himself lying in the hammock, field recorder in hand, his voice murmuring out a string of memories from the previous week. When he'd tried to write, his fingers curled away from the keyboard like a mimosa pudica plant. The swing rocked back and forth, a thin line of smoke trailing from the tip of his Camel.

Fracturing of consensus

                                   epistemic challenge

presence of governments slowly diminishing

                        neighbourhood scale alliances

       plethora of local trade

                      effects of twentieth-century

               move like virus

His phone ringing cut the momentum.

'I'm passing through the Green. Do you mind if I come over?'

'Sure, I'll buzz you in.'

When he opened the door Anya looked flustered; an emotional state that didn't suit her.

'Hope I'm not interrupting your work.'

'Not at all,' he lied, 'did something happen?'

'No, well yes, sort of. Yes and no.'

They took a seat. Carl waited for her to gather her thoughts. For a second he glanced around at the almost animalistic untidiness of his flat: wilted watermelon rinds and overflowing ashtrays strewn out around his swing. Only Anya's disquiet told him these things probably didn't matter.

'Nothing happened to me, I mean I wasn't hurt or caught up in the chaos of it. But just *being* there, being so close to the action, it turned something in me. Something I haven't felt in a long time.'

'Wait, back-up a second, where were you?'

'On Oxford Street. Where the protests are happening. Can I take some water, I feel really nauseous?'

'Of course.'

She drank in silence, savouring the water with her eyes closed, breathing deeply.

'Sorry I didn't give you any context. So I was with a few members of the VFL earlier. We had to meet to go over a press release we want to send to out.'

'Ah, I think Sofia mentioned this had started.'

'I'll tell you more about it later. But when I went to get the tube, that's when it really hit me: that nausea we spoke of before.'

Carl nodded, looking down at the floor.

'I had this sudden flashback to that night when you told me about your... well what would you call it, *memoir*, I guess? I suddenly saw myself as part of the crowd, and in my head I was describing it in the collective first person. I had this inability to detach myself from them. It was only when they were out of sight that they became *they* and not *we*.'

Reaching for an ashtray, she lit a cigarette and continued:

'Do you remember when we wrote down what it would have been like if we had both actually gone with our groups to carry out the attacks?' Anya asked.

'Of course, I still think about that every week, or *at least* every month. I think about it a lot.'

'I reread the text a few weeks back.'

'You reread them?' he asked, taken aback.

'Yes, why? Are you annoyed at me?'

'No, not annoyed. Just surprised. How come you went back to them?'

'With these recent protests taking up the news, I haven't been able to stop thinking about it. It really is some kind of PTSD syndrome. It makes me feel physically sick, not because I'm disgusted with the protesters, or what they stand for. Far from it. But it's that same kind of deep, all-encompassing nausea that I felt the night I lied to Marco. I remember telling him to give me a week to organise myself, and even as he was hugging me telling me that was fine, I remember trying not to be sick.'

'It's quite eerie how specific that type of nausea is. I had it the other day when I passed the protesters in Parliament Square. I went just to listen to what they were saying to see if it evolved into discussions rather than mantras. Like you, it's not that I find the crowd or their demands sickening, but there's something about the way in which this collective consciousness forms that puts me into the fight-or-flight mode. As you said, it's identical to the feeling I had when I lied to my group. I remember feeling like some undercover cop, going through all the details for hours, *days* even. Then just assuring them I'd be at the pick-up point the following week. Four nights later and I was already in Prague.'

'I think what still haunts me to this day, more than anything, is the fate of the two who took our places. Those ones that got away and that the police never found. It's too surreal for me, like it feels as if that girl in Brazil who fled before the attack either never existed, or was in some way a part of myself.' Anya said, fiddling with her lighter.

'I still ask myself the same question about the third guy in my case. The fact the police never got a profile on him: I think that's what scared me more. I mean, I had my alibi, being documented boarding a plane and landing in Prague a week before the attack happened. But it always felt that the fact he was never identified meant that, in a sense, it could always come back to me.'

'Part of me wonders if I were ever capable of something that direct. I think I see that in both of us, this tendency to over-analyse everything which makes it hard to... well I guess hard to see one clear solution.'

'It's what I fear when I see these crowds turning violent in London. I know how easy it is to feel part of something larger, where you have this temporary support network from all the other members around you. But you can't act collectively; it always requires one member to take the first step, to throw the first punch. Then this member gets singled out and the crowd disperses. The fact that those two members of my former group still face almost a decade in jail, when those days feel so distant to me, says it all.'

Standing up, she walked over and took a seat in his swing, gently rocking back and forth.

'It was so interesting reading your version', she continued, how you wrote it almost as a sort of short story, whereas I wrote mine as a report. There was almost no superfluous description in mine. I wanted to be more direct and blunt, sticking to the trajectory and facts, rather than imagining it in this almost cinematic way that you did.'

'Perhaps that was a way of making it less real to myself, I'm not sure.' Carl replied, rubbing his eyes, before continuing, 'It's strange, the more I read in the news, the less real it became. It was only when I sat down and wrote the whole event out, as if I was recollecting it from memory, that I managed to integrate that part of my life. I think that's where the blue light comes from. I have no idea exactly what happened at the scrap yard. No more than what I read. I imagine one of the men must have seen the lights and got away through the woods. So I've always imagined myself as him, seeing that blue light and fleeing. But that's the strange thing; since I wrote that piece, I actually have suffered from a blue-light related anxiety.'

Walking to the balcony door, he stared out at the sky.

'Even the small details, like the trace of blood they found on the wire fence from the guy who must have pried it open and forced himself through it. That detail was *weirdly* what gave me the most comfort. It took a while for that to be discovered — or mentioned in the news at least — but even with my alibi, just knowing that it wasn't my blood meant that I could never be linked to that scene. I think having all those details in the report gave me the means to imagine all the small twists and turns of the narrative. I remember I wrote so much, that I just couldn't dispose of it. I felt that having it was what allowed me to integrate it, even if being in possession of something like that felt really stupid.'

'For me it was the other way round. As soon as I read what I'd written, I just sort of wanted to burn it. The act of writing itself seemed enough to integrate it. But the paper itself, beyond the risk of incrimination, just felt haunting. But I'm glad you made me save it on the hard drive.'

They both paused, looking down at their feet. He remembered how strange he'd felt showing Anya what he'd written. He *hadn't* been the one that had carried out the attack. He *hadn't* been there when they'd fled across the North Sea or across the coastal road. He'd been in Prague where he'd fled to a week before. So why would he write it in the first person, as if it had actually been him? Nor had Anya gone to the north of Brazil. So why would she want to write a personal account of a crime she never committed?

'You were more descriptive, but in in a way, less *personal* than me. I felt mine centred so much on Marco and his perception of me. Even though I wrote it in the first person, it was almost through his eyes. I remember thinking it was such a strange thing for you to suggest. Like, why would I want to write a fictional account of myself as that missing girl? But you were right, ever since that week before their attack, when I fled from São Paulo, the whole narrative still hadn't been processed. Writing as you suggested sort of helped me to integrate that shadow I'd been trying to suppress.'

He turned to face her, feeling the same nausea creep back into his stomach. Somewhere in the distance sirens started to rage. The dim lighting flickered, for a split second turning the apartment blue.

'I asked myself, 'what *type* of person is vulnerable to those ideas?' I think you have to recognise that it doesn't necessarily take a certain type

179

of person. That's why I had to write it in the first person, to situate myself *in* the text, turning it into a sort of false memoir, or *memoir that could have been*. At first, I typed *they*, then realised it was *we*. Same with the protagonist: I typed *he* before realising I needed to type *I*.'

The news that their next immersion date had been pushed forward worried him. He wanted to be pissed-off, to email Anton back telling him that cutting their writing time by a week was unacceptable. It was *them*, after all, that had insisted the testers needed three weeks off. This was as much for their writing as it was for their health. This insistence that they rush into the next stage felt suspicious. He could picture Anton switching between the caring, compassionate researcher and the cut-throat, almost business-like persona he adopted in smaller groups. He wished he could see how the other testers had responded. But the message, although not personally addressed, hadn't been sent as a group email.

He thought about messaging Sofia. She'd surely have some objection to this. But as quickly as he reached for his phone, he changed his mind. While unjust, the project being stepped up was actually in his interest. He wanted the testing finished as soon as possible. Let the analysts decipher the algorithms. He'd be there after to help write up the findings. But that wouldn't be until next year and he needed a break.

He didn't even need more time to write up this second report: he'd finished it a week ago, feeling ever more impressed with the complexity of the software. One element he'd been obsessing over for the past week was the presence of a tank that had been occupied by a rogue group of vigilantes. He recalled spending much — much more than he *should* — of Wednesday's immersion following this group. At first he assumed it had been hijacked from an abandoned military barracks. In this world, such a crime would have been more than plausible. But it wasn't this alone that made it so surreal. The design, far from anything cutting edge and contemporary, looked as if it had been plucked from the Cold War and transported to this future world. He'd questioned whether such historical discrepancy should even be flagged up as some type of visual discordance? It was then that he realised the huge difficulties in pinpointing such discrepancies in the virtual world. Did it even matter? Perhaps that was a better question.

As he boarded the overground at Hackney, he covered his mouth; the smell of the hot metal tracks was almost sickeningly sweet. Despite the protests, some areas of the city were starting to feel almost abandoned. On the weekends, those who didn't work stayed indoors: knowing it was late autumn seemed to overpower the fact that the temperature remained in the forties. There was something about the workings of this deep biological rhythm that felt so out of touch with the present chaos. It wasn't just visible in those he perceived, but also in his own actions. His decision to spend the day at Hampstead Heath spoke to this: it was, at least for him, inextricably tied to autumn. He hadn't been there in years; not since before he left for Prague.

During his adolescent years in London, the Heath had become a place of repose, a small arcadia reachable by tube. But it was always during autumn that he most appreciated the garden. There was something in the dying of the previous season that seemed to resonate with where he found himself; this sort of cinematic fade to black as one part of himself slipped away and another emerged. Watching from the window, the sight of passersby in t-shirts made him uneasy. The image simply clashed with the low afternoon sunlight, the actions of London's inhabitants suffering from a seasonal latency.

The fact that he was arriving there sweating instead of shivering made the familiar sight of the entrance seem foreign. It was then, as he entered the garden, that for the first time in his life he felt an acute sense of climate-induced loss. The dry ground remained firm, dust kicking up under his feet. All around him, the forest carried a gross mixture of vibrancy and exhaustion. These contrasting states unbalanced him as he looked out across the green, wilted canopy. The floor remained bare; no leaves had fallen. Sagging, the vegetation seemed almost listless.

He'd found that over the previous years, climate change had become something purely political: a grave problem that needed addressing and solving. But there had remained little, if any emotion in his approach. When he read about swathes of people in the southern hemisphere having to abandon their homes, he felt compassionate, often overcome with a drive to do *something* to change what was happening. But these issues were always happening at a distance, meaning that they remained just that: *problems*. There was no sense of loss in something happening on the other side of the equator, only of a sense of injustice and guilt. But now, as he walked through the same tracks he had followed so many times before, his inner dialogue silenced itself. He found a spot just off the path and took a seat between the trees. As he opened his backpack to take out his winter coat and headphones he couldn't tell if he felt more relieved or sad that it had come to this. Placing his headphones on and selecting *Credo*, he wrapped his winter coat tightly around his shoulders and waited. Following the lento opening, his core temperature gradually dropped.

Only hours later, when he opened his eyes, shivering in the night sky, did he begin his walk. In complete solitude, he could feel each footstep passing under the dry soil. For a moment, he felt he could hear the spark of information passed along mycorrhizal roots. Each time a gentle breeze brushed his cold skin, he paused, watching the silhouette of the canopy swaying against the backdrop of a muddy night sky. With the sounds of a distant Tallinn now over, he rubbed his ears, feeling his temperature gradually rising. Part of him wanted to ignore everything and delve back into that world; to just sit all night shivering in Lahemaa national park. But he hadn't come here for that. He needed to read over his report. Taking

The fact that the cold climate allowed them to cut down on air-conditioning also came back to bite them. It was there, in Keflavik, that the first centre went into overload, leading to a system crash that spread throughout the nation.

a seat at an opening that looked out onto central London, he reached in his bag for the printed report. Brightly lit skyscrapers protruded into the low clouds; the Shard standing as a suppressed trapezoid. The noise of the nearby roads brought him out of his melancolia, almost reminding him that he had work to do. Lighting a Camel and straightening out the pages, he flicked on his portable lamp.

ooooo

As he leafed through the pages, he couldn't help but recognise two competing emotions inside him: dread and hope. There was something about this quite brutal report that he found almost comforting, something about the sheer perseverance in the face of resistance that the human race seemed to possess. The immersion had been rough, and he could still feel it. Visions of aggressive tribalism growing out of wide scale poverty had, initially, turned his stomach.

Just seeing such panic, such instability and above all else *uncertainty* was harrowing. Yet there was a faint light present in such a deathly landscape. Witnessing the creative and innovative ways humans found for survival made him question whether there was any catastrophe that could ever wipe *all* humans out? Despite the hardship, the lives he'd encountered existd in a type of animalistic ontological mode, in which mere survival was where life's meaning was found.

As he read over his case study entitled 'A Football Net Floating in the Ocean', he felt the cold winds of the Norweigan sea hitting his cheeks, his eyes watery as he strained to listen to Olaf's explanation of the abandoned crypto-currency factories. All around him, the world as he'd known it was crumbling. Remnants of territorial disputes, in the forms of blood stained tarmac and burnt out cars, littered the landscape. But these battles weren't fresh, Olaf had assured him. It was just that no one had the time to worry

185

about cleaning up public space. They were too preoccupied with sourcing the necessary materials needed for survival.

With all factories having been out of action, the simplest things, such as fishing nets had become a sought after luxury. He remembered how Olaf had laughed as he said this, the harsh wind tugging at his thick blonde hair and turning his cheeks red. Along Norway's west coast, one of the tools that had always been in abundance were fishing nets. It was unthinkable not to be able to buy one. But as soon as the fear set in that tools were becoming scarce, looting ensued, followed by a descent into stockpiling and aggressive small-scale trade wars. It was during that era that the most desperate sort of innovation sprung into life, with every corner of the cities being ransacked. He'd seemed hopeful for a better future; at least that was the impression he gave off. This became evident when he led Carl down to the coastline and pointed out towards the clusters of rocks that jutted out into the dark, foaming waters.

'Look, do you see what I'm pointing to? It's right there, half floating in the water, half tangled on the rocks. That's the football net from the Aker Stadium. Someone got so desperate that they managed to break in and steal the net, hoping that they'd catch something big enough to not slip through those wide holes. We all say that when this crisis ends, when Norway is actually a functioning, united nation again, that net is going in our national museum as a memorandum of these times.'

He stopped reading and closed his eyes; his memories seeming to hold more depth than the words on the page. As he trawled through the images of the deserted cities and abandoned towns, he found himself back at a bar in Soho, engrossed in a conversation he'd once had with a close friend about her father. He remembered it so vividly that he could feel the bar stool beneath him, hear the chatter of other groups and the clinks of their glasses. He ran his tongue over his lips, which tingled a little as the taste of the overly-spicy bloody mary he'd been drinking all surfaced at once.

He'd been in that state of intoxication where outwardly no one could tell he was drunk, but inwardly his filters were warping. They'd been discussing what economic vulnerability actually consisted of, and whether the amount of money you had in your account *really* signified anything. He'd been adamant, perhaps a little *too* adamant, that you can't judge someone's security based solely on this.

'Take me for example', he'd offered, placing his fingers on his chest and taking another swig from his drink, 'I may not have much money in my account, in fact I have quite little. But the fact that I'm here in this bar, paying nine pounds for a cocktail says quite a bit. I've never really worried about money. To be honest, I'm *quite* bad with it. I just spend freely when it's in my account, then I'm happy to live humbly whenever I don't have it. But I think that carelessness, that blasé attitude of knowing I'll scrape by, really stems from privilege. I know that if I really fucked up and couldn't pay my rent, I have such a wide safety net around me that I'd never end up on the streets. I've got my parents place in Highgate, I've got loads of friends, who are all from similar backgrounds, and who always have enough money to lend me. So I'd have plenty of time to get back on my feet. But imagine you don't have that. Imagine everyone you know is also hard up and none of your mates, even if they wanted to, could actually lend you any money. If you come from that walk of life, then just spending freely and not forcing yourself to be rigorous with your own buffer is out of the question.'

He noticed himself getting drunker, his cheeks becoming more flushed. Whenever he noticed himself becoming drunk and talkative, he'd drink even more as a way of compensating. This was a tendency he'd had since his teenage years, and often resulted in him becoming flippant, coming out with statements that his sober self was too reserved to ever say. The following morning would always be ridden with paranoia and a harrowing sense of guilt that he'd overstepped the mark. The worst of all was that his memory would be too fragmented for him to really know *what* he'd come out with. Did I *really* say that? he'd ask himself while rubbing his eyes.

Then the slightest sense of hostility between him and whoever he'd spoken to would send him into a frenzy, making him believe he'd said something truly appalling. Despite being well aware of this tendency, it seemed to inevitably reoccur, time and time again.

When his friend still hadn't commented on his theory, he felt himself becoming neurotic and questioned whether he should backtrack. Soon after she broke the silence:

'Did I ever tell you what happened to my father?'

'I don't think you did, no.'

'I don't normally talk about him, but I think his story is quite pertinent to this argument. Well, not *argument*, but *idea*, let's say. The reason I bring it up is because I used to think just like you do. My parents used to be *loaded*, so when I was growing up money was never something I worried about. They didn't exactly spoil me. They always wanted me to work from a young age so I knew the value of money: something I always rolled my eyes at and resented having to do. But as I got older I understood why they made me do it.

My mum came from a rough background, one of those families who never had much and never knew anyone else with much money. But she managed to climb her way up from quite a young age. She started working at the local Northern Rock in Doncaster where she was from. But her family, well, they sort of *hated* her for it. This was during the eighties so pretty much everyone in her community despised Thatcher and hated everything to do with neo-liberal politics. I think my grandfather, who had always worked in the steel industry, was quite torn. In a way he was proud that his daughter was providing for the family and actually earning well, which was really uncommon in that area, especially for women. But I think there was an underlying shame and resentment he held for her, firstly because she became the main breadwinner, but mostly because he saw the banks as an embodiment of the politics that were, in his view, destroying communities in the north.'

She paused, taking a sip from her drink and slowly stirring the last of the ice cubes at the bottom of the glass. Carl hadn't moved a muscle, his chin rested on his fist, the vein on the left side of his temple throbbing from all the alcohol.

'Anyway, the nail in the coffin was when she left Northern Rock, moved down to London and took a job with JP Morgan. In essence it wasn't *that* different, but without the 'northern' element to it she was just another member of the southern elite who were crippling the north. I've spoken to her about this a lot, and while she says she did what she needed to do to create a better life, I can tell she's hurt that her family still look down on her. If you ask me, I completely respect her. I didn't when I was young, but now I see her as a role model: a woman who went her own way and didn't heed to the pressures of her dad and brothers.'

The barman politely interrupted, asking if they'd like the same again. They looked at each other and nodded to him. The story wasn't anywhere near finished.

'So anyway, early nineties in London. She meets my dad, another investment banker and they end up having me quite soon after. I think they liked the idea of having a kid more than they enjoyed raising me. Not that they didn't do a good job, but I think it was almost another *thing* to invest in. They didn't want their lifestyle to change, and didn't realise it would dramatically until I was there, kicking and screaming and needing twenty-four hour attention. I think that's definitely why they didn't have another child. Once I started school and they were both back at work, they weren't gonna give up big chunks of life rearing more kids.'

Two fresh bloody marys were placed in front of them on black coasters. She barely noticed hers, while Carl resisted the urge to drink straight away.

'*Well*, I could go on for ages about my childhood, but that wasn't why I brought up the subject of my dad. What I wanted to tell you about was his *fall from grace*, so to speak. The reason I'm bringing this up is because everything you just described; the vast safety network of wealthy friends, the money in the bank, the quite literally *huge* buffer he had in place, in the end, couldn't stop him hitting the concrete. It *wasn't*, as you might have guessed, in two-thousand and eight, when the financial crash happened.

In fact, it was the year before, in September. I think his dismissal from the bank had been a long time coming. Mum and I had noticed his health getting slowly worse, not so much physically, but mentally. He was becoming forgetful, often with trivial things, such as forgetting they had organised a dinner or that the car, or *cars*, needed to be serviced. But this was just the beginning.

Soon it started to filter into his work life: forgetting meetings, or remembering to go to meetings but not being able to remember anything after. When his colleagues started to notice, they urged him to go to the doctor but he was too proud, his answer always being that he needed to 'pull himself together' and just focus more. This didn't work, obviously, and things just spiralled. One time he'd been on a trip to Shanghai and apparently couldn't recall anything from the trip when he returned to London. His boss sort of gave him an ultimatum, told him he needed to get medical help to figure out what was going on or he'd be dismissed. It's kind of gross in some ways, that only through the fear of losing his job, and not his *memory*, did he actually go to the doctor.'

She paused, taking a long, slow sip from her drink as if she really, really needed it. Carl, who still hadn't moved a muscle, also took the pause as an opportunity to drink.

'It was bad, like, *really* bad. The Hippocampus region of his brain was plastered with beta-amyloid plaques.'

'What's that? I mean, what does that region of the brain do?'

'It's the region of your brain that allows you to form new memories. If you don't get enough sleep, which he never did, then in the short term the brain can't transfer memories from that region to the rest of the brain. But in the long run, well it can't clean out this protein and then it's a quick descent into alzheimers.'

'I see.'

'So, he had no choice. His company demanded the medical report and once they understood the state he was in, they had to 'let him go', as he put it. I've never felt so distant from him as during that period. I remember him sat on the couch sobbing, not because a heavy onset of *alzeheimers* was approaching, but because he'd lost his fucking job. *Can you believe that?* It was as if all meaning in his life had been taken away and he no longer had anything to live for. But do you wanna know what's so weird about this whole story?'

'Of course.'

'The same day he was fired was the same day that the queues started outside Northern Rock's branches. I mean, don't get me wrong, they're *obviously* not related, but there's something eerie about the first step of my mother's journey starting to crumble happening on the *same day* as the start of my father's descent towards a miserable death.'

'Death?'

'Yeah, I mean from there it all happened quite quickly. As I said, without his work he had quite literally *nothing* to live for. He never had any hobbies or interests. If it didn't relate to finance he didn't see any use in it. Even *us*, his family, just seemed like an extra, something he had put time into because he knew, essentially, that it was just a thing you did.

But anyway, his descent didn't really have anything to do with money. Not to say he didn't squander tens of thousands during that self-destructive streak. But we were so loaded and he got such a big payout from the bank that ending up homeless was never on the cards. Unfortunately he realised that the only way he could still engage with the financial world, or more with money, was through gambling. They might have refused to let him work, but casinos couldn't care less how mad you are. If anything, the madder and more unstable the better. So we didn't see him for a while. Everyday and night he would basically live in one of those twenty-four hour casinos, gambling until he desperately needed to eat, which he'd do at the restaurant inside the casino, then just keep gambling until he fell asleep. I'm surprised they never kicked him out, although I think they made so much money from him everyday that they could turn a blind eye.'

By the look on Carl's face — one he wanted to be perceived as sympathetic, but came across more like a mixture of anguish and slight disgust — she could tell he felt uncomfortable.

'Don't worry, by the way. I'm fine talking about this, it's been so long and we were so distant that I don't have any emotion attached to it anymore.'

He nodded silently.

'Well, the story ends with my mother leaving him after begging him to seek help. She told me that one time she stood next to him in the casino imploring him to come home but he could barely recognise her anymore. The saddest, or perhaps most tragically amusing part of this is that he could only play roulette. His memory was so fucked that any game requiring concentration and any level of skill was beyond him. So he just sat in his chair, placing thousands on either red or black and watching the ball spin. My mother told me he was utterly manic, even though he never touched a drop of alcohol. I don't know if that's better or worse. But she said he would pull her roughly by the shoulders and shout that he was 'onto something', there was some pattern he'd found whereby he could predict red or black better than anyone else.'

'Textbook gambler's fallacy, no?'

'Exactly. There's nothing more to it other than a fifty-fifty throw of the dice that resets with every new turn. But you start to believe that if it's been red eight times in a row, *it just must be black this time!*'

'Or that in fact red is on a winning streak.'

'Precisely.'

They both laughed, each thankful that the other could see the humorous side of it.

'So can I ask how it all ended?'

192

'Of course. So one night he decided to leave. No idea why, but I think he was heading home. He was at one of the Murker Casinos, this time in Putney. That's what was also so tragic, that he believed he had better luck in certain Casinos, still playing the same roulette game. Anyway, he felt that this one was *particularly good*. So he'd been there all night, as usual, throwing thousands into the machines. Then even though we lived in Highgate, which is over an hour cycle away, he jumped on one of the Barclays bikes and started his cycle.'

For a split moment, the smile and humor vanished from her face. She took a long sip from her drink, looked down and continued.

'He didn't get very far. I only know because the police told us they had CCTV footage of his journey. He was approaching Putney bridge, but at the last moment just veered off the road and hit the wall. I've never seen the footage — didn't want to. But they said he went head over the handlebars and into the Thames. They found his body washed up downstream along the edge of Battersea Park.'

Carl looked down at his hands, as if in mourning, then looked back up to catch her eyes.

'The only poetic thing about it, despite the utter destructiveness of his tragic fall from grace, is where his body lay before it was found.'

'In the park you mean?'

'Not the park, but the statue it lay in front of. It's the London Peace Pagoda at the edge of the park. It was given to the city as a gift by Nichidatsu Fuji, a Japanese buddhist monk. I've been there many times since, as to me it feels like his gravestone and it gives me some comfort when I look at the statues on it.'

'Why so?' Carl asked, a little sheepishly.

'It's cheesy, I know, but the series of statues on it represent the stages of Buddha's life, moving from his birth, to contemplation leading to enlightenment, his teaching and eventual death. I've never been into Eastern philosophy, but I've always liked to think, as highly improbable as it is, that during his descent down the river he had a moment of clarity, a moment to contemplate that before his fall, he'd loved his life and really been quite happy.'

He opened his eyes, the sight of London's bright lights glinting back at him. Glancing at his watch, he realised he'd had his eyes closed for almost an hour. It had felt like a kind of meditation, or if not meditation, a sort of memory realignment which allowed him to see his report more clearly. Leafing through the pages, he found his conclusion. Was it *that* naive? To think that such a world was so improbable? The collapse of the international community, the sharp fall into tribalism and chaos? Were these conditions really so unimaginable? He'd been skeptical of the first phase, but in that case it was somehow easier to see why: a world which essentially looked like a manifestation of luxury consumer communism would always be hard to strive towards. But it's counterpart, this world of looting, tradewars and the quick destruction of civilised culture? Why had he found it so hard to believe? He stood up and grabbed his rucksack, knowing that the report needed rethinking before its submission.

'*In other news, tens of thousands of inhabitants in Mozambique's rural areas surrounding the 'Parque Nacional das Quirimbas' are heading south towards the capital, Maputo. Mozambique's national government has requested foreign aid from G7, insisting that the desiccation of their land is a direct result of global climate change-*'

'*All across Central Europe, the fear of economic collapse, due to the vast fluctuations in exchange rates and property prices are causing many to descend on the streets of their capital cities, demanding answers from those in power. From Prague to Warsaw to Belgrade, hundreds of thousands are marching towards their parliaments-*'

'*Public transport throughout London is at a standstill as drivers refuse to work in such conditions. A representative of the RMT has demanded that due to the ventilation conditions, sustained hours on the London Underground pose a grave risk to workers' health-*'

He locked his phone screen and leaned back in his swing. He understood their arguments but still, it was frustrating to hear that the city's most vital transport system was out of action. Even the short journeys he took were enough to make him feel nauseous. He could only imagine what a days driving would do to you.

Walking through to the kitchen, he placed his coffee cup in the sink and turned on the tap. After the initial spluttering, the water began shooting out, spraying cold splashes of coffee around the metal basin. He cupped some in his hands and brought it to his cheeks, which already felt flushed and sore. The idea of having a headset on for the best part of a week felt almost too much to stomach. Probably better not to dwell on it. It wouldn't be long until his main role was over. Anton had even said that they would proceed with the data analysis as soon as the fourth reports were in. Everyone agreed it felt like crunch time. The hotel had been hired out for the next six weeks solely for the VFL to finish this initial testing phase. They were clearly eager to get the ball rolling.

He had no idea how the other testers felt about this. Part of him still found it unacceptable, even insulting that the process was being ramped up with such ferocity. Who the fuck was Anton, after all, to decide how much rest they should get? But at the same time it was in his interest to motor on. He felt that dragging it out would only make things harder, given the current political conditions in the UK. The sooner they had the initial work completed they could step back and wait for things to cool down before trying to launch the project in other institutions. He wasn't averse to intense periods of work, and in a sense the brutality of needing to spend the best part of a month locked in a hotel churning out the reports felt good. He wiped his face and made his way onto the terrace.

Despite having been chained up for months, his bike didn't seem to be in bad shape. The chain was dried out and rusty, but once he'd applied some oil it seemed to turn smoothly. Now the only problem facing him was that he didn't have a clue where his keys were. Lighting a Camel, he took a step back and eyed up the lock: a flimsy chain secured with a thin padlock. He gave a quick tug, assessing the weight. There was no chance of him finding the keys, that much was sure. But he couldn't walk from Bethnal Green all the way to Monument in the heat.

As he wrenched open the large metal tool box in his flat, he turned it on its side, emptying the contents noisily on the floor. Broken lighters, screwdrivers, lecture notes and chopsticks scattered across the wooden floorboards. Rummaging around, he found the small hammer he had been looking for and strode out into the stairwell. His neighbour, an elderly lady from Tunisia, whom he never spoke to, opened her front door.

'What's with all the banging?'

'Nothing, just fixing something upstairs.'

She glanced at the hammer, scowled at him and slowly closed her door.

The first blow did nothing to the chain; it just shifted its position on the bike. He gave it a few more attempts, and only succeeded in denting the frame as well. Eventually he managed to position the chain against the wall, securing the bike with his foot. One, two three, swing! The hammer came thundering down on the metal. Something cracked. One, two, three, SWING! Same link, another crack. One, two, three SWING! He shouted out and flung his hammer with full force against the chain. A loud crack sounded and he grabbed his face, keeling over backwards. Cursing, he pulled his hand away from his cheek. He resisted the urge to hurl the hammer and just let it drop to the floor. Back inside his flat, he stared in the mirror, examining the small shard of metal protruding from his skin. There were no pliers in sight, but he was sure he'd seen some in his tool box. With blood dripping over his old lecture notes, he trawled through the objects until his fingers gripped the small metal pliers.

It took him almost half an hour to remove the shard, his plucking exacerbating the pain and irritating his skin. By the time he was ready to leave, he realised that cycling with such rage inside him wasn't a good idea. He took a seat in his hammock, lit a cigarette and closed his eyes. He went over his checklist on his phone, making sure he had everything he needed to stay at the hotel for the next month. There wasn't much he *really* needed. Only his dictaphone and a hammock. Everything else they had covered. Standing up and flicking his cigarette towards the large plant pot, he untied the hammock and folded it into a small canvas bag.

ooooo

'Carl! Didn't have you down for a *cyclist*!'

He didn't respond to Anton, just laughed and nodded as he wheeled his bike into the hotel lobby.

'How was the journey over?'

'Wild, to be honest. Everyone's cycling. It's like we've suddenly copied the Dutch but haven't bothered with the infrastructure. The roads are dusty and the tarmac's wilting, but it was actually quite fun.' Carl responded.

'Bit of a,

well, what would you say,

adventure?'

He'd grown to distrust everything about Anton. After his last outburst, nothing he said, even when seemingly friendly, sat well with Carl. Although he recognised that it was more in his head than an actual character trait, his theatrical way of speaking just pissed him off. It was only with Sofia that he felt any sense of connection. She spoke her mind and didn't care if she seemed cynical or pessimistic. But he hadn't formed a real connection with any of the others. He no longer cared about any niceties or friendly rapport between him and the higher members of the VFL. He'd rather just treat them as colleagues and cut out all the 'we're in this together shit'. He parked his bike against the wall and turned to face Anton.

'I'm just gonna head up to my room to get cleaned up. Do we have a meeting today?'

'No no, not a meeting per se. But we thought we'd,

well

take a drink

— soft in your case —

in the bar a bit later on?

'Sounds good. I'm gonna need an early one before tomorrow, but I'll see you down there later.' Carl said, moving towards the lift.

'Of course!

   Catch

        you

down

                              there.'

When he reached his room he slumped on the bed, wheezing a little. The fan above his head circled lazily, the white porcelain blades gliding like an albatross's wings. The faint smell of the air freshener hovered around his nostrils; mandarin, or maybe even grapefruit. Bit of an artificial smell for an expensive hotel. He closed his eyes, inhaling slowly. Even after a short cycle he felt congested; minute dust particles clinging to his vibrissae. His lungs burned, as they often did. He'd need to start looking after himself better. Stop smoking as much, start exercising. But maybe not just now. Not until this whole immersion stage was over.

Trying to relax his body, he reached for the fan controls next to the bed and slowed it down until he could no longer feel any breeze. Closing his eyes again, he listened to the fan's rhythm and tried to match it to his breathing. He could feel the vein in his left temple pulsing, its metronome-like beat gradually dropping its bpm. His body temperature started to fall, as melatonin rushed through his bloodstream, slowing down his brain waves.

ooooo

He watched the clear water running over his bare skin, washing the sand from between his toes. He looked up at the ocean, searching for markers. A rusty pier, an abandoned tea room on a deserted promenade. Somewhere on the west coast, perhaps Blackpool. Further down the beach, he could make out a light flickering against the overcast sky. He wandered across the sand, stepping through the small clusters of pebbles protruding like tumors. When he reached the source, he remained at a slight distance; enough to see it clearly, while hiding in the shadows.

A large group, perhaps two hundred, were gathered in a huge semi-circle, facing the ocean. Dressed in white, they resembled angels, their faces glowing, illuminated by the small candles they held like an offering. They stood there in silence; the only sound was the waves tentatively falling on the sand. He couldn't tell how long he'd been watching them when a woman stepped forward. She had an almost shaman like energy to her; placing her candle in the sand and raising her arms above her head. With her back to the ocean, she started to chant a short refrain, which the other members then repeated back to her. He strained his ears to hear the words. Were they singing in Latin? Turning his right ear to catch the sound, a deluge of aquatic echoes flooded his eardrum. It were as if their words just liquified into one viscous harmony, with the original meaning being contained in the frequencies that passed through the water. Somehow, even without the words, he knew he recognised the music. As he stood facing them, a faint light started to appear on the water's surface.

The clouds above the water didn't shift; a blanket of dense iron on which the candle light danced. As he looked closer, it seemed like the light's source was actually within the water. The choir's chants grew in intensity. He crept forward to the water's edge, his vision almost blinded. Peering through slightly parted fingers, he squinted at the swell. Shards of light flashed across the waves as a thousand boats rose from underneath. He stood static, watching the small fleets erupting. Churning in the dark foam, all of them were empty. Wading out into the water, the choir continued to harmonise behind him, their candles creating a path of light into the shallows. As his knees submerged, he felt something sharp hitting against his legs. All around him, dark masses of metal were tossed violently. Only when they protruded from the water, did he recognise them as bicycles. He held out his hands, trying to get hold of one. There were thousands and they were all identical: a wide handlebar Batavus model from The Netherlands. Plunging his arms into the water, he grabbed at a frame but the wet metal, eel-like, slipped out of his hands.

Behind him he heard the choir's collective voice rising in volume. He turned to face them, stumbling on the uneven seabed. Suddenly the beach was lit up, their candles rising above them, floating up towards the sky. A wave hit against his back, sending him tumbling forward. Metal pedals clanked against his legs. He stretched out his arms, diving into a front crawl and kicking out behind him. As he did so, the music shifted. The choir started to scream in a sort of cacophony — dissonant notes shrieking out and blending with the crash of the waves. Kicking as hard as he could, he felt himself lifted into the barrel of a wave. There was a moment of complete darkness, as his tired body came crashing down on the shore. He lay there on his back, panting. Every time the waves spat out bicycles onto the shore, the bells clanged and rang out.

There was no rhythm, no harmony, just a wall of ear-splitting noise. The choir continued to hold their hands in the air, their candles floating like a halo above them. He sat up to face the water, awaiting the climax. And that was when he saw it: thousands of eyes looking back at him through the its surface, flowing around in between the debris. A huge wave started to form, a thousand pupils dilating. When it crashed against the sand the scene cut, like a power-failure.

ooooo

Four hours later he found himself at the bar with Jakob, one of the VFL's data analysts. Almost the whole team were there, picking at the buffet and knocking back iced-tea as if it were G&Ts.

He'd never spoken to Jakob before, but there was something about him he liked. He was incredibly intelligent and precise with his words, but in a way that didn't come across as too sharp or intimidating. Carl had watched him give a talk at one of the smaller conferences the VFL organised after their first immersion. What struck him was not how much he knew, but how he managed to expound such complex ideas in a way that made him seem humble. When he spoke about data analysis — which would really be the make or break of the VFL — he presented his ideas without the audacity of Anton. What was most reassuring was that he recognised how difficult it would be. Rather than trying to convince everyone that he and his team had it all under control, he made sure to highlight the unexpected issues that had compromised his previous work. For Carl, this uncertainty was fundamental: they all knew the project was a gamble, and trying to pretend that there was no room for failure would only make it more probable.

'So how have you been managing to juggle this with university? Sofia told me you were still lecturing?' Jakob asked, helping himself to an olive.

The only thing about Jakob Carl struggled with was his persistant interest in those around him. Rather than talking about himself and his own work, as most others did, he seemed to prefer listening. Carl also preferred to let the other person do most of the talking. But he felt at ease with Jakob and didn't want to seem aloof.

'Well, to be honest I only gave one lecture before the university put everyone on study leave. So many people were getting ill from the heatwave and even those that did make it to class were so lethargic it almost wasn't worth it.'

'Ah I see. Well I guess that's no bad thing, especially for you.'

'Completely. I'm not really built for this weather either, so having less on my agenda came as a blessing.'

'I mean, are *any* of us really built for this?' he let out a little laugh.

'You've got a point there.'

They both reached for their drinks. Carl sensed it was his chance to turn the conversation towards Jakob's work.

'I never got the chance to speak to you after your talk last month. But I really enjoyed it.'

'Oh, really?' He raised his eyebrows and smiled.

'Absolutely. I'd never come across the term 'apophenia', which is surprising because it's so relevant to the work were doing here.'

'It's strange, isn't it? I think even for people who work *with* but not *in the field of* data analysis, often they understand the concept but just don't have the word for it. But it's something we have to talk about, because believe me, it's a danger that simply *plagues* my type of work.'

'I particularly liked the metaphor you gave for a sea; just having to search for that *actual* signal within the waves, while the waves themselves create patterns that resemble signals. It's quite poetic.'

'It's exactly that. We always say we're drowning and that the signal is the lifeboat we're searching for. It's kinda morbid, but that's always how it feels.'

He paused, taking a sip of his drink.

'Let me show you what I mean. Take this image for instance. We took this sample earlier today. On first glance, it looks just like visual noise. There's just a chaos of data. When this set started to form, you could clearly see the patterns, but quickly after entropy followed. Now, if it were *humans* that had to find the code, we'd be struggling.'

Sitting his drink down, Carl peered at the image on Jakob's tablet.

'Am I meant to be looking for something?'

'You tell me.'

Carl raised his eyebrows, peering at the small white spaces that seemed to shift in between the letters.

'You just tell me what you see.' Jakob said, looking away.

Folding his fingers in the palm of his hand, his knuckles let out a muffled crack.

'Ah okay, hold on. Well, I'm guessing there's nothing I *could see,* but already there's patterns forming.'

'So you've found something?'

'Not really. But at the bottom of the left page, all the white lines form a sort of halo, with thin lines all leading towards the word...*human?* Is that what it says? I'm guessing it's probably nothing.'

'Well, you've spotted something I didn't.'

He sensed from his tone that he wasn't serious.

'Wait, so what was I meant to be searching for?'

'Nothing. There's nothing there. It's just a sea of random words — computer-generated data. It's one of the first ever images they showed me on my computer science undergrad.'

Carl felt his cheeks flush a little and reached for his drink.

'Look, I hope you don't think I did that to tease you. It's not that at all. Pretty much every person you show that image to will react the same way. We're hardwired to search for patterns. And this image is just one of the many ways to demonstrate how easy it is to find meaning in random data. It doesn't reflect badly on you, honestly.'

'Fascinating. So when they showed this image to your cohort, everyone found different patterns, or *meanings?*'

'You bet. You should have heard some of the elaborate readings. The funniest thing was the complete turn of the table when they revealed the truth. I always remember there was this girl in the class, Lucia, *I think...* and she was the only one who said she couldn't find anything. I remember these two guys almost smirking, until our lecturer revealed that she was the only one who wasn't misled. Well, anyway, the point is that it's quite hard to grow out of these kind of errors. Experience teaches you to be wary, but the golden rule is that you're never immune to this natural tendency for pattern recognition, or *mis*recognition, I should say.'

'Are you worried that will be a problem with this work? — if you don't mind my asking?'

'Not at all, I'm happy to share my concerns. Well, in the case of the VFL, it *shouldn't* be as difficult because the signals we're taking won't actually have to be deciphered.'

'Because the AI already does that for you?' Carl asked.

'Pretty much. It will spill out a load of code, which we translate into data about our present world. Then, as you know, we have to work out how to act on this data.'

'What decisions the international community can take, how we should go about this, etc?

'Exactly. Now, *my* only worry is that given the instability of these last few months, the data is going to shift so rapidly that we won't be able to secure a foothold.'

'How do you mean?'

'Well, it would be different if just a few nations were in panic mode and only a few areas were experiencing deep shifts in their politics and economies. But, I mean, you've seen the news. This is happening *everywhere*. If not everywhere, it's at least becoming the global norm.'

'So essentially, the AI, or at least you, the analysts, need some level of stability to be able to map out the instructions the AI is giving us?'

'You've got it. Now, that isn't to say we *won't* be able to do it next month. But it *does* mean that it might be much harder than anticipated. The security we have — and this is something I've stressed to Anton — is that the AI continues to adapt to all the information its automatically fed about our current world. So, yes, while the worlds you and the other testers are visiting will shift and there'll be new iterations, unless there are *huge* shifts in today's world, your reports should hold up and we'll know what we're aiming for.'

'Got you. So it's really just a delay that we need to be worried about?'

He took a sip from his drink and gave a quick glance to his left.

'It's always going to be a possibility.'

ooooo

After the third immersion Carl found himself sat alone at the edge of the hotel swimming pool. Located on the top floor with glass walls stretching around three sides, the faint glow of stars blinked behind London's thick smog. All around the pool were white vases in which green, almost artificial looking plants stood. The whole setting felt slightly surreal to him: the light blue water, the dimmed lighting and empty bamboo sunloungers. He felt like he had been transported into a David Hockney painting; the gentle ripples in the water like brushstrokes that perpetually shifted. There was something clinical about the space: the warm sterile water, the scent of lemongrass and the meticulously trimmed plants.

Despite the previous yoga session, his whole body ached. Running a hand across his shoulders, he tugged at the edges of his neck and upper back. Every now and again, he would cough violently, his lungs throbbing with each expulsion of mucus. The combination of heavy smoking with the high levels of pollution meant he was constantly short of breath. He ran water over his head, tucking his thinning, sandy-coloured hair behind his ears. For a while, he sat kicking his feet, watching the small undulations beneath the water's surface. He heard a door open behind him.

'Hi Carl, mind if I join you?'

'Not at all', he responded, secretly annoyed that he now had to engage with someone. He hadn't spoken extensively with Irma, but she seemed like a quiet, pragmatic type. Usually when the group dispersed after the immersion he wouldn't see her again until the next day. She took a seat beside him, carefully sliding her bare legs into the water.

'How are you getting on today?' she asked.

'Feeling a bit rough, but that's more to do with my lungs than with the effects of the immersion.'

'I've been the same recently. I had to quit smoking earlier this year because that, mixed with the pollution, really messed me up. One day I woke up coughing and could barely breathe. Ended up in A&E where a doctor basically *scolded* me until I agreed to kick the habit. It was so humiliating. I felt like I was back at school again.'

'I should take a leaf out of your book. Or I'll probably be in for the same reprimanding.'

'If you can manage, then you should. I don't think I could cope with this smog otherwise.'

He glanced at her and smiled. The sight of her in her bathing suit, with her toned physique, suddenly made him self conscious. He looked down at his pale skin and loose stomach and forced himself to sit up straight.

'I'm quite looking forward to the immersions being over, to be honest. When Anton sent us the email saying it was being pushed forward I thought it was strange, but was actually quite pleased.'

'Same for me,' Carl nodded, 'Even with it making this final month quite intense, I think there's something about waiting for it that makes me as exhausted as actually *being* in the VR.'

'Totally. My partner's been saying how I seem on edge constantly. I don't know how you've found writing up the reports, but some of the scenes have made me feel physically ill.'

'I know the feeling.'

'What's strange is that it isn't actually during the VR experience. I think when I'm in the immersion, I'm so keen to gather as much information as possible that I keep pretty focused. It's afterwards, when I'm at home trying to put it into words that it really hits me.'

Pushing a strand of hair from her face, Irma turned to Carl.

'It's going to be interesting when we get to read each other's takings. Anton was saying that we'll be meeting with the data analysts after we've finished our final reports and we'll get to see how they're deciphering the information about each one.'

'Definitely.' Carl nodded in agreement, but failed to add anything more. A short silence hung between them.

'Anyway, I'm gonna take a dip.'

'I'll be in the sauna if you fancy it after?'

'Sure. Catch you in there.' she said, dropping into the unbroken water.

The heat felt good against his skin. His body was still dripping from the cold shower, beads of water slowly evaporating from his legs. He took a seat. Placed his head in his hands. The sound of feet hammering on dry earth reverberated in his head. The thrashing of limbs in choppy waters. Violent winds carrying sandstone dust, dancing between lifeless trees. Disused cameras hanging from abandoned buildings. Dark stone walls and barbed wire metastasizing; an iron cancer spreading across coastal borders. A bike bell jingled, and outside the sauna he heard a splash.

Raising his head, he stared through the glass towards the pool. A bike floated on the water's surface. Not a single ripple broke the stillness. Irma floated face down, her long black hair flowing around her in thin, tentacular-like threads. He jumped up from his seat and stumbled out of the sauna, his head spinning violently. Stepping forward, he felt a wave of hot darkness engulf him and fell to his knees. Moments later cold water splashed against his skin. He opened his eyes and met Irma's, who was now perched at the edge of the pool.

'Are you okay? Bit too long in the sauna?'

'For a moment I thought you'd drowned, I just saw you face down in the water.'

'Oh, I'm sorry. I didn't mean to scare you — I always do this. It's something I've been doing to strengthen my lungs. I just float face down and count for as long as I can. But you're right. I'm sorry, that was stupid to not let you know I was alright.'

He glanced out at the empty pool, then back at Irma.

'No it's fine, honestly, just glad you're okay.'

'I think I'm gonna give the sauna a miss and get showered before eating. See you down at the bar in a little bit?'

'Yep, I'll catch you there.'

The sun had barely risen when he stepped out onto his balcony. He resisted the urge to smoke, having decided to limit himself to four a day: one with his morning coffee, one after lunch, one after dinner and then a final one before bed. Despite being up until the early hours working on his report, he felt fresh. Part of him wanted to stay at the hotel for as long as possible after the final immersion. Even though he'd been apprehensive to live in such close proximity to the others, the place itself was doing him good. He was eating well, swimming everyday and smoking less. This alone was a huge improvement. But it went deeper than that, and even if he didn't really want to admit it, he'd started to feel really proud of the VFL and what they were doing. His conversations with Jakob and his avoidance of Anton had really helped. He no longer felt like a cynic, but instead recognised that his doubts were not only valid, but that the other members also shared them. In a counterintuitive way, this uncertainty made everything feel more possible. The fact that a delay in the results didn't signify a failure assured him that what they were striving towards was worthwhile.

Bending over and reaching towards his toes, he rested his hands on his shins and tucked his chin into his chest. Holding the pose, he breathed slowly through his nose, recognising how much better a little exercise had made him feel.

After a cold shower, he got dressed and made his way downstairs. He'd agreed to meet Anya at a café near London Bridge. He was excited to catch her, as they hadn't seen each other since he arrived at the hotel weeks ago. She'd also been tied down with helping to organise conferences for potential VFL investors who wanted to meet some of the project's researchers. From what he could gather from her messages, it had been going well.

In the lobby, he gave a nod to the woman at reception and walked through the revolving glass. Knowing that his report was almost finished, even though four days still remained before the final immersion, calmed him. There was no rush today. He could spend as long as he wanted with Anya, and perhaps spend the afternoon reading. Recently he seemed to write better during the late evening, at the time most others were finishing their days work. At first, this technique had felt a little risky. What happened if he spent the day doing as he pleased then *couldn't* manage to write in the evening? But within a week of working at this rhythm, almost like clockwork, he no longer had any concerns.

∞∞∞

'So you're all just *living* there? I mean, it sounds pretty desirable. You get to really take care of yourself and be catered for during the whole process?'

'Yeah I had my doubts, but it's definitely doing me good.'

'I can tell. You're looking really well. I hope you don't mind me saying, but I'd started to worry about you.' Anya said.

'No, that's fine. I mean, I'd started to worry about myself. I've felt like shit these past few months, so I think treating the time at the hotel as a mix of intense work and rehab has sorted me out.'

The waiter placed their drinks in front of them. Carl reached for his packet. First of the daily four. As it was still so early, most of the tables around them were empty. A few cyclists passed by, along with different groups of workers carrying food deliveries into the adjacent restaurants.

'How have you been? I feel like you've been so busy every time we've spoken recently.'

She raised her eyebrows and turned her head slightly to the side, her way of nodding.

'It's been non-stop. Every week there's been a conference or a meeting or even just a dinner I've had to attend. I can't complain, though. I think until recently, I didn't really know what my role was at the VFL. Just being a 'researcher'... it's quite *vague*. In your case, you actually know what you're there for. But for me it's only since they've had me speaking with potential investors or just representatives from other institutions that I finally feel like I'm *doing* something useful.'

'That's great to hear. I'm sure they must think highly of you, otherwise they wouldn't want you acting as the face of the project.'

'Thanks, I'd like to think so', she smiled. They both sat silently for a moment, watching one of the delivery men carry boxes of greens into a small grocers. Exhaling smoke, she continued to speak without looking at him.

'Carl... I've been meaning to ask you something. I think I need a bit of time out of London. It doesn't need to be far away. I'm happy to stay in the UK and it doesn't need to be for long; even just a long weekend would do. But I've been sleeping really badly recently, waking up every hour or so, often confused and not knowing where I am.'

'Do you want to go away together?'

She laughed a little, 'I mean, I wasn't just going to ask you to water my plants — wait that's a good point actually, they need watering.'

'I think I could do with that as well. Perhaps once the final stages at the hotel have finished, and if you aren't busy with the conferences, we can head to Cornwall. You've still never been there, no?'

'No, never. But I remember you speaking about it — that could be perfect.'

'Do you have any idea what might be affecting your sleep?' Carl asked.

'Stress, I guess. I mean, it's hard not to be concerned when you wake up each day to the news that this chaos is spreading like a virus. But that's what's puzzling me. You know me — I'm really good at taking the news quite pragmatically and it doesn't usually affect me *that* emotionally.'

'But something's changed?'

'In my waking life, no. Nothing that I can really perceive. But this hidden... I don't know, *anxiety* I guess you could say... it seems to be manifesting in my dreams. There's really not a night that goes past in which I don't wake up from some grim scene.'

He reached for his coffee, finishing it in one gulp. Without noticing, he'd lit another cigarette but decided he didn't care. Perhaps five today was okay.

'Did you want to share any?'

'I mean, there's been so many. But one *really* stayed with me. It wasn't that the dream itself was particularly horrific, but I felt it was trying to tell me something.'

'How so?'

'It was a reference, or at least it *felt* like a reference to an artist I'd come across some time ago. The meaning of this reference, in terms of my dream, I still haven't figured out. But when I saw the parallels it really unnerved me, because I felt like I *had* to understand it.'

'What was the dream?'

'It was based here in London, and as far as I could tell it was in our present world. Everything looked uncannily similar to how it does. Even small things, like the saxophonist that's always busking in front of Southwark Bridge was there, playing the same music.'

'That Coltrane piece?' Carl asked, before waving away the question, realising it probably didn't matter.

'Yeah, the one from Blue Train. But anyway, the main part of the dream was that everyone, like pretty much *every* person I saw, was riding a bicycle along Bankside. Then all of a sudden, as if they'd all received a signal, they started cycling over the small wall and fell into the Thames. I remember just standing there screaming but no one could hear me. And they just kept going, cyclist after cyclist just careering over the walls and off the bridges into the river. Then when I ran to the edge to look down, the water was perfectly still, as if the bicycles had just slipped right through it without breaking the surface.'

Carl sat motionless in his seat. A long finger of ash hanging at the end of his cigarette fell to the floor.

'But anyway, when I woke from the dream I wrote the whole thing down — well as much as I could remember. And I just *knew* that it was familiar; that there was something about it I'd seen before. It took me a few days, but then one evening I was walking towards Blackfriars and I saw it.'

She paused, finishing her coffee, looking down at the ice in her glass. The waiter paused near them, until Anya told him they'd have the same again.

'You've got time for another, right?' she asked.

'Yeah I'm in no rush today. So what did you see?'

'Well I can't have actually *seen* it. Because it didn't happen. But it was sort of like a hallucination, one that only lasted a few seconds. Suddenly the Thames became a canal in Amsterdam and I saw a man driving his bike into it. I knew instantly who it was. It was the Dutch artist Bas Jan Ader. Do you know his work?'

Carl shook his head.

'Well there's this one piece, or performance I guess, where he cycles along the edge of the canal and then suddenly turns his handlebars and falls straight in. He did a lot of similar pieces in which there's always this moment right after the fall where he's just floating in space before he lands. They're really beautiful, but I still don't know what the meaning of any of this is.'

'But you said you had a sort of hallucination, that's what aligned the memory?' he asked.

'Exactly. Until then it was just a weird dream that *felt* familiar. Now it's just a weird dream about Bas Jan Ader's work which still doesn't make any sense.'

They paused as the waiter put their coffees down on the table.

'Yeah that's really strange. I actually know someone whose dad died after riding a bike into the Thames. I hadn't thought about it in ages, but the other day it came back to me. Not that it's related, just a strange coincidence.'

'What? He just rode right into it? Why?'

'Oh he was long gone already. Lost his job, had alzheimers and a gambling addiction. I doubt he even knew where he was cycling.'

'Jesus. That's so...' she looked up to the sky, hunting for the right word in amongst the clouds.

'Have you had any more of these hallucinations?' he asked.

'Not really. There's been a few instances where I've felt like I'm missing something or that I'm repeating a certain action. I used to get déjà vu a lot when I was younger. Not so much anymore, but I think it creeps back in now and again.'

'Mine have been all over the place.'

'Oh really?' she asked, leaning back in her chair.

'Yeah. I mean, physically I feel much healthier after the past month. But mentally, I've been getting them all the time. Sometimes I just sit and close my eyes and it's like I go into a dream for half an hour or so. Then when I'm awake, things I've dreamt about crop up unexpectedly. It's nothing *too* severe, I mean it doesn't really hinder me. But the fact that it's there... yeah I don't know. I might see someone about it after this whole work stint comes to an end.'

'Yeah, that could be a good idea. I also think you shouldn't underestimate what prolonged time in a VR can do to you. Maybe that's causing it?'

'I mean, it's probably not doing it any good, but to be honest, these have been happening since I got back to London. Strange, as I never experienced this in Tallinn. But within weeks of being back in London this all started. At first it was really subtle — I guess it still is to some extent. But they're certainly more frequent.'

'As bizarre as mine?' Anya asked.

'Would you believe me if I said that bikes have been a recurring theme running in mine?'

'Well, *have* they?'

'Bikes *and water*, to be more precise.'

'I don't know if I believe you?' she laughed.

'Honestly. That's why I looked so unnerved when you told me about yours. The themes are eerily similar.'

'Go on.'

'The other night, well actually it was during the day, I fell asleep for an hour and dreamt that I was at a beach. I don't really remember anything leading into it. I was just *there*, nothing more. One minute I was in the hotel room, lying on my back trying to focus on my breathing. The next, I was standing on the beach, looking down at my feet. I remember standing completely still, just watching the water running over my skin, washing the sand from between my toes. It's quite a lot to explain, but essentially there was a choir dressed as angels, holding candles to the sky. I couldn't make out what words they were singing, but it felt familiar. It was like I knew the music *physically*, but not mentally.'

'That's exactly how I felt.' Anya interjected, 'It was as if my body was reacting to something my mind couldn't process. But anyway, carry on.'

'So yeah, I stood on this beach with the choir, and then I saw a light out at sea. But it was coming from *under* the water, not above it. Eventually I waded out into the waves, and thousands of lifeboats started to emerge from the surface, along with thousands of bikes.'

Anya leaned forward, her eyes narrowing.

'But the sea got quite rough and I needed to swim out. I don't remember everything, but a wave picked me up and threw me onto the shore. At this point the music just *turned*. It went from beautiful harmonies to the most abrasive, harrowing type of cacophony. Suddenly all the bike bells started clanging and making this horrendous noise. Then I turned and looked at the sea. There was a huge wave forming, and I could see thousands of eyes blinking back at me like stars. I knew it was building into some kind of climax, and sure enough, as the huge wave broke down on me the choir just erupted into screams. Then it was just total blackness: the kind of silence that cuts so deep you can hear your own pulse. But I knew I was still at the beach. I suddenly felt freezing, and could still feel the cold sea air against my skin. All of this happening while my heart rate slowed. The only thing left was the sound of a gentle thud slowly decreasing until the gaps in between each pulse felt like years.'

After a few minutes Anya still hadn't spoken.

'Maybe that's not what you needed to hear. I know it's quite an intense dream.'

'No no, it's not that. I'm glad you shared it with me. It's that there's more to it than you realise.'

'How so?' Carl asked.

'It's the link to Jan Ader. I mean, who knows, in both our cases it's just a dream. But I feel almost sick after hearing that. It's *too* accurate.'

'Wait, I really don't know what you mean?'

'It's the end of his life. It's like you were there, Carl. I don't know what any of this means but it couldn't be more uncanny.'

∞∞∞∞∞

The bright light of the laptop screen stung his retinas as he scrolled through images of Jan Ader. Rubbing his eyes, he glanced around the room. His tracksuit hung from the wardrobe door like a thin, lifeless figure. White mugs stained with dry coffee stood like islands in amongst the sea of paper inundating his desk. He could hear the slow dripping of the tap coming from the bathroom. He stood up, switched on the fan and stretched his arms above his head as he looked through the dusty glass doors. What the fuck did any of this mean? The ocean, the bikes, the choir? Each element felt like a worn-away puzzle piece that couldn't connect to the other. He perched on the end of the bed, running his fingers along the cotton sheets.

Bas Jan Ader, he discovered, disappeared after setting sail across the Atlantic Ocean from Chatham, Massachusetts, on July 9th, 1975. His journey to Falmouth, England, was estimated to take two to three months. Ten months later, one hundred and fifty nautical miles from the south west coast of Ireland, his small sailing boat, *Ocean Wave,* was discovered by a Spanish fishing trawler, named *Edoardo Pontal.* Documentation confirming it was his boat was discovered by the crew, alongside cans of food and other nautical equipment. His body was never found.

But this in itself wouldn't have caused him to see a parallel between his dream and Jan Ader's death. It was the ceremony that was held before he commenced his journey. The work, entitled *In Search of the Miraculous,* took its name from Ouspensky's work of esoteric philosophy in which he documented his time spent with the philosopher and mystic, George Ivanovich Gurjieff.

The artwork was composed of three parts: first, on the night before he set sail, a choir sang sea shanties in a gallery, the second was his journey across the Atlantic and the third, which never occurred, would have been a choir in Falmouth welcoming him with the same sea shanties. Had it been sea shanties they were singing in his dream? He felt he'd recognised the music, and before reading that article he'd never heard of the word 'shanty'. The more he strained to remember the finer details of the dream, the quicker the images turned watery. When he heard the voices of the choir, it sounded like they were submerging under the waves, like a slow removal of high frequencies.

Did it even matter? Although he'd always felt that the ambient, dreamlike states he entered into were what allowed him to make certain connections, this time it only felt confusing. Perhaps it was an example of what Jakob was speaking about. *Aphenia,* or *apophenia*? He couldn't recall the exact word but remembered the concept. Jakob had said something about two different types. Was it type one he said was more common, seeing patterns where patterns didn't exist? Or was this a case of type two, with him failing to see a pattern when there *was* one? The more he thought about it, the more his left temple throbbed.

He continued running his fingers along the sheets, watching the curves rise and fall under his touch. The dream, which he'd written down, contained all the information he needed. Perhaps a connection would come to him later on, but for now he couldn't waste more time mulling it over. Returning to his computer, he opened his report for the third immersion and started to read through it.

Two weeks later he found himself sat in the same position, staring at the computer screen.

The blending of one stage into the next was contained in the objects that made up his surroundings: the same tracksuit hanging from the door, the same pile of papers and empty coffee mugs, the same orange dust clinging to the glass doors and the same dripping echoing from the bathroom. The only difference now was that the end was in sight. His report, entitled 'Phase Four — Advanced Algorithmic Capitalism and Cultural Pastiche' was underway. With three reports already completed, he felt more comfortable with the last, knowing that he was capable of putting into words most of what he'd experienced in the phases. He even found that during his writing of the last two reports, he'd entered into a mode which felt like auto-pilot, with his feet gently kicking the chair back and forth.

During this process, he would write for hours at a time, not pausing for anything. Only when he did eventually stop did he realise his body had been crying out to him: his throat would be dry or he'd be desperate for the bathroom. When he read back over the reports, it was as if he were hearing about the immersion for the first time. His memory of what he'd written was frequently blank, and only when he went back through the report did everything fall back into place. Perhaps the funniest realisation was how much of a waste of money his swing had been. He could write perfectly well sat in his chair, as long as he gently pushed the balls of his feet against the carpet. He didn't actually need the chair to rise and fall, but something about the tensing and untensing of his thighs and calves gave him the notion of movement. Oh well. He liked the swing and was pleased he had it as a place to rest in the flat. If winter ever came, it would become his new hammock.

The energy at the hotel had been pleasant, even jovial after the final session of the fourth immersion. It was clear that all of the testers were pleased to have it out of the way. Most of them had managed to do each eight hour sitting without interruption, but during the final phase Irma had removed her headset early, complaining of motion sickness and a painful headache. But as Sarah was quick to assure them, one early exit out of four long weeks of immersions was much better than they predicted.

After the final session, Anton had told them that the bar was open for the evening and anything they wanted was on the VFL. They deserved to kick back after such a long, condensed workload.

That evening Carl noted that his mood had shifted again. This time, Anton seemed to take a back seat in the conversations, nodding along and laughing when the others did. His often dominating, performative way of interacting was completely absent, and for a moment Carl wondered if there was something bothering him. Was he keeping quiet and letting them celebrate because he knew something was wrong? For a moment, he suspected this generosity of the open bar was a sort of last supper before the fall, a way of letting them down kindly. Would everything be different tomorrow morning? He imagined Anton telling them that there'd been a gross problem with the software, that the project was as good as worthless and everything they'd achieved counted for nothing. The Negronis he liberally knocked back weren't helping this paranoia, and while he excused himself to use the bathroom he resolved to approach Anton and see if something was wrong. When he returned, he placed a hand on Anton's shoulder.

'Can I offer you a Camel, Anton?'

'Well, seeing as we're celebrating, I would *love* one.'

He got to his feet and walked behind Carl towards the terrace. They took a seat at one of the outside tables and Carl lit his cigarette for him, something he tended to do only when he was drunk.

'Thank you, Carl,' he replied, leaning back in his chair and looking up towards the sky. The sound of muffled chatting behind the windows accompanied the faint hum of traffic. The streets seemed quieter lately. There had, in fact, been a huge reduction in traffic due to the government's new regulations: London was becoming unbearably polluted, and there was a need for stronger reforms. They'd placed a ban on any vehicles other than delivery lorries and public transport in the city centre. While the pollution was still butter-like in its thickness, everyone agreed this was at least a step in the right direction.

'Well, Carl, I can't thank you enough for all the hard work you've put in over the last few months,' he paused, taking another long drag on his cigarette. His speech remained soft, less jumpy.

'I'm sorry if I seem a little quiet this evening. It's just been a really emotional day for me. To see how much dedication you've each shown, especially living here over the last month... well it's made me so proud to be a part of the VFL'.

Were his eyes growing moist? He had no idea how to respond to this new Anton. He felt slightly ashamed of being so mistrustful.

'I appreciate you saying that. I'm just glad we've made it through this first testing phase. Oh, and about us being dedicated... honestly, living at the hotel, it's been the best thing for me, really.'

'Is that so?' he asked, a smile forming across his face.

'For sure. I've not been in the best health and living here seems to have put me on the right track. I'm smoking way less — except for tonight — and swimming everyday. I feel great in all honesty.'

'Well, I'm glad to hear. Too bad we can't all keep living here after the New Year!'

They both took a sip of their drinks.

'So what's next for you, after Jakob and the others have analysed the data?' Carl asked.

'It's hard to say, I'm afraid. All being well, the software will give us these reports documenting the changes and we'll just take it from there. Nothing's really changed with the original plan.' His words slurred a little.

'Anya, who I believe you've met, said she's been really busy recently with organising VFL conferences.'

'Ah Anya, yes we met quite recently. She's been working *non-stop* this last month. The amount of interest she's fostered in us has been unbelievable. Everyone on the publicity team have been saying how natural she seems when it comes to presenting the project.'

'I'm sure she'd be pleased to know that.'

As he placed his hand in his jacket pocket, fishing for his cigarettes, his phone started to vibrate. He pulled it out and saw Anya's name on the incoming call.

'Speak of the devil, that's her just now. Will you excuse me while I take this?'

'Of course. I'll catch you back inside.'

As Anton reentered through the glass doors, Carl swiped his screen and answered the call.

'Hey, we were just speaking about you.'

'Oh, who's we?'

'Anton and I. He was saying how everyone's been really impressed with all the work you've been doing.'

'Oh, well that's always nice to hear. Look Carl, I can't stay on the phone for long, but do you have a minute? It's kind of important.'

'Sure.'

'Well I've just got back from the hospital-'

'Shit, did something happen?'

'It was because of the hallucinations I told you about. They got quite bad today and I had to leave one of the conferences early. I thought it was just tiredness combined with a bad headache, but then I started to lose my hearing and my vision became, well, *watery*.'

'*Jesus*, sounds bad.'

'It was. I thought I was losing it. But the reason I called you was to warn you because I know you've also been getting them. I spoke to a doctor and she told me that there's been a steep rise in the number of people suffering from this condition.'

'What's the condition?'

'They said it doesn't have a name yet, but it's a type of psychosis which is induced by air pollution. She told me that thousands of people have been treated for this throughout London in the last few months.'

'Right. That's scary, but kinda relieving to know that there's a reason behind it.'

'That was how I took it as well. But regardless, she told me to wear a face mask at all times when I'm outside and also said that pharmacies are providing inhalers which help to clear out the dust from your throat. I've already picked mine up and I think you should do the same as soon as you can.'

'Ok, yeah that's good to know.'

'Anyway I need to go soon, but is everything okay with you?'

'Yeah I'm fine. We had the final immersion today so we're all at the bar celebrating.'

'Oh, that sounds fun. Well you deserve it and I'm glad you all got through the final phase.'

'Thanks, I'm sorry to hear it's been a stressful day. Let me know if you have some spare time this week and I can always come meet you again.'

'I will do, thank you. And don't forget about the inhaler.'

'I won't. Take care and let me know if you need anything.'

'I will, of course. Speak soon Carl.'

She hung up and Carl lit another cigarette. He could feel the alcohol flowing through his blood stream and his cheeks burning a little. He glanced through the window into the bar and noticed that some of the others had already left. The urge to order another drink and remain outside all evening, falling deeper into the honey-like waves of inebriation tempted him. Only the thought of having to get started on the final report told him it was a bad idea. He stubbed out his half-smoked Camel and made his way to his room.

∞∞∞

During the final week at the hotel, he found that beyond showering and sleeping, he couldn't be in his room for anything other than writing. Each morning he woke up naturally at seven a.m., took a cold shower and ordered breakfast to his room. While he drank his coffee and ate his way through the small pile of fruit, he read over his report, often pausing to take down more notes. He usually found that he could sit there and write until midday, pausing only to read through other notes or listen back to fragments of audio on his dictaphone. When he reflected on this change in routine, he couldn't understand how such a drastic shift had occurred: only a month ago, he was staying up all evening to write and not touching his report during the daylight hours. He preferred his new routine, but found it strange how quickly he could change his habits, especially during such an important stage.

In the afternoon, he ate lunch by himself in the restaurant and watched the news updates flooding in on the large television above the bar. Europe remained in a state of chaos, with talk of another financial crash ricocheting throughout the continent. Muted scenes of protesters demanding immediate elections, as a surge of support for extreme green but also extreme nationalist parties became clear in the polls. Mass migration from those fleeing the scorched earth of the southern hemisphere was coming; that much was sure. Now it was time for nations to decide how to deal with the new arrivals. The rise of nationalist platitudes seemed inevitable, as the fear of overpopulation and hyper-inflation paved the way for a rise in border controls. Cropping up in nation after nation, populist leaders repeated the mantra 'Our Nation First'. In defence of the global community, green parties stressed that now more than ever required international cooperation and a resistance to protectionist politics. The arguments carried on unabated, as orange dust nestled into the cracks of the wilted roads.

When he finished eating, he tended to swim and pass the afternoon reading by the swimming pool. Often the other testers would be there, and he found that talking to them, even if they couldn't say *exactly* what they were writing about, helped him to work through his case studies. Often they chose not to speak about their reports at all, with all of them admitting that despite their excitement, they needed time to clear their heads. These became known as 'phase-free' afternoons, whereby any conversation was permitted as long as it didn't include the VFL.

One afternoon, all four testers Carl, Irma, Sofia and Kristen, were sat reading in silence in their sunloungers. The reflection of the water flickered on the veiny leaves of the philodendron and ficus plants. After submitting their final reports that morning, all four of them agreed to spend a last afternoon together by the pool before the data analysis meetings commenced the following day. Now that the immersions were over, they could speak freely about their findings. But it seemed no one was really in the mood. Only when Kristen broke the silence, did they all look up from their books.

'That's an interesting tattoo', she said, pointing at Sofia's ankle.

The others glanced over, noticing a small, blue tattoo above the bone: a circle with thin hair-like strands splaying off in all directions.

'This one? Yeah I got it when I was in my early twenties. I was diving near the Mariana Trench in the Pacific Ocean- '

'Oh, I didn't know you were a diver.'

'Well, I *used* to be. I started out in marine biology before doing a bit of a u-turn and going into literature, then another smaller turn into psychology.'

'Ah, I seem to remember you mentioning this.' Kristen said.

'But yeah, while I was in the Mariana Trench I spent a lot of time filming jellyfish. One of them was a hydromedusa, part of the genus Crossota.'

'Ah, so it's a jellyfish. I couldn't make out the shape.'

'Yeah it's not the neatest of designs. Just a small stick-and-poke someone did for me. But I really like it. It was such a magical time in my life. They're such an interesting type, as they emit this really faint glow. So when there's a bloom of them, it's as if there's a cluster of lights flickering.'

Irma, who hadn't said anything, stretched her leg forward towards Sofia.

'Want to see something strange?' she asked.

'What is it?'

'That scar on my ankle.'

All four of them peered at the white scar tissue that meandered around her ankle bone.

'How did you get that?' Sofia asked.

'A jellyfish.'

'No way.'

All four of them sat up to take a closer look.

'*God*, it's even the same shape' Sofia said. All of them laughed a little.

'I've never scuba dived, but when I was a teenager my dad took me and my brother to Falmouth.'

'*Falmouth*?' Carl asked.

'Yeah, it's a small town in the north of Jamaica. Have you been?'

'No, never. Sorry, go on.'

'The reason we went was because my dad wanted to see something called *bioluminescent dinoflagellates* — that's a mouthful. The area is really good for it, as the brackish water is a mix of fresh water from the Martha Brae River with the salt water from the Caribbean Sea. It's supposed to combine with nutrients from the red mangrove trees and creates the perfect environment for these dinoflagellates.'

'What are they, exactly?' Kristen asked.

'Mostly marina plankton. There's definitely a better scientific answer but I can't quite remember.'

'So how did you get the scar?' Carl askeed.

'*Well*, we went out on this small sailing boat at night. And sure enough, the whole ocean was glowing. It was as if there were thousands of blue and green lights shining out from under the surface. I was quite scared when my dad suggested we all take a swim. I mean, it's just plankton so it can't harm you. But it was so otherworldly I felt that anything could be down there. So we all put on our masks and jumped overboard. For half an hour it was one of the most amazing sights I've ever witnessed. The thing is that the more you disturb the water, the more they shine. So we all just thrashed about as if we were drowning, watching the threads of lights shoot out from below. Then I felt something on my ankle.'

'And that was the jellyfish?' Sofia asked.

'Yep. Didn't know until I got back to shore, because I never actually *saw* it. I went into complete shock and had to spend the night in the hospital.'

Carl, who hadn't said much until this point, broke in:

'Would any mind if I broke the 'phase-free' session and spoke about my last immersion? It's sort of relevant.'

'Yeah, sure.' they all nodded.

'It's just that in this immersion, right at the end during the last session, I found myself at a beach with glowing waters, just like you described.'

They all turned their bodies towards him.

'I'm not sure where it was, but I found myself standing on a beach with the water washing over my toes. There was a choir behind me and I thought I knew what they were singing, but it was more of a *physical* recognition, like my body, not my mind, recognised it. Anyway, I

229

eventually walked out into the shallows, and these bright lights started to shine from underneath the water.'

He shifted in his seat a little, looking down at the sunlounger.

'Soon after, loads of empty lifeboats started to emerge from the water, but all of them were empty. Then I started to hear bells ringing. I thought they were coming from the shore, but when I looked down I saw hundreds of rusty bikes clattering against each other under the water's surface. I can't quite remember all the details, but eventually I ended up on the shore looking up at a huge wave forming. At this point the choir's chant rose to a crescendo and I saw thousands of glowing points in the face of the wave. For a moment they looked like eyes. Then the wave broke on me and everything went black.'

'Wait, so that was the end of the immersion?' Irma asked.

'I must have hit the relocation button because next thing I knew I was back in a city, staring up at a highrise building.'

'Did you include it in your report?' Kristen asked, warily.

'I did, but in a way I don't know why. It was such a short experience compared to the rest of the immersion. Also, I have no idea what relevance it has to the phase itself.'

'I think you were right to include it', Sofia cut in, 'I won't bother going into the finer details, but there were some moments in my last immersion that seemed totally absurd. When I was writing my report, I had no idea how to analyse them. Funnily enough the weirdest one was also in water.'

'Care to share it?' Carl asked.

'I mean, it's hard to really *explain* what it was. I'd been in a small town, somewhere that looked faintly middle-eastern. Then when I hit the relocation button, I was just in a raft floating downstream somewhere. There weren't any signs of human life. Just mangroves lining the sides of the river. But I could hear something emanating from the water. Then when I looked over the edge, there were clusters of rotting cellos bumping into each other like driftwood. I stayed there for a while — probably longer than I *should* have — because it was so... well, just fucking *weird*. But like you, I don't have a clue what it meant. I also put it in my report. So I wouldn't worry if there's some elements you can't get your head around. I think those moments are unavoidable.'

Sirens howled abrasively outside the hotel, blue lights flashing against the foggy glass. From the spacious conference room on the twenty-second floor, the team at the VFL could make out the throngs of protesters flooding across London Bridge. Placards had made way for projectiles, dialogue for brute force. The Shard stood static, penetrating the dense sky, as a helicopter's shadow reflected off its glass. All around them the London they knew was collapsing: all transport was at a standstill, looting of shops couldn't be contained and the MET were dangerously overstretched. News of hyper-inflation hitting southern Europe sent surrounding nations into panic, with most believing their economies would be next. Food shortages brought on by widespread crop failures were leading to tactics of aggressive stockpiling. The next wave of climate migrants were already arriving on the shores of Italy and Spain, with pocket after pocket of the southern hemisphere becoming completely uninhabitable.

Anton stood at the head of the table, sipping his mineral water garnished with a slice of cucumber. Everyone else sat in silence, waiting for him to commence. With all sixteen of the reports having been read and analysed, it was now time for Jakob and the other data analysts to step up to the plate. The presence of Carl and the other testers wasn't required, but they were welcome to remain at the hotel. With the fans above the table whirring, Anton placed his glass on the table and looked back at them.

'Well, *here we are!* It's been a long time coming, but we've all made it through the testing phase and now comes the real challenge.'

Carl couldn't be sure what the others were thinking. But surely the fact that mobs were forming in the streets required immediate attention? Or did it? Was there anything that they, a group of academics could really do to quell the violence? Perhaps blindly sticking to the plan really was the best option. Sheepishly, he looked back up at Anton.

'So, as we predicted, there was a clear correlation between your reports. All of them, while offering different examples in your case studies, showed four *clearly* distinct worlds. *Now*, while we are all probably in agreement about which one — or maybe *ones* — we should be aiming for, this isn't our immediate priority. First, we need to have clear-cut and comprehensive reports which document *what* actions we would need to take to either reach or avoid each of these future scenarios.'

They all nodded in agreement; there wasn't anything new in his dialogue. Carl glanced at Jakob who stood awkwardly behind Anton alongside two other data analysts. He couldn't tell if he was imagining this, but he looked nervous. Turning to Jakob, Anton beckoned him to the head of the table.

'Anyway, that's enough from me. I'll let Jakob explain the next stage.'

A little hesitantly, he smiled and nodded at Anton.

'So great to see you all here. Now, the important thing to start with is what Anton mentioned — the reports themselves. Well done all of you, I'm very excited by what I've read. Now comes the harder part. Well, erm... there's no easy way to put this, so you'll have to excuse my bluntness. Things are going to be a little trickier than we imagined.'

Carl glanced at Anton, whose face was stiff. It wasn't quite a glare, but he could sense the tension in the room.

'The good news is that the software is designed in such a way to deal with the issue we're facing-'

'Sorry, cut to the chase, Jakob', Anton blurted out. 'None of us know what you and the other analysts know, so don't beat about the bush.'

'Yes, you're right, my apologies. I'm getting there,' his cheeks flushed a little. The other analysts looked down. 'The best way I can describe it is through a metaphor. You've all seen a musical tuner before, right?'

Everyone looked around the table, nodding in quick succession. Anton kept his eyes fixed on Jakob.

'So when you're tuning up an instrument — let's say a cello — you need to let each note ring out a little before the needle in the middle hits the tone. When you first pluck a string, the needle will flit from side to side before it lands on the spot that indicates the frequency. Now imagine you've only got one tuner, and you're trying to tune up a hundred cellos at once.'

A few members leaned forward, puzzled.

'Essentially, if you keep changing string too quickly, the needle will keep jumping back and forth but it won't ever land in one position, so it's impossible to know if a string is in tune-'

'So what are you *saying*, Jakob? I'm not following.' By now everyone could sense the aggression in Anton's voice.

'It's to do with information overload, but, *in particular,* information that's perpetually in flux. That's what I mean with the cello example. You could tune a thousand cellos with the same tuner. But if they're all played too quickly, then the notes keep changing and it's impossible to decipher one tone from the next.'

'Right, *thanks* for that. But you still haven't said how this relates to *our* software?'

'Perhaps that's not the best example. Essentially, with the AI we're using, it's designed to process huge amounts of data. But the issue now is that the information it takes in which tells us what steps to take in order to move towards — *or avoid* — each of these worlds, is changing too rapidly.'

'Wait, you mean the information about our current world?'

'Exactly. The economies, the food sources, the political landscapes, the movement between nations... it's all shifting drastically from day to day.'

'So you're saying you can't figure it out, *that's* what you're getting at?' He was now making no attempt to hide his anger.

'Imagine an ocean during a storm,' Jakob continued, in an attempt to pacify Anton.

'No! No more *fucking metaphors*, Jakob. Tell it how it is.'

'Please, Anton, it's the only way for any of us to understand it.' As Anton didn't respond, he continued with his explanation.

'Imagine you're trying to read the GPS and figure out the best route out of the storm. But the waves keep shifting the boat and changing its direction. It's the same with the tuner. The navigation needle will just keep flying around and it's near impossible to determine what direction you should follow. So the only solution is to keep yourself afloat and weather the storm, so to speak. Then when it's calmed down, *only* then can you start to read the data and proceed.'

'So, you're saying that until things calm down — and let me just remind you it's fucking *anarchy* out there — *your* AI isn't able to identify *any* solutions?'

'No. That's not the case. *Our* AI can identify *all* the solutions-'

'So what's the issue, then? You just said it couldn't figure it out until the conditions had settled down?'

'No, that's not what I said. The AI can identify all the solutions in real time. *It* is smart enough to process literally *tonnes* of data each minute, *even* if that data is constantly shifting. The problem is us. We *can't* process data that quickly. So no matter what instructions the AI spits out, they'll change so rapidly from minute to minute that we won't be able to follow. It's the same as the tuner. It's not that the needle won't continuously follow the exact frequencies. It's that to the human eye, the needle is just dancing around erratically.'

'So all we can do it wait?' Sofia broke in.

'I'm afraid so. We, and when I say *we*, I mean the global community, need to get a foothold. But the good news is that even if things get worse, they tend to plateau at some point.'

'Right, so once it's got *so* chaotic that anarchy is the new norm, *then* we'll be able to find solutions.' Anton shouted.

'It might not get to that', Jakob tried to assure them. 'But for now all we can do is wait. But it's important to recognise that this isn't a system failure. It's just a delay. The issue now is that if we try to read the data, we're inevitably going to run the risk of apophenia. It's too chaotic and there are too many shifts. So if we try to read it, we might start seeing patterns where there aren't any. It's best to wait, you just really have to trust me on this one.'

Anton, who had sat with his forehead resting on a clenched fist pushed his chair back from the table and stood up.

'I think it's best that everyone except Jakob goes downstairs.'

'Should we wait for further updates at the hotel? Do you know when they'll be a definitive answer?' Irma asked.

'Mind your own *fucking* business, Irma. Now all of you, get out. You'll hear from us once we've found a way out of this shit.'

Downstairs in the bar, the four of them sat around a small table. On the television, a panicked news reporter wearing a helmet spoke into a headset: fires were breaking out around Parliament Square.

'Do you remember what I told you about AlphaGo, Carl?' Sofia asked. She didn't sound disappointed, and Carl sensed that she'd been preparing herself for the worst.

'Yeah, I do. It was exactly what came into my head when Jakob mentioned that it wasn't an issue with the AI, but an issue with us.'

'Wait, I don't know the story? What's AlphaGo?' Irma asked.

'It's Google's AI that was designed to play Go. It beat the world champion in a way no one predicted.'

'How's that relevant?' Kristen asked.

'It's not that it just beat the Go champion. It's that it played Go in a way no one has ever witnessed before. Obviously it could plan hundreds, even *thousands* of moves ahead. So it played a game that seemed almost alien. But the point of the story is that no one, not even the programmers at Google, know how it formed its strategy. So it's an AI that can play Go better than anyone else, but only the AI knows how it went about it. Or perhaps it *doesn't* know. It just plays, plain and simple.'

'I see,' Irma said. 'Yeah, I guess that is quite analogous.'

'I don't think we should be too disappointed', Carl said, 'I mean, like Jakob said, it's a *delay,* not a system failure-'

'Oh *come on*, do you really think things are going to stabilise in time for this project to be of any fucking use?' Sofia asked, placing her head in her hands.

'I really do. I think in a way the AI was telling us this during the immersions. Do you remember the scene I told you about, when I was at the beach?'

'Yes, but Carl, that was just a small section of the immersion. It doesn't necessarily *mean* anything.'

'No, not *necessarily.* But there could be something in that. I really think that was the point of that one scene. It didn't make sense at the time. But when Jakob gave the metaphor of being lost at sea — I think that's really it.'

'What *exactly* do you think it is?' Sofia snapped.

'I think it was a warning from the AI. It was telling us that we need to weather the storm. But as soon as we have, we'll be able to read the data. There's no point giving up now. There's something in it, I'm sure.'

'Well I'm not, I'm afraid. Sorry to be the pessimist, but just *look* outside. There's riots in the streets and we're expected to just *wait for things to calm down*?'

'What else is there to do?'

'I don't know, Carl. I don't think any of us really know.'

ooooo

Stepping out into the street he lit a Camel and looked down at his watch: it was still early afternoon. He'd take a walk, clear his head a bit and return to the hotel later. Somewhere in the distance he could hear the scream of car horns, blending with the chants.

He continued along Lower Thames Street towards London Bridge, stepping around the broken glass and litter that lined the pavement. Carried by the wind, a wave of dust kicked up from the concrete and choked him. He suddenly remembered Anya's recommendation and decided to look for a pharmacy. As he wandered, somewhat aimlessly, the myriad patterns and possible connections from the VR circulated in his head. He felt confident in an almost intoxicated manner; his steps were light and airy, his mind mulling over the scene at the beach. Surely there had to be *something* in it? Too many clues pointed towards the beach: the choir, Irma's scar, Jan Ader's final destination... As he turned into Cannon Street he could see the crowds in the distance. It should have been sobering. But it wasn't.

And he continued to amble along the empty pavement until a blue sign caught his eye. It was a pharmacy, its windows completely smashed open. An alarm inside rang out. The shop was deserted. When he saw the face masks in the window, he paused, not wanting to be seen stealing. He reached in his pocket and fished around for small change. Other than a few twenty-pence coins, he only had a ten-pound note. Surely that was *more* than enough? He reached in and replaced one of the masks with the note. It would probably be stolen if anyone saw it, but at least if *he* was on camera, they'd notice he had honest intentions. Placing the mask over his face, he inhaled deeply and flicked his cigarette onto the floor.

He passed Mansion House Station and continued along the same road. St Paul's Cathedral stood to his right; the grass surrounding it was brownish and bare, covered in bin liners. Only when he reached Warwick

Lane did the source of the chaos become visible. The crowd was one entity: a faceless cloud of black balaclavas and fists gripping glass bottles. All around the street people scurried into shop doorways, searching for cover. Carl looked up at a helicopter circling above in the overcast sky. The cloud cover was thick but consistent. A steel blanket pulled taut across the city. Suddenly black shapes started to flit across it, and he realised rocks were being thrown. The sound of smashing glass reverberated around the streets. With no direction and no clear enemy, a sense of restlessness festered in the crowd, as no one member knew where to direct their anger.

Carl ducked inside the closest building — a large two storey McDonalds. Running up the stairs, he passed by workers who rushed to lock the main doors as paving stones hammered against the glass. An alarm sounded, and all around him screams of fear blended with the Muzak. He took a seat in the corner and looked down onto the street. No police in sight. The alarm continued to ring, followed by thick shoots of water that sprayed out across the restaurant floor. He looked up, shielding his eyes from the spray and clambered under a large table. When his phone started to ring he answered it without looking at the screen.

'Carl? Are you there? What's the ringing?'

'It's a fire alarm. Someone must have sounded it in McDonalds. Where are you?'

'I'm at the Tate, had to take some guests from the VFL here. What are you doing in McDonalds?'

'I'm hiding.'

'Hiding?'

'There's a crowd outside. They're really going for it. Taking aim at anything. They've smashed the windows, and the sprinklers are-'

'It's... *flooding?'*

'Barely. Just some water around my ankles. But it's running down the stairs so I'm safe.'

'But I mean, that's *uncanny*, no?'

'Look, I think I've realised what the AI was trying to get at. We almost wrote it off earlier. Said it was another case of AlphaGo.'

'AlphaGo? Wait, what do you mean?'

'It's got the answers but we can't see them. We can see the results in the VR, but not the process. The instructions are all there in the algorithms, but we can't decipher them. The data's shifting too quickly so we can't get a stable foothold.'

'But wasn't *that* the whole point?"

'Absolutely. That's why everyone's so pissed. Anton kicked all of us out, told us to mind our own fucking business and stop being so impatient.'

'*Mind our own business?* But this is *our* business?'

'I know, but there's no getting through to him just now. The data analysts were the only people he kept in the conference room.'

'Against their own will?'

'They didn't seem to object. But they weren't in any position to. Either way, my work was done. He's got my reports, but I realised earlier that I missed it. Couldn't see the wood for the trees.'

'What do you mean?'

'I think we already reached the conclusion earlier. It's just that we didn't *know* we reached it.'

'How so?'

'Jakob, one of the data analysts, hit the nail on the head. When Anton started shouting at him, he said it was impossible, because we were essentially searching for a signal in a sea of noise. I think that's what my dream was telling me. That the answers are right there in front of us, but we just can't perceive them. Right now it's frustrating, because the technology won't allow us to find them. It can't point out what we need, only we can decide that.'

'But I thought that was part of the package, that all the information would be laid out in front of us? They made it *sound* so straightforward, so what changed?'

'The way that information moves. It's updated in real time, so the shifts and fluctuations we're seeing across the world means the system can't calibrate it. It's moving like waves, just undulating back and forth, so the code we're being fed changes as rapidly *and* as dramatically.'

'I see. So the project's essentially got no use anymore?'

'No, on the contrary. I think it *will* have a use. But only when the current conditions settle down. There needs to be *some* stability for us to be able to read the data. Then we can work with it.'

'But wait this doesn't make any sense. Wasn't the idea that this technology was meant to be the *means* for us to stabilise? That was their whole pitch, *no*? That this would provide answers to *current* problems? What use is it if it only works when things are fucking stable?'

'I know it seems like a lost cause but it's really not, I promise. I think that's the lesson from the whole process. It's the same that happened with Arvo Pärt. His tools, the musical knowledge he had, no longer worked, couldn't keep him afloat. I never got to tell you, but I remembered what the piece was that the choir was performing in my dream: it was *Credo*. The whole piece is about disintegration, collapse and despair. It was when he'd given up on what he thought he knew. Composition couldn't take him any further and only isolation and silence allowed him to recalibrate his approach. That's when he reappeared eight years later with *Tintinabuli*.' By now his words were slurred, his ears throbbing.

'But what does Pärt have to do with any of this?'

'I think that's what the dream was saying. That we're going into a period of silence. That we won't find the answers we need until we take a step back. It's not about the tools, it's just how we're *using* them. The technology itself, like Jan Ader's boat, might make it over the finishing line. But until we move back from it, our vision will be too narrow and we'll be lost at sea, just like him. I think that was the meaning of all the empty boats. Then the bike bells and then the light going into the sky. It *has* to be that. The eyes, the drowning bodies as the music hit its final conclusion and everything went dark. It's telling us that this technology itself won't suffice *unless* the needle stops shaking. We need to calm the storm, wait until the water is less choppy and we'll be able to see clearly.'

All around him the water continued to rise. Metal poles smashed against the glass as a few workers backed away from the locked doors. The skies opened above the metropolis, with huge drops of rain bouncing against the pavement, forming syncopated rhythms with the crowd's projectiles. His trousers soaking wet, he sat still in the water, observing the small ice shards forming puzzle pieces that hit against each other. Behind his swollen eyelids, a photographic reel softened, oil paint metastasizing across the celluloid. Coughing violently, he leant back and slid into the deluge, his vision dropping like a server.

'Anya, are you still there? Do you see where I'm coming from?'

'I'm still here with you Carl. It's just that I'm not sure anymore. I'm just not sure.'

But behind his eyes, he was somewhere quite distant, sat perhaps at one of the small cafés in Kadriorg Park. As he walked his loop around the dry, dusty grass, he would see snow covered parts of Tallinn, the thin frosted branches of the leafless trees and small air pockets trapped underneath frozen puddles.

VFL — Four Immersions

Carl Campbell

Phase One — Ecological Harmony infused With a Post-Human Equity — An Elusive Utopia

The following report documents my week spent visiting the first phase of the VFL's Immersion Testing Programme. Before focusing on specific elements, ideas, cultural traits etc. that I encountered, I will proceed by offering a condensed overview of the society, focusing on the overall organisational structures and visible ideological frameworks pertaining to this given population.

Perhaps the most striking observation one can observe upon entering this first phase is a deep and overarching commitment to the notion that both land and resources should not only be distributed equally among the members of the population, but that with this equitable access comes a responsibility for each citizen. The right to access a given space or resource is inseparable from the responsibility to maintain this right for future generations. This notion of cooperation between the present and future generations is evidenced in all areas of the society's formation. The result of this is that privatised property, in the form of ownership, is made prohibited. While the members of the society have access to apartments which they are entitled to call their 'home', the underlying principle is that they do not in fact own the property. It is registered to their name, but this registration is valued for the way in which it allows the society to organise itself. No one citizen is permitted to be registered at more than one property, facilitating a system in which the primary objective is to house people, at the expense of impeding any one citizen from owning more property than they need.

One does not need to spend copious amounts of time in this society to perceive the highly advanced relationships between humans and technology. However, every element of this post-human harmonisation is predicated upon a systematic organisation which values the commons over individual gain. That is to say, the distribution and integration of these smart technologies form the infrastructure of this deeply equitable society. Therefore these technologies, far from merely offering the citizens additional benefits, are the basis through which the ideology of equity and ecological harmony are able to shape the organisation of society on all levels.

Within this society, the state as a visible, located institution is not apparent. Systems of voting, or even political parties, are non-existent. The state, if we shall refer to it as that, is perhaps best described as an autonomous organisation that is distributed amongst the population, with each citizen owning a stake in it. If there were once any opposition to this form of distributed governance, it seems to have died out: those leading the charge have either been outnumbered or have themselves come to accept the benefits offered by this form of governance. However, it is hard not to view this model with skepticism: while on the surface everything appears to function equitably, there was really no way of knowing how such a peaceful, internationally unified planet would react to any nation or group that threatened the status quo.

It would seem that it is only through this organisation — whereby it is in each citizens interest to maintain a form of stable governance — that the state itself is permitted to exist without having to intervene, unless completely necessary, in the lives of its members. Many people, when I asked them about the role of the state, took some time to respond, it being evident that they no longer thought of the state as an institution *per se*. Yet, rather than serving as an encouraging example of how a state can exist without intervening, it seemed instead that too many questions were left unanswered. If there is a state, and it *can* intervene, who takes these decisions? Why would an invisible — but still powerful — state be in any sense *better* than one we can see?

Perhaps one of the key roles almost every government has always had to fulfil comes in economic management. In this system it would appear quite different: a form of deeply matured blockchain functions not only as the society's economic pillar, but too as a form of managing production, distribution and disposal.

Instead of being viewed as corporate giants, intent on economic gain at the expense of the environment, autonomous companies 'work in harmony' with the citizens that use their services, this bond forming a carefully constructed mode of collaboration, in which both parties help to find the most equitable and sustainable solutions to the citizens' needs. These advanced blockchains coexist alongside a system of algorithms that predict consumers' needs and fulfil them by automated production. Running alongside these production systems are equally matured disassembly systems, which collect and recycle products when they have reached the end of their lifespan. Any parts that can be reused, in whatever way, are fed back into to the assembly system, thereby minimising waste to a percentage nearing zero.

Such intelligent systems of material recovery are made available through the careful tracking of all manafactured products. In a similar way to ISBN numbers, each item is given a specific geometric code which can be scanned and tracked, allowing the recycling methods to not only track waste, but to carefully modulate how any given product can be improved to increase its lifespan. In stark comparison to the widespread use of built in obsolescence that pervades every area of our current system, the given notion here is that an item should be valued not only by what it permits its user, but also for how long it will permit this. Yet such a neatly organised and clean system - while systematically impressive - fails to answer many fundamental questions, the most important being energy consumption. On the surface, everything functions immaculately. But where is the power for these energy-consuming blockchain systems coming from? Where are the enormous warehouses and server farms that would be needed to make such a system possble? Outwardly everything may appear sleek, clean and beautiful, but something so technologically complex would require ugly superstructures of satellites, undersea cables and complex networks of distribution factories. If these systems — like the state — are simply present but not visible, we should ask why is it that they are kept carefully out of sight?

In an equitable system as methodically organised as this one, there is apparently no need for universal basic income, as the material demands of each citizen are systematically realised through this carefully constructed, interwoven network of demand, supply and reproduction. Perhaps the most far-reaching result of this society is the gentle erosion of commodity capitalism, there being no need for materialistic endeavours when the products of the society are essentially all low-hanging fruit.

With an ever-expanding population, the question of how to equitably organise the remaining space was one of the key ecologcial questions. With both regional and international coordination, widespread city planning vowed to make both urban and rural environments available for every citizen. The one cost, as with all other elements, was that all new infrastructure had to fit in accordance with the careful monitoring of each ecosystem it affected. Of course, this was more than one person or group could manage. So the implementation of these new systems was left to AI architectural planning, which could not only monitor how each change would affect other nations and their ecosystems in the present, but also decades into the future. While the processes were near incomprehensible, the results were truly fascinating. In the cities themselves, a deep and careful planning of the general infrastructure has resulted in the construction of huge high-rise buildings in which intricate systems of disposal ensure that every household can function without generating unnecessary waste.

Beyond the walls of solar panels which power the building (seemingly throughout all seasons?), each of the high-rises' walls have been infused with trees and other vegetation which function as a CO_2 vacuum for the small amounts of pollution the city does produce. Running alongside the trees, being fed from large rain-collectors on the roof are filtration systems which ensure the trees are carefully watered, maintaining a structure of healthy, flourishing vegetation. Based on a system of bio-architecture that values a building for its 'ability to coexist with the non-human populations of a given urban space', these AI-designed units are built to house both humans and non-humans alike. The rooftop of each building, also infused with vegetation, are designed to be resting grounds for the city's bird populations. With perching spots built into the trees, alongside water baths and small hanging food containers, the bird populations which previously relied on scavenging in the city's waste (waste no longer available for the taking), exist in harmony with the unit's human population. These buildings are integrated throughout the entire city, viewed as the most equitable and sustainable forms of living available to an ever-growing population.

In both the natural and urban landscapes, the use of smart technologies to aid the recovery of previously damaged habitats are one of the core focuses of this new society. In the city itself, small, inoffensive machines running on algorithms move freely among the city, performing the role of street-cleaners and garbage handlers. This job serves as a pertinent example of a role that has been passed on to automated machines due both to its simplicity, as well as the collective recognition that it constitutes a job few humans wish to do. Considered not as an eye-sore or nuisance, the city's inhabitants hold a deep respect for the twenty-four hour shifts put in by such machines, as it is this work that makes possible the generally clean and hygienic society in which they live. It is quite common to see a group of people step aside to let a small cleaning bot move past them; a sense of respect and shared harmony existing between human and machine. But again, we must ask, what is the system that makes such an enormous, algorithmically-mapped cleaning system possible? Surely the energy and materials such a system requires outweight the need for robots to maintain what already appear to be really clean streets?

In the more rural landscapes, automated AI systems monitor all fluctuations in the environment; from pollution, to air pressure, to changes in sea levels. Supposedly set up in such a way as to inform humans before any harm or instability has the chance to escalate, this deep meshing of human organisation with machine learning only helps to further infuse the deep value humans place on the role of technology. From the predictions offered by those working in the area of biosphere restoration, the human population looks set to continue further along the path towards complete ecological harmonisation with the natural world, with all fears of implosion consisting of well kept records of a past world that narrowly avoided such collapse.

As this society continues to direct its efforts into such ecologically harmonising endeavours, the traditional notion of progress, as framed by neoliberal capitalism, has taken on a radically different form. Progress is not synonymous with growth, but is instead seen as a quest towards the biosphere's stability, material security and the development of intelligent methods of sustaining the deeply hospitable world which this society has succeeded in creating. Thriving throughout all corners of phase are new forms of creative endeavours (which we shall come to see in a later case study), the coexistence of humans and other forms of life, and perhaps, above all else, a deep-rooted sense of satisfaction with the present state of affairs. Notions of war, conflict or civil unrest, while being concepts all citizens appear to be familiar with, are framed as elements of the past. The population emphasise that maintaining this world will take dedication, compromise and responsibility, and the recognition that this is a small price to pay seems to be widespread. How such responsibility would fare under harsher environments didn't seem to be an important talking point: why worry about civil unrest or a shortage of resources when everyone has everything they could want?

When it comes to creative pursuits and the exploration of what it means to be human in this world, the results are multifaceted. With traditional politics having gradually eroded, so too have the notions of countercultures, cultural subversion or even trend-setting. Society welcomes the liberation of genders, new forms of relationships or even familiar structures. The deeply libertarian value of allowing people to do as they please as long as it doesn't infringe on others rights is taken as pure common sense. Perhaps predictably, in my entire time in this phase, no one ever mentioned a conflict of interests — something that seemed to have been smoothed over like all other forms of friction or dirt. Rather than serve as an inspiration, I couldn't help but consider the ironing out of all human conflcit to be almost intoxicating in its dreamlike simplicity.

In this world, if your way of living is in harmony with the natural world and your fellow citizens, there is really very little you can do that will raise any eyebrows, let alone fists. Running alongside this exploration of cultural liberation is the endorsement of a post-human politics of anthropo-techno fusion. Bodily augmentation has long since moved beyond a medical procedure to grant disabled citizens the ability to walk, hear or see again. Advancing both this technology and its societal acceptance, citizens are actively encouraged to explore such augmentation in the same way they might choose to explore their sexuality.

The same playfulness and liberation with which people approach this exploration is also manifest within their notion of work. Perhaps the most striking signifier of this blend comes through a common slang heard in this society, to swoop. Having heard this word used in multiple different contexts, I came to understand that the verb can be used interchangeably to signify 'to work', 'to play', or 'to create', all three being viewed as consisting of essentially the same type of endeavour, each notion feeding into and harmonising with the others.

While my relocation switch didn't appear to take me to different nations within the week long immersion, the general history of this new type of global restructuring dated back to Japan. It was, I was informed, the first society to reach such an advanced state. Once the pursuits of this nation were recognised internationally, its ideas are said to have spread across the Internet, reaching all corners of the developed world in a time of ecological crises when nations were desperately searching for answers. With its steady implementation in south east Asia, it eventually spread to the Americas, Africa & Europe, the logical procession of such an equitable system being the harmonising of the global population with the planet's ecosystems.

According to many in this world, while there has been inevitable teething problems and perhaps unavoidable conflicts of interests in the internationalisation of such radical societal shifts, the international community, by and large, appears to have accepted this new form of planetary organisation as the favourable option to the sixth mass extinction. Yet the mere fact that the relocation switch didn't lead me to any other 'nations', but instead kept me floating in this dreamy smart-city which people claim was based on the 'Japanese Model', seemed deeply suspicious. Has the whole world really merged into one homogenised automation? And is a world void of conclift also one void of cultural differences?

Case Studies

Absorbing the Sun into Vertical Lawns — The High-Rise Tenement Buildings

Perhaps the most ubiquitous structure of this society is the high-rise building; huge, carefully constructed and well integrated living quarters for the city's inhabitants. When I first had the opportunity to enter one, the careful division of space reminded me of Le Corbusier's *Unité d'Habitation,* the physical embodiment of his idea that 'the home is a machine for living in'. Yet it would be inaccurate to suggest that there is anything brutalist about these housing units. While being recognised as a careful and functional division of space, the integration of natural light, vegetation and aquatic installations gives one the impression of being inside a contemporary rehabilitation clinic. Lining the walls of each high-rise are trees and other vegetation, the space for such intertwining carefully built into the structure of the building itself. The result is that each small apartment sports a shaded balcony, with the natural greenery providing protection from the sun. Each building takes the shape of a hollowed-out cuboid, a small recreational garden being the centre point for each space. The four inner walls of the building, looking down onto the garden, are made entirely of glass, allowing for the building to be well-illuminated during the day. When the sun has set, the light captured by the immense solar panels built into the roof provide the building with energy during the night. As I walked through the building, it felt like the whole city consisted of cleanly cut glass and steel alone, with all mess or waste evaporating into thin air before it could tarnish the clean surfaces — as if human touch itself were too indecent for such minimal spaces.

Perhaps one of the most cinematic moments of my whole immersion came when a resident invited me to join them at one of the city's hilltop look out points for the fortnightly bird dance. Sat in a huge crowd, we waited patiently for a group of musicians to broadcast what they informed me was a new type of bird calling, 'a certain chant the flocks responded to'. Set against the backdrop of a crisp mauve sky, a series of high-pitched melodic calls reverberated through the urban space, triggering the simultaneous take-off of thousands of birds from several rooftops. For a moment, I saw the buildings almost as huge chimneys, the birds as black embers pouring from them, before recognising the inappropriateness of such a simile. When I turned to my fellow spectators, asking who organised it, they responded that it was a community initiative, again using the verb 'swooping', both to describe the birds movements, but also as a way of referring to this activity as one of work, creativity and play.

This type of shared creative activity is a common phenomenon inside the high-rises. Beyond the shared garden spaces, each building boasts a spacious hall one that is used for a huge range of activities, from performances, to group exercise, to regulation meetings. Having the opportunity to attend various activities, what stood out to me was the versatility of the space and the inhabitants willingness to continuously share their creative endeavours with each other. At one event I attended, a young girl had built a small wind-chime instrument which could be attached to the ventilation shafts at the buildings exterior. If each one were carefully constructed to chime a certain series of notes, each building in a given area could have its own distinct melodic loop, thereby, she believed, making it easier for each buildings' cat population to recognise their home. While I didn't remain long enough in this area to see this design put in place, what was memorable was both the willingness of the building's inhabitants to test out schemes like this, as well as their excitement for such inventions that dissolve the border between work and play. Of course, a society that *swoops* — instead of working in any traditional sense — may appeal hugely. But the question of where such resources were being magically produced still remained unanswered.

Pine Leaves Floating Between Veins — Bodily Augmentation & Societal Restructuring

One of the most striking elements witnessed in this phase was the experimentation at the edges of the human and the self. For anyone visiting this world, it would seem that the traditional notion of familial structures have been totally reshaped. While family structures do still exist, many members of this society choose to form relationships based on what they can 'gain' together from sharing a space or entering into agreements together. This sense of the word 'gain' is tied more closely to the word 'create'. 'Creative gain', as I will now refer to it, is a central tenet of this culture.

There seems to exist an underlying level of respect between different groups who chose to restructure their relationships in such radically different ways. As with most other innovations, if it is harmonious with other citizens' lives, there is little other criteria on which it can be scrutinised. Interestingly enough, these different groups, rather than seek out isolated spaces in which they can form a majority, appear to be quite content sharing their space in high-rise buildings with those who choose to pursue the traditional family structures. If both parties admire what the other does for its creative value, a natural respect forms between them, there being no need for distancing.

One group I encountered, a collection of roughly a dozen citizens whose gender identities were almost impossible to distinguish, cohabited a small apartment in which they viewed themselves as a 'creative unit', their bonds being formed based on the creative utility of each member. Having freely adopted other more common forms of bodily augmentation and decoration, such as the insertion of leaves under the skin as a type of tattoo, the groups enthusiasm for pushing the limits of the human's aesthetics and capabilities was instantly patent. When questioned about it, they seemed to fear a comparison between their goals and the transhumanist strive for corporeal transcendence offered through the Singularity. Their vision, they made sure to inform me, was not intent on *transcending* the body, but on enhancing it to 'benefit the largest possible number of life forms on Earth'. Yet while being deeply impressive on an aesthetic level, how such augmentation benefited other life forms — or even other members of their comunity — just wasn't tangible.

In some sense, their activity could be compared to an art collective in our society. Yet their cohabitation and sense of each member's creative utility seemed to pervade every element of their daily lives. In the case of this group, their focus was on the augmentation of the human voice to communicate with animals that were located in their city. Small voice box enhancers, or 'VBHs' as they referred to them, had been surgically input into their larynxes, allowing the members to sing bird songs, communicate with cats and even imitate the sounds of insects, such as grasshoppers and crickets. When I first came across this group, they had started their training to communicate with each other in bird song. While they had arrived at a point of being able to comprehend simple questions or directions, their focus was on trying to find ways of expressing parts of their personality through this new language, an endeavour they stressed was intended to better understand the personalities and desires of animals. Presenting their findings and updates on a monthly basis, I happened to be present for their demonstration in their high-rise's communal space. Consisting of a small lecture alongside a series of performances in which the augmented members sang a series of gentle melodic lines, the audience followed the subtitled words moving slowly along the projected screen. After explaining how they envisioned the possibility of being able to discuss elements such as urban planning with the bird populations, the audience broke out into applause, many parents encouraging their children to sign-up to the workshops offered by this group.

Automated Rafts Drifting In The Sun — Casual Coastline Maintenance

One of the areas I had the chance to visit, a weather monitoring centre located along this island's south coast, served as a case study into one of the most common occupations found within this society: supervision and monitoring of AI decision making. The humans who worked in this centre described their work as 'keeping an eye' on the large autonomous rafts floating in the oceans which measure currents. While monitoring this is their role, their day-to-day usually consists of reading or playing games together. This is what they described as the 'perk' of their job — the fact that while someone has to be here in case any unusual activity is detected, these detections are so uncommon that their role grants them ample time to educate themselves and dedicate time to their interests. Assuring me it was not always so easy, they recounted the hardship not so distant generations had gone through during the installation of such systems in a time when the oceans and coastal habitats were in serious degradation. While they recognised the benefits of the free time offered to them by such a position, they took their jobs 'very seriously', making sure to regularly stop their activities to examine the data coming in from the rafts. Akin to all other unsightly or undesirable elements of technology, it would seem that in this world the dangers of planet Earth itself have been muted out of existence. The idea that any natural disasters now consist of subdued tremors that can be tended to while painting or reading felt more sinister than any other element of this world.

The group's supervisor, a woman named Irene, spent her days stood outside the centre, painting the coastline, often inserting loose fauna in the images. Yet every hour, without fail, she would jump back into the control room to check on her colleagues, making sure there were no 'peculiarities' in the rafts' movements. When I asked her colleagues what the rafts were actually doing, I was surprised to see how well-informed they were, each of them being able to explain the processes of measuring coastal erosion, water pollution and even changes in the currents and seabed pressure. Even with the chaos of the Anthropocene apparently being many generations in the past, 'you can never be too careful,' they warned me, highlighting that all it could take is a change in the current to go unnoticed, and thousands of lives, human and non-human alike, would suddenly be put at risk.

Many of them spoke of other monitoring centres they'd worked in, noting how the routine was essentially the same, it was just the knowledge of a given system that you would need to learn. One man described his time supervising the smart systems of autonomous robots that worked specifically in land maintenance. These robots, he informed me, were designed to move through rural areas, digging through the Earth's surface to collect any waste that was hidden. Due to the huge damage that occurred in the previous century, the planet was still recovering, and part of this recovery was the gradual expulsion of plastic and other waste material buried deep in the surface. His role at this centre had been to monitor where the robots were harvesting the biggest yield of waste material, as this often indicated that it could have been a landfill site. As I nodded along, he apologised, before going on to explain what a landfill site was, evidently assuming that I had no idea.

Fluorescent Beaks Prizing Open a Can — The Evolutionary Research Centre

The final case study obtained during this immersion covers the workings of a specific centre located on the outskirts of the urban metropolis; the Evolutionary Research Centre. This location was recommended to me by the same group mentioned in the second case study. Catching one of the city's free electronic trams to the suburban neighbourhood, I came across the centre. As with everything in this phase, all places seem to be open for visitors looking to better understand the workings of their society.

Explaining that I wished to have a tour of the centre, two assistants said they'd be willing to show me around, just as the VHB group had assured me would be the case.

The centre was opened two decades ago by a team of scientists who perceived the necessity for certain animals to undergo a process of recovery that would help them evolve to their present day conditions. These centres are apparently now located all throughout the world, with a strong chain of communication being held between them to closely monitor vulnerable populations and to chart all evolutionary developments of these groups.

Many of these animals, they explained, were forced to evolve during the waning stages of global capitalism, an era in which systems of waste disposal had fallen into decline. The result of this was that many animals, birds in particular, had evolved specifically to feed themselves in those harsh environments. In one case, the Atlantic Puffin had developed a particularly long and thin beak which allowed it to prise food scraps from half opened metal tins. While such a beak was 'likely what allowed the bird to narrowly escape becoming extinct', the effects of such adaptation are now inhibiting this bird from flying long distances. Showing me their operating rooms, they allowed me to watch the careful process of trimming the birds beaks before returning them to their temporary habitats where they drink and eat small fish from wide water bowls.

We walked through the centre, passing by tanks filled with strange mammalian creatures I couldn't recognise: dolphin-like creatures with long tusks; different species of fish pulling at food with tiny, wafer-thin hands; cats with large, feathered ears. When I asked them what they hoped to do to help the animals that had evolved to such extremes, they informed me that not all of them were actually in need of assistance. The Bottlenose Dolphin, with its new trunk, was in many respects more efficient now than it had been before. When I enquired as to why it was being kept there, they assured me it would only be there for a short period of time while the local schools came to visit and learn about evolution.

'It's part of their curriculum, you see.' one of the assistants clarified.

Eventually we stopped in front of a series of tanks that housed large, muscular rats. At first the only immediate difference I noted from the ones I am familiar with was their size and physical build. It was then that the assistants pointed out the pouches on their stomachs, such as those found on marsupials and monotremes. These rats evolved such pouches as a way of storing food scraps in an era of scarcity. However, despite the obvious utility of such pouches, the waste scraps left inside often caused infections and were a perfect incubator for contagious diseases. Yet these rats, they noted, were quick learners, and through a series of games had quickly learnt the value of washing the insides of their pouches. What was beautiful, they said, was watching the mother rats start to teach this game to their children, indicating that their work at the centre would, they hoped, continue to pass from generation to generation.

When asked if their results had been predominantly positive, the assistants smiled, shaking their heads a little.

'You see, it's only really now that we're starting to rewild many of these animals. It's a long process, one that takes continual efforts not just on our behalf, but on everyone's.'

When I asked them to elaborate, one of the assistants highlighted that unless the conditions in their urban spaces remain constant, the efforts to help, for example, the Atlantic Puffin, would be in vain. They mentioned the new waste recycling systems they have in place, noting that even in a circular economy like theirs, if people aren't fastidious with their disposals and other cans end up in the ocean, it would be easy for other animals to continue trying to feed from them.

I left the centre perplexed, unsure of how such a centre fit in with the evolutionary time-frame of previous decades. When I had first arrived at this world, it seemed evident that the final stages of late global capitalism were not so far in the past. Yet these animals, unless evolving at radically new speeds, would have surely taken thousands of years to reach these new forms? Something was clearly off, either with the AI's temporal mapping, or with the narrative offered by the centre. Moreso, their process seemed based on a type of evolutionary morphic-resonance, whereby altering one animal would somehow alter the entire species over time. Neither of these questions were ever answered, and as the final scene started to fade to black, I left the world feeling disconcerted.

Final Reflections

For anyone visiting this world, the quest for universal bounty coupled with the strive for ecological harmony make instantly apparent the allurement such a system offers. This society, which could accurately be described as fully-automated luxury communism, provides its citizens with economic and ecological stability, high living standards and perhaps one of the most cherished luxuries of all: that of time itself to explore creativity and play. Even without reaching the same level of technological and ecological maturity as this society, there are myriad lessons to be learnt from the ways in which it has organised itself to achieve greater equity for all life on Earth. The cohabitation schemes, the erosion of the border between 'work', 'play' and 'creativity', and the perpetual strive for biosphere restoration through smart technologies are all notions we should look to learn from.

However, becoming enamoured with such a system without grasping how it came to be would be irresponsible. It would seem that our AI has merely spat out a lucid — but also textbook — example of Silicon Valley's dream of digital utopia. The same loose promises offered by the Singularity find their form here in an equally unconvincing manner.

While yes, there seems to be an awareness of the dangers of climate change and the need for global vigilance, there seems to be a outright blind spot when it comes to the question of energy — how is everything being powered, if running on complex, energy-consuming blockchain technologies? These are questions that couldn't be answered, and while it might be fun to imagine a population that *swoops* all day, it doesn't explain how this could lead to well-formed, pacified societies in which everyone has adequate material resources to sustain themselves. It also fails to answer how such international unification could sustain itself without the excessive ironing out of cultural and political differences.

Clearly, the very much extropian excess enjoyed by this society is not something we could arrive at by chance. Without a fully-formed and mature analysis of the data on which this world came to be, the setting will exist as nothing more than a techno-utopian dream, relying essentially on a cornucopian form of resolution in which technological growth will save us from ourselves. This is an ideological stance which we should treat with the greatest caution, as any optimistic reliance upon AI to offer us universal solutions to complex, multifaceted problems could undoubtedly lead us into greater confusion.

On a deeper, psychological level, this world patently adheres to the position that existential fullfilment and societal cohesion can be neatly managed through algorithms, urban planning and citizens' cooperation. Yet the darker and more sinister elements of human nature appear to have been simply erased in what we must surely consider a reductive manner. If, as it seems, our AI has chosen to create a virtual future governed by the philosophical stance of extropianism and transhumanism, it has performed exceptionally well. But it is crucial to note that the map is not the terrain. So for those of us who view these promises with skepticism, such an elusive utopia begs the question of whether technological advancement can ever alter human nature to such a radical extent?

Phase Two — Innovation, Local Alliances & the Failure to Coordinate in an Age of Societal Collapse

Throughout the time I spent in this second phase, the imminent sense that all stable forms of societal coordination are balanced on a razor's edge pervaded every element of daily life. The ghosts of a not-so-distant past continue to plague this world's global community, both structurally as well as psychologically. In short, this is a world of widespread chaos, collapse and a perpetual struggle to find stable ground on which new societies can be built. Only through understanding what came before can one really understand how the citizens of this world find themselves in such a fraught and turbulent situation. While the conditions somewhat vary from nation to nation, concurrent issues of energy shortages, organised crime, looting and a harrowing descent into tribalism were consistent in each nation I visited. This is a world of local alliance, brutal trade wars and a perpetual inability to coordinate in an age of societal and ecological collapse. Before exploring different facets of this world, it is necessary to first describe how such a society came to be. This is based on the reports and testimonies I received from a variety of sources.

In each area I visited, I informed the members I spoke to that I was a journalist — a profession which almost everyone values immensely. By inference, it seems that although most people don't think it's possible, hope for a larger, civilised society still burns strong. While the Internet remains active and there are still networks of journalists reporting online about the state of affairs in other countries, most of the coverage is lost as there are only a privileged few who can afford time online. Among these journalists, there are attempts made to foster relationships, but these are almost always made in vain as people are too preoccupied with creating stability within their small regions to focus on the larger picture.

When Blockchain Undercuts

For decades before the collapse occurred, investments were made in various economic blockchain technologies, moving the world towards the original techno-libertarian idea of a truly free market where governments were unable to interfere. With a new way to trade without the need for banks or third party ledgers, these new forms of tender undercut the official free market and took away one of government's main functions.

Huge data-mining and cooling houses began to spring up all over the globe, where such a technology was welcomed for its promise to democratise the market and remove third party interference. For many of the early instigators, this fringe philosophy of cyber-libertarianism that grew out of Silicon Valley in the nineties had finally found its place on the world stage. Heralded as a liberator of the masses, many thought that traditional economics was over.

However, the huge data houses required to sustain such a rapidly growing blockchain economy were simply too energy-consuming. Warning signs indicating that this new economy was utterly unsustainable were simply ignored. While this collapse was simmering, almost all governments worldwide refused to fund or support blockchain technologies as they were not 'technically' a public asset, even though everyone used them. If a crash were to occur, they would not be bailed out with public funds. Many economists warned that this was imminent, but were dismissed as politically-motivated critics intent on keeping the global community locked into an outdated and corrupt monetary system. In short, they were ignored.

Over time, an area in the black market opened for electricity hacking, with groups able to pay for illegal syphoning of electricity as a way of running these large data-mining warehouses. This over consumption led to inevitable power failures and eventually blackouts. As energy prices soared, so too did the cost of keeping this new economic model running.

Warehouse after warehouse were abandoned, as innumerous blockchain companies fled into new corners of the dark web, investing their cryptocurrencies into material assets and leaving their waning systems to crumble.

Suddenly, the radical new form of currency started to shut down. As the vast majority of the world's population had become so dependent on cryptocurrencies, the previous banks and forms of cash currency had grown near obsolete. With traditional economics as good as extinct, region after region suddenly became unable to source anything from outside their local periphery. Across all continents, where almost all nations had decided to jump on board the cryptocurrency trend, the results were devastating. With the system crashing, people scrambled to assemble any form of tender they could. Whether it was recognised by any official body was irrelevant: the point was to be able to use accumulated wealth to buy food.

Unfortunately, for many who had invested heavily in cryptocurrencies, all their money vanished into a void as the online platforms abandoned ship. The most brutal irony of all was that the sudden disappearance of value was akin — if not identical — to the catastrophic consequences of hyper-inflation. For those that spent their lives saving and investing, all was in vain. The only winners were those that had no savings but had put their wealth into material goods. Yet winning came with a price. From the information I had gathered while speaking to Olaf, a young Norweigan and one of the only people willing to speak at length about the crash, the transition to local currencies was one of the darkest periods known to that region.

Before any suitable form of tender could be established, those with the means to survive, principally farmers, made a literal killing through selling their produce at heightened prices. The main way to purchase these goods was either through a bailiff style, whereby electronic goods, cars and even property could be transferred for a steady income of food. But in many cases, Olaf informed me, violent theft of the most brutal kind proliferated at a quite uncontrollable rate. It was not uncommon to see armed mobs ransacking their neighbours' houses in order to feed their own families. This widespread adoption of tooth and nail violence was just one of the harrowing elements of a post-cryptocurrency and pre-local tender society. Olaf, whose detailed explanations stood in stark contrast to the hostile suspicion of most others, often stopped mid sentence while explaining these scenes, and just stared into space. When he did speak, he often repeated the same line: 'Much blood was spilled, often over something so insignificant'.

When I asked him to elaborate, he explained that before there was any currency, there were two options: an attempt at a civilised trade of goods, or crime. In most cases crime prevailed. Often someone would refuse a trade offer, perhaps a car for six months of fresh bread, and the person making the offer would become desperate and steal what little they could, using nothing but brute force to overcome the owner.

For a relatively short period, but one that felt like decades, Oslo became a city that never slept. Armed gangs would descend from nearby towns, ready to steal whatever provisions they could and kill anyone who tried to stop them. This movement worked both ways, as often many people from the south would ascend to the fishing villages along the west coast, ready to either barter or loot whatever they could from the storage units. Anyone with any control over any part of the food market, no matter how small, had to adapt. This in itself opened up a new found demand for bodyguards, a profession that the many took up. Fierce battles ensued on a regular basis, with throats being cut for the most meagre amounts of food.

You might be thinking, where was the government, the armed forces and the police during all of this? A problem that seemed to have ensued in each of the areas I visited, from Norway, to Chile to Algeria to Ukraine, was that before the crash, the need for and thus the presence of governments had been slowly diminishing. It wasn't so much that they had become extinct, for each nation, I have been told, had still resembled a nation with a ruling political party. But with the market completely undercut by cryptocurrencies, their roles were more as official overseers that regulated public assets, such as the health services. However, in perfect harmony with the ideals of techno-libertarianism, most of these assets fell into the hands of private companies who also traded in cryptocurrencies. When the crash did finally take place, those in government, i.e. the only ones who officially had any authority, retreated, taking what they could and looking to resettle in poorer, underdeveloped nations where blockchain had yet to colonise the economic system. There, a life of moderate wealth with no responsibility or need to solve the chaos of the rest of the world awaited them.

Case Studies

A Dormant Tank Awakens — When Artefacts Become Weapons

Nowhere was such a descent into tribalism more apparent than in Eastern Ukraine, where the presence of a previous military dictatorship came back into being in the most sinister of ways. In the centre of Konstantinovka, surrounded by desolate grey buildings, a group of men clad in black tracksuits and balaclavas clambered up onto a World War II memorial and repurposed an old tank that had stood static for nearly a century. All around the city, signs of civilised life hung in tatters. Abandoned apartment blocks with broken furniture littering the nearby pavements were the last signs of domesticity. Looted shops with smashed windows and empty shelves marked the streets where trade used to be conducted. Alongside old advertisements for clothes, electrical goods and even holidays, there were myriad signs advertising the very blockchain companies responsible for the collapse. The odd few had been graffitied with anti-libertarian slogans, with the call for strong socialism and a top down style of governance now desperately sought after. No such signs of systematic organisation were anywhere in sight. As I watched this group of vigilantes appropriate this historical artefact, I could only guess at their intentions. As the engine was filled with petrol from metal canisters, the tank which had stood lifeless for decades reemerged, ready to descend on whatever group this men were intent on overpowering. As I paused in a shop doorway, watching it roll across the broken concrete, an elderly woman (the only person willing to speak to me) informed me that ferocious battles were ensuing in the rural villages where agriculture was still the main industry. The para-military groups, according to her, had been employed by the farmers to protect their livestock and their crops. In return for their services, daily meals and living quarters were provided. When I asked her what she was doing in this abandoned city, she told me that she needed to return to her apartment to gather whatever was left: she now lived permanently in Armiansk, a small town in western Crimea where fishing was now the main source of food. She agreed to let me accompany her to the apartment block.

Inside the building, which used to house thousands of urban workers, almost every front door was kicked in, each apartment having been ransacked for any small resources left behind. When we reached her home on the twenty-second floor, the door had been ripped from its hinges, the small apartment mercilessly raided for its contents. I watched her step through the trail of broken material strewn out across the floor before she reached the bathroom. She told me she had expected nothing less, but was happy that the people who had raided it hadn't been as resourceful as they could have been. Bending down and removing a modest array of tools from her bag, I watched her remove all the screws and washers from the bathroom taps, pilling all the metal pieces into her small bag. When she had scaled the apartment, taking any tiny piece of equipment that could be reused, we climbed back across the broken door and left the apartment. In the distance you could hear gunfire erupting. From the hallway windows flashes of light lit up the overcast sky, as birds circled the disused buildings. She paused for a moment, patted down her pockets, and nodded to me emotionlessly as we left the building she had lived in almost all her life.

A Sword Fight In Algiers

What became most distressing about this experience was the parallel between what I witnessed in Ukraine with that in Algiers. In Algeria, the government and military seemed to have taken a leaf out of the European's book: fleeing the chaos with what commodities and wealth they could. In a strikingly similar way to the Arab Spring, young revolutionaries tried to utilise social media to coordinate a large scale takeover of the city. But with power failures constantly crashing the Internet connection, any widespread alignment was rendered impossible. The same plague of tribalism that swept Europe manifested in Algiers, leading many groups to take up arms and prepare for territorial disputes. It was then that the ransacking of the Museum de l'Armee Alger ensued. Suddenly, groups of youths armed with weapons as archaic as swords took to the streets, ready to form alliances and establish strongholds. These alliances, their formation based on necessity and a demand that each member can provide for the group, seemed to hold stronger than blood and lineage in many cases.

I had a chance to speak with one group who had survived the transition to local currency. Akin with Ukraine, these groups situate themselves between the cities and the rural areas, either protecting local farmers or heading to the urban areas to search for raw materials. What seemed different about Algiers was the level of coordination and the size of the groups. Here, the populous seemed more adept at coordinating across larger groups, with some contingencies consisting of thousands of members. While the difficulty of such large scale coordination was evident, the stability and safety offered by these memberships seemed widely desirable. Each member had their role, and was guaranteed security and fair access to the group's resources. The danger, they informed me, came when disputes happened between groups: while everyone seemed committed to resolving territorial or material skirmishes through the ambassadors of each contingency, it was near impossible to ensure that small-scale battles wouldn't break out when different missions were sourcing materials. This led to inevitable rivalries, vendettas and orquestrated attacks that could rapidly escalate without any clear way of finding a peaceful solution.

E-Ghosts of Techno Libertarianism — Abandoned Mining Towns

Before the aforementioned collapse, many of Scandinavia's rural landscapes were transformed into contemporary mining towns. With the landscape acting as a natural fridge to cool down the energy-consuming buildings, places such as Norway's west coast became a prime location for private companies to locate their data-mining warehouses. When the erection of thousands of such buildings occurred, each supported the mining and maintenance of multiple crypto-currencies. These centres, analogous with traditional mining towns, opened up a huge space in the market for new jobs in the industry.

Throughout many of these data strongholds, small towns were revitalised, with homes and public utilities being constructed for the new workforces. When the collapse did occur and the same companies that had funded these warehouses went into free-fall, the funds that were used to support the buildings vanished along with the necessity for such centres. In the short space of a year, prosperous towns that were thriving with vitality and economic possibilities suddenly lost their function. As industry dried up, so too did any reason to remain. Olaf gave me a tour of many of these ghost towns, telling me the story of their sharp descent into collapse and abandonment.

As we drove from town to town in his small jeep, it felt as if we were passing through a completely uninhabited part of the world. Barely a single other car passed us on the roads, with petrol now in such scarcity that people only used it when it was absolutely necessary. When I asked Olaf why he was using fuel chauffeuring me around on a tour, his response was that beyond surviving, the next most important element for almost every citizen was revival. When I asked him to elaborate, he explained that journalism fell into the field of revival, as communication — and in particular communication between nations — was of the utmost importance. Other endeavours, such as community rebuilding, coordination between disparate groups, the creation of a national currency and the distribution of goods in a manner that resembled the previous socialist scheme of state support were all considered vital. Even those involved in organised crime, he insisted, actually wanted a return to order.

Located in each town we stopped at, huge warehouses stood static, the cold winter batting against their iron walls. These buildings used to house thousands of computers, each of them burning through enormous amounts of energy in a race to 'mine' specific cryptocurrency e-coins. Every hour, different computers would 'win' a small bundle of coins, each prize signifying an enormous monetary value.

When we entered one warehouse, the insides had been torn apart, with wires, computer boards and bits of glass covering the damp concrete floors. Olaf informed me that there were two main reasons. Initially, people were so angry at the crash that they stormed the factories, damaging as much as they possibly could as a futile way of 'getting-back' at the companies. Not so long after, people realised that the raw materials could be stripped down and used for something: they returned on mass to loot anything they could find, even objects that had no apparent use. Each site had the feeling of a technological scrap yard; a mere dumping ground for disused electrical equipment that sat rusting in small puddles. While Norway had been hit hard, things were much worse in Iceland. According to him, the nation had started spending twice as much money on data-mining than on its other infrastructure, gambling away public funds on any company that wanted to set up a new factory. Eventually the hydroelectric and geothermal power sources that had provided the small nation with buckets of cheap, renewable power simply couldn't keep up with the demand. The fact that the cold climate allowed them to cut down on air-conditioning also came back to bite them. It was there, in Keflavik, that the first centre went into overload, leading to a system crash that spread throughout the nation. When I asked him if this was the global catalyst, he looked almost surprised. No, he told me. According to reports, nations worldwide were playing the same dangerous game. What happened were identical and concurrent collapses occurring independently of each other in multiple different nations. Iceland's disaster was simply the first, but no one thought the same thing could happen in *their* nation.

A Football Net Floating in the Ocean — Innovative Repurposing

One of the most widespread practices I witnessed during my time in Scandinavia was the innovative repurposing of raw materials. If there are any positives to take away from this phase, none are more patent than the sheer sense of resilience and resourcefulness shown by groups of humans when faced with societal collapse.

My first taste of this came when driving with Olaf back from one of the mining towns. Even in small areas, remnants of territorial disputes — in the forms of blood stained tarmac and burnt out cars — were ubiquitous. People simply didn't have time to clean up public space anymore. Moving through the depraved towns, Olaf explained that with all factories having been out of action, the simplest of things, such as fishing nets, had become a sought after luxury. Olaf had laughed as he said this. Along Norway's west coast, one of the tools that had always been in abundance were fishing nets. It was unthinkable not to be able to buy one. But as soon as the fear set in that tools were becoming scarce, looting ensued, followed by a culture of stockpiling and aggressive small scale trade wars. It was during that era that the most desperate sort of innovation sprung into life, with every corner of the cities being ransacked. He'd seemed hopeful for a better future; at least that was the impression he gave off. This became evident when he led me down to the coastline and pointed out towards the clusters of rocks that jutted out into the dark, foaming waters.

'Look, do you see what I'm pointing to? It's right there, half floating in the water, half tangled on the rocks. That's the football net from the Aker Stadium. Someone got so desperate that they managed to break in and steal the net, hoping that they'd catch something so big it wouldn't slip through those wide holes. We all say that when this crisis ends, when Norway is actually a functioning, united nation again, that net is going in our national museum as a memorandum of these times.'

From the ingenious to the bizarre, I came across all types of innovation which Olaf was always ready to explain. One small house we passed stood out because of its yellow metal roof. It turned out to be made from the shelves of a local supermarket, the stickers indicating sales still plastered across its surface. More extreme, but no less resourceful was the ransacking of contemporary art from the Institute of Modern Art in Stockholm. Almost smiling, Olaf explained that it was broken into when people realised one of the exhibitions, named *Circuitry,* consisted of huge quantities of raw materials presented as sculptures. Vicious fights were said to have broken out among people who entered, with blood stains still apparently covering the gallery's white walls. I asked Olaf if anyone saw the humorous side of art being reused for its original purpose. He didn't, saying that it was just another example of the animalistic nature of their society. It didn't matter that at one point the building was one of the most prestigious cultural centres in Scandinavia. Now it was just another looted building, no different from the innumerable empty supermarkets, restaurants and shops that just hung in the street, their windows smashed and lights permanently out.

Catching the Cloud with Weathered Hands — The Last Ambassadors of Globalism

Although for most humans I encountered, survival and local alliances were the key focus, there are still tiny contingencies that together constitute what I will refer to as Ambassadors of Globalism. These are small groups who dedicate their time to attempting to restore international communication and in particular the stability of the Internet. From the short time I spent with one group in Panama, I learnt that their responsibilities consist of maintaining online spaces in which communication between global journalists is fostered, as well as keeping track and monitoring the members that dedicate their time to safeguarding the material infrastructure of the Internet itself. This last responsibility may seem peculiar, but after witnessing the aggressive repurposing of raw materials in Scandinavia, it became immediately evident *why* the materials that actually make up the Internet would be sought after.

Mateus, one of the key coordinators in Panama, explained that in many areas of Eastern Europe, the ripping up of underwater ethernet cables had already led to 'dark-zones', the name given to areas completely cut off from the online world. If rubber couldn't be found from car tyres or other sources, cables in any form would run the risk of being torn up and melted down for reuse. The fact that the international community's ability to communicate depended on these cables simply wasn't important when winter storms were blowing ice-cold water through leaks in your roof. The same could be said for the warehouses that contained huge quantities of e-data. While many of them had, inevitably, temporarily shut down due to power failures, there were still enough operating so that the Internet — in a more restricted form — could still function. But these warehouses could also fall victim to looters at any moment, and the ability to communicate internationally remained balanced on a razor's edge.

When I went with Mateus to visit one of the warehouses, he gave me a journalist's visitors pass and I was greeted warmly by the armed guards who granted us access. Akin to Norway, journalists were treated with the utmost respect and lenience due to the service 'we' were seen to be paying to the global community. It was here that I learnt just how fearful this group were of digital collapse. Thiago, another coordinator, explained that since the late nineties most of the information that constitutes our global history is in digital form. Covering such disparate pools of knowledge, from birth records, scientific data, cultural documentation, almost all art and music along with historical, political and economic records, the evidence of most of humanity's activities for the past seventy years would be wiped. The problem was also that there was no way of storing such huge amounts of data beyond how it currently was: stored as data in warehouses. Thiago looked almost nauseous as he told me this, stressing that the human population faced a memory wipe on an unprecedented scale.

'You have to look at it this way, before the crash, the amount of digital data had been doubling every three years. Back fifty years ago around two-thousand and fifteen, we hit two thousand exabytes of stored digital data. To put it in perspective, that's equivalent to the entire USA being covered in sixty layers of encyclopedias. We kept growing, and now we're at seventy-three *million* layers, give or take a few. I mean, much of that data is just noise, but there's all of our signals in amongst it. That's what we need to search for and protect. So we've got teams looking to search out for the most valuable information in this sea of data so we can get it stored in the safest place possible. There's been huge chunks wiped out with the looting, but we could be facing systemic amnesia at any moment.'

When I asked Thiago if there were any personal losses, he explained to me that he'd been printing out what little he could with the small supplies of printer ink he sourced locally. With print books having gone extinct thirty years ago, all publications existed as e-books, floating in an unstable online space. He now had a small library, consisting of stacks of office paper on which works of literature, biology, anthropology and cultural history were printed. If everything collapsed and people resorted to looting the libraries for flammable material, there would still be some knowledge he'd cling on to.

Final Reflections

Perhaps what makes time spent in this world so harrowing is the unambiguous path that led to such a catastrophic turn of events. Audacious and careless investment into blockchain technologies, at the expense of both local and global ecologies, led to the gradual erosion of any safety net that could have caught humanity when the system eventually overloaded, as it seemed perhaps destined to do.

What has emerged in the remains of this system of advanced techno-libertarian capitalism demonstrates how unregulated technological and economic growth is unsustainable on a planet composed of finite resources. In this world, the global population suffer in lives which are gruelling, unpredictable and which show no signs of improving, so deep rooted is the damage. All of this can be fairly interpreted as the result of their ancestors irresponsibly spending their planetary inheritance, consuming huge amounts of energy and failing to match the economic boom with suitable infrastructure.

Yet, there are positives to take from such chaos. The ingenuity, resourcefulness and creative innovation of many groups demonstrate their ability to survive and coordinate in the face of societal collapse. The same can be said for the dedication and perseverance of the Ambassadors of Globalism, without whom this population would be moving dangerously close to collective amnesia. But how humans act once faced with such abhorrent conditions should not be our focus. Instead, it is crucial that we carefully consider what type of investments are being made in energy consuming technologies, especially ones on which the world economy and international relations rely. As witnessed in this world, such collapse can happen in a matter of days, foreseeable but also unpredictable in many senses. That we want to avoid such a condition is irrefutable. How we will restrict and regulate the technologies that could pave the way to such a future is another question.

Phase Three — Bird's Eye View of A Haunted Archipelago — The Cancellation of the Future across Isolated Islands of Nationalism

Life continues, but has somehow stopped.

— Mark Fisher

It is difficult, perhaps even illogical, to begin any analysis of this third phase without reference to the preceding one. In the previous world, we witnessed the remnants of a society that had gambled on blockchain technologies, one that led to (perhaps) inevitable societal collapse. While this world significantly differs in myriad aspects, what is patent is the strive for technological mastery present in each corner of this world.

Whereas previously, the overarching grand narrative was centred around blockchain's ability to liberate the world from the corruption of neoliberal market politics, in this world the narrative is one of national sovereignty made possible through each individual nation's strive towards technical independence. The irony is that in both worlds, these unabated propulsions towards technologically enhanced societies has come up against a brick wall that cannot be overcome: the ecological instability of the planet.

I would like to propose that somewhere along the path to both these worlds, a certain forking of ideas occurred, whereby phase two moved forward internationally, embracing techno-libertarianism, while phase three followed a different prong, pursuing a more protectionist path, working at the national rather than the global scale. The results in both worlds are cause for huge concern, with the destruction and depletion of natural resources leading the techno-infused ideologies of both movements towards implosion.

In this world, ideological nationalism and economic protectionism reign like a cold shadow across Earth, compelling the erosion of free trade and free movement, as each nation appears to adhere to the age-old dogma of 'our nation first'. This narrative moves insidiously and pervades all areas of life, from the obvious, such as fastidious border controls, to an unbounded descent into nostalgia on a cultural level. In a world where people struggle to imagine how the future could be better — or even *different* — there appears to have been a descent into a type of history tourism, whereby people indulge fully in the past as a form of escapism. Afterall, why look forward when there's nothing ahead of you?

One of the most alarming elements of this phase is the implementation of certain technologies that were manifest in the utopian world of phase one, such as material tracking devices. Whereas in phase one, these unique user codes for each material product were used for recycling and repurposing functions, in this world the same technologies are implemented to track the origin of each product, making sure that no 'foreign' materials, cheap or expensive, manage to slip into a nation's economy without being viciously taxed. These commonplace tracking devices are just one of many examples of the smart technologies being concurrently implemented throughout the global system.

While I highlight many of these in my case studies, it is worth mentioning the sharp rise in surveillance, such as through the proliferation of drones equipped with facial recognition technology. In many of the cities I found myself in, the continuous hum and bird-like movements darting across the sky felt at first invasive. Yet by the third day of immersion, the buzz had become so ubiquitous that I barely noticed it. Needless to say that for most citizens, the drones were now as good as invisible, perching like birds atop of buildings throughout the urban landscapes.

Such internalisation of surveillance technologies is also felt at ground level, where the proliferation of CCTV cameras is so excessive that I began to question whether these cameras actually functioned as cameras. One woman I spoke to in London, who refused to give her name, told me that the British government had imported tens of thousands of fake cameras from India, with the aim not of watching people's every move, but of making people consciously aware that they could be being watched at any given moment. According to her, only one out of every hundred cameras was actually a camera. The others were mere replicas which were impossible to tell apart from the real ones. The effect, like Jeremy Bentham's Panoptican prison, was that even if you probably weren't, you simply never knew if you were being watched. In times of energy scarcity, it was more efficient to have the illusion of surveillance on ground level and leave the high energy drones for real threats. What these threats actually were was unclear.

When I asked her if there had been any protest against this, she informed me that it was quite the contrary. With the possibility of international warfare still simmering, along with the perpetual fragmentation and weakening of global food supplies, people were no longer concerned with surveillance. A technological arms race, along with vicious trade wars meant that stability was the most sought after privilege. Most people, for better or for worse, had internalised the narrative of 'nothing to hide, nothing to fear'. Highlighting this shift in values, she explained that crime had hit an all time low. Not because everyone had suddenly become morally averse to criminal activity, but because the sentences were simply too high to risk it. In an age of chaos and shortages, something as small as shoplifting could land you seven years in jail. And given the foul conditions, even a month locked up with others who weren't 'team players' was enough to avert most temptations. Before she left me, she said that that the sign of a healthy democracy is one in which someone can commit a crime and get away with it. When I asked her to elaborate, she laughed and told me it needed no further explanation.

The maturation level of many of this phase's technologies suggest that it exists in a future harrowingly close to our present day world. Emerging technologies of deep fakes and their ability to render objective reporting obsolete has run its course, meaning that news, in the most literal sense, has become a means purely for disseminating narratives. With video footage no longer carrying any claim to truth, people are left to believe what they want to believe, not out of laziness, but simply because no other alternative exists.

Whether fortunately or not, most people appear to be aware of this and seem to ignore mainstream media channels all together. The news itself seems to be a mere way for different governments to save face, bolstering up national politics and drawing heady comparisons between their agenda and those of other nations. The citizen journalist, in a similar way to the previous phase, is still a role highly valued by many who want to search for truth: in a world not of collapsing communication, but of collapsing consensuses, the rise of voices that at least attempt to offer uncoloured perspectives gain traction online.

When I first heard about these independent journalists, I imagined they would be cracked down on by government surveillance and therefore nearly impossible to locate. Yet what is perhaps most sinister of all is that despite their work at illuminating the inconsistencies of such narratives, there is a widespread recognition that such accusations and clarifications are simply drops in a choppy ocean. To put it simply, everyone knows that their governments lie, and everyone also seems to believe that the international cooperation needed to combat systemic ecological collapse will not be brought about through grass-roots movements. If governments don't cooperate, no level of citizen engagement, no matter how popular, will break the deadlock. Such a fatalistic, despondent approach, while disheartening, seems also painfully accurate.

Such despondency regarding planetary stability manifests on both the micro and the macro level. In the same way that ordinary citizens recognise the inability of independent journalism to counteract fake news, individual governments seem to also acknowledge the tragedy of the commons that has manifest across international waters. With the need for international cooperation drowned out by the ever-increasing drive towards national sovereignty, much of international governmental communication revolves around perpetual blaming and accusations. If ocean life is on the brink of complete collapse, the fault must lie somewhere. What has ensued is a situation in which the only remaining surfaces of the world which technically belong to all nations are now actively avoided. Why bother pulling your weight when other nations won't follow suit? Act locally, think globally loses all tread. Such atomisation and bordering has led to one of the greatest tragedies of the commons the global population could conceive of: that of our waters and our air.

Case Studies

Brainless Occupation — Oceanic Collapse and the Tragedy of the Commons

It has been known to us for some time now that one species more than any other benefits from rising ocean temperatures. While coral reefs suffer from extended bleaching and other marine life are thrown dangerously out of balance with their natural habitats, the biggest and most patent of these changes is the disappearance of the artic sea caps.

Yet little attention was paid to the life that would actually flourish under these new conditions. Enter the new oceanic global player: the jellyfish. This creature, suited to warmer waters and which can reproduce throughout much of its lifespan, has now become the dominant force in the oceans of this phase. It is crucial to note that this is something scientists have noticed in today's world; something which only serves to make this manifestation more harrowing. So although presently we know of this possible rise in jellyfish activity, we have yet to see the outcome that

283

decades of temperature increase would incur. What some of the possible effects are form the basis for this first case study.

One of the areas I visited in this third phase was the Greek island of Crete. Having found myself ankle deep in the warm Mediterranean waters, I noticed a tangle of small purple threads moving close to the shoreline. Stepping back, I couldn't make out where the small threads were coming from. Soon after, my thoughts were interrupted by a young boy shouting at me from close behind, gesturing for me to move away from the coast. As I stepped backwards, I then realised why he seemed so concerned. The tangle soon started to multiply, with large dome-like heads eventually protruding from the sea foam. When he caught up with me, the boy pulled me back from the water and shook his finger in what I assumed meant 'do not enter'. He lead me back up to the house where his elder brother was waiting for us.

The waters around Crete, like so many other coastlines along the Mediterranean, are now 'no go' areas. Not only are the waters dangerously polluted, meaning that submerging oneself could lead to fatal infections, but are now home to these new deadly inhabitants. With a sharp decrease in all other marine life, the occupying force in warmer climates consists of all different types of jellyfish. Having killed off all coastal activities, leisurely and otherwise, the surge in their population has also brought with it huge infrastructural problems to many coastal cities.

One of the biggest issues continues to be drainage blockage, which happens on regular intervals as the creatures move from the waters through many of the pipes leading to the ocean. Councils of the affected cities tried vastly different measures, from wire meshes surrounding the drains to chemical substances designed to kill off and dissolve the jellyfish. With the fishing industries in these areas now extinct, there seems to be an almost fatalistic recklessness with which governments and councils approach oceanic problems.

When I asked my hosts what they thought of the chemicals being used to eradicate jellyfish, they told me that the waters were already so damaged that anything you could catch was probably contaminated anyway. As for swimming, they stuck to chlorinated pools only.

Xander and Elias, the two brothers I met at this location, offered to take me out on their boat to show me the failed technology the Greek government had funded in an attempt to clean up the island's shores. Around each of the islands, huge wire fences just under the surface had been erected in an attempt to both trap jellyfish and to prevent any more entering. The idea, they informed me, was that once the fence was up, the remaining jellyfish would die off and new ones wouldn't be able to enter. Eventually the coastlines would be clear of this invasive species and the beaches would be habitable again. Yet, as with many large-scale technologies developed to serve one cause, the outcome turned out to be both drastically and ironically different. The fence did serve to keep jellyfish from leaving, but the downfall for the designers was a failure to really understand how jellyfish reproduce. For adult, or medusa jellyfish, the process involves the release of sperm and eggs into water, forming what is known as a planula. In this larval stage of their life, the planula hooks onto any smooth surface and grows into the polyp, something which resembles a small sea anemone. During this process asexual reproduction occurs, with the polyps cloning themselves and entering the next stage of life named ephyra. This form then grows into an adult medusa jellyfish. So while the Greek engineers who designed a fence with minute holes believed they would prevent jellyfish from entering, they failed to appreciate that the eggs themselves would pass through the holes and cling to the fence. The result is that each island now effectively has a breeding fence surrounding it, creating a insulated tank of jellyfish that cannot move away from the island. The Greek government, they told me, were waiting to find out how best to remove these long, expensive fences, spanning the hundreds of kilometres around each island.

From what I gathered from Xander and Elias, these fences are just a further extension of border controls that are now present in all nations. Where huge fences have been constructed on land to curb immigration, these large underwater fences are seen as defences against 'foreign forces'; in this case, the jellyfish. It is not, in their view, that consequences of global irresponsibility have lead to this level of oceanic destruction, but instead that neighbouring states have acted rashly and now they must pay the price. There could not be a clearer image of an international tragedy of the commons. National and international waters alike are falling prey to the damages of post-industrialised societies, but the blame will forever lie 'over there', absolving everyone and no one simultaneously.

Artisan Populism — A Virus Hidden in a Jar of Sauerkraut.

The preference for local in this society seems to have pervaded all levels of cultural life. From the obvious areas such as food and community politics, the UK seemed like any other nation pushing through the wave of nationalism that seems to be moving on a global scale.

One group I stumbled across were members of a local ceramics club in Blackpool. Having accepted their invitation to a workshop, I was granted a look at the rise in local artisan trades, where such members make 'authentic' and 'unique' artefacts that they sell at local markets. This obsession with everything local, with the handmade and the regionally sourced came, however, with sinister undertones. Whereas at first I took it to be a quaint local initiative, it seems more to be a rejection of global, mass produced products than it did a celebration of the local. I heard many of the dealers making quite brazen remarks that 'no foreign hands had touched it', so there were no diseases coming hidden inside the small ceramic pots. What I took to be a rather trite xenophobic remark turned out to have a much more complex source: a deadly fungal virus of supposedly Polish origin had in fact broken out in Cornwall less than a few years ago, wiping out a sixth of the population. The fungus had apparently been living inside a jar of Sauerkraut, and spread from one person to the next once the first victim had been contaminated. People jokingly described it as similar to the plague, with bile being built up and eventually choking those suffering from the illness. It had been nicknamed 'global melancholic', almost as a warning to people not to be nostalgic for a system which could so easily bring foreign diseases to your land.

Yet later on, when I spoke to a group of teenagers on the beach, a girl named Cara told me that some believed it had actually come from water contamination, but had been sold as a foreign disease to further strengthen the government's protectionist policies. This seemed like a much more plausible explanation, but one not shared by the majority of the population.

Catching Bygone Waves inside a Headset — The Virtual Tourists of History

One definition of VR: Hope for a medium that could convery dreaming,

— Jaron Lanier

Jaron Lanier once wrote that virtual reality is the most humanistic approach to information, as the technology allows you to feel your consciousness in its most pure form. You are the fixed point in a system where everything else can change. For Lanier, VR is the technology that highlights the existence of your subjective experience: it proves you are real.

While already making waves in our current era, virtual reality tourism seems to have been marketed as the perfect form of escapism in a world void of hope or novelty. Rather than as a form of technology which proves you are real, the use of VR in this world appears to be a desperate strive towards escaping reality through dreaming. Yet from what I gathered, this form of dreaming — or existing in past worlds — feels more like a form of cultural inebriation than any attempt to envision a better future.

With travel permits even for tourists now proving to be either extortionately expensive or impossible to obtain, many people I discovered now choose to spend their time in the past. This form of cultural nostalgia played out most clearly in many people's desire to switch off from the world by losing themselves in the archives of the Internet. In many bars or cafés I walked past in Los Angeles, it was common to see people sitting with their tablets, journeying back to other eras or spaces less harsh and restrictive than their current one. One of the most common and saddest forms was seeing many adults scrolling around on what looked like Google maps, dropping their pins and wandering virtually through distant corners of the globe, perhaps revisiting places they knew were no longer reachable.

Yet a more advanced form of cultural ennui and escapism was evident at Long Beach on what I assumed was a summer's afternoon, as the climate seemed to be relatively akin to our current one. As I walked along the coastline during the morning hours, plastic and litter churned up on the shores. Teams of workers who clear the beach of debris every morning worked as if they were shovelling snow, making the waters moderately presentable for people to simply look at. With water and air temperatures now incredibly high, these beaches are thriving during the summer months. It was here that a deep desire to flee — both in a spatial but also temporal sense — was made present through the possibility of virtual reality travel.

All along the beach, crowds of people slouched in their deck chairs, their skin gently burning in the low afternoon sunlight, creating goggle lines above their eyebrows. Some sat with their feet resting in paddling pools of water, while others picked at wilting ice creams or cold drinks. When I asked a few red-faced members who had removed their masks where exactly they'd been, they remarked that they couldn't tell exactly where, but some place that looked like Machu Picchu. Another informed me that they'd been at a drive-in cinema watching a horror film, sometime back in the eighties. The location didn't matter to them as much as the era. Others that stood with their feet water in shallow pools told me that they'd been at a *BTS* music concert in Seoul, something that 'never got boring'. Another young woman standing by herself showed me a new catalogue of 'exotica' locations that had been developed by that year, crassly covering everything from Amazon rainforest excursions to surfing in Bali.

As I sat watching the clusters of people locked in their headsets, I couldn't decide whether such VR tourism seemed therapeutic, or was merely nostalgic escapism as a form of inebriation. Was there any essential difference between watching a music video from the eighties on Youtube or 'attending' one in a headset? It seemed understandable that people wanted to escape their spatial surroundings, but also wanted to journey back in time as virtual tourists to enjoy the pleasures of a world not plagued by international tensions and widespread restrictions. With their future having been cancelled, time seemed to stand still, and any movement — even one towards the past — appeared to be less painful than stagnation.

A Desolate Uranium Jungle — Nuclear Power Breakdown in France

In the late 1980's in Ukraine, not so long after the nuclear accident of 1986, two opposing movements surged throughout the nation: ecological nationalism and economic nationalism. After the disaster, many writers who had championed the nuclear plants in Ukraine as emblematic of the nation's prosperity and wealth quickly re-evaluated their position and became champions of Ukrainian ecological-nationalism. The rhetoric was inherently anti-Russian, with the central government in Moscow being blamed for allowing such a badly equipped and under-staffed plant to be run on Ukrainian soil. The consensus in Kiev was that no nuclear programmes should ever run in Ukraine after such a catastrophic distaster had rendered huge areas of the country uninhabitable. But how would

Ukraine then bolster up the economy, and would such ecological stances provide the nation with alimentation and job security? It would turn out that, in fact, it couldn't.

During the nineties, less than a decade after the Chernobyl disaster, the construction of new power plants on Ukrainian soil went underway. The same academics and politicians that had argued for ecological solutions and green politics suddenly changed their rhetoric, highlighting the necessity of a strong economy in which people could receive a decent living standard, regular meals and job security. Such a case study has provided us with a clear insight into the huge challenges facing those that lobby for sustainable economies.

When I found myself standing in a small, abandoned port town in Le Havre, the tragedy of Chernobyl was fresh in my mind. France — that for many decades has been one of the world leaders in clean nuclear energy — fell from grace when a declining economy forced them to ramp up their nuclear programme at the expense of safety measures. From what I gathered from locals I spoke to, the arguments for more power plants were supported by the majority of the population. The country needed energy and couldn't function if its grid went down. Now, following the same trajectory as Ukraine, the rise in green politics and a demand for more safety measures was present. Extreme rates of thyroid cancer, international trade sanctions and huge areas of uninhabitable land meant that the country needed a new approach. Yet, I wondered how many years it would take before the demand for energy started overshadow such ecological leanings.

As I walked through this desolate, devastated area that spans from the northwest of France all the way to Lyon, Bilbao and Zaragoza, I was surprised to see that many humans were present. I'd heard of the nuclear collapse from Cara in Blackpool, but wasn't sure if I'd get to visit the area of the disaster. While all dressed in rubber suits fitted with face masks, many appeared to be going about their daily lives. Amongst them were investigation teams that appeared to be collecting data on the state of the city: officers spoke with local residents, informing them that scientists would be measuring levels of radiation in the atmosphere to ensure the city was fit for habitation. From a distance I watched them examining both the air levels and also placing large metal rods into the soil in the local parks.

From what snippets of conversation I could listen into, I gathered that the meltdown, in a similar fashion to Fukushima, had been caused not by human error, but through a natural disaster. In this case, winter storms coming in from the Atlantic had caused powerful waves which flooded part of Brest. The question was not whether the meltdown could have been prevented, but whether a power plant like this should have ever been built so close to the coastline in the first place. Thinking back to the stories I'd heard from England, it seemed that this was the most likely cause of all the deaths in Cornwall, even despite the winds and currents carrying the radioactive material towards the south. The story of contamination from Polish goods suddenly seemed like a desperate political move to shift the blame.

Dust Settling on a Lens Façade — Fake Cameras and Advanced Surveillance Capitalism in India

I will have spent my life trying to understand the function of remembering, which is not the opposite of forgetting, but rather its lining. We do not remember. We rewrite memory much as history is rewritten. How can one remember thirst?

— Chris Marker

Whereas time spent in Europe and America presented me with a view of receding economies and cultural stagnation, my time in two other continents painted quite a different picture. In Europe, failed technological

291

projects, scarcity and bitter trade wars between isolated nations seemed to be the new bedrock. The story in India was quite different, where an access to a wealth of natural resources now paved the way to economic sovereignty. I will focus on the brief spell I passed in Mumbai, where a taste of India as a global superpower came hand in hand with sinister politics and a strong rousing of nationalism.

The first thing I noted after my relocation button landed me in India was a large camera staring back at me. It was a rampantly busy street in what I afterwards learnt was Kandivali West. A small red light flashed on the camera, which instantly made me feel that I was being registered. Yet what was strange about this camera was that it couldn't have been recording me: coated across the lens was a layer of orange dust so thick that nothing could have been detectable. It may seem strange for me to be focusing on this minor detail. But such a camera is emblematic of this new India, in which state surveillance, citizen registration and a vicious point scoring system which ranks all members of society seems to have long passed the level currently established in China.

Akin to the UK, part of this new system is an embodiment of the adage 'nothing to hide, nothing to fear'. Only after some brief and restricted conversations with a few journalists did I discover that cameras such as this one were not cameras at all: they were simply replicas. As in the UK, hundreds of thousands of fake cameras are positioned around the city. Dispersed amongst them are highly advanced facial recognition cameras, running around the clock and gathering data about every citizen they view. If London had given me a taste of the Panopticon, the idea had been followed to its extreme here.

Perhaps the next question should be, 'why is India implementing such a ruthless surveillance system? What does it have to protect?' From what I could gather from local news channels, India was now sitting on a goldmine of oil reserves, guarding itself against other nations by investing heavily in bio-weapons. It was reported to be in first position when it came to the global arms race. Any nation that wanted to trade with it would only reach a deal on their terms. And with global oil supplies now at an all time low, any nation that suddenly discovered it was geographically located on top of such a gold mine would find itself calling the shots. Yet that still doesn't answer the question of surveillance? Only late into my visit in Mumbai did it all become clear.

One afternoon (it is hard to tell exactly how long days last in this immersion), I found myself at a government rally in Dadar, where a huge screen showed a government spokespersons relaying news of the police's latest catch: a Chinese spy sent to gather information about their nuclear programme. A multitude of supporters filled every corner of the street, and when a man who I assumed was the president appeared on the screen, a wild, almost frenzied energy broke through the crowd. Supporters shouted words of praise for a leader that was 'keeping the nation on top of the world'. There was something about this spiritual, almost magical realm of political support that nauseated me. The video itself, which had the aesthetic of a livestream — while also being cut up with previous recordings and formed from multiple sources — morphed and warped in a way that almost anyone today would recognise as constituting a deep fake. Yet here there seemed to be no protest at such clearly synthetic media. Whether this was due to a lack of perception, interest, or simply because this was now the normal way of delivering information, wasn't obvious.

As I spoke to many members of the crowd, their explanations for why such crackdowns were necessary seemed to be based on loose excerpts of information regarding previous tensions. Yet even when one group tried to explain the political happenings of the previous month, there appeared to be a constant need to correct each other, to recall other information or reframe how the other person was recounting the events. In this sense — along with their continuous reference to the videos playing on the screen — it seemed that their very memories of the recent past were being updated in realtime.

While I saw too little of this nation or its politics to be able to really comment on the population's condition, I felt while standing there that a new narrative of worldly dominance and entitlement had awoken within them. When this synthetic video of their president, posing as a spiritual leader of sorts, spoke to them of their strive for economic and global dominance, the crowd seemed to transcend to a state of berserk ecstasy. Although I didn't experience this in any other place I visited, it seemed that such conditions for the merging of synthetic politics with spiritual self-realisation would perpetuate as a threat to the stability of international relations, wherever it happened to spring up.

Liquid Tender Hidden in Stone — The Rise of Central Africa as the New Global Mineral Basket

If access to finite materials has become the measure of a stable society, following shortly behind India were many nations in Central Africa. While I only spent a very brief period in the Democratic Republic of the Congo, I was told through an acquaintance I made that the nation was not unique in its new position as a dominant force on the global market.

With huge sources of nickel and ore springing up all across the central African nations, new alliances had formed between them in which they privileged trade between neighbouring (or close to neighbouring) states and rose their prices for other continents. The result, while not as technologically infused as the society I witnessed in the first phase, evidences much of the same ethos. Along with intricate 'climate agreements', a focus on creating gregarious societies in which natural wealth is pumped back into the economy and social infrastructure has prevailed.

Davina, a young woman I spoke to in Kinshasa informed me that these agreements were to ensure that with the fluctuating climate, no nation would, in theory, be left to suffer during particularly difficult spells. The agreements were based on reciprocity and a sort of pan-continental unification, in which multiple African nations agreed to distribute resources and materials to ensure the health of the alliance as a whole. She explained that in Tanzania, for example, such severe droughts and crop failures due to climate change would have left the majority of the nation without food. But new freedom of movement laws, alongside a reciprocal trade deal, meant that resources were dropped in from neighbouring states.

When it comes to trading with nations outside of this new alliance, the rules are slightly different. There seems to be a more subtle system of loyalty to one's 'own'. This comes through the prioritising of sub-continental stability over global trade. In short, the resources and goods extracted from these nationalised mines seemed to remain where they originate. If they are traded to any other nations, the prices are astronomical, the idea being that the huge amounts of economic profit gained will be directed back into their economy.

Life is by no means care free in these nations. With the threat of unprecedented damage and loss from climate change always in sight, they have learnt to prioritise the type of climate preparation that was not successfully established in other continents. Huge food banks of dried produce have been erected through the nation, along with seed vaults, shock-proof irrigation systems and underground bunkers filled with medical supplies.

When Davina invited me to see her small rooftop garden on top of her apartment block, I felt a certain sense of déjà vu for the apartments in phase one. From the top of the building, I noticed that each apartment block had a similar system of greenery growing from the rooftops. Part of their new social system, she explained to me, was not merely to produce food in the cities, but to help the urban population to learn basic agricultural skills as part of the national curriculum. With the possibility of harsh droughts always present, the government wanted as many citizens as possible to know basic horticultural skills which could be used in the proliferation of 'cool-houses' spread throughout the capital. These were, as they sounded, carefully controlled environments in which produce could be grown without being affected by soaring temperatures. While the produce from these couldn't feed the entire nation, it provided huge amounts to the system each year.

Unfortunately, questions of how to power and sustain such enormous cooling stations again were not part of the conversation. So while the system may have looked carefully organised, equitable and ecological, was the energy powering it still coming from those same sources that caused the droughts, forstest fires and soaring temperatures? If the same system that necessitated such cooling stations now enabled them to function, what had actually changed? Was everything locked carefully in a carbon loop? Or was it just as polluting as before?

As I stood with Davina watching birds take off from the rooftops, I had to say that overall I understood why they had preferenced such a system of reciprocity. Through trading only between the nations in this alliance, shortages seemed to be kept mostly at bay. The only price paid, at least in this moment, was a lack of international goods. But when the richness of their lands provides them with sufficient alimentation and raw materials, preferencing stability could seem logical.

However, even if the results did seem to speak for themselves, in a world in which ecological stability feels deeply fragile, the longevity of any system that preferences the local over international felt questionable. Akin to the first phase, much of the technology such a system would surely depend on seems to be either non-existent or kept neatly out of sight.

Final Reflections

What must be taken away from this phase is how dangerously close it is to our present world. While far more extreme, many, if not all of the elements present in this phase have already emerged in a more premature form in the twenty-first century. From the international arms race and rise of state nationalism, to ever-more sophisticated surveillance technologies, the world as we see it here is frightfully similar to our own. Most alarming of all has to be the epistemic collapse of a shared narrative, caused in most part through the proliferation of deep fakes and an unwillingness by most nations to engage in international cooperation. The message reads clearly: with the track we are presently on, this third phase seems quite plausible.

Phase Four — When Transparency Becomes Mirror — Advanced Algorithm Capitalism and Cultural Pastiche in a New Planetary Cognitive Ecology.

From a cluttered desktop whose complicated topography acts as an external memory device for its messiness-inclined owner, to the computer on which I am typing this, to the increasingly dense network of "smart" technologies that are reconfiguring human lives in developed societies, human subjects are no longer contained — or even defined — by the boundaries of their skin.

— N. Katherine Hayles

The above quote was published in 2017, when many digital theorists were stressing the importance of rethinking how we, as human beings, conceive of other actors that are cognisant. Hayles put forward the idea of 'unthought' to mean a mode of interacting with the world enmeshed in the 'eternal present' that forever eludes the belated grasp of consciousness.

As our societies become ever more interconnected, with cognition manifesting in the assemblages of technical actors that make up our lives, there is a pressing need to reconsider not only what these assemblages represent, but also what the human represents *within* these planetary cognitive ecologies.

In our fourth and final phase, we have come to see the mature stage of such technical assemblages. Before us sits a world of heightened interconnection, where the complete amalgamation of the political and economic spheres with AI modulated capitalism now dictates and governs all areas of life. Before I commence my analysis and specific case studies, it is worth reminding the reader that the technological structure of our first and fourth phases are uncannily similar. The focus point will be on how these technical systems have produced significantly different cultures and global economic structures.

Currently, advances in machine learning are coming to dictate much of the world's decision making, as throughout our smart cities, the embedding of AI in all aspects of our lives continues unabated. If our current investment and prioritisation of this mode of management continues, it is possible to see how we could find ourselves in a world similar to this phase.

In this global structure, the disparity witnessed between nations in the previous phase is simply not present. Akin to the first phase, where heightened uses of technology seemed to spread and stabilise across all nations, here the use of AI as a tool for societal structuring has been pushed to its logical extreme. It could be said that heightened surveillance has created a system similar to the surveillance state we witnessed in our previous phase. However, the surveillance in this world comes not through facial recognition cameras, but through algorithmic tracking and monitoring. This happens on all levels, but most crucially through the use of AI to distribute and monitor work tasks.

One of the key issues resolved in this global society was the balance between universal economic security and a sense of purpose. The key to this was a careful rethinking of UBI as a form of societal structuring. One of the questions that both UBI advocates and opponents have examined is whether populations at large can find a purpose when everything is provided automatically. As the old adage goes, people will still revolt with a full stomach, so economic security in itself will never be enough: there has to be some sense of belonging, value and above all motivation to contribute to society.

Another issue has been the question of UBI dependency. Alaska during the 2010's has proved to be an invaluable case study, demonstrating that once UBI is a given, it runs the risk of overriding all other political issues should any party want to take it away or even reduce it. So how has this society faired differently? One key element is that UBI is still what is purports to be: basic income. While it has sufficed to almost eradicate poverty from all corners of the globe, there is still a sense that a better life depends on the individual's desires and goals. The result is a secure safety net from which each member can pursue prosperity and personal growth. However, for much of the population, time has become the new sought after currency, with the vast majority recognising that minimal work, alongside their basic income, paves the way for a life of leisure in which there is little if any interference from external governing forces.

With most jobs taken by automation, many governments set about creating a scheme whereby every citizen has to work one day a week, with each day being different. Some days consist of factory work or in cleaning the streets, others are spent supervising AIs running restaurants or bars. Any low skilled work that can be done with no training makes up this programme. The continuous changing of jobs 'functions as a way of preventing the boredom that comes with the repetition of monotonous work'. When I asked one of the academics I met at a government think-tank to elaborate, she told me how the AI had calculated that a one day week, or 'micro-job', was optimal. She explained to me that after much trial and error, one day a week seemed to be the perfect balance between feeling useful and feeling liberated. Any more and people slowly started to resent the work. Much less and people would feel useless.

When the workings of this system were first explained to me, I found it hard to believe that such a widespread societal infrastructure could function without the predictable pitfalls of crime, corruption, or nepotistic management. I also found it hard to understand how a system could keep itself afloat when much of the population seemed to only work four days per month. Then I discovered that the governing body of each interconnected system was not made up of human actors, but of coordinated AIs that worked as number crunchers. When it comes to decision making, AI dominates this society on almost every level.

Rather than individual companies or businesses in which employees learn specific trades and apply them accordingly week in week out, much of the functioning of the society works on algorithm based work assignments that are spread equally throughout the populus. Perhaps the most impressive thing about such work is that no one is exempt, as every member of the society, no matter how wealthy, is obliged to do their mandatory monthly work days to gain their UBI and be entitled to basic rights, such as free health care.

Of course, there are those who still choose to work other jobs or to work six day weeks in order to gain capital. But at the baseline, each member is obliged to their four days per month, the reward being that they don't *need* to work any more: it is purely their choice. In essence, the system is not so different from that found in our contemporary factories: workers clock in at warehouses, carry out tasks alongside machines which track their work and monitor their progress. Each shift is carefully documented and stored, meaning that there is always documentation of a worker's presence or absence. Such a system is at play here, with each member's UBI only released once their four days are completed each month. You might think, what does this matter if they have another job? The answer is that clocking-in and out doesn't only release their UBI. If this work isn't completed, a person's government issued bank account, linked to them as an e-passport, is locked. If it sounds sinister and oppressive, the workers I met evidenced no frustrations.

My next query was to do with crime, and in particular money laundering. How could such a society protect itself against the seemingly inevitable human desire to cheat the system and jeopardise the stability of such philanthropic economic policies? The answer, again, comes down to advanced AI systems that track all movement of goods, including money itself. As the world now trades solely in e-currency, it is near impossible to move money through any online platform while evading the fiscalisation of AI monitors that work specifically to crack down on financial crime.

Again, this may sound extreme, but the population seems to show no distaste for such supervision. The key to understanding this widespread acceptance can only be reached by examining a term which has been passed around in the AI community for the last decade: the alignment problem.

The idea of AI alignment comes to do with recognising that AI can never really be 'evil', but can only be misaligned with out goals. Yet if we ascertain to align our desires and aims as carefully as possible with such advanced AI systems, the results *can* be of inestimable benefit. Such a deep trust for and recognition of AI as a means to emancipate humanity from many of its former problems is accepted unwaveringly amongst this population. From AI judiciary systems, to the normalisation of driverless transportation, all areas of this society have become not only digitalised, but algorithmically dictated. So if a crime does occur, and an AI system catches the culprit, the evidence is usually plain for the courts to see. Should such an incident occur, an AI judge which functions, ostensibly, without the bias of previous AI systems, will be able to decipher a fair sentence. How such 'neutral' or unbiased code could be created through AI wasn't exactly clear.

This is taken to another level when it comes to government decision making, where groups of elected officials function as spokespersons and overseers of AI based decision-making which organises all areas of commerce, industry and agriculture. The government officials, elected through online survey type pages that are completed when receiving UBI, are seen as mostly insignificant actors fulfilling a function like any other. With full recognition of the AI's superior decision-making abilities, the role of the politician need not entail anything other than a spokesperson.

In a sense, it would be wrong to say that the populous simply trust the AI. Their belief in its abilitities to deliver tend more towards a sense of faith. Even with complete transparency, there seems to be a blindspot when it comes to the comprehension of AI *processes*. If you want to see the results, you *are* able to examine the open government pages. But most people don't, and have little interest in such matters. If it works, why waste time examining the workings?

It is here that the title of this report was taken from, as akin to present day Estonia, perhaps the most sacred element of this system is its transparency. Almost everyone I spoke to referred to it. Many even showed me on their tablets how easy it was to log into any government page to view exactly what it had been doing, what decisions were taken by the AI and what the predicted changes would be. This is merely one example of such transparency and whether it worked on all levels is, undoubtedly, impossible to say. But in line with the techno-utopian dream of a fair, open and transparent society in which every member has the right to track (and thus, the responsibility to accept *being* tracked), this system seemed to be held in the highest regard. With everything functioning so well, the dangers of such a system weren't as easy to locate. So how does transparency become a hall of mirrors?

Case Studies

Automated Voices Sealed in Latex — A Sex-Doll Factory in Detroit.

One of the most memorable locations I visited during my time in this phase was a series of factories located on the outskirts of southern Detroit. The factories themselves functioned like all others: automated robots completed almost all the tasks while a few humans oversaw the process, ready to take note of any irregularities. Their position was, it seemed, really void of any technical skill: they filled in electronic forms and monitored machine activity following basic guidelines. When they told me that their shift was part of the one-day-a-week scheme, it became evident that they weren't needed there at all, but were instead there to 'give them a sense of purpose'.

When it comes to understanding the products being manufactured, it is necessary to note the philosophical framework which has allowed such products to become readily available. Currently in the United States, AI sex dolls are not illegal, as under the First Amendment of the constitution, no harm comes to anyone in the creation or use of such devices. Other nations, for example many in the European Union, have banned them outright, claiming that, especially in the cases of child-sized ones, they normalise and even promote peadophilia. Now let's jump however many decades down the line to this fourth phase, where the American liberalist approach has prevailed. Not only are such sex dolls now readily available on the market, but such models have become highly advanced. For those with the money to spend, such dolls come fully equipped with voice recognition, deep learning memory capabilities and touch sensitivity. They are, to put it simply, lifelike.

So when I asked the group of factory workers what they thought, most replied that they didn't see an issue with it, it just 'wasn't their thing'. Only a few workers spoke out against them, saying that especially in the case of child-sized dolls, they served as a temptation for some people's darkest desires which shouldn't be let out, even through 'safe' technological means. This sparked a short debate between them, with some citing how cases of peadophilia had been sharply declining for the last decade. The others not only questioned the data, but suggested that as the doll's AI became more advanced, wouldn't it be similar to *actually* abusing a child? Only if they had artificial *general* intelligence, one woman replied, making sure to point out that while the AI was narrow, it didn't matter if it could form a relationship with you. Its intelligence wasn't *consciousness,* merely synthetic dialogue. The discussion went on for another half an hour or so, before they realised they had forms to fill out. Leaving me to my own devices, I wandered through the rows of pristine limbs soon to be attached to their new bodies.

Although an extreme example, my time in this phase showed me that no matter how controversial or taboo a new technological pursuit can at first seem, if the results suggest that less people are harmed through its use, people tend to support it here. In the same way that the use of sex dolls had apparently reduced cases of peadophilia, the widespread use of driverless cars and planes now meant that far less people died in traffic or aviation accidents. When mistakes did occur, the population seemed quick to remember that data was more important than anecdotes. What was interesting here was not the technology itself — which is no different from our current driverless cars — but the attitudes towards it. I was genuinely surprised to see the evolution of such acceptance, as for some time I had believed that no matter what the data showed, an automated car running over a child would quickly turn society against such technologies. Evidently, it seemed, I had underestimated how quickly society at large can come around to such new technological advances.

A Drone-Delivered Ballroom Dance

The mounting mass of memories leads to an enormous growth in historiographical knowledge. But untrammelled dedication to the past, instilling the belief that we are its late-flowering fruits and epigones, ultimately undermines history itself: 'at the point of a certain excess of history, life crumbles and degenerates, as does, ultimately as a result of this degeneration, history itself'.

— Paulo Virno

One group I visited, who assured me they were one of many, consisted of a small village of people who had chosen to live their lives outside the city in rural (but no less technologically-advanced) communities. In contrast to the atomisation witnessed in the cities, in these small enclaves there was a deep-rooted desire for social relations, community and above all else a sense of belonging.

To say that there is a longing for the past would only be partly true. For similar to the VR tourists in phase three, here it exists in the plural, a perpetual and ever-changing longing for different *pasts*. This group pick different eras on a regular basis, adorning their shared spaces with the aesthetic of that month's chosen era. 3D-printed replicas of objects and props are delivered by drone and assembled using online instructions. The only break form this faux-reality comes when each member must momentarily pause their activities and head towards the nearest city to complete their weekly eight hour shift in a factory, hospital or restaurant.

These outsider groups create the crassest of historical amalgams, blending different eras into new hybrid forms. For them, there is no way of imagining a future different to theirs. They have, essentially entered a 'post-historical age', whereby everything becomes pastiche.

Ironically, these groups seem to place a huge focus on the 'authenticity' of each aesthetic they choose to inhabit, yet have no problem with crassly blending these different aesthetics into new formations. The fact that the amalgams are anything but authentic seems completely unimportant to them. It is all about having the 'right authentic materials' from the start. This mode of thinking inevitably leads to the equation that one authentic stlye, plus another authentic style, no matter how incongruous they may be, inevitably leads to a new 'authentic' hybrid.

Many of these citizens express an extensive knowledge of different eras and cultural epochs. Yet their speech jumps erratically between past and present, such eras appearing to be indistinguishable from their current world. When I asked them if they ever thought about the future, they struggled to comprehend my question, as if something had realigned in their brains to keep them forever looking backwards. Far from viewing my question as a provocation, they simply didn't possess the cognitive capabilities to imagine that their future would be anything other than a continuation of the present.

In one village, I encountered a 1930's style American ballroom with a jazz band playing. At first it really did feel as if I had stepped back into that era, as each detail, from the cigarettes they smoked to the shoes they wore, seemed harmonious. Yet when I looked closely at the tables and the art on the walls, there was something of a Parisian café to the style. I eventually concluded that this amalgam was nothing more than just another 'back-then': a reformulation of a past not dominated by technology, with no care being put into making it a realistic replica.

Algorithm-Based Crop Rotation, Bio-Engineering and Widespread-Seed Vaults — The New Global Food Chain

Throughout this planetary system, huge areas of land are dedicated to bio-engineering farms run by human workers but dictated by algorithms that decipher export prices. While there is a slight mistrust evident among many of the agricultural experts, they do admit that everything functions optimally and without animosity. So while global food chains strengthen and produce standards continue to rise, the global agricultural community are prepared to place their trust in AI.

Worldwide, there seems to have been a recalibration of expectations, whereby people no longer try to think of new, perhaps 'fairer' or 'purer' systems, but instead focus on how their living standards can continue to improve. In a quite utilitarian sense, the end — in this case well-fed nations — justify the means: AI organisational softwares. If the chain is oiled and running smoothly and a clever network of emergency seed vaults, dried goods and extra land have been put aside, there really seems little more this system could do to ensure the alimentation of an ever-growing population.

With crop failures, drought and global pandemics always considered an existential threat to humanity, huge measures have been taken to ensure that one weak link won't break the chain. If one area were to to suddenly fail to produce sufficient food, advanced AI systems will recalibrate and reroute the supply and demand procedure, similar to how when a car takes a wrong turn, the GPS immediately figures out the next best route. To ensure that each country works in cooperation with the others, a union of seed vaults has been established, whereby whenever a new strain of modified seed is created, identical samples are sent to each nation for storage in their underground vault. The idea, I was told, is to both ensure that no one nation can gain a monopoly on available produce, while also encouraging nations to recognise that cooperation is in everyone's best interest.

I had the opportunity to visit two of these large farms, the first in Urimán, eastern Venezuela, the second in Douala, Cameroon. Both sites provided evidence of the highly advanced and wildly intuitive ways of farming that the AI systems of each nation had devised as the most viable, profitable and sustainable solution to those specific landscapes. While both locations had the look of futuristic factories, the products they were producing seemed akin to the fruits and vegetables we see on our supermarket shelves today. The difference in these cases was that although they retained a 'natural' or organic appearance, they were advanced produce packed with high levels of nutrients.

In Urimán, where sugarcane still stands as the staple of the country's produce, a new range of modified fruits have taken off, gaining popularity mostly in Europe where such high nutrient, yet sweet-tasting foods simply cannot grow. *Sandía Violeta,* or Violet Watermelon as it's known globally, contains a profusion of antioxidants, but most importantly one called anthocyanin. This plant pigment gives the inside fruit of the watermelon a violet colouring, with a rich yet fresh taste. I of course couldn't taste these virtual fruits, but I heard them described as giving instant hydration with a soft tannin, similar to a light red wine.

I only saw a fraction of the farm, which spanned over three-hundred kilometres squared. All around the land, workers moved across the rows of heavy watermelon plants, loading them into driverless cars that moved them to the washing and sorting facilities run solely by automated machines. Yet despite the highly advanced machinery and infrastructural organisation, I found it slightly peculiar that none of the staff could adequately explain what was actually being produced. They knew that certain minerals and oils were added to the original plants, and that with strict regulations, each seed would eventually grow in to a huge *Sandía Violeta*. But that was all they could tell me. As for the actual science behind the process, the AI knew best and could provide evidence as to *why* this fruit was so beneficial to the human immune system, but without revealing the highly-complex algorithms that had determined this to be true.

Akin to Urimán, the workers at the hydro-farm in Douala recognised that they were not there to find solutions or create new innovative alimentation, but to strictly follow the rules set forth by the AI that governed their sea-fruit farm. Located across the Manoka Reserve, thousands of huge glass tubes run into the South Atlantic Ocean, at times stretching as far as two-hundred kilometres. Inside each of these tubes are seeds which will germinate underwater, eventually growing into plants which are known by their supermarket name as 'Ocean Potassium'. Specifically, they are modified banana plants engineered to grow underwater alongside algae. Not only are these bananas rich in micronutrients, the levels of potassium mean that one banana can give you all the Vitamin B6 and C1 you need in a week. Visibly, they appear as unripe bananas; their skin being a shade of dark, earthy green. But on the inside, the flesh is a cream colour with thin cyan lines running like marble stains through it.

Thousands of workers run these plants each day, collecting the bananas that are drawn out of the tubes on conveyor belts and shipping them to the long list of global suppliers. Yet what was most impressive about these structures was not just that enormous quantities of high-quality food was being produced everyday, but that these glass tubes held a second function. As has been known for some time, algae works as a sustainable method for reducing toxins and pollution in the waters. Not only do these tubes contribute to the reduction of CO_2 in the Guinean Gulf, but the algae plants, once past a certain lifespan, are removed and used for biofuel to run the very factories which produce this alimentation. The result is a fully self-sustaining eco-system, which needs no outside energy sources and continues to produce masses of high-nutrient food every day. One of the farm's supervisors, Sianga, was proud to tell me that their farm has been used as a model in various other countries as evidence of a highly profitable, carbon negative system.

While impressive, I left Douala with the same uneasy sensation I experienced in Urinám. Was it an issue that no one actually knew how decisions to build these farms were taken? It seemed that the longer I spent in this phase, I felt almost ridiculous for taking issue with the fact that algorithms dictated so much of this global system and that *most* people trusted it unwaveringly. If everything functions so well, is it logical to question the computer behind the decision making? Or should we all just be thankful that most of the issues facing us at the start of the twenty-first century seemed to have been solved?

Vorsprung Durch Technik — Inter-Governmental Decision Making Under A Glass Ceiling

Perhaps one of the most iconic symbols of unified Germany is Norman Foster's glass dome that sits above the Reichstag building. Dazzlingly futuristic and a symbol of transparency in the politics of a re-unified Germany, the design is both aesthetically powerful and environmentally friendly. Perhaps the most impressive feature is the mirrored cone in the centre which uses daylight to create energy and reduce the buildings carbon emissions. Through tracking the sun using a large shield, direct light is blocked so as to simultaneously reduce solar gain and in order not to dazzle anyone inside the dome. Inextricably tied to this new ethos was the catchphrase linked to Audi Motors, but also borrowed by John Hegarty of BBH and used in Britain in the mid 1980's: 'Vorsprung Durch Technik', 'Advancement Through Technology'.

When I noticed the catchphrase glowing on the glass floors, I asked one of the assistants working there why this (seemingly) outdated catchphrase was engraved into the glass ceiling. Smiling, she informed me that many first time visitors had the same question. But it was quite simple: in post-war Germany, the nation had needed not only a new economy and infrastructure, but a new ethos and way of showing the international community that they had moved on from the horrors of the Holocaust. 'Vorsprung Dutch Technik' acted as an ethos for a new, technologically advanced but green thinking and democratic Germany. So when, after the horrors of the mid 21st century, the global community needed a catchphrase to encapsulate the new global ethos of stability, green thinking and technological advancement, they turned to a government funded AI to conjure up a new slogan. They had, understandably, all been quite surprised when it has chosen 'Vorsprung Dutch Technik'.

In its reasoning, the AI explained that the globe's new governing ethos needed two things: firstly, it had to recognise that advancement could only come through technology, but secondly it needed to be trustworthy, relatable and above all, timeless. The AI itself described its choice as 'retro-futurist', continuously looking forward to a better, more technologically advanced future while also playing on people's nostalgia for the promise of technological prowess on a consumer level. So rather than creating a new phrase, the AI went for recycling as a symbol of renovation, a metaphor for the times in which these people lived.

In this phase, the Reichstag has two functions: not only does it still act as the official parliament building for the German nation, but it has become the centrepiece for international AI decision making. Before I visited the building, the notion of an AI that determines world decisions had remained rather abstract: I saw the results, but had no reference or localisation point for where this actually happened. Only during my final immersion was I fortunate enough to sit in on a viewing session at the main theatre to catch a glimpse of how the AI communicated its decisions back to the global population. This theatre was one of many thousands that are located in government buildings around the globe. There is a strict calendar for news updates, meaning that specific journalists or officials can attend only the screenings that are relevant to their respective areas.

During the viewing, a large audience of journalists sat scrawling away on tablets while watching series of code run across the screen. Every now and then, the large streams would be punctuated by pauses, in which an automated voice would read out in English the key areas of focus. When the man sat to my left turned to me and asked what I thought of the AI's decision to move from fission to fusion nuclear energy in Karachi, I had to confess that I hadn't understood the information being relayed. Seeming a little surprised, he told me that if I wasn't yet fluent in *Xigo-i* (which I subsequently learnt was the official international governmental AI code), I could always listen to the live translation in English on the headset. He seemed to gather quickly that I was essentially a tourist, and invited me outside for a coffee.

It was late afternoon in the phase, and I knew from my headset clock that this would be my last experience in the VFL's testing period. He ordered two *Abiespressos* for us, telling me that I simply *had* to try it. It was a new strain of bean they had released last week, the product of a crossbreed between the Abies Guatemalensis tree and their local coffee plants. Resting his glasses on top of his head and taking a sip, he almost shivered, noting how there was something oceanic about the taste. Lighting a cigarette, he rubbed his eyes and we returned to the subject of code.

'Don't be intimidated by it. It's just like any other language. Once you get to grips with the grammar, the vocabulary will soon follow and you'll be set. Weird how at times I even catch myself cursing in it.'

'*Cursing* in it?' I asked.

'Yeah, you know like how when you learn a second language, the sign that you're really becoming fluent is when you start cursing in it. That's when the language has reached your primal fight-or-flight circuitry response. So you don't even think, you just react and there it is! Fuck! Joder! Scheisse! In Xigo-i, we say '*xixke*!"

I started to laugh, and realised I would have liked to spend more time with this man. But knowing the phase was drawing to a close, I decided to ask a question that had been on my mind since the first opening.

'So let me ask you something. As someone who understands the code, to what extent do you *actually* understand the AI systems that govern the global system. From my perspective, it seems that we see the results, but not the workings or the reasoning?'

Mid-toke, he nodded his head and coughed as he exhaled a thick cloud of smoke.

'Need to quit these. Doctor suggested virtual cigarettes but there's just something about the old-fashioned burning that I can't let go of. *Anyway*, to answer your question, I think you're coming at it from the wrong angle. To be honest, it's been a while since I've heard that question — but that doesn't mean it's no longer an important one. Here's my take on it.

Understanding the reasoning — or the 'workings' as you put it — is an unachievable goal if we want to maintain the excellent quality of life that pretty much every person alive enjoys. Understanding the workings slows us down. Not just slightly, but drastically. There's no possible way even the most proficient group of highly intelligent humans could configure the right algorithms and methods that our AI does. And that's before we even get to the problem of national, let alone international coordination.

So to answer your question, I don't understand the AI systems. No one does. For a while people wanted to, but after the horrors of the

313

21st century, no one really trusts humans to be in charge of politics. I understand your point, in an ideal world it would be best if we could have both. But we can't. And there's no getting around that. Either you leave it to AI, accept a certain level of ignorance, and everything functions near to perfectly. Or you prioritise human intelligence and a system in which we can all, to *some* extent, understand decision making. But no one wants that. *I* happen to find it interesting, but most people couldn't give a shit whether Karachi is moving to fusion or fission nuclear power. We just trust that in the grand scheme, it's the right choice.'

I felt the world fading to black and realised that in the final minutes of the immersion period, I had managed to snatch the most valuable insight into the bedrock of phase four's global ideology. Looking up to the sky, I could feel the fibre optic synapses flickering throughout the airways. A flock of birds erupted from the Reichstag, and his voice dissolved into noise as the 'immersion ending' tag brought me back to the hotel.

It would be impossible to list here all of the writers, thinkers and speakers who shaped this novel in its entirety, but I would like to give special mention to Adam Greenfield's work listed in this bibliography. While differing in content, it was Greenfield's imagining of different possible technological futures that provided me with many core ideas for the four case studies in this novel.

The Future — Marc Auge. *Verso, 2015.*

The New Dark Age — James Bridle. *Verso, 2019.*

The Longing for Less: Living with Minimalism — Kyle Chayka. *Bloomsbury Publishing, 2020.*

Ghosts of My Life: Writings on Depression, Hauntology and Lost Futures — Mark Fisher. Zero Books, 2014.

Radical Technologies: The Design of Everyday Life — Adam Greenfield. *Verso, 2018.*

How We Became Posthuman: Virtual Bodies in Cybernetics, Literature, and Informatics — N. Katherine Hayles. *The University of Chicago Press,* 1999.

Unthought: The Power of the Cognitive Nonconscious — N. Katherine Hayles. *The University of Chicago Press, 2017.*

Typewriters, Bombs & Jellyfish — Tom McCarthy. *The New York Review Books, 2017.*

To be Machine: Adventures Among Cyborgs, Utopians, Hackers, and the Futurists Solving the Modest Problem of Death - Mark O'Connell. *Granta Books*, 2018.

Duty Free Art — Art in an Age of Planetary Civil War - Hito Steryl. *Verso*, 2019.

Life 3.0 Being Human in an Age of Artificial Intelligence — Max Tegmark. *Vintage Books*, 2017.

Déjà Vu and the End of History — Paolo Virno. *Verso, 2015.*

All quotations on pages 38-40 are in direct reference to the Superflux video work, Drone Aviary, 2015.

Lightning Source UK Ltd.
Milton Keynes UK
UKHW010639290721
387974UK00002B/472